PENGUIN BOOKS

CITY OF TINY LIGHTS

Patrick Neate is the author of three previous novels: *Musungu Jim and the Great Chief Tuloko*, which won a Betty Trask Award, *Twelve Bar Blues*, which won the 2001 Whitbread Novel of the Year Award, and *The London Pigeon Wars*. His last book was *Where You're At: Notes from the Frontline of a Hip Hop Planet*, an exploration of the global proliferation and appropriation of hip hop. He lives in London some of the time.

City of Tiny Lights

PATRICK NEATE

PENGUIN BOOKS

PENGUIN BOOKS

Published by the Penguin Group
Penguin Books Ltd, 80 Strand, London WC2R ORL, England
Penguin Group (USA) Inc., 375 Hudson Street, New York, New York 10014, USA
Penguin Group (Canada), 90 Eglinton Avenue East, Suite 700, Toronto, Ontario, Canada M4P 2Y3
(a division of Pearson Penguin Canada Inc.)
Penguin Ireland, 25 St Stephen's Green, Dublin 2, Ireland
(a division of Penguin Books Ltd)
Penguin Group (Australia), 250 Camberwell Road,
Camberwell, Victoria 3124, Australia (a division of Pearson Australia Group Pty Ltd)
Penguin Books India Pvt Ltd, 11 Community Centre,
Panchsheel Park, New Delhi – 110 017, India
Penguin Group (NZ), cnr Airborne and Rosedale Roads, Albany,
Auckland 1310, New Zealand (a division of Pearson New Zealand Ltd)
Penguin Books (South Africa) (Pty) Ltd, 24 Sturdee Avenue,
Rosebank, Johannesburg 2196, South Africa

Penguin Books Ltd, Registered Offices: 80 Strand, London WC2R ORL, England

www.penguin.com

First published by Viking 2005
Published in Penguin Books 2006
1

Copyright © Patrick Neate, 2005
All rights reserved

The moral right of the author has been asserted

Typeset by Rowland Phototypesetting Ltd, Bury St Edmunds, Suffolk
Printed in England by Clays Ltd, St Ives plc

ISBN-13: 978-0-141-00907-0
ISBN-10: 0-141-00907-1

Acknowledgements

I'm grateful to all who support what I do. Most of the criticism's appreciated. All of it's necessary. Special thanks to my family, Simon, Juliet, Nots, French, Ils, Sam, Trusters and Miss M. Thanks too to everyone @ Cherry Jam and Trevor the web fairy (www.patrickneate.com).

Another Tommy Akhtar investigation

I

I have sometimes wondered how it might have been if I hadn't opened my door that morning; hadn't said, 'All right, Trouble? Good to see you with your jabbing fingers, swinging fists and no insurance, household or medical.' Isn't that the way a cartoon story like mine's supposed to begin?

Problem is, the door of my shoebox flat opens right into the waiting room of my matchbox office and I wasn't going to sit in all day like some retired middle management with the complete works of Gilbert and Sullivan on leatherette boxed set. Problem is, I always leave the waiting room unlocked because mine's a shy kind of business and you got to cajole clients in like you would a forkful of Alphabetti Spaghetti into a reluctant kid's mouth. Problem is, my bedroom stank like a pub ashtray at chucking-out time and the living room was just as bad so I needed to get out. It didn't occur to me that this stink was oozing out of my pores like butter through the holes in a cheese cracker.

I'd been with the old man the night before; sat up with him and Trinidad Pete and watched the tape of Viv Richards taking England to the cleaners in a one-dayer in '84. When King Viv stepped outside leg stump and creamed Bob Willis high over extra, Farzad said, 'That's the secret of greatness, Tommy boy. Quick feet.'

Trinidad Pete only half agreed. 'You gotta have fast feet and your head steady,' he said.

Me? I didn't say nothing and we watched the whole of Viv's knock in real time (including the lunch break) and sank a bottle of Scotch (their choice) and a dozen cans of Genius in the process.

Farzad always says, 'You can learn everything you need to know about life from the game of cricket.' I'm sure he's got a point but, that morning, as I stumbled to the bathroom with my head pounding like the bass bin in some junior gangster's souped-up Saab 900, I figured not for the first time and not for the last that I wasn't such a quick learner.

I brushed my teeth and combed a parting on the pelt on my tongue. I splashed my face with cold water only because that's what you're supposed to do on a hangover, right? It's not like it made me feel any better. I doused my body with deodorant and slung on a fresh polo shirt and last night's jeans. I checked my reflection in the mirror and pushed a damp hand through my hair. The barnet did as it was told. My eyes were like two fag burns in the carpet, my complexion was dirty as usual and I had stubble to send a film star screaming to his agent about the injustice of the ageing process. I was as pretty as ever. Oh, yeah.

Then, Hush Puppies on my feet and shrapnel in my pocket, I opened the door. I was ready to face the world; ready like a junior colt standing short leg to King Viv in expansive mood.

She was sitting on my pew bolt upright like a candle. She had her feet flat on the floor and perfectly parallel. On her lap she had a copy of the *Screws* from the table. She was reading some story about a pop star who'd had an affair with another pop star. Big deal. The rag was at least six months old. Like that made any difference. The two protagonists were most likely having affairs with two other pop stars by now. Either that or they were practising their diction and stage-school smiles on 'Do you want fries with that?'

She was wearing a long denim skirt above box-fresh trainers and a tight white crop top beneath a fitted corduroy jacket that did little to discourage her chest. Her breasts were round like two moulds for birthday jelly and just as plastic. Somebody else's ringlets were hanging off her head. She had skin the colour of toffee but her complexion wasn't so great, pebble-dashed with pocks like peppercorns along her cheekbones. This was her day face and I didn't reckon many geezers got to see it. Even from where she was sitting, she managed to look down on me; like I was detritus in the plug-hole. She had that about spot on but I was yet to be convinced she was more than a moist wipe better. I had her number straight off. I'd done my uncharitable sums: two plus two equals whore.

She said, 'Your door was open.' Her voice was a surprise, like a tide across a shingle beach, rough but kind of soothing. Uncharitable Tommy wondered whether she worked chat lines on the side.

'So *that's* how you got in,' I said.

Either she didn't get it or she chose not to bother. I'll admit it wasn't one of my best. 'I was looking for TA Services.'

'Tommy Akhtar,' I said. 'At your service.'

She rolled a pink tongue round her dark purple lips. A geezer could get hypnotized by a tongue like that. 'I think I made a mistake.'

'Suit yourself.'

She made to stand up but gave me one more chance. 'You look like crap.'

'You can't kid a kidder.' She got that one all right and I reckon she enjoyed it too. This bird was no fool. I said, 'You want to step into my office?' I held the door for her.

She walked like she was used to being watched. So I watched her. Just to be polite. Good manners cost nothing.

I took a corner of the desk and she sat down in the client's chair. Like the pew in the waiting room, it was another relic I'd salvaged when the Romans decided to shut down Holy

5

Trinity on the Attlee Estate. I liked the associations. Father Tommy Akhtar as confessor. Why not?

'How did you find me?' I asked.

'*Yellow Pages*. I picked three names, called three numbers, got three ansaphones and chose you. You sound better on your machine.'

I chuckled. I was getting to like this bird and in a way that didn't strike me as too unhealthy neither. I sparked my first Benny of the morning. I call it my thermometer because it usually gives me a fair idea of just how sick I am.

She said, 'Do you mind?'

'Uh-uh.' I shook my head.

'You better let me have one, then.'

I offered her the packet and she snaked one. Her fingernails were long and fake and the same purple as her lips. I flicked my lighter and held it out to her. She leaned forward and cupped my hand in hers. It was unnecessary but she didn't mean anything by it. Just force of habit.

She sucked that smoke like it was country air. Mine tasted like poison and churned my fragile stomach. I guess I was running quite a fever. I took to the chair behind my desk like a pensioner to his rocker. I got out a pen and pad for show.

'So what can I do for you, Ms . . . ?' I began, but she was having none of it.

'First things first . . .' She blew a pretty smoke-ring. 'What are your charges, Mr Akhtar?' Her formality didn't fit.

'It depends on the services required. I'm sure *you* understand that.' I guess I was trying to be funny. I shouldn't have bothered. She ignored the attempt in the same way she stepped over tramps in the gutter.

'What's your day rate?'

'Three hundred. Plus expenses.'

'That's a lot of cash.'

'I'm a lot of man,' I said. I must have been sicker than I thought. Nothing from the bird. I decided to play it with a full face. 'Look,' I went on, 'no offence and feel free to stop me if I'm barking but I reckon you either earn that in an hour or in a week. If it's an hour, I'm loose change in your copper jar. If it's a week then, sorry, Ms Whatever, but you never gonna afford me anyway.'

She levelled her deer eyes at me. A few punters must have dived into those pools and never come up for air. 'Which do you think?'

I pretended to ponder a moment. Call me a naughty boy but I was playing along. Then I dropped it cold. 'No idea. Frankly I never understood the business and I never been good at valuing a hooker. I've met girls who charge more than a grand a night who've got more tracks on their arms than Virgin got trains to run them and I've seen sweet meat under King's Cross that will get you off for a Lady and a lolly to take the taste away. It's always been a trade that could use a regulator, right? "Off-whore". Something like that.'

I guess I was hoping for the thrill of a slap or at least she'd storm out with shoulders back and chin high. In my experience, women all got overblown views of themselves; prostitutes to princesses. In fact, scrub women. *People.* But this classy bird stayed serene, serious. 'I can afford you, all right. Don't you worry about that.'

'Cool.'

'But don't expect no payment in kind. I got principles. One of them is I ain't sleeping with no ethnics. There's one exception. But you ain't it.'

'Ouch!' I laughed out loud. 'Why's that? I thought us brown skins were supposed to stick together.'

Now it was her turn to laugh. 'I don't wanna stick to no brown skin,' she said. 'It's the white dudes that slide off nice and easy, right back to their pink wives with their tails limp between their legs. Besides, Pakis always wanna bargain and half the time they sweat last night's curry.'

'You a lovely tom,' I said. 'You cut me right down to my English-Ugandan-Indian core.'

'Indians? Pakis? What's the difference?'

'Tell that to Kashmir,' I said. 'When the missiles start to fly, you can ride one and drop leaflets.'

I was having fun. I could have gone on like this for hours. Fast talk with a fast woman? There are worse ways to play out an idle hangover. But the whore suddenly got serious. 'Let me tell you the particulars of my case.'

'Your *case*?' I said. 'For real. Tell me the particulars.' I had my pen poised like a starter pistol. 'First things first. How about you let me in on your name?'

'Chase. Melody Chase.'

'Right.' I scribbled it down. My pen stumbled with a suppressed ha-ha. Let me tell you something about hookers. Black hookers? Got about half a dozen names. There's Melody, Harmony and Bianca (don't ask me why) and there's Ebony (obvious). Then there's Naomi and Tyra. Blondes? Marilyn, Caprice, Helena and Elle. Sultry Hispanics? Sandra, Salma and, bizarrely, a bunch who appear to be named after cars (like Fiesta, Sierra and Cleo). Petite girls? Kylie, one and all. Kylie, Kylie and Kylie.

The classification system is mostly self-explanatory. These days even whores know the value of a good brand, no different from the geezers selling knock-off Gucci outside Oxford Circus. I once met a black girl who worked under the name of Katarina. It threw me big style, serious.

I pulled on my fag to stop my lips quivering. 'So what can I do for you, Ms Chase?'

'A friend of mine's gone missing.'

'A friend? Who's the friend?'

'My flatmate. Natasha.'

'A Russian bird?'

'Right. How did you know?'

Her eyes were wide and she seemed genuinely impressed. I flashed her my best fillings. 'My job,' I said. 'I got an HND in this stuff. I was gonna hang it on the wall but that seemed kinda naff, know what I mean?' She blinked slowly. Like, *really* slowly. I knew I couldn't take the piss too much. But what the hell? 'Look. One question springs out already. Your stable-mate's gone missing –'

'My flatmate.'

'Flatmate. Stable-mate. Whatever. My first question is this: why do you care? What's going on here? Honour among whores? I'll admit I'm an old-fashioned kinda geezer but I never heard of it.'

That really seemed to needle her. I was surprised. She threw some proper filth my way; the kind of stuff Mum never heard her whole life (and probably wouldn't have heard even if she'd made her three score plus ten). The gist was something like, 'You wanna hear my f——ing story or not?' Fair enough. I gave her the mysterious Asian eyebrows by way of an apology and she hushed up and started talking.

The God's honest truth is I took notes but I barely heard what she said. I'd stepped over Mr Sick's doormat and was beginning to feel the sandpaper side of rough. I might have got past the Guinness but now the Scotch was kicking in. It's not my drink and it has a tendency to repeat on me. I was dry and sweaty all at once, like a Christmas goose come New Year. What follows, therefore, is lifted straight from my pad. Lucky me that my biros come with cruise control fitted as standard.

Melody and Natasha had a rule. Not hard and fast. More

like a principle. If one of them was seeing a punter for the first time and it was an outcall engagement, the other would tag along for company. If they were going to the horny geezer's house or hotel room, the other would sit outside and wait for a call to say it was all hunky-dory (or blimey-slimy at least). If they were meeting in a bar or restaurant, the other would take a corner table and sip water and wait for the nod. Like I said, honour among whores. Who'd have believed it?

Two nights ago, Natasha was meeting a newbie at the bar in the Embassy just off Shepherd's Market. I knew the spot: exactly the kind of high-class hangout where you always find the real lowlife. Media bum bandits, minor celebs and Arabs who pissed oil hung out there in gaggles and cliques. They drank non-vintage Moët at a ton-fifty a bottle and pretended not to notice let alone recognize each other. It had a cokey reputation too. You sat on the bog too long and your arse got high.

Although Melody had a gig herself, she put him back half an hour and took a seat near the door and batted off the chirpsing drunks and chancers. Natasha's punt turned up on time and she soon gave the signal. Melody left. It was the last time she'd seen her.

Judging by the automatic writing, I must have started asking a few questions. You can figure the kind of thing.

Melody was worried because of the second part of her and her ho-buddy's pact: if one was staying out overnight, they checked in with the other. They always stuck to the principle. Of course Melody had tried Natasha's phone but it had been going straight to voicemail ever since. No, Natasha had no other place to stay besides their apartment. No, she had no other friends or family as far as Melody knew. She'd only been in London a couple of months. Before that, she'd apparently had a spell in NYC. Yeah, she had a coke habit. A lot of girls did. What of it?

Apparently, Natasha said she was twenty-three. Melody figured she was more like twenty-seven or -eight. Sure, I could see some pictures. I could check out www.sexyrussian.co.uk. There weren't any headshots but I'd get a fair idea of the girl's upholstery if I could see past the quoted stats and the webhead's airbrush.

I was going through the motions, for real, like I was padding out the last hour of a tame draw against the opening bat's occasional offies. For starters, the idea of searching ditches and municipal tips for a flash of pale flesh hardly tickled my prostate. I had better things to do with my time. I could catch up on some paperwork, some reading, some zees. I could wallow in self-loathing. I hadn't done that for a while. For seconds, my migraine was now galloping and my belly a washing-machine on long cycle. I'd never puked in front of a prospective client before but there's always a first time.

I stubbed my fag and wiped the back of my hand across my forehead. It felt like yesterday's frying-pan. I coughed and spluttered a little. I had to swallow a mouthful of God knows what. I tried to dream up some more queries. I asked Melody if she knew blokey's name.

'Blokey who?'

'Natasha's punt.'

She pulled a face at me. 'John,' she said. Yeah, right. It was a dumb question.

I asked what the geezer looked like and got a lot more than I had any right to expect. White, forty-five to fifty, five-ten and a disorganized fourteen stone. Thick, jet-black hair (probably dyed), parted on the left to a curling pile on the right temple. 'Not a style,' she commented. 'He's probably had it like that since he first felt his mum's brush.' A sallow, sunken complexion with bloodhound eyes over shadowed cheeks sinking into jowls that tickled the white collar of an otherwise navy City shirt. His tie – she couldn't make out the pattern – poked from the pocket of his charcoal grey suit. The suit was good but he wore it like a bin-liner. He had expensive shoes that were carelessly scuffed at the toe and socks marked with a small crest of some kind.

I said, 'That's quite some description.'

And the tom shrugged. 'Some girls let them blur into one. But I remember details. Just in case. Besides, it passes the time, know what I mean?'

I checked her out some more. This bird was extra. On another morning, in another lifetime, I might even have given a toss.

'He wasn't Tasha's usual kinda trick neither.'

'Why?'

'He was English.'

'So?'

She gave me a look that made me feel about twelve years old. I kind of liked it. 'So let me tell you how it is. The English rose type? She sees Americans, Dutch, the odd German. Fat chicks? They get skinny nerds with a stiff little needle in their boxers. Brassy blondes? City whiz kids, Nigerians and Pakis. And exotic girls like me? We're talking middle-aged gents with colonial fantasies, Vi prescriptions and balls like peanuts. The basic rule is a trick goes for what he don't never get at home. But Russians are the exceptions that prove it. Those guys get off the plane with their pinched faces and their brand new D&G jeans and the first thing they're looking for is a familiar piece of pie. Preferably corrupted by the West but Russian pie all the same. I guess it's kinda patriotic.'

'So Natasha mostly sees Russians?'

'You're fast. You should be a detective.'

'And how do you know blokey was English?'

The whore smirked at me. 'The guy was a mess. He looked

dirty. He needed a shave. Foreign men wouldn't see their missus looking like that, let alone a pro.'

I stared at her. I was feigning thoughtful but I knew it was time to stop with the games. I'd decided way back that this wasn't my cup of tea, pint of lager or even slug of Turk. Who wants to be employed by a hooker? You know that even the maids and sticker-boys dream of something better. I wasn't thinking pride. Oh, no. My pride's all locked up in my overdraft. I was thinking squalor. Sure, I'm paid to get my hands dirty but that doesn't mean getting them bitten off by vermin.

I was about to send Ms Melody Chase on her way with no ceremony. Her fake chest could show her the door. But then a new tide of nausea washed over me and I knew I had no time to play Canute. I had to get out. I stood up shakily and navigated round my desk. The bird looked at me in surprise.

'Coffee,' I muttered. 'Place across the road. You want one?'

'No thanks. You gonna find Tasha, Mr Akhtar?'

'Sure,' I said. 'You wait there.'

Is there a dumber way to take a case? Put your answers on a postcard. Mark it Tommy Sucker. It should find me, serious.

2

I stumbled down the stairs two at a time and out into the street. The London morning smelled like a London morning – bitter, charred and artificial – but it was good enough for me. My face fizzed like a chemical reaction and my guts slowed to a gentle spin.

A couple of the drivers were lounging in the office doorway: Swiss Chris and Big John. Swiss Chris is a vast West African who apparently picked up his nickname because of the regularity and verbosity of his bowel movements. Something to do with some old-school laxative. I didn't get it. Big John's a tiny Pole with round shoulders that look like they've carried the weight of Soviet oppression on their own. Nobody can pronounce his real name. It hasn't got no vowels. But apparently he's got a porn-star dick that he's not ashamed to flash. So Big John it is.

'Easy, Mr T.' Swiss Chris winced as he dragged on his butt. He must have been anticipating his first dump. The sewer rats would be running for cover.

'Morning, Tommy.' Big John's moustache curled up with his leather lips.

I took a deep breath. My head was clearing. 'All right, Swiss? John? How's it hanging?'

'Fine,' said Swiss.

And, 'To my knees.'

I took out a Benny from the spares in my pocket and tapped it on the packet. Then I reholstered. I didn't want to push my luck.

I heard a familiar voice barking over the intercom. 'Two-five! Two-five! You clear? Where the f___ are you? I got a pick-up. Bevan House.' Then, still through his loudspeaker for the whole street to hear, 'Jesus H, bruv! You look like turd. You look like less than turd. If Swiss dropped you he'd be straight to A and E.'

I peered into the office and could just make out my brother's smug teeth and pudgy cheeks behind my own reflection in the Perspex window. I gave him a jolly grin and I gave him a jolly wave. 'Lovely morning, Gundappa.' His hand squeezed through the small money-hole between the Perspex and the Formica counter. He gave me the finger.

I put on my best Indian accent. It's not up to much but, in this instance, it served a purpose. 'I saw Farzad last night, brother,' I said. The finger waggled at me.

My office is just above my brother's cab firm in a two-up-two-down terrace at the unfashionable end of Chiswick. This is Farzad's legacy to his two sons. I reckon we make him proud, for real.

I know the story off by heart. I should do. I've lived it. But to me it's just a story.

Dr Farzad Akhtar arrived in this country with his wife, Mina, and sons in '72. He left Kampala in a real hurry. He wasn't no big shot, just a competent GP. He likes to say, 'Competence is the most underrated virtue, Tommy boy. Just look at Steve Waugh.' As I said, the old man thinks all life can be explained through cricket and the former Aussie skipper is one of his favourite sources of metaphor.

Farzad wasn't no big shot but he knew some, including his mentor Dr Arshad Patel. I don't remember Dr Patel. He was one of the few Indians who thought he could exert influence over Amin. He never made it out.

The Akhtar family moved in with a white couple in

Norwood. I can't remember the connection. There must have been one. We lived there for the best part of a year. Farzad sent to Uganda for his certificates. There was no reply. He sent again. His qualifications, his past, his mentor had gone up in smoke. Farzad was an unemployed Ugandan-Indian clutching a British passport. He was an unemployed Paki.

Farzad had his travelling suit lined with US currency. Some of it was his. Most was Dr Patel's. Idi allowed the Indians to leave with two thousand shillings but most of them were robbed blind on the road to Entebbe airport. Farzad got lucky. He opened a bank account in London. Dr Patel had disappeared and his family disappeared with him. Farzad bought a small premises just off Chiswick High Road, the Gunnersbury end. It wasn't his money. He got the guilts. It was a short-term thing, until he proved his status. He's still got the guilts. For different reasons, I know the feeling.

Farzad opened a Paki shop. He sent his sons to the local school. He served briefly on the PTA. He thought better of it when he got to know the other Ps and Ts on the A and he vowed to teach them at home. He didn't have time. 'Akhtar's' opened at six and closed at ten. Ten thirty. Eleven. Farzad's home tutorials, therefore, consisted only of throwing quotations at his sons and then demanding, 'Who said that?' These quotations came from all sorts of people although, for some unknown reason, a lot of them seemed to be from military leaders. When, for example, I complained about stacking shelves after school, Farzad might say something like, ' "England expects that every man will do his duty." Who?'

'Lord Nelson.'

'When?'

'Trafalgar.'

'Good. But you know cereal doesn't go next to the bleach, Tommy boy.'

Akhtar's sold milk and washing-powder and toilet-paper. It sold Marathons and Space Dust and Chewits to the local schoolkids. Later, because of the shoplifters, there was a sign saying, 'Only three children at one time. The management'. Gangland, serious. But it didn't stop the thieving. Most of it was down to Tommy and Gunny. It sold lightbulbs and fuses and plugs. It sold plantain and Nurishment and Jamaican bun. It sold cheap Dutch lager and cheap Polish vodka and knock-off supermarket Scotch. It sold everything. It was a short-term thing, until Farzad proved his status.

The Akhtar family lived above the shop. My bedroom was once my parents'. In fact, my bed was once their bed. For most of our childhood, Gundappa and me shared a bed in what is now my office. I once hung him out of the window by his underpants. Unfortunately they'd made the elastic strong. My lounge with the kitchenette in the corner was once half our lounge with the kitchenette in the corner. The other half is now my waiting room.

It wasn't as bad as a lot of immigrant families had to put up with back then. Still do. But I figure the Akhtars were used to the open spaces of our 'Kampala mansion'. That's how Farzad remembers it. Certainly we got under each other's feet. But it was only a short-term thing, right?

Farzad thought his certificates would come through. Then Farzad thought his sons would go to university. Then he thought they'd become professional English gentlemen; lawyers or accountants, perhaps even doctors. Farzad began to imagine retirement with Mina to Gravesend. He imagined becoming active in the local mosque (which was strange since Islam had always been for him only a question of culture rather than faith). He'd wear dapper three-piece suits. His sons would bring their wives and grandchildren and Mina would cook up a storm. One of them – back then it was most likely

17

yours truly – might play silly buggers and marry a white woman and that would cause a kerfuffle. But he'd get over it with Mina's gentle reasoning. That's what he imagined.

Farzad never did retire to Gravesend. He lives in Brixton. Tommy and Gundappa never went to university but to the dogs (metaphorically in my case, mostly literally in Gunny's. Every Friday. Trap five or six on the nose). Mina died suddenly and everything changed. In fact she died in my bed. Farzad went Tonto. Tommy played the Lone Ranger. Gunny went native.

I turned my back on my brother's middle finger and crossed the road. I was heading for Khan's; another Paki shop that sells everything. It opened two weeks after my mother died. Us Asians can spot a gap in the market, serious.

There was some lanky geezer hanging about on the pavement. He had slick hair flicked behind his ears and a razored goatee just so. He wore a suit that shimmered like Cellophane. It was brand new and spick and span but hadn't been cool since '83. He wasn't your typical Chiswick blokey. A yummy mummy fresh from the prep school run passed with a pram. She kept her expensive hairdo out of her face with a pair of expensive shades on her forehead. Blokey let her by with expansive good manners. Yummy mummy kinked her head and flushed a little embarrassment. As I pushed the door and chimed Khan's bell, the geezer gave me a look. I couldn't be bothered to meet it. I was still sick like Monday morning.

Mrs Khan peeled her teeth at the sight of me. They were crooked against fleshy pink gums. 'Hello, Tommy. And how are you this morning?'

'Cream-crackered, Mrs K. But mustn't grumble, eh? You?'

'Mustn't grumble. Mustn't grumble. Av's in trouble again.'

'Yeah? What now?'

'Same trouble. Always the same trouble with that one.'

'Right.'

Av was junior Khan; fifteen or thereabouts, with the fixed indignation of a post-office queue and stretched tight like a catapult ready to let fly. Who knew where he'd land? He was running with the local thug-lites who fancied themselves as proper little gangsters: text messages meant pb fghts n wd by d oz. Mrs K was getting desperate. She wanted me to have a word. That's how desperate she was.

Mrs K's shop was suffering. Chiswick was heading up in the world – even our end – and Khan's was strictly low rent. It couldn't compete with the new batch of health-food shops and delicatessens that sold all kinds of products that were high in this and low in that. I went into one once. I was confronted by sun-dried tomatoes, dried peach halves, prunes and raisins. It caught me right in the gut. I might have been thirty plus years out of the Ugandan sun but I'd never seen such a selection of unhappy fruit.

Mrs K was flogging dead horses to try to turn things round. The latest was fresh coffee in Styrofoam beakers and she'd bought an espresso machine and milk frother. This scheme was already rigor-mortised with its legs up in the air. I reckon I was her only customer.

I chose a newspaper while she busied with a double espresso, heavy on the sugar. I never read the papers but today I made an exception. Trying to impress the whore, I guess. Who was I kidding? I scanned the front-page headline and photo. Well. Would you Adam and Eve it? Ten minutes down and I was half-way there with a case I didn't want. I'm good. Yeah, right.

I slipped Mrs K a couple of nuggets. Even the smell of the coffee was beginning to perk me up. I was feeling half-way evolved: past Neanderthal and almost erectus.

I stepped outside and eighties blokey was gone. Maybe he was chasing yummy mummy around a stripped-pine kitchen.

Mind the Aga. I checked the far side of the road. There, at the window of my office, I could see the whore peering out. She must have wondered if I'd done a bunk.

Around where her purple toenails raked leather soles, Gunny's sign was still hanging squonk. It said 'Phoenecia' in blue italics with a silhouette of a trireme. Not 'Phoenecia Cabs', mind. Just 'Phoenecia'. I swear I'd cry for my brother if I could only stop laughing.

Cab companies are called things like 'SOS' or 'A+', right? Maybe even a simple 'Chiswick Cabs'. Gunny's was called 'Phoenecia'. There were two reasons for this. In the first place, he got the sign cheap from a bankrupt Greek restaurant. In the second, he fancied himself as some kind of Mediterranean. No complicated cultural questions for him. No way José, Jorge or Juan. Hence 'Phoenecia' (cabs). Hence the open-neck shirts. Hence the East London wop accent. Hence the dolly blonde girlfriends. Hence Gunny. Hence I only ever called him Gundappa.

Tommy and Gundappa Akhtar; named against Mina's better judgement and the religion of their birth for Farzad's favourite comedian and favourite middle-order bat – Tommy Cooper and Gundappa Vishwanath. Sometimes acquaintances would ask Farzad how he'd come up with their names and he'd say, 'Just like that!' and kill himself laughing. A tangential geezer, my old man.

I'd have loved Gunny's name. Vishy's feet were quick and his head was still and the willow was like a brush in his hand. Vishy had steel wrists, immaculate timing and an imaginative eye for the gap. Vishy was an artist.

I swigged my espresso. It was scalding. It cauterized my tongue. I jumped the road and two-timed the steps to my office. I'd come over all business-like.

Melody Chase glanced up when I came in. She was back in

the client's chair and puffing on a cig; one of mine. Her eyes looked kind of wet. She smacked kind of vulnerable. It was probably just the smoke. It gave the whole scenario a *noir* gel.

She said, 'You took your time.'

I said, 'You miss me?'

She tut-tutted and breathed more smoke.

I sat behind my desk. I blew across my coffee. I played it slow. I said, 'OK. Let's recap. You want me to find Natasha, your ho-buddy. She disappeared two nights ago after a gig with some geezer. He was a new punter, English, white, forty-five to fifty, well fed and with black, black hair. That about the size of it?'

'Sure.'

'Cool.' I sipped my espresso. I furrowed my brow. Meditative, for real. 'You catch the news last night?' She shook her head. 'Seen a paper this morning?'

The bird stared at me like one of those beady-eyed parrots: all fancy feathers and not a lot upstairs. I unfolded the front page across my desk. She studied the picture. I studied her. There was a flicker of something, all right – like the cowardly plantation rapist in her genes had blanched a shade – but then it was gone. She was cool, for real. I'd had that right.

Her head bobbed. Just the once. 'Yeah,' she said. 'That's the guy.'

'You reckon she did it?'

'Who?'

'Don't be funny. Sexyrussian.co.uk.'

'I dunno.' She shrugged. 'I doubt it. But I wasn't there. You're the detective, Mr Akhtar. Find Tasha and you can ask her yourself.'

I was dubious about this, serious. My mind was now crystal but it needed time to pulse. I sat back and cracked everything that would crack: my knuckles, my wrists, my neck. My jaw went too. That was a first. 'This smacks trouble,' I said. 'This smells dirty. This looks like a mess.'

The whore smiled. There was a daub of purple lipstick on one of her front pearlies. She polished it with that dextrous tongue. I looked away. I looked out of the window. Eighties blokey was back outside Khan's. He was scanning a tabloid sports page. I could see the same photograph staring off the front: the geezer. The geezer what's now dead, I thought. It sounded right with wrong grammar.

'You telling me you don't like dirt?' the tom was saying. 'You telling me you don't like mess?' There was a ha-ha in her voice and her head lolled back as she checked out the dirt and mess of my habitat.

'They're OK,' I muttered. 'But I don't need no trouble.'

Her head snapped round then and her eyes pinned me. I liked it. She leaned forward and her breasts made the arse crack of a heart above the neck of her top. Silicon Valley, I thought. Ha-ha of my own. I should be on stage. She reached into her handbag and fetched out an envelope. She counted out bold pink Elizabeths, thirty in all. 'Fifteen hundred up front, Mr Akhtar. There's more as you need it.'

'I'll poke around. But I ain't making no promises. Bill will be all over this like –'

'Like flies,' she finished my sentence.

'I was fishing for something better,' I said. 'But yeah. Flies will do.'

'I'll be waiting for your call,' she said. She stood up. She handed me her card. It read: 'Melody. Exotic Beauty'. There was a mobile number. There was e-mail. There was a web address. You can figure the URL.

I shook her hand. It was cool and dry. She turned for the door and shimmied her way out. I watched. She had an arse like an executive toy. Left cheek down, left cheek up, left cheek meets right cheek. Right cheek down, right cheek up, right cheek meets left cheek. You could watch an arse like that for ever. You could lose your executive job and it would cost you three long for each and every hour.

3

I let it lie for an hour. Don't ask me why. I tied Cub Scout knots in loose ends instead, made calls that had been on the list a couple of days.

I belled Mr X. I had his Beamer stashed in a garage round the back of my gaff. His wife had run off with some scumbag. He wasn't too vexed about that but there was no way he was gonna let her half-inch his pride and joy.

The job had gone smooth like cream cheese. I had a name, I pinned it to an address, Swiss Chris and me tailed the beloved motor into a West End NCP. I always use Phoenecia on a job. A real 'spread love' kind of geezer, me. I tipped Swiss a nugget and waited at the exit.

Scumbag and Mrs X were taking in a musical. Scumbag turned out to be a loss-adjuster from Cheam with jam-jar specs and a comb-over. There's no loss adjustment of taste. I watched them buy ice-cream and a family box of Maltesers: Lloyd-Webber romance for fifty quid, tops. I went back to the car park and bought myself a ticket. I was buying myself a motor. I had the Beamer started in a tick, no problem. I had Mr X's keys, didn't I? I gave the geezer at the gate my ticket and pulled out. Smooth like cream cheese.

I got the ansaphone. I left a message. Mr X would be chuffed. Money for old rope.

I belled Mrs Y. I'd been watching her old man. She was late twenties with a sprog on the way. She did tennis lessons, bridge and casseroles frozen in Tupperware. She was a late-twenties woman who discussed stuff like 'how you always used to keep your door on the latch'. She was a relic of another age. She was almost mythological. Her husband was forty plus, a banker, and his hours were stretching. Hook's Spring Law: they'd reached their elastic limit.

She'd wanted to know if he was seeing another woman. I queried the small print at the outset. 'What if it's not another *woman*?'

'He's not a bender if that's what you mean.' Bender? I didn't know people still used words like that. I wasn't sure people had ever used words like that. My cartoon life.

I mollified her. I came over all metaphorical. I said, 'I'm not saying nothing, Mrs Y. I'm just pointing out that your rooster's spending a lot of time away from the hen house, know what I mean? Perhaps he's fluffing another pillow and perhaps the pillow's pink. Or perhaps he's shooting dice or perhaps he's shooting smack. Frankly, I've no idea. Perhaps . . . just perhaps, mind . . . he's overtiming to surprise you with that farmhouse Provençale . . .'

'Do you think so?'

'I've no idea. What I'm saying is that if he's not seeing another woman, do you really want to know what he's up to?'

We'd to'd and fro'd for twenty minutes. Eventually we agreed that I'd tell her if it was 'something sexual'. That was the week previous.

Turned out this rooster had a thing for young bamboo and hard sports-lite. Turned out this rooster spent most evenings with a couple of teeny Thais round Bayswater having his nuts dipped in wax. They were now red raw. I had the pictures to prove it. Clearly blokey wasn't getting any marital or Mrs Y would have noticed. But he never shot his bolt with the bamboo; not once. So how do you define sexual?

I talked to Mrs Y for time. I skirted the subject and weighed the pros and cons. I made a value judgement. I said, 'It's nothing sexual.' When I put the phone down, I traced the rooster's e-mail and dropped him a note; friendly, for real. I told him about the pictures. I suggested he best start saving for a breath of Le Mistral. I shut down my computer. Call me the marriage counsellor.

I belled Mrs Z. Her sixteen-year-old daughter had run away. That was three days before. She'd called the Old Bill but what were they going to do? I'd done nothing. I knew there were pennies to drop.

I said I'd drawn a blank. Mrs Z was all apologies. Apparently Sophie had come home last night. It was all a misunderstanding. She'd meant to call me. She'd pay me for my time. A cheque was in the post. Easy money.

And so I finally turned to the newspaper. I read the whole story. There was Natasha's punt in grainy black and white. It was an archive shot. I stared at his boat for a full minute like it might reveal some secrets. I didn't pick up much beyond the way his eyebrows raised a little in the middle and the corners of his lips twitched upwards. He looked like a smug so-and-so. I wondered how smug he'd looked when he was eye to eye with the business end of a hammer.

The geezer's name was Anthony Bailey. He was a government MP – hence my 'this smacks trouble, dirt, mess' kind of take; an understatement, serious. He had a constituency somewhere up in Leeds. He was also a junior minister in the Foreign and Commonwealth Office. He'd been found beaten to death with a blunt instrument – probably a household hammer or similar – in a sixty-quid-a-night 'Businessman's Special' at the Holiday Inn Express just south of Battersea Bridge. His wallet was gone, his wedding ring, his watch. It had taken some time to identify the body. It seemed that his Palm Pilot had gone too. A government spokesman said this was a personal machine and contained no sensitive information. As yet, there were no witnesses. As yet, nobody was helping the Old Bill with their enquiries. As yet, there was no motive; none except the robbery.

Bailey had a house in the Leeds suburbs. There was a picture of that too. You could just make out his widow ducking inside. She wore a Barbour, a headscarf and shades. She'd issued a statement. My heart popped. Oh, yeah. It had been written by a Whitehall suit. It revealed nothing.

Bailey also kept a flat off the King's Road. It was being renovated and was currently a building site. For the last few weeks his London nights had alternated between family friends in Islington and odd nights at the Chichester, a boutique hotel in Pimlico. He'd never stayed at the Holiday Inn Express before. The paper pointed out that it was walking distance from his flat. Perhaps he'd planned to check up on the building work. The paper was filling space. The paper didn't have a clue.

I pondered. The story didn't tell me much. But that told me something. All the info was police release – no newshounds allowed – and the Bill were clearly playing it close to their chest.

I ran the X+Ys and came up with a few general equations.

Bailey meets Natasha in the Embassy. It's a public place and hardly smart on his part. Maybe it was his first punt and the bar gave him easy breathing. Unlikely. More likely he figured he was hardly *OK!*-famous so what the hell? Nonetheless, he's somewhat cautious. He's not going to take her back to the Chichester. They know him there. He's not going to take her to no other chichi joint in the neighbourhood neither because (1.) he might be recognized and (2.) the whore might start to get comfortable. So he takes her for a 'Businessman's Special'. It's south of the river. It's anonymous. It costs no more than an Ayrton in a cab. The sheets are clean.

They get to the room. They do the do. Or they don't. Perhaps Bailey gets a little rough and Natasha gets nasty. What? So she beats him to death? It didn't sound so likely. I've never heard of no whore carrying a blunt instrument in her handbag. Mace without a shadow, even a Tazer gun, but not no hammer. Whatever. Never rule it out. It didn't sound so likely but it wouldn't even touch six on the freakydeak barometer.

More likely Thug #1 turns up. He gets into the room – how? However – and introduces Bailey to Mrs Hammer. They kiss kiss – Mwah! Mwah!, two pecks and job done. Thug #1 scarpers.

Four questions. What was Thug #1 after? This didn't sound like no robbery to me. No jobbing crim walks into a hotel, takes the lift, picks a door and beats the occupant to death for his wallet and his palmtop. How did Thug #1 know where tom and punter were holed up? Bailey had never used the Holiday Inn Express before. So Thug #1 must have followed them; probably from the Embassy assuming they stopped nowhere else on the way. Either that or he was tipped off. Did Thug #1 get what he was after? If he was after Bailey, then a cautious 'yes'. Otherwise he wouldn't have pulped the politician. If he was after Natasha, then God knows. Because this led to the big Q. Where was the hooker? She wasn't dead. Nobody leaves no minister mangled in a hotel, then takes the time to dump a whore's corpse elsewhere. So maybe Thug #1 was looking for sexyrussian.co.uk after all and ushered her out with a bow and an ostentatious swish of the blunt instrument. Or maybe Natasha escaped somehow. Questions, questions.

I had a think. It wasn't too painful.

I called Cal Donnelly. He's a DS I know at the Battersea factory: Irish, drunk, dusty as a seamer's paradise at the Oval come August. A charming combo, for real. We get along fine.

When work is thin, I scour the London locals for juicy stories and prospective clients. Then I bell the nearest nick. I've got tame coppers at most of them. Cal Donnelly knows the drill. A good bloke.

'Donnelly?'

'Is that my immigrant friend? How you finding the weather?' He was one funny geezer, serious.

'Chilly. You?'

'Home from home. What you want?'

'Just fishing.'

He sighed. I could hear him chomping gum. A while back he'd told me CID had gone smoke-free. He was still suffering. 'I got a mugging. Some lawyer lost his watch among other things. He wants it back and he's willing to pay.'

'Flash piece?'

Chuckle. 'Some Timex crap. An heirloom. You know the score. Sentimental value.'

'No such thing. It's already down a drain. Along with the photos of Zak and Daisy.'

'Zak and Daisy?'

'His kids.'

'Aren't you the cynic? Might be worth a shot.'

'Cool,' I said. 'Thanks.' He told me the name. I paused like I was writing it down. I said, 'So what about Bailey, then?' I'm so subtle. I might as well have been whistling Stan Laurel-style.

His voice thinned. 'What about him?'

'Just making conversation. It's all over the papers. It's on your patch.'

'It's nothing to do with you, is it?'

I laughed. 'Just making conversation, Cal.'

'I said, it's nothing to do with you, is it?'

'You asking me? Course not. I don't even chase ambulances. I can't keep up. You know me, I'm small-time. I'd be small-time

29

on Lilliput.' He ha-hahed. He was sweet. 'So when am I gonna buy you that drink, then? I been promising since time.'

'You're telling me.'

'So how's about today? I'm gonna be down your neck of the woods as it goes.'

'Today it is. School's out at six. I'll meet you over the Hope and Anchor.'

'Later, then.'

I hung up. I checked my wrist. I wasn't wearing my watch. I fired up my desktop again. It's as knackered as its owner and took a minute or two to whir into life. I checked the time. It wasn't even midday. I opened the desk drawer and took out the Turk. Wild Turkey is my friend. Old friends can meet any time. They're easy together like that. I poured myself a large one and lit a Benny. Brunch.

I went online. The connection was slow. I don't surf. I pothole. I checked out sexyrussian.co.uk. There was Natasha interlacing in various poses and outfits: Natasha legs akimbo in a black leather thong, Natasha in school uniform bent over a desk, Natasha in a negligé looking as seductive as a chip shop after a night on the sauce. In all the pictures, her face was pixellated but I could make out her hair: blonde and limp. Her body was pasty and scrawny. Her breasts barely troubled the material of her black leather bra/cut-off white blouse/lace negligé. Her hips looked like the back end of an Indian cow. She needed a good feed. I pictured her raised on cabbage soup in Moscow, twenty degrees below. She had a tattoo round her belly button. Some Hindi writing. Classy.

I swilled my Turk and tugged on the cig. I pulled an expression like someone was watching. My stomach felt like it was chewing itself.

I had a thought. I reached in the pocket of my jeans and pulled out Melody's calling card. I tried another URL:

exoticmelody.co.uk. My new boss. I checked out the photos. As expected. Nutcracker thighs and ten to two nipples riding high on zeppelin breasts. The over-employed airbrush smacked eighties erotica. The pictures did nothing for me. I was somewhat disappointed.

I was more intrigued by the blurb. An hour in the 'company of a high class, exotic escort' was 250 notes incall, 300 out. She was 'educated to O level' but would 'consider A-level tuition with regular clients'. She was a non-smoker (apparently). She kissed. She liked to cuddle. She offered a 'true GFE' (whatever that was). All activities were covered 'for my safety and yours'. My favourite part was the following rider: 'No fantasies described in these pages should in any way be construed as an offer of sexual services for financial reward. I am a high-class escort. Anything that happens on our "date" [her quote marks] is a matter of choice between two consenting adults.' Check out all those euphemisms. I found them kind of touching. We live in a world of phallic chocolate bars, soap lathered over shadowed breasts and male genitalia straining the white cotton of designer underwear. But a whore still beats around the none-too-proverbial bush. Enjoy the incongruity.

I zapped the browser and checked my mail. I was offered 'snapshots the celebrities don't want you to see', a master's in psychology, a bank loan interest free for ninety days, the opportunity to sign a petition supporting the release of Burmese political prisoners, the opportunity to help the widow of a Nigerian dictator funnel cash into a Western bank account. The latter was 'no joke. No joke at all!' The information super highway. Super information. Super. I zapped the computer. I had lunch. The Turk was tasting good. I was killing time. It died slowly.

4

Time died and I died with it. We called a truce and elected to resurrect around half four. I struggled to the bathroom. The Turk was two-thirds done. I threw up. I remembered that Dean Jones once made a double hundred on the sub-continent and spent every interval with his head over the pan. One tough geezer. They breed them like that down under. I threw up again and felt a little better.

I took a shower. The water was needles that pin-pricked me to something like life. I scraped a razor across my face, I moisturized, I rinsed my mouth peppermint fresh. All the products were the same brand. My cheeks weren't smooth, my skin didn't glow and there was no sunbeam glistening from my pearlies. I looked nothing like the adverts.

In the bedroom, I chose my clothes careful: a tired navy suit, frayed white shirt and brown tie. I looked something like a school teacher on the pull, serious. It was the desired effect. I headed out.

I took Mr X's Beamer – perk of the job – and headed across the river. I got stuck on the South Circular. I got frustrated. Generally I avoid the rush-hour the same way I avoid pork; a question of taste masquerading as principle.

I gagged on exhaust and drive-time radio. I fantasized about an accountant losing the plot in his Audi and leaping out to batter a few of his fellow motorists with the wheel spanner. I might have joined in; egged him on at least.

I clocked the faces of executive gents, fixed on the brake-lights of the car in front as they pictured their frumpy wives at suburban doors, their aortas choking on business lunches and lost love. I clocked the faces of school-run mothers, half turned and hushing brats, their tendons strained at the neck as their petrol gauges began to flash. I clocked the faces of white-van drivers, indicators flicking impatiently as they planned their next short-cut, their veins pulsing the same rhythm at the temple. Welcome to the city of tiny lights. It takes you a lifetime to get somewhere you've no particular desire to go. You're welcome to it.

It was twenty to six before I pulled into the car park of the Hope. I was angry. I'd have mown down some pedestrians but there were none around so I just parked up.

The Hope and Anchor was your average London boozer; the kind you don't see so much these days. The décor was brown, the lighting murky, the gents' stank of warm beer and the saloon stank of warm piss: it was a typical coppers' hangout.

I'd timed my arrival just right. All chance, no design. The day relief must have knocked off at five and they were deep into their third and fourth pints. They were huddled around the pool table like a gang of playground bullies on a school trip. You can smell Old Bill in mufti. They can't get rid of the institutional stench. If you want an easier method of ID, just look out for the burly geezers in crap threads wearing expressions by turn shifty and dumb: coppers every time.

I leaned on the bar. My sleeve soaked up some lager. No problem. It all added to the image.

The barmaid was so tired and so filthy I wasn't sure whether to order a drink or propose. We were made for each other.

I said, 'You got bourbon?' and she curled a lip like I'd asked for a cocktail with its own pink umbrella. 'Wild Turkey?' I tried. She tutted and a fleck of her spittle spotted my cheek. I didn't wipe it away. 'Give me a Jack,' I said. 'Ice.'

'Single?'

'Double. Double JD on the rocks.' She looked at me like I was an idiot. I wasn't going to argue. Sometimes I say stuff and I don't know where it comes from.

I sipped my drink and sparked its condiment. Jack and Benny go together like salt and pepper, like Benny and Turk. My stomach was calm. It's about time of day; the body's natural cycles.

I turned to the plod playing pool. I bided my time. Plod #1 sank a long black. I applauded, made sure they looked round. They racked up another game. Early on, Plod #1 was umming and erring over a shot. It was the closest he'd come to thinking all day (in both the pluperfect and conditional senses of 'he'd').

I idled over and checked his angles. 'Take the double,' I said. 'A little left-hand side.'

Plod #1 stared at me like I was some kind of Martian. I stared back. We come in peace. He took it on and the ball fell with a pleasing 'thunk', leaving him perfect on the next solid on the balk.

Plod #2 was checking me out. I returned the favour. I said, 'You know Donnelly?' He pulled a so-what-if-I-do? kind of face. I smiled and shrugged. 'Easy, mate. I'm job. DC Akhtar. Shepherds Bush.' I offered him a hand from the sleeve of my crappy suit. He took it.

'You seen Donnelly?' I asked. 'I was supposed to meet him down here at half five.'

The geezer was still cagey. 'I'm sure he'll be down. The DS likes a sherbet.'

'At least you guys mix.' I laughed. 'Uniform and CID. That's healthy.'

Plods #1 and #2 were softening. I recalled Donnelly's war record. I told them we'd been probationers together down in

Streatham. I told them about our day on the front line at the Brixton riots. They lapped it up.

Plod #1 said, 'That must've been tricky for you. Being coloured. No offence.'

I said, 'It was. None taken.'

These guys were hardly fast-track material. I hoped I never had no grief on their beat, serious. These were the kind of geezers who thought 'common sense' was a class insult.

I bought a round. They were lubricated. I asked them about the Bailey case, just like that. They couldn't wait to talk.

'F__ing crazy,' Plod #2 said. 'That MP had his head beaten to mush. His own mother wouldn't have known him. I mean, what kind of person does something like that?'

Plod #1 said, 'Some f__ing cracker', and we all nodded and swallowed our drinks; respect.

Donnelly came in about five past six. I saw him first and clinked the lads farewell. 'My date's here,' I said, and gave it the ha-ha. The plods pumped my hand and clapped me on the back.

I bought Donnelly a drink. He joined me on the Jack. He came over all suspicious. 'Making friends?'

'Told them I was Old Bill,' I said. 'You know my kind. We love to fit in.' He left it alone.

I stayed forty-five minutes and bought two more rounds. Me and Donnelly chatted about not much. I gave him a tip about some shebeen I'd been to round Vauxhall. It was hardly serious crime but it would boost his stats. Donnelly told me that his missus had upped and left a couple of months back. He said that if he'd met me just afterwards he'd have probably clutched my arm and shed a booze tear. I was glad he hadn't. We weren't tight or nothing. He shrugged. He said she was back now anyway. He said he couldn't remember what all the fuss was about. He couldn't remember why she'd gone and he couldn't remember why she'd returned. He smiled. 'I doubt it was for the company,' he said.

I left before seven. I knew where I was heading next but there was no hurry. So I decided to stop round the old man's gaff, seeing as I was in the area. Someone's got to keep an eye on Farzad. He won't do it himself.

His yard is ex-council in a quiet side-street off Acre Lane. It's a cool enough area, although the recent influx of yuppies has somewhat lowered the tone: mostly shaggy-haired graduates with media jobs and a taste for perceived authenticity. You should see the faces of the locals when these pasty Bohemians make for the takeaway for a polystyrene carton of jerked this or curried that. Nobody does bemusement like Jamaicans.

Brixton: I wondered if this was exoticmelody's original neck of the woods. Could be, could be not. London's not so ghettoized these days. Check me out in my Chiswick pad.

I pulled up outside Farzad's. Trinidad Pete was sitting on the wall outside. He was swilling from a can of the black stuff. There was a dead one next to him and a fresh pair in a plastic bag at his feet. At the sight of me, he gave an expansive swish of his forearms. 'Picked up from off stump right over mid-wicket!' he said. 'King Viv.'

'King Viv,' I agreed.

'Nice motor, Tommy. You win the lottery, man?'

I slammed the driver's door. Even the sound it made was chunky and expensive. I beeped the alarm. 'Not mine,' I said. 'You keep an eye on it, Trinidad?'

He sniffed and dipped his head. 'I gotta couple appointments.' He was being abstract. I didn't get it. He stared at me for a minute, then nodded at the plastic bag at his feet. I got it. He smiled and I smiled back.

'You're a good man,' I said.

'Sit still long enough and generally speaking you get the chance to do somebody a fine turn.'

'And a philosopher too.'

'Sit still long enough and generally speaking you get the chance for some philosophizing.'

'Right you are,' I muttered. I walked past him and made for the front door.

Without looking round he said, 'The old man's not answering. Not to me anywise.'

'Right.'

I banged on the door. There was no reply. I dropped to my haunches and pushed open the letterbox. 'Farzad,' I shouted. 'It's your number-one son.' Still nothing. 'Dad. It's me. Open the door.'

I heard the clink of glass. I heard the patter of the old man's feet. I heard him wheezing. I straightened up.

Farzad looked worse than usual. That was saying something. He looked older than his sixty-six years, shorter than his five foot four and lighter than the eight stones he'd weighed last time I asked. He looked washed out, like his aged Ugandan-Indian skin had begun to fade with wear. As a kid, I remembered him dark and glossy like oiled leather. Now his face looked like a scrunched-up ball of paper ready for tossing, like a cricket ball after twenty overs of Tendulkar fireworks. He looked shrivelled. If you'd dropped him in a vat of olive oil in a Chiswick delicatessen, you could have sold him to rich housewives at a fiver a pound: 'sun-dried immigrant'. He was wearing his enormous old T-shirt with a picture of Bob Marley on the front and a pair of pin-striped boxer shorts that hung to his knees. His 'outfit' was covered with various-coloured blobs of paint. So were his hands and arms and legs.

'What do you want, Tommy?' he snapped. 'Can't an OAP be left in peace? I'm working, for goodness' sake.'

He was drunk. When he was sober, he slept or sat melancholically mournful in his armchair (a threadbare, brown velveteen number – his first purchase on British soil). Mostly he was drunk. When he was drunk, he watched cricket or painted. Mostly he watched cricket. Today he was painting.

'What are you working on?'

'What do you think I'm working on? A cure for cancer? I'm painting, Tommy boy. I'm working on a picture. What did I ever do to deserve two bleeding numbskulls for sons?' He kissed me. His cheek was rough and clammy. It had the texture and stink of a beer cloth after a hard night's mopping. 'I suppose you're coming in.' He looked past me to where Trinidad Pete was perched on the wall. 'What are you staring at, you black bastard? Go home.' Trinidad raised his can. Cheers.

After Mina died, the men of the Akhtar family splintered. It's not surprising. Death is a Spaghetti Junction with many slip-roads. These lead past familiar houses, parades of shops and so forth into new and surprising landscapes. They're trippy tours, serious, but travel them long enough and they'll generally find their way back to that same junction. Or, to put it another way, most roads don't lead nowhere special: they just pass places. You'll see what I mean.

Gundappa, for example, was vexed with his mother for dying and he told anyone who'd listen. Over the next decade, he'd developed a view of himself as essentially hard-done-by. He's not interested in nobody else.

Gunny discovered dope and he discovered blondes. Roughly in that order. The former just about financed the latter. He denied everything that he was and assumed a vicarious identity that required an enormous amount of puff for its upkeep (both literal and metaphorical, as it were). He got a reputation as a minor hooligan of note. He had minor law trouble. He should have turned to what was left of his family but they had problems of their own. He moved to Harlesden, then Wood Green, then Hackney. Finally he settled in Leytonstone. He spent most of his time at the dog track. He enjoyed its arbitrary justice. He learned to back traps five and six, he learned to fleece a punter with a smile on his face and he was taught to nobble a greyhound with no more than a bucket of water by a man called Miami Tony on account of his orange tan. He hung out with proper geezers and began to talk the talk. He watched the Hammers at Upton Park, and when black players touched the ball, he joined in with the monkey noises. This wasn't an act of race hatred but of belonging.

He raced GT Turbos recklessly and didn't think about no consequences.

One time, his opponent hit a concrete bollard, headlonged through the windscreen and landed faceless on the tarmac. Gunny and his boys legged it sharpish. The car was hot and the geezer was dead so there was no need of an ambulance. Now, when he gets drunk, he tells that story like he's some kind of war hero. Sometimes he adds gory details that never happened. Somehow he recalls a severed hand lying on the tarmac, its fingers flexed like it was trying to crawl away.

Now, when he gets really drunk, he remembers his mother. The pictures are numerous and fleeting but one stands out. He was about ten years old when a couple of squaddies came in the shop. Farzad was at the cash-and-carry, Gunny was hidden behind the counter, Mina was at the till. The squaddies were laughing and nudging each other. One of them muttered, 'Watch this.' He turned to Mina and said, 'Give us a pack of blue Rizla, you Paki bitch.' His face was straight, his expression didn't flicker. He paid with a ten-pound note. Mina handed over the Rizla and carefully counted out the charmer's change.

Nine pounds and ninety-two pence. She looked at Gunny, squatting on the floor behind the counter, and her eyes were dry and sleepy. He is ashamed of this memory. He is ashamed of his mother's weakness. I guess he's scared it's genetic. He's done everything he can to squash it.

Back in Leytonstone, Gunny got in with organized crime. One of the big families was moving into the area from their traditional Essex stomping-ground. The boss had finally come round to the idea that drugs were a virtue and he planned to muscle the Yardies out of their monopoly in a none too subtle way. To describe crime as 'organized' has always been a contradiction.

Gunny was no more than a body, a cog in the creaking machine, but he started driving for one of the old timers from the family and they got kind of close. The war got ugly. There were a couple of shootings and a lot of beatings and torchings. Even the Bill couldn't ignore this kind of trouble. The old timer asked Gunny about his background. Gunny said nothing. The old timer suggested Gunny should get out while he could. A week later, the old timer had his skull cracked in an alley behind Safeway. The family took out their revenge on three teenage mules in Peckham. Gunny got out.

Gunny took time off. He started dealing weed again. He couldn't rinse it no more. There were younger geezers with better contacts. Besides, he'd lost his enthusiasm. He had some money saved. He spent it on indistinguishable blondes in West End nightclubs. One of them gave him the clap. He only went to the doctor when his piss burned him to tears. He got a course of antibiotics and went to stay with Farzad. He didn't talk to his father much and he didn't think about him at all. But he thought a lot about his mother. He decided he hated her.

Gunny stayed with the old man pushing three years. Eventually Farzad suggested he move out and offered him the chance to start a business in the Chiswick shop, which had been boarded up a long time. Farzad said to him, 'Do you think this is what your mother wanted for you? To be a layabout?' Gunny didn't care what his mother wanted but he moved out nonetheless, partly because his brother was now staying round Farzad's too and partly because it all helped his own sense of injustice.

As for Tommy, he knows something about his mother's death that he's never told nobody. In the last decade, he's developed a tendency to describe subsequent events in the third person. He feels like he's describing someone else.

Tommy discovered guilt and he discovered religion. Roughly in that order. The latter was fuelled by the former. He decided he was nothing and assumed a piety that required an enormous amount of prayer and denial for its upkeep. He got a reputation as a young Muslim of note. He had a minor mental-health episode. He should have turned to what was left of his family but they had problems of their own. Instead he travelled to Ahmadabad, then Lahore, then Peshawar. Finally he set out for Zhawar. He joined the mujahideen of Gulbuddin Hekmatyar. He was part of a just war. He learned to use a Chinese 7.62 RPK, he learned to live off tea and rancid *nan* for days at a time, and he was taught to slice a man from 'his navel to his chops' by a former English teacher from Riyadh. He prayed and he trained and he began to see action. He watched the Soviet personnel carriers flounder on the rocks. Those machines were nicknamed 'mobile coffins' by the Hizb-e-Islami and each time a rocket found its target he whooped with the rest and picked off the Red Army boys one by one. This wasn't an act of religion or politics but belonging.

He watched his new brothers die in droves and found he felt nothing.

One time, he slipped as they were attacking a column and

he shot the Saudi English teacher through the back of his head. Tommy swept past his body without looking down. The bullets were zipping and popping around him so he had no time for self-recrimination. Now that he gets drunk, he often pictures the English teacher's face. Sometimes he recalls the sound the man made as he fell. Somehow, over the shooting, his last breath whined like the string retracting into a plastic doll's plastic guts: 'Mama'.

Now that he gets really drunk, he tries to remember his mother. But his efforts only ever produce the same image again and again. He was about thirteen years old and sick in bed with the flu. While Farzad was at the shop and Gunny at school, Mina had stopped home to look after him. He was woken from a feverish sleep by her standing over him with a tray. 'I brought you some potato soup,' she said. 'You must eat something, habibi. To keep your strength up.' His face was clammy with sweat and his vision was blurred. As Mina bent over him, she was silhouetted against the grey light of the window behind. His head was suddenly filled with her various smells: of shampoo, cardamom and rose petals. In his delirium, he didn't recognize this figure as his mother but mistook her for some kind of angel. She set the tray down on the bedside table, wiped his forehead and, as she turned to leave the room, she affectionately patted his erection, which was pressing up from beneath the blankets. He is not ashamed of this memory. He is not ashamed of his mum's love. Sometimes he wonders if it's a part of him too. He's never seen it.

Back in Afghanistan Tommy fell out with the radicals and got in with the Yanks, mostly loud-mouthed charlies with designer shades and a deathwish but sprinkled with the occasional taciturn and thoughtful geezer who'd figured the real deal. The Agency had finally come round to the idea that direct involvement was a necessity and the number of so-called advisers increased tenfold. To describe the CIA as an 'agency' has always been a euphemism.

Tommy was dispensable, no more than an ant crawling over the Red Army's picnic, but as an English speaker he started driving for one of the Yanks, Agent Stanton, and they got kind of close. The war got uglier still. A nation was reduced to craters and rubble and dusty kids with guns for crutches. Even the world's press couldn't ignore this kind of trouble. Stanton asked Tommy about his background. Tommy told him everything. Stanton told Tommy to get out and arranged passage back into Pakistan. Stanton was blown to bits by a PDPA landmine not far from Kabul. The Agency was relieved that his corpse was mutilated beyond recognition. Tommy fled about the same time as the Soviets.

Tommy took time out. He stopped praying. It didn't work for him no more. There was no connection, no spark, no enthusiasm. He was broke and sick to the core (head and heart). He made it back to Blighty and slept in West End doorways with Falklands vets. One of them held a knife to his neck and stole his shoes. About a year later, another asked about his family and led him to a night shelter. Tommy got a shower, a new set of clothes and a care worker. He went to stay with Farzad and Gunny. He didn't talk to them much but he thought about them a lot. He thought about his mother too. He decided that if her death was his fault, he might as well give up now, and if not, her memory deserved better. But he wasn't sure he had it in him.

Tommy stayed with the old man pushing three years. Eventually Farzad suggested he move out and offered him the chance to move into the Chiswick flat, which had been deserted a long time. Farzad said to him, 'Do you think this is what your mother wanted for you? To be so unhappy?' Tommy didn't care about unhappiness but he moved out nonetheless, because nothing mattered more than his mum's wishes.

And Farzad? He was confused when his wife left him behind. He found alcohol and art at about the same time. At first the latter financed the former. He recognized everything that he was – a Ugandan, Indian, Paki and Englishman. A doctor, shopkeeper, widower and father. An immigrant, citizen, *émigré* and refugee – and the weight of it exhausted him and squeezed out pictures. He got a reputation as a post-colonial artist of note. He had some minor press. He exhibited in bars, community centres and warehouse spaces. Eventually he was even part of a major collection: 'Winds of Change'. He learned to paint by numbers, he learned to conjure Gauguin exotica from some alchemy in the logical synapses of his doctor's brain, and he was taught to press pink flesh and smile by a Zimbabwean sculptor called 'Hondo', which means, he was told, 'war'. He pressed and he painted and he began to shift canvas. He watched geezers with cigars and comb-overs gush over his political perspective and when they demanded to meet the artist he treated them with semi-shrouded contempt. This wasn't an act of integrity but marketing. He watched his work sell in droves and found he felt nothing.

Briefly, until the drink made it impossible, he took up cricket again. One time, he made a chanceless ton on a sticky wicket in Hounslow. Farzad swept their leggy to distraction. Wickets tumbled around him but, the oldest man in the side, he kept his concentration intact. Now, when he gets drunk, he tells you he cannot remember one of those sweep shots. Instead he remembers only a single off drive dispatched from the returning seamer's loosener. Somehow he can always re-create the synchronicity of movement, balance and timing in that one stroke. 'The oldest man in the side by twenty years,' he reminisces. 'It was a moment of perfection.'

When he gets really drunk, he recalls his wife. But it is as if his memory is a Pathe newsreel that is looped to infinity. It can't have been more than a couple of years before they left Uganda and they were driving home from supper with Arshad Patel. Tommy was asleep in the back seat of the Land Rover, Mina was chattering next to him and she was heavily pregnant with Gundappa. The road was pitch black and his beam didn't pick out the street dog in time and it took a hideous glancing blow. They heard it yelp and whine and he could see it in the rear-view mirror. Farzad would have driven on, of course, but Mina insisted, 'Stop the car, habibi!' They got out and examined the animal. It was more dead than alive, its breathing shallow and uneven, its ribs flickering like an eyelid in deep sleep. While Farzad watched, Mina fetched a heavy stone from the side of the road. She hitched up her sari to gain more leverage for her strike, and although Farzad was a doctor, he looked away as she brought the stone down into the poor dog's skull. They didn't talk all the way home. He was deeply moved by his wife's intuitive courage and he is still deeply moved by this memory. Sometimes he thinks that his own bravest day was spent on one knee in Hounslow, paddling the furious spinner to the leg-side sweeper for one comfortable single after another.

Back in the art world, Farzad got in with the cognoscenti, mostly fey middle-aged men who dressed at least fifteen years too young or highly strung women whose intellects flickered like a nervous twitch. Some of these people were journalists and they were eager to know about his childhood, his flight from Amin and the loss of his wife. Once Farzad commented that to describe his pictures as 'post-colonial' was 'like describing tea as post-prandial'. This remark was widely quoted. To describe these hacks as cognoscenti was a joke.

Farzad was flavour of the month but he was wise enough

to know the clock was ticking. He hated the endless rounds of meet and greet and he was drinking heavily to get through it. The backlash was ugly. His last major show was rubbished by all those who'd fêted him, even the gaggle of queens for whom previously he could do no wrong. Farzad didn't care. There was drinking to be done. He retreated.

Farzad took time. He stopped painting. It didn't work for him no more. There was no connection, no spark, no enthusiasm; not even for cricket. He'd made some good money and bought the house off Acre Lane; anything to get away from the Chiswick flat, which was haunted by his dead wife, of course, but also by the compromises he'd made in the name of his family that now seemed to mean nothing. After a while his sons moved in with him; first Gundappa then Tommy. He didn't talk to them much but their presence eventually made him paint again. He thought about Mina and he painted her on his living-room wall whenever the mood took him. If he didn't like what he'd done or he was bored with it or he was just feeling particularly cussed, he'd whitewash it and begin again. He started to believe that white was the wall's pure state and that his compulsion to paint it denoted his human imperfection.

Farzad couldn't tell whether it was his sons' presence or the painting that was driving him crazy. Eventually he suggested they move back to Chiswick, first one then the other. Farzad said to himself, 'Do you think this is what your wife wanted for you? To be broken?' But he couldn't care about the answer and he kept painting nonetheless; because nothing mattered more than this regular, endless cycle of sin, redemption and rebirth. It had been revolving for almost a decade but Farzad had lost any sense of time.

So you see what I mean. It's not the arriving but the journey: life as tourism.

I walked into the living room and found that the old man was working frenetically. The picture was clearly my mother but the style was unusual. She was in profile, her skin tone was oddly pink and her eyes sleepy and placid. Around her, there were pencil sketches of what appeared to be Africans beating each other with hoes and spades and impaling each other on forks.

Farzad was pouring himself a drink. He said, 'What do you think? My wife as Frida Kahlo. Myself as Rivera. I don't have an original bone in my body.'

I didn't reply.

He said, 'So what do you want, Tommy boy?'

'I was just passing. I'm on a case.'

'What case? Another missing poodle for the great detective?'

'A disappearance,' I said. 'And a murder.'

Farzad rinsed his mouth with whisky. He wiped it on Bob Marley and peered at me. He said, 'You'd never have made a proper batter, Tommy boy. Too tall. No good against the quicks. You know the best player of fast bowling I ever saw? Sunny Gavaskar. Five foot four or thereabouts. My height. All of Thommo's bumpers flew way over his head. But you? They'd take your teeth out.'

Five minutes later I left.

5

I met this bird once in a Chiswick bar-restaurant. It was one of those *faux*-American rib joints that seem to breed in suburbia. She was mid-twenties with pin-prick eyes, a Spam complexion and a heavy masculine jaw, like she'd spent her whole life chewing calamari. She'd been drinking margaritas and approached my table unsteadily. She said she'd seen me watching her. I didn't set her straight. She asked me what I did and I pondered the options. I settled on lawyer and flashed her one of the business cards I keep for these and other deceptions. I said I worked with asylum-seekers, human rights, fighting deportations. She was half-way impressed. She told me she was a freelance fabric designer. I didn't know what that was. She said she designed the patterns for carpets in chains of shoe shops, the seating on fleets of coaches, car interiors, that kind of thing. 'The new Ford Focus,' she said. 'That's one of mine.' I pointed at the stitched diamond pattern that backed every chair in the bar. She shook her head. 'Looks in-house to me.' We left together. I was going to head back to her place. I couldn't bring myself to go through with it. I called Phoenecia. She was driven home by Big John. Next day he told me he'd pulled. Her little eyes must have popped.

I thought about her as I stared down between my feet at the carpet in the lobby of the Holiday Inn Express by Battersea Bridge. I wondered if she'd designed the intricate swirling patterns of greens and greys that hid the dirt and branded the chain all at once. Or maybe it was designed in-house. I wondered how you tell. These days people do peculiar things to earn a crust. These days there are peculiar forms of expertise. When I was a kid, Mina taught me the nursery rhyme about the butcher, the baker and the candlestick-maker. I remember thinking, What? This guy *only* makes candlesticks? It had sounded so unlikely. Now a bird's paid to design corporate homogeny. How unlikely is that?

I checked in about half eight. Before doing so, I sat in the car park for a couple of minutes and studied my reflection in the rear-view mirror. I made the necessary adjustments. I straightened my tie and tightened the knot at the collar. I took out a comb and gave myself a perfect side parting, pushing my fringe into a clump above my right brow. I licked my right palm and pasted it across my barnet until it glistened. I looked square, serious. I got out of the car and rolled my neck a couple of times. Then I rolled my shoulders before pushing them forward in a tired kind of hunch. The final touch.

I walked in past a camera crew packing up. The reporter was a smooth-looking geezer with slick hair and a slick suit. Blokey looked pleased with himself. One of his eyebrows appeared to have been stapled up just about an inch below his hairline. It gave him an expression of unruffled, sardonic surprise. I guessed he was a minor BBC hack. I guessed he'd been to a minor war or two. I guessed he'd been fitted with a flak jacket and heard the occasional bang. Blokey had world-weary down pat. I knew his type.

There was uniform either side of the automatic door, standing to attention and suppressing yawns. A glance to my right took in a couple of guys in narrow suits lounging against the flank of a navy saloon; maybe a top of the range Vauxhall. One of them was talking into a mobile phone. Special Branch.

I took a Businessman's Special. Sixty notes. I asked for a room on the top floor for the view. The spotty teen was impressively efficient. No problem. I clocked the CCTV cameras on either side of the lobby. Their lights were dead. Either they'd never worked or the cops had taken the tapes and not turned them back on. I looked up at the kid and decided to get conversational. 'All the police,' I said. 'What is happening, please?'

'We had a murder here last night. An MP.' The kid was so frank I almost cracked up. I don't reckon his candour was company policy.

I played the shock-horror: gob-smacked-of-Gujarat. 'Blimey!' I exclaimed. 'Will I be safe in your establishment?'

The kid laughed: 'Safe as houses. Look at all the coppers!'

'And I notice you have security cameras and such technical wizardry.'

His eyes levelled. 'Yeah,' he said. 'Right.' I took in his expression from a long distance, way behind my own. It didn't take no mind-reader to figure the cameras were just for show.

I signed the register. Younis Khan. Leicester. The kid asked me for ID. I played a little indignation. 'For what purpose, please?'

He shrugged apologetically. 'The police told us. After last night. I think they're worried about journalists.'

I tutted. 'The tabloids are the curse of our country,' I said and produced a driving licence from my wallet. He took it and noted down the details.

Let me tell you something. Whatever anybody says, it's no joke getting fake documentation in the UK. Passports, National Insurance numbers, even birth certificates: you can track them down if you have to but you pay through the nose. So you need to think about your purposes. Like, I've got all kinds of fake this, that and the other but, for my purposes, a driving licence will almost always suffice. The old-style licences are just pieces of pink paper. You borrow a licence, take it to a colour photocopier and you're sorted. You fold it into eight and slide it into a cheap plastic wallet with the name and address showing. Who's going to take it out and give it a proper gander? Nobody, that's who. I've got about twenty. They've worked in banks, hotels and even, when push once came to shove, with the Old Bill when they decided to give me a tug for no more than the colour of my boat. And the only time I've been caught out? By some jumped-up little tart in Blockbuster. I was up for a night of *Star Wars* and a Chinese. I had to make do with TV.

I paid in cash and was chuffed when the kid gave me one of those credit-card-style keys. It would make my job a whole lot easier. I took a stroll round the ground floor. It didn't take long. To the left of Reception, there were double doors with a sign on them saying, 'Bar/Breakfast Room/Lounge'. Multi-tasking, serious. I pushed through them and had to take an immediate right, which opened up into a festival of Formica functionality. There were half a dozen ugly lounge chairs surrounding a couple of varnished pine coffee-tables littered with the day's papers. Bailey's face stared up from every one. There was also an orderly arrangement of upright chairs surrounding small tables. Only the plastic menus that stood vertical on each table and the small bar at the far end distinguished this place from a recently refurbished sixth-form common room.

Three hacks were huddled round one of the tables. One of them was scribbling in a notebook. The other pair were chatting conspiratorially. They were all smoking hard and swilling from tumblers of double this or double that. Living the dream, for real. Apart from those guys, there were a couple of Asians leaning over the bar. They looked like south Indians to me. Trinidad Pete once told me that in this country black people usually acknowledge each other across a room and if they don't there's probably a reason. I reckon it works the other way round with Asians. It's not that we don't want to stick together but we don't want to be seen to. These two glanced up at me and quickly looked away.

I approached the bar. I was tempted to have a swift one but thought better of it. I talked to the barman. He was a middle-aged Geordie with blond highlights in his hair. I wondered how he'd ended up there. I asked him how long the bar stayed open. He said, 'As long as there are people drinking.' He didn't look best pleased about it. I nodded and about-turned.

I took the lift to the sixth floor. I briefly clocked the layout. It was an L-shaped corridor of around twenty rooms. It matched the plan of the lobby and multi-functional bar exactly. That meant every floor was just the same. The lift was near the corner of the L. I checked my bearings. It was facing out towards the car park.

At either end of the corridor there was an emergency exit leading to stairs that headed, I was guessing, outside to the car park on one side and the street on the other. The doors were wooden with glass panels surrounding wire mesh. They were the kind that deadlocked behind you. That was inconvenient. I needed some kind of plan.

First things first: I had to locate Bailey's room. I chose the emergency exit at the end to the left of the lift. I kept it open with a wedge of paper and went down the stairs. I peered through the panes at every floor but no joy. The room had to be on the other side of the L. I went back to the sixth and repeated the process from the emergency exit at the far end. At the fourth floor I found what I was looking for. I could see a single line of police tape strung out across a door counting five down. Next to it there was a single PC. He was sitting on a stiff chair like the ones in the bar and reading a paper. I watched for a couple of minutes but nobody else came. That wasn't surprising. Two uniform at the hotel entrance and one at the room sounded about right.

I had one more preparation to make. From my own floor I took the lift down to the fourth. The door slid open and I took an immediate left. I knew the copper couldn't see the lift but he could certainly hear it and, unless he was seriously dozy, he'd have to check. I idled down the corridor but was only twenty feet from the emergency exit before I was called to a halt.

'Excuse me, sir?'

I turned round abruptly. I dropped a little shock and then an obsequious Paki grin. 'Yes please, Officer?'

'This floor is closed to guests.' He checked me up and down. I kept smiling.

'Sorry. Please?'

'I said the floor's closed to guests.' He'd raised his voice a notch or two. I wanted to say to him, I'm playing foreign not deaf.

'Please? The four look like L for lobby.' I sniffed dramatically, gargled a ball of phlegm into my mouth and swallowed heartily. I pointed to the exit. 'Car park?'

I turned down the corridor. I knew he was watching me leave. I knew he wouldn't wait to check. At the door, I glanced back and sure enough he was gone. I opened the door and shut it with a bang. I listened. After a moment or two I heard the creak of his chair and the rustle of the newspaper. He wouldn't remember me. For all the talk of Muslim this and fundamentalist that, in this country nobody can be invisible like a Paki (of whatever nationality . . . Pakistani, Indian, Ugandan or even English). It's ingrained in the national psyche. Whites can be threatening, blacks can be threatening but, most of the time to most people, Pakis are just Pakis, even to Pakis. I'm only telling it like it is. That's the trouble with kids like Av Khan (maybe older kids like Gunny too): they're desperate to be conspicuous.

I gently eased open the fire exit again and secured it with my wedge of paper. I headed downstairs to the car park, back in through the lobby and up to my room in the lift. All this toing and froing and downing and upping. Nobody wants to know the layout of a cheap hotel that well. It gets kind of depressing.

I set the alarm on my mobile and lay on my bed. I kipped easy. I dreamed about my client: the hooker, exoticmelody. In the dream, she was one of those cardboard cut-out dolls you used to get free with girls' magazines in the seventies. She was in her underwear and then you could dress her in all sorts of different outfits by folding cardboard tabs around her shoulders, waist and hips: a nurse, a ballerina, a princess, that kind of thing. God knows what the dream was about. Apart from the obvious.

My phone beeped at one thirty. I sat up. I felt like crap. I gathered my thoughts. There weren't many so it didn't take long.

I took the lift to the ground floor. Surprise, surprise . . . there was the plod who was supposed to be guarding Bailey's room chatting idly to his mates at the entrance. Farzad has it right: competence is an underrated commodity and, what's more, it's rare too.

I headed straight to the bar. The tables were already set out for the morning. At one side, the breakfast buffet was ready to go. There were large bowls of bran cereals, yoghurt and tinned fruit covered with clingfilm wrapping. The Geordie was nowhere to be seen. I rang the bell on the counter but he didn't show up. I guess he was dreaming of his own cardboard cut-out. I went behind the bar and helped myself to a large Turk. I left a lady poked under the drawer of the till.

In the lobby, PC Halfwit and his friends gave me the once-over. I nodded respectfully, raised my glass and called the lift.

'Trouble sleeping, sir?' one of them said.

'Most problematic,' I agreed.

Halfwit said, 'Must be a guilty conscience.'

I forced a smile. 'That's a good one. Guilty conscience. Yes, indeed.'

I pushed button six while the plod watched. The Turk was done before I hit my room. I left the glass by the basin and picked up my gloves. They're cricketers' inners; thin brushed cotton so that the batter doesn't lose his feel for the blade. They're perfect for what I do.

I took the stairs down to the fourth floor. The emergency exit was still wedged open as I'd left it. I walked down the corridor. I could hear my heartbeat thumping. I had that nervousness, that exhilaration: the kind that makes you feel the breath go into your lungs, the oxygen pump round your veins and your heart thud like a fist on an oak door. It was the same feeling I used to get thieving from Akhtar's. It was a feeling I'd never had in all my months in the Kush: not when a bullet bit the rock behind my head, or when I blew a point-blank hole in a Soviet trooper's chest, or even when I accidentally shot the Saudi English teacher. How do you explain that? I checked the lights above the lift as I passed. It was still stuck on floor six. I wondered if I'd hear it beep and whir from Bailey's room. I doubted it.

At the room, I carefully unstuck the strip of police tape. I checked myself. You might wonder what I was looking for. I wondered the same, for real. I didn't expect to find anything but I needed to see nonetheless. I wanted to build a picture.

I was inside no more than five minutes. I didn't learn much but I learned something. It's often the way. By the time you're an adult, learning usually means confirming what you already know. You don't learn nothing new.

The room was stripped bare. The furniture was still there but linen, mattress, pillows, towels, tooth-mugs, shower curtain and the like had all been taken away. On the desk in the corner, one of the forensics boys had left a couple of empty sample bags and a pair of plastic gloves. They were scrunched up and half inside out in a way that made them look peculiarly arthritic: like an old man had been clinging to the desk for dear life at the moment his hands were severed at the wrist. Strange the things you think.

The first bloodstain was no more than a couple of feet inside the room. It was less a stain than a splattering that had even made it to the frame of the bed. Looking at the base of the door, there was a sizeable dent on the inside and the chipboard was splintered. The main area was in the very middle of the room. There was a damp, reddish-brown puddle about a foot in diameter. It looked like some geezer had upturned a bucket of the stuff. There was a different stain next to it. I squatted down and had a gander. Seemed like Bailey had pissed his pants too. Isn't my life charming? Finally, there was another substantial patch of the MP's life beneath the window-sill and a few spots climbed the pane like some kind of freaky decoration. I took a look at the foot of the bed on the window side. A neat square had been carefully cut away from the wooden leg. What was that about?

I pondered the ponderables. This was what I came up with. There was no sign of forced entry so Thug #1 must have knocked. Bailey opened the door. He had his foot behind it so, when Thug #1 dropped his shoulder, Bailey's foot must have got stuck. Hence the dent at the bottom. Bailey probably yelped so Thug #1 needed to land a blow sharpish. Thug #1 was right-handed. Whether it was hammer or fist, Thug #1 swung and caught the minister nice enough; nice enough for the blood to reach the bed anyway. The force of it turned Bailey right around. That's what I reckoned. I pictured him lying on his front in the middle of the room. Thug #1 shut the door behind him and got ready to do the business. He raised the hammer high. Maybe it was at this point that Bailey wet himself or maybe it was after the hammer fell. It didn't much matter. It would have taken one blow if it was good and clean but he probably dropped a second, just to make sure.

By now, Bailey was dead. Only he didn't know it yet. He couldn't see the back of his own head so he didn't see his cerebellum staring at the ceiling. I guessed some kind of misplaced survival instinct raised him to his knees and he crawled towards the window. He tried to pull himself up on the sill. Thug #1 took his time. Maybe he was savouring the moment or maybe his stomach was churning now. Even the toughest geezers get nauseous. He lifted the hammer above his right shoulder and brought it down one more time. That explained the spots of stained glass and it explained the piece the Old Bill had removed from the bed frame. It had probably been embedded with shrapnel: hair and scalp and a shard or two of Bailey's skull.

Conclusions? I didn't know about conclusions but there were a couple of best guesses. (1.) This confirmed it wasn't no frenzied attack by some crackhead nutter. Sure, it was violent but there were no signs of real struggle and none of the tell-tale marks of savage lunacy. To me, Thug #1 was clearly just a geezer doing what he came to do. (2.) I figured the whore wasn't there. Why? Let me put it to you like this. First, they didn't find her sorry corpse. Second, there are degrees of viciousness that, generally speaking, preclude the possibility of witnesses. There are some things so grotesque that people don't do them in front of other people unless they're making a point. I figured that this clumsiest form of brain surgery was one such thing. Maybe you think I sound kind of naïve but I'm talking from experience. I've seen religious types rape wives in front of their husbands and castrate husbands in front of their wives. But that's different because they were making a point to spouses, themselves and to God. There wasn't no point to be made to a strung-out Russian whore: they're a penny a pop. So the whore wasn't there. So where was she?

I took the stairs back to my room. I slept like a baby. I didn't dream.

I was up at six thirty. At Reception, I dropped my key into the box. There was a new kid at the far end of the desk but she didn't even glance up. I had a thought. I walked quickly and quietly to the exit before I looked back. The kid was still flicking idly through a Rolodex. My thought was confirmed: you could certainly come in and out of this hotel and never be seen. I nodded at the plod as I left.

I sauntered across the car park but for the moment ignored my ride. Instead I ducked down the short alley that led out to the main road. I didn't know what I was looking for but I knew there was something to see. In the alley, I paused over three clean squares of tarmac against the fence from where three hefty objects had recently been moved. I did some figuring. I guessed these were where the hotel's wheelie-bins had stood. I guessed the cops had taken them away and were currently hunting through crap for the murder weapon. I guessed they'd have no joy and were most likely looking for the wrong thing in the wrong place anyway. No imagination, coppers.

At the main road I looked left and right: left to Battersea Bridge and right towards Clapham. A couple of cabs passed, heading into town for the early-morning City trade. Their lights were bright through the dawn mist.

I turned towards the bridge. Fifty yards up there was a forlorn parade of shops: a bookie, a greasy spoon, a news-agent's and the ubiquitous and so familiar sell-everything-and-nothing Asian-owned grocer's. This one had a dull yellow sign that said, 'ABC Minimart (24 Hours)'.

Outside the shops, there was a pair of dustbins. This was where the Old Bill should have been looking. I pulled on my gloves, I pulled a face, I poked around. Don't call it instinct, call it experience.

Beneath the newspapers, discarded chicken bones and burger cartons, I found a generic blue plastic bag with no high-street branding. I dragged it out and let the bin juice drip. I opened it up and peered inside. There was a receipt. It didn't say what the receipt was for, just the shop, the price, and the time and date. ABC Minimart (24 Hours), £5.99, 11.45 p.m., three nights previous. Another cab drove past and over Batter-sea Bridge. I watched it disappear. I reckoned I had the whole story.

Bailey and sexyrussian made it back to the Holiday Inn Express around eleven thirty. They didn't know they were being followed by Thug #1. I figured Bailey started pawing the whore in the lift. She fended him off. His breath was sour with alcohol and his clothes reeked of smoke. By the time they got to the room, he was all over her like a rash. She said she fancied another drink. She *needed* another drink. She said she'd nip out; maybe she suggested he take a shower. Sexy-russian left the room. Perhaps she headed down to the bar first. Probably not. She knew hotels like this and she knew there'd be no one serving. Instead she went to the ABC Minimart (24 Hours) who sold her a hooky bottle of wine (Bulgarian red, I was guessing) for £5.99.

She went back to the hotel. Nobody noticed her. Why would they? By now Bailey was chin-wagging with St Peter.

She saw the damage. Maybe she panicked. Probably not. I doubted she touched the body but she almost certainly lifted the wallet, watch and Palm Pilot. Then she shut the door behind her and legged it: straight down the fire escape, across the car park, down the alley and into the street. She was still clutching the bottle of wine. She looked left and right. She was scared but she was thinking. A steady stream of cabs was heading into London from suburban drop-offs. She flagged one down. Where did she go?

6

I found Avid Khan making himself comfy in my waiting room. I'd known Mrs K wanted me to have a word but she must have set the time unilateral. Av was smoking a chunky reefer. He looked me up and down like a casting agent. 'Nice suit, Tommy.' Sarky kid, serious.

I snatched the reefer from his hand. He tried to resist but I caught his finger and told him I'd break it. I led him into my office by his pinky and stubbed his dope in the ashtray. I handed it back to him. 'Not in here,' I said. 'This is where I work.'

I sparked a Benny. He helped himself to one and I didn't say nothing. We smoked at each other a little while.

Av was a Christmas tree. He wore pristine trainers and logo sportswear but what caught your eye were the baubles, trinkets and touches. He had heavy rings on every finger, a gold chain at his neck and a diamond stud in his ear. He'd even shaved go faster stripes into his left eyebrow. Av pictured himself the junior don.

I said, 'So what you doing here, Av?'

He shrugged.

I said, 'So what you done this time?'

He kissed his teeth. I flicked my ash.

'Keeping shtum? That's fine. Let me tell you something. There's nothing about you that impresses me, Av. Not one single thing. But you know that already. What you probably haven't figured yet is that there's nothing that distresses me about you neither. I've seen it all before. I've *been* it all before.

You can't surprise me. You think you're some tough geezer? I'm tougher than you. You think you're so smart? I'm smarter than you. You think you're misunderstood? Mate, you're an open book compared to me. You think you're out of control? You're not. You're tame. Tame. You're so tame that if I opened the cage door I'd find you cowering at the back.'

Av said, 'F— you, Tommy!' That cracked me up.

'You giving it the stroppy Paki, Av? Damn. I ain't never seen that before. You must be the first stroppy Paki in the whole of London. You a real bad boy.'

'F— you!'

'Let me set it out for you. You're sitting in my office because Mrs K told you to come and see me. She told you to come and see me because you done something stupid again. You came because you couldn't handle any more of your mum's mouth. You want your mum off your back? I can get your mum off your back. Or I can do that whole shaking head "well, Mrs K, the boy needs discipline" routine and you'll be lugging your mum around the manor until you're twenty-one. Up to you. So you may as well tell me what's going on.'

Av kissed his teeth. Av stared at the ceiling. Av played with his diamond. Av scratched his balls. I yawned. I needed a drink. I could smell the Turk in my desk. I'm a role model for young London.

'It's that girl Michelle. She's extra, man. You know Michelle?'

'Who's Michelle?'

'That blonde girl. Lives on the Attlee. Hangs around with Romeo and them.'

I shrugged. I said nothing but I was thinking, *Romeo*? For real?

'She been running her mouth, man. She been saying what what what. Av this, Av that. I admit that I been chirpsing her.

But that don't give her no right to give me grief in front of my boys, you get me?

'Now I know that she been saying all of that but I'm, like, "f__ her." But then she comes up to me one time when I'm hanging outside the Horse and she's brought some geezer with her. She's, like, "This is Bubble or whatever." She's, like, "This is a mate of Romeo's." Only I ain't never seen the geezer in my life. Then she's, like, "I told him you could sort him out." I mean, that's bang out of order, right? So Dave and them are all like, "Av, man. Who this bitch think she is? You gotta handle your business."

'So I take Michelle to one side. And I'm calm, right? I say to her, "Who the f__ you think you are? You can't come down here with some stranger and think you're gonna score off me. That's extra. That's *delusional*." But then she goes off on one. She's all, like, "You said this, you said that, you're not even nice, what what what." All of that. And my boys are staring at me, going, like, "Handle your business, bruv!" You get me? So what else am I gonna do? I give her a slap.

'Only trouble is, Benzi's hanging around with the other kids nearby and she sees everything. So she runs home and tells Mum. So Mum goes off on one, what what. So here I am. F__ mother's man. No wonder Dad bailed. F__ing women.'

I stared at Av. I felt old, serious. I only understood about half what he'd said and I didn't like it and it made me suspect that I wouldn't like the other half either. I could hear the Turk calling me and I couldn't resist. Turk may taste of bourbon but it's got a voice like syrup. I pulled out the bottle and poured myself a gentle introduction. Turk and Benny. Benny and Turk. Tag-team action.

Av kissed his teeth at me. 'That shit rots your brain, man.'

I rinsed it round my gums. I swallowed. 'Trying to come down to your level,' I said.

I'm so funny you could pop me in a cracker.

Av kissed his teeth and cupped his balls possessively like they were his favourite new toys.

'Let me tell you something,' I said. 'You know what? You can't tell how much of a man you are until you've smacked a bird.'

Av said nothing. He wouldn't even look at me. He was staring at the floor and sniffing his fingers. One minute he's cupping his balls, the next he's sniffing his fingers. Teenage boys need to be bussed out to the jungle, serious. The chimps could teach them how to act like human beings.

'You can't tell how much of a man you are until you've smacked a bird.' I said it again. 'You agree with that, Av?'

'Whatever, man.' Av shrugged. 'Sure.'

I gave it the ha-ha. I needn't have bothered. This kid was not conversant with what you might call the finer points of irony. 'Let me tell you a story,' I said.

I told Av a story. I told him the one about the housewife from Nangarhar. I've got a lot of stories. Some of them are true. Most of them contain some truth.

It was when Tommy Akhtar was driving Agent Stanton. They were dirt-tracking it at dusk, Tommy's foot flat to the floor to make it back to camp before the sun failed. They didn't want to be using no headlights or they'd have been catching skyers from the mortars nearby. They were crossing what was called no man's land. This was some kind of joke. Afghanistan? That whole gravel pit was no man's land.

The gauge was flickering sixty when a small shadow flashed in front. It was a boy. Could've been eight years old, could've been fourteen, it was impossible to tell. Tommy slammed the brakes and skidded to a halt, almost catapulting the Yank over the dashboard.

He said, 'What you doing, Tommy man? You wanna get us killed?'

He had a point. A couple of weeks later when things got really feisty Tommy wouldn't have stopped. He'd have squashed that kid without a second thought.

The boy was screaming blue murder. In fact, Tommy wanted to drive on and it was the Yank who decided to take a look. They followed the boy back to a hamlet a hundred yards off the track. There were women rushing here and there. They didn't see a single man.

They ducked into a house after the boy. It was lit by one flickering oil lamp. They couldn't see jack. Suddenly there were a dozen women all clamouring around them. Tommy didn't catch a word they were saying. There was a smell that was hot and sweet like cooking chocolate. He'd brought the flashlight from the jeep. He swung it round the room. There were two women bent over a bed in the corner. The chatter was spooking him. Tommy couldn't hear himself think.

The Yank was already over at the bed. The two women were talking to him. They were calmer than the rest, speaking in urgent whispers. Tommy wondered how much Stanton understood.

It took Tommy a minute or so to figure what was going on. His light illuminated an uncovered face on the pillow. She couldn't have been much more than nineteen. In the beam she looked pale like a City gent. There was a stripe of dirt on her cheek, a smudge of bloody vomit on her chin. She was taking short, shallow breaths. He scanned down her body. She was heavily pregnant. She'd also lost both her legs around the mid-thigh. Must have been a landmine.

The women were pressing bundles of rags into the wounds. The Yank had his knife out. One of the women saw the glint of the knife and she gasped. She was talking so quick

Tommy had to tell her to slow down. She must have relaxed her pressure on the stump. A fountain of blood spat out from artery beneath the dark cloth and sprayed Tommy's face. Tommy said to Stanton, 'She wants to know what you gonna do.'

He said, 'How pregnant is she?'

Tommy asked. Eight months, they said. Tommy passed it on.

He said, 'What do you think I'm gonna do? I'm gonna get the baby out. That's what. Tell them that's what I'm gonna do.'

Tommy translated.

The Yank said, 'Tell the girl. Tell her she's gonna have to stay still, then hold her by the shoulders. Tell her she's gonna die anyway. Tell her to stay still.'

Tommy knelt down next to the girl's forehead. Her eyes flashed like the moon on deep water. She was terrified. So was Tommy. He said, 'Your baby's dying. You'll die whatever we do. Your baby can live. We have to cut it out. Do you understand?' She blinked. She was crying. Tommy was crying too.

He went to the head of the bed. He pinned her down, his full weight pressing in to her shoulders. She looked up at him. He looked away.

Stanton was already poised with his knife.

Tommy said, 'We've got morphine in the jeep.'

'That's my morphine, Tommy man. What if I get shot? I need f__ing morphine, man. I'm an American. This girl's gone. I'm sorry but that's the way it goes.'

Tommy couldn't fault the Yank's logic.

Tommy said, 'You not going to sterilize nothing?'

He said, 'Shut up! Shut up!' Tommy had never seen Stanton lose his cool. 'What for? She's got half an hour max. I just gotta get on with it.'

Tommy had a field dressing in his pocket. He stuffed it between her teeth and she bit down hard. He held her as the Yank operated. Her shoulders bucked. She swallowed half the dressing. She wouldn't take her eyes off him. He whispered to her. All kinds of prayers and other nonsense: 'Paradise awaits the righteous. You're a good girl. You're a good girl. Be brave. Keep looking at me.'

The Yank was dextrous with his knife. He had the baby out in less than a minute. The girl was spewing blood. The Yank slapped the baby and it screamed into life. Tommy looked down at the girl. His tears were falling on her face. He said, 'It's a boy.' But her eyes were opaque, her face the colour of paper. 'Paradise awaits the righteous,' he whispered.

The men left quickly. The women were saying they'd killed her. Tommy tried to explain that they'd done the best they could but the women wouldn't listen. The Yank didn't seem to care. He sparked a cig. Tommy wasn't smoking at the time. It was against his beliefs. But he really wanted one then.

They drove away. They'd almost made camp before Tommy had to pull over to puke. When he got back in the jeep, the Yank had his needle out. Tommy said, 'You ain't been shot.'

Stanton said, 'After what I just did? I need it, man. You want one?'

Tommy said no but he changed his mind later that night. The drugs made everything go away. The drugs let Tommy recall that girl's face in his mind's eye and think only about how pretty she looked, so pale like a sculpture.

As Stanton dosed his sidekick, he gave him his philosophy. 'You know what, man? Don't you worry about a thing. That girl didn't need it. It would have been a real waste, I tell you. Pregnant women? They can take anything, man. Their hormones kick in and they can deal with pain that would kill

you and me at the thought of it. That's why I'm no feminist.
I don't trust people who don't have the same fear as me.'

Benny and Turk. Benny and Turk. I stubbed my Benny and
downed my Turk and held Av's eye. He was trying to puff
out his fifteen-year-old chest but it wasn't working and he
knew it and he knew that I knew it too. He said, 'You f___ing
with me?'

I shrugged.

He said, 'You a nutter, Tommy. You done some f___ing
crazy shit.'

I nodded.

'So what you saying, Tommy?'

'You ever watch cricket?' Av looked blank. 'You should.
You should watch cricket. Teach you everything you need to
know. Like Graeme Hick, right? Stick him on a flat pitch with
a friendly attack and he's the don. He just swings that timber
and the hot-dog men and geezers flogging scorecards are
running for cover. But put him on a fast track with the likes
of Ambrose and Marshall running in? The guy's a pussy.'

Av gave me the what-you-on eyes. I shook my head. 'I'm
just saying you can't tell how much of a man you are until
you've smacked a bird. If you think you're a man after that?
You're still a kid, serious.'

You wondering what I was talking about? You and me both.
But there ain't no need to reason with no thug-lite; only blind
them with a little bait and switch. So I just had to deliver the
punchline. I did it nice and quiet with a hum of menace: 'I
ever hear you hit a girl again, Av? I'm not your dad. I'm not
gonna give you no slap. I'm not gonna send you to live with
no aunty in Lahore. I ever hear you hit a girl again and I'll
beat you so hard you'll be living with your mum till she pegs
it and then you'll have some Estonian home help wiping your
backside for the rest of your natural. Just so you know.'

As far as I was concerned that was the end of the conversation. I find morality tiring and I had work to do besides. But Av didn't seem in no hurry to bounce. I'd made a fan. Av figured I was the Shaolin master he'd never had, serious.

'I gotta go,' I said. 'I got an appointment.'

Av helped himself to another cig and sparked it. He sat back in his chair. Kids aren't sensitive to even the simplest niceties of social situations. 'So what you working on, Tommy?'

I couldn't resist it. I smouldered my mysterious immigrant eyes. 'A murder,' I said.

'So who's the appointment?'

I stood up and shook my keys. 'I gotta see a whore about a whore.'

Av loved that. He dragged on his cig like a proper little gangster. 'I could help you out, Tommy man. You should let me help you out. Undercover. What what what.'

'Right,' I said. 'And I'm sure Mrs K would approve.'

I stood at the door and held it open until Av finally got the message.

7

Swiss Chris took me. I meant to bell Melody on the way, let her know I was coming, but Swiss was telling me stories about his missus, the prosaic day-to-day stuff that nobody wants to hear. People talk to me. Father Tommy Akhtar as confessor? Who am I kidding? People don't confess. They only lay blame.

I called the hooker from the pavement outside her South Ken mansion block. It went straight to voicemail. She was probably seeing someone. I decided to stick around.

South Ken is a strange neck of the woods as it goes. I don't reckon one Londoner lives there. There are cheap and not so cheap hotels filled with Russian Mafiosi, African dictators, Indian arms-dealers and other similarly lovely clientele. There's Arab money that's followed the original Arab money that first heard in the seventies that this was where the money lived. There are language schools for priapic Mediterranean boys with too much confidence and Dutch girls too suss to fall for it. There's the occasional aristocratic shire widow who knows she's out of place and out of time. And there are the hookers, of course, in sparsely furnished one- or two-bedroom joints with mini-fridges and DVD players churning out 24/7 porn. Some of them may be Londoners. But they're unlikely to live in the area.

I watched the people come and go from the front door. I played 'spot the punter'. It wasn't so hard. After about ten minutes, a tall white dude in a City double-breasted emerged. He was younger than the usual; maybe no more than late twenties. But there was something in the way he looked left and right, something in the flush of his face, something in his swaggering shoulders that left me in no doubt. The fact that he then adjusted his tackle none too subtle like was only the umpire's finger. Owzat? Sweet relief.

I called up. She answered. I told her I was right outside. Melody didn't sound so pleased to hear from me. I said it was no problem. I could come back another time; it was her money. She laughed. She said she'd forgotten that. She had another client in a while but she could spare me fifteen minutes. She apologized. I was kind of getting to like her.

She buzzed me in. Flat six. First floor. The atrium was knackered glamour: big double doors, leading to wide marble stairs with a uniformed concierge catching a nap in an office on the right. He was a fat geezer, his forearm resting on the desk and his head on his forearm. One of his epaulettes was hanging loose and his heavy breathing was gently puffing ash from an overloaded ashtray a couple of inches from his mouth. Real classy. He didn't stir when I came in.

On the left of the stairs was a rack of numbered mailboxes, each secured with a small padlock. I glanced at the concierge, I glanced at the boxes. I looked out into the street and up the stairs. I went over to the boxes and checked out number six. It had a flimsy key padlock. I found a paperclip in my pocket and sprang it in a second. This is less illustration of my professional skills than the redundancy of such low-level security.

It was full of all kinds of junk mail to any number of different addressees; something that suggested sexyrussian and exoticmelody hadn't been resident too long. There were numerous mail shots from estate agents, a posturepedic mattress catalogue for Mrs Schiliro, an air-miles statement for Mr Mahmoud, Ms M.A. Kuntz was offered twenty pounds off a mixed case from the UK's largest direct wine suppliers.

Mr Francis Siame was pre-approved for a platinum Visa with 0 per cent credit transfer. This is the nature of the Western world. You accumulate junk whether you're there or not, alive or dead. There's just too much stuff. The waste is enough to make me come over all fundamental.

I flicked through, and bingo. I found a bank statement in the name of Natalya Kuzmin postmarked yesterday. It had to be Natasha, sexyrussian.co.uk. A careful whore has aliases and she has to stash her money somewhere. My job's too easy. I tucked it into the pocket of my jeans, refilled the box and relocked the pointless lock.

I was feeling kind of sprightly so I took the stairs two at a time. It was a mistake. By the time I reached the first-floor landing I was blowing hard and seeing stars, serious. You got to know your limits in this life.

Melody answered the door quickly. She was wearing a white cover-all bathrobe, the kind you nick from a hotel when you're a bored tom. She smiled. I smiled back. I checked myself. We weren't friends.

She looked different. In bare feet she was shorter and the bathrobe hiding her super-sized chest made her look smaller too. She was wearing so much makeup that she looked like a cartoon. Her eyebrows, lips and cheeks were all painted on. I hate that look. It would've taken a hammer and chisel ten minutes to find flesh. Not so much warpaint as battlements.

I followed her inside. The air smelled sickly; somewhere between a florist and a gym. I began to feel a little nauseous.

It was a typical mansion-block flat designed around a single dark corridor. There was a claustrophobic hallway holding a coat-rack, mirror and the entry-phone (there were no coats and the mirror hung an inch low on the left). Then, straight ahead, the corridor passed one, two, three rooms before opening up into the living room at the far end. The first door was shut. The second, half open on to a bedroom. I caught a glimpse of a mirror that reflected a double bed, its turquoise sheets rutted and rucked, overlooked by a Gauguin print, *The Seed of Areoi*. The last door was shut too but the wet footprints on the pale blue carpet told me it was the bathroom.

The living room was bright and spacious and semi-inhabited. On the left, there was an open-plan kitchenette with a fridge decorated with a few magnets that said things like 'Be real' and 'Be safe'. Behind 'Be free' and 'Be alive' there were postcards: another Gauguin and a Hopper. There was a break-fast bar that held a couple of grubby wine-glasses. There wasn't much sign of no cooking. I've seen bachelor pads with more pots and pans.

On the right, a TV was pushed back into the corner. It was showing daytime chat on mute. Two fat birds were going at it all wagging fingers and ugly sneers above a strap line that said, 'When good husbands go bad!' DVDs and videos were strewn around the base. I could read the titles of *Baby Got Back 31*, *Buttman 16* and a rental copy of *Titanic*. Next to the telly a micro hi-fi sat on the floor with no more than half a dozen CDs stacked on top. They were all bootlegs.

There was a magazine rack stuffed with glossies and a cheap coffee-table holding a half-full ashtray, a tube of KY and a bottle of poppers. Domestic bliss. The table's surface was marked with careless ring stains. There was a bunch of wilting flowers haphazardly drowning in browning water in a make-shift vase cut from half a plastic bottle; some kind of gift expressing some kind of gratitude. On the far wall a low sofa was covered with a cheap beige throw. Melody sat there. Her legs were crossed, right over left, and her robe rode up over her knee and thigh. I perched next to her. There was nowhere else to sit.

Melody said, 'So, you found Tasha for me, Mr Akhtar?'

'Call me Tommy,' I said. 'Everyone calls me Tommy.'

I was staring at the caramel of her thigh. Whatever you might think of me, I wasn't catching no freebie; just checking out the pale scars that striped her leg. She caught me at it. She said, 'You wanna good look, Mr Akhtar?' She pulled aside the material of her robe to reveal numerous further scars and blemishes, more thin contours and the occasional circular mark: the kind of freakishness that gets called 'culture' in African photos from the *National Geographic*.

She said, 'Mum was handy with the flex.' With one false fingernail she traced the outline of one rough circle. It was sort of erotic, for real. 'The cigarette lighter from the car,' she explained. 'You didn't want the front seat in my family, know what I mean? You wanted the back seat. Out of reach.'

'That's charming,' I said. 'Life-affirming.'

Melody covered up her legs, looked me in the eye and gave it the whatever shrug. 'Didn't do me no harm.'

I laughed at that, didn't I? I said, 'So says exoticmelody the whore.' Like it was a punchline. Sometimes I figure I'm the type of geezer who'd cut himself just to test the sharpness of a blade. But Melody didn't react beyond a smile that told me nothing.

'You got a cigarette?' she asked. I gave her one and sparked it.

I told her what I knew. It didn't take long. I told her Natasha didn't kill Bailey. I told her Natasha was still alive. I told her I'd find her friend soon. She said, 'That's it? You couldn't say that on the phone?'

I said I'd wanted to see her place, see Natasha's place, ask her a few more questions. She sucked deep on her cigarette. The air in the room was still and the smoke hung between us like a net curtain. 'You better make it quick,' she said. 'I haven't got much time.'

I asked her how long she'd lived in this flat. She said she didn't. Natasha stayed here but she just used it for incalls. I asked her where she lived then. She told me to mind my own business.

I asked her about Natasha's coke habit. She stared at me and gave it the slow blink: 'What you wanna know?' She said that sexyrussian was better than some and worse than others and that was about the size of it. I nodded and played thoughtful. I asked if Natasha owed her money. She licked her lips and folded her arms. She said she did but it wasn't so bad and what had that got to do with anything? I gave it a minor funny and a 'no big deal'. I was just clearing something up. I felt a lot better knowing that Melody's motivations for finding her ho-buddy were less than altruistic. Honour among whores? My brown backside.

I asked her about her pimp. She said, what pimp? I gave it the 'You trying to tell me you work out of this flat with some Russian bird and you ain't got no pimp?' You can see the angle. She did the feisty feminist and I let her get on with it without pointing out the bleeding obvious. When I could get a word in I tried, 'What about security?' She snapped, 'I got my driver and before you ask he's got nothing to do with anything, OK?' OK. Enough said.

I got on to the night of the murder, the night sexyrussian disappeared. I told her I figured punter and tom must have been followed out of the Embassy and back to the Holiday Inn Express. I told her that she'd most likely seen Thug #1 in the Embassy herself. Was it my imagination or did she look a little too spooked at the prospect? I pressed: 'You remember anyone in particular?'

'Not really.' She shook her head jerkily. 'I don't remember. Look. What difference does it make? I asked you to find Tasha, yeah?'

I nodded. She nodded. I shrugged. She shrugged. It was 'Simon says'.

'So, let me get this straight. The only people you remember being at the Embassy that night are yourself, sexyrussian and Bailey the punter, right?'

'Right.'

'And then Natasha gave you the signal to say everything was cool.'

'That's right.'

'How did she do that? Just throw you a thumbs-up?'

'No. I was sitting by the door. She had her back to me. She got up to powder her nose. She gave me the look and a smile and I left. End of story.'

'Because you had a gig of your own, yeah?'

'Yeah.'

'And who was that?'

'That, Mr Akhtar, is none of your business.'

I stared at her. She stared back. Simon says be inscrutable.

She was getting a little impatient. I gave her another cigarette. She lit it. It didn't seem to help.

I asked her who was the Gauguin fan. She raised her eyebrows at me and said, 'Exoticmelody, who else?' I liked the third person. I knew how it felt. Like I said, she was no fool.

I asked her if she knew Natasha's real name. She said she thought it was Natalya something or other or something like that. I suggested Natalya Kuzmin and she nodded. She was impressed. I told her it was my job to know and she nodded at that too. Even the unfoolish are suckers.

I stood up. I asked to see Natasha's room. I said it would only take a minute. Melody's mobile rang. It was her next punter. He was downstairs. When she talked to him her voice changed. It got coquettish and smooth with the light vibrations of a bass drum. She said she'd be ready for him in two shakes. She called him 'baby', 'darling', 'lover'. There are all kinds of sexual relations but only one language to describe them.

Melody said I could check out Natasha's boudoir while she changed. I did. I worked fast.

The room was a contradiction undoubtedly explained by the fact that it was, as it were, both home and office. The bed was black linen with a red duvet. A huge mirror covered the wall opposite and from its corners hung a pair of handcuffs, a leather mask and some other form of elaborate restraint. There was a chest of drawers littered with perfumes, lubes and a trade delivery of condoms. Among the debris I found one small, creased photograph of Natasha cradling a baby. Perhaps a niece, perhaps her own. Sexyrussian was laughing up at the camera and her eyes were shining. It was my first look at her face. She was wearing a T-shirt that said FCUK across the front. For a moment I imagined her sitting on this bed and staring at this photo. It would be late at night after her last punter when her last fat line of charlie was flying around her synapses. The picture would be pinched so hard between thumb and forefinger that her knuckles would whiten. I didn't take the thought any further than that. I pocketed the picture for future reference.

Next to the chest of drawers, a pair of thigh-high boots stood to attention beneath the window. Next to the window, there was a narrow closet. I took a peek. There were a lot of outfits hanging up; a lot of rubber, a lot of plastic and a lot of black. Amid them all there was one summer dress, a vibrant yellow print with blue and green flowers. It looked as shy and out of place as a church girl in a shebeen. I shut the closet door.

I dropped to my haunches and went through the chest of drawers. I opened the top drawer. There was much crotchless this and tasselled that and plenty of sensible St Michael's besides. Sexyrussian was clearly a tidy tom because her underwear was neatly folded and stacked. But someone had beaten me to it, no doubt. There was just enough disorganization among the order to tell me that someone else had been rummaging. Exoticmelody, I guessed. She wanted her cash, serious. Fair dos.

The second drawer was pretty much the same. It was the last that interested me. This was where Natasha kept her own stuff. It was crammed full of T-shirts and tracksuit bottoms and the rest of her 'I'm no whore' garb.

There was a bundle of letters. They were all in Russian. No use to me. There were four or five Russian books. God knows. There was one book in English, *The Road Less Travelled* by M. Scott Peck. Self-help for the helpless. There was a small box containing a religious medallion – St Whatever – on a cheap silver chain. There were more photographs: Natasha and middle-aged woman with desperate eyes (Mum?); Natasha and old geezer in a wheelchair (Grandad?); Natasha among a bunch of flat-faced youths smoking fags and drinking wine; Natasha hog-tied in this very room, biting on a gag, her eyes wide and fearful.

I closed the drawer. There was nothing for me to find. It was OK. I reckoned the bank statement would provide clues enough.

I stood up. I glanced at the upright chair that was in one corner. It was covered with soft toys. There were teddy bears, puppy dogs, a reindeer with a bright red nose, a lion wearing a T-shirt that said, 'I love London'. In spite of myself, my imagination kicked in again. I was too sober. I saw sexyrussian sitting on the edge of her bed, staring at her photo, which was now in my pocket, ruefully rubbing her stomach, squeezing her arms across her chest. I saw her close her eyes and fall back against the pillow, her knees drawn up all foetal. But the cocaine is still fizzing her head and the stench of men is thick in her nostrils. I saw her struggle to her feet and choose a favourite animal from the chair in the corner. She stumbles to the living room. She pours herself the dregs of a bottle of wine and opens all the windows. She curls up on the sofa holding the teddy bear like she once held that baby.

I blinked. I needed a drink. I pictured myself taking guard at Lords in fresh whites. Wasim was coming round the wicket and bowled me an in-ducking toe-crusher first up. I adjusted my feet quickly and clipped it to the mid-wicket boundary.

I took another look at the chair. Among the teddies, puppies, reindeer and lion I noticed for the first time an enormous, fluorescent pink dildo. It was as thick as my wrist, a size to carve a bird in two and leave her bandy for a week. It was a toy among toys. It was enough to break your heart. Not mine.

I exited the room and ran straight into exoticmelody. She was in full combat gear. Literally. She was wearing jackboots, tight camouflage trousers, a khaki vest knotted at the navel and light webbing. She'd tied her plaits back with a green scarf and smudged black lines beneath her eyes.

She said, 'You done?'

I cracked up.

She said, 'What?' But I was giggling like a fool. She looked down at herself. She smiled. She said, 'You don't like my outfit?' Then she packed up laughing too.

I was all, like, 'Geezers like this stuff?'

She was all, like, 'Different strokes, you know?'

I gathered myself. I was smiling down at her. I could smell her perfume. It was surprising: fresh, lemony, almost childlike. I smoothed out my smile.

I told her I hadn't found anything in sexyrussian's room. I told her that I'd taken the photo. She said fine. I told her I'd find Natasha in the next few days, no problem. She said no problem. I told her I'd be in touch.

I took the stairs slowly. The concierge had woken up. He gave me a look. He lit a tab. His eyes were too small for his puffy face. I gave him a look right back.

There was a geezer hanging around by the mailboxes. I didn't want to stop to check him out. I wondered if he was the army fetishist. Out of the corner of my eye, I didn't think so. Out of the corner of my eye, he looked vaguely familiar. I flipped through some mugshots in my mind but I couldn't find him. I didn't dwell on it.

On the steps into the street, I looked left and right. I couldn't see any obvious punter. He was probably in a nearby pub downing a stiffener. The thought of alcohol made me salivate. I found a pub myself and joined Benny and Turk at the bar.

I tore open Natalya Kuzmin's bank statement. There you go. A withdrawal of fifty pounds at Waterloo station at seven a.m. the morning after the murder. Another withdrawal at four p.m. that afternoon: two long that took her to her overdraft limit (£300). But the point was the whereabouts: Lymington, Hampshire. It looked like I'd be getting a train myself. I was on a mad roll of competence. Call me Steve Waugh.

I checked the clock behind the bar. It was already past four: teatime. If I caught a train now I'd be squashed in with the commuter suits braying long vowels into their mobiles. That would do me about as much good as another large Turk and I knew which one appealed.

I drank until eight; until I was brassic and my innards were going cannibalized. I took a tube to Stamford Brook and passed out for ten minutes or so. When I woke up, I found I'd dribbled down my shirtfront and my section of the carriage had been taken over by half a dozen toffs evening-dressed for a night out who-knows-where. They were laughing at me.

One, a smug little so-and-so with gel in his hair and buck teeth, kept on whispering to his mates and glancing at me sideways; real subtle. They giggled. I began to stare at him. I stared at his girlfriend too: the flash of her cleavage and the promise of a glimpse of stocking via the slit in her dress. Buck Teeth stopped laughing then all right. I hoped he'd say something, get a little confrontational, give me the chance to take some exercise. But he didn't. The English ruling classes that Farzad so admires (and there's so much potential therapy in that statement) don't exist no more. Once they ran the world. Now they couldn't even run a drunk Paki (excuse my shorthand) off a train. They make me ashamed to be English, for real.

I stumbled home. Gunny was still in Phoenecia, holed up behind his Perspex window. I hadn't seen his legs for so long I was beginning to wonder if they'd dropped off. He shouted through his loudspeaker, 'Jesus Christ, bruv! Pissed again?' Then, 'Pissed again! Again! He's only f___ing pissed again!' He's got a great line in repartee.

There were three messages on the ansaphone. One was from an elderly-sounding lady who'd lost her dog. I deleted it. There are some problems even I can't help with. Old age and loneliness are just two. The second was Mr X. He wanted his Beamer back; said he'd collect it in the morning. Shame, but I could hardly argue, could I? The last was Cal Donnelly. He wanted me to call him back, soon as. This was unusual but not unheard-of. Maybe the plod in the pub had told him about my questioning. He probably had some work to sling my way. It could wait. I was busy.

I was in bed by half nine, asleep by ten and awake by midnight. I found myself thinking about sexyrussian's bedroom: the photographs; the soft toys; the dildo, cuffs and mask. For some reason best known to the night, I felt a well of sadness in my gut. I was becoming soft as a toff.

I chose to open the batting against the Windies attack from the mid-eighties: Holding, Garner, Roberts and Croft. It was a fast track at Bridgetown and we had to bat out two days to save the match. I was 123 not out, past lunch on the last day, before I fell asleep a second time.

8

Next morning Mr X collected his motor bright and early. He was all smiles with his hair freshly cut and wearing a natty leather jacket. He looked ten years younger for the lack of wife. I'm not making no point here; not the obvious one anyway. It does occur to me, however, that you don't know the strength of your cards until the hand is played out and you don't know the value of your runs until the opposition bats. Even a pair of twos can clean up in the right circumstance and 120 can be a tough chase on a muggy day green top. Think Headingley '81.

I was at Waterloo for the nine fourteen, arriving into Lymington at one minute to midday. The train left closer to eleven and arrived closer to one but I'd still found sexyrussian before four. I'm good, serious. It panned out like this.

I walked straight into the town centre. It was no more than five minutes but I felt a little heady. Maybe the fresh air blowing in from the Solent was a shock to my city system. More likely, though, I was brought up short by what I saw.

I don't get out of London much. Occasionally my work takes me to other cities – Hull, Leeds, Manchester in the last few months – or more often, truth be told, to the ring of grey commuter towns in the Home Counties gangster belt. But never to the coast. In fact, apart from occasional trips with the old man to check on Gravesend house prices, I think the only time I've visited the great British seaside was a school trip at fourteen.

We went to Bournemouth, just about ten miles or so from

Lymington along the Hampshire cliffs. I remember we went swimming, ate ice-cream and played cricket on the sand. Kenny Garrigan stood on a broken bottle and needed fourteen stitches, Anjan Patel took a beating from a bunch of Paki bashers in the arcade and Wayne, Lovely, Stuart and me prowled the pier for hours trying to find them. Typical kids stuff.

But most of all I remember that everybody wanted to buy presents for our mums and brothers and sisters. Like we'd been away on some grand adventure that required material evidence. We took to the high street clasping sweaty Alans in our mitts and bought sticks of rock, test tubes full of multi-coloured sand, painted pebbles and the like from curious little gift shops run by old women who smelled of camphor and lavender.

More than twenty years later, I guess I expected Lymington high street to be the same: quaint and cutesy and kitsch. Instead it looked kind of like salty Chiswick with nothing to see but the familiar logos above chain outlets flogging greetings cards, mobiles and alcohol.

As London unravels into ribbons of suburbs and market towns coagulate into perfect globules of homogeny, I can get a little nostalgic for the England I grew up in. This is ironic for an immigrant Paki who arrived in the aftermath of Rivers of Blood. But I can't help but think wistfully of days playing 'hunt the skin' when we'd catch some scrawny geezer in DMs and braces, with 'NF' in felt tip on his knuckles, and batter the little pillock to a colour not far from my own.

I headed to Sainsbury's. I bought a cheese sandwich. I don't eat much. A couple of bites reminded me why. I sparked a Benny and took up position by the cashpoint. From there I could see everything. The Benny tasted good. Cleared my head.

A cop car did a couple of circuits on the one way past the entrance. The driver looked my way. He had sleepy eyes and a moustache. Rural Bill look like porn stars. Rule of thumb.

I watched the comings and goings – locals from the nearby New Forest in corduroy and wellingtons, deck shoes up from the harbour, family holidays in people carriers with roof racks – but I knew what I was looking for.

After half an hour I spotted them, three tearaway teens (or so they figured) sitting on the railing beneath the Perspex-covered enclosure purpose-built for the trolleys. They were laughing. One of them had a skateboard, one of them had a two-litre bottle of Diamond White, one of them was tugging on a joint. A dad in a sports jacket returned his trolley and ushered his eight-year-old away with a sideways glance. A blue rinse stopped to wag her finger at them. They laughed some more. As she walked away, one of these charmers spat in her general direction. His phlegm fell, as he knew it would, fifteen feet short. Maybe England's not so homogenous after all. A London kid like Av Khan would have eaten those little sociopaths for breakfast and spat out their fillings like pips.

I strolled over to have a word. They looked nervous, shifty. It couldn't have been the colour of my skin – ask any middle-Englander, my type gets everywhere these days. So it must have been my attitude. Good. That was the plan. I was giving it the full swagger.

One of them stubbed the joint and looked away to some point in the mid-distance, another swilled deep from the bottle, the third pulled up his hoodie high around his head. See no evil, speak no evil, hear no evil. Only these monkeys weren't so wise.

I stood in front of them and flicked my butt. It landed at Cider Boy's feet. 'You all right, lads?' I didn't get no response.

The skater was smirking. I said, 'You get good shit round here?' Cider Boy looked up at me, a reflex action. He was younger than I'd realized, younger than the other two. He was crapping himself. 'What is it? Slate? Black?'

Now the skater looked at me too. His smirk had stretched into a grin. He looked cocky. 'F— you, man,' he sneered. First rule of adolescence: don't be cocky. When I've met one who's learned it the easy way, I'll let you know.

I grabbed him. I had his throat in my fist. He tried to scream. How did he think he was going to scream when he couldn't breathe? Beats me. His mates looked ready to bolt. I gave them one eyebrow each and they thought better of it. I checked left and right but no one was looking. I gave his skull a couple of friendly taps on the enclosure. The Perspex cracked. Shoddy workmanship. This country is falling apart.

I had what I wanted in five minutes flat. I told them I wasn't interested in their teenage kicks. I told them it was charlie I was after. I told them I was Met. They didn't ask to see my badge. They were puppies. I've washed my face with flannels more abrasive. They told me to check the White Horse on the Brockenhurst Road, no more than half a mile along Cider Boy's quivering finger; a greasy biker who hung out by the fruity and went by the name of Dirty Harriet. I cracked up laughing at that. I thanked them for their time.

The skater spluttered that I should let him go. I apologized and released my grip. His eyes were streaming as he gingerly fingered his neck. Two dark welts were rising either side. I told him they'd pass as lovebites. 'You're the real Lymington Lothario,' I said. It didn't raise a smile. I don't think he had the vocabulary.

I left them to their childhood.

The White Horse was a boozer that signified its clientele by the plaque nailed to the door: 'No Hell's Angels, no leathers, no soiled denims'. Yeah, right. Two dozen high-powered machines lined up in the car park told a different story.

Inside, the air was thick. I had a Benny in my mouth ready to fire but what was the point? The light through the murky window gave up trying before it stretched half-way across the brown carpet.

I was feeling frisky so I ordered myself a lager. Aren't I the cosmopolitan? The lager was brewery's own, too thin and too fizzy, so I had to chase it with Jack. Good intentions frequently founder on external incompetence.

The whole pub needed a haircut and a shave. There were huge, bear-like men who could have been all muscle or all fat beneath their leathers. I couldn't tell and I had no desire to find out. They looked to me like a waste of half-decent genes. There were skinny women in grubby sleeveless T-shirts that revealed bushy armpits and zombie flesh. They had a uniform hairstyle: a limp two-month-old perm that frizzed out to peroxide ends. Styling it in my loafers, jeans and navy shirt, I felt quite the snappy dresser.

It didn't take much in the way of investigation to spot Dirty Harriet. She may have been surrounded by Dirty Sue, Dirty Dave and Dirty Tony (or whatever) but she had her back to the fruity and was dealing to Dirty Denise (or whatever) as brazen as you like.

I strolled over. I was going to have to play this careful. This was a grown-up game; the kind of game where you can all too easily end up spewing blood in a car-park dustbin.

I sidewaysed between the two geezers and flashed Harriet my estate-agent smile. She didn't know what to make of it but she knew she kind of liked it.

I was holding a nugget in my fingers and I gestured towards the fruity. I heard the geezers behind me begin to grumble, like they were trying to invent language. But I kept my cool and Harriet moved aside. I dropped the nugget in the slot. Only four plays.

It was one of those fancy machines that's all lights and music, the sort that requires a degree in loafing to figure out. This one was called 'The El Dorado'. It had a Wild West theme and it occasionally whinnied, whip-cracked and 'yee-hahed'. I slapped the button and the reels spun. 'Yee-hah!' Bar, bell, bell. One nudge. No use. Second play. Watermelon, lemon, dollar bill beneath a bright red two. I was on to the Gold Rush special feature. I held the two. Third play. Bell, triple bar, watermelon. Nothing doing. But I still had a hold. I pondered. I was about to slap the button when I heard a voice next to me: 'Hold the bar!' It was Dirty Harriet. I had her attention. Or, at least, the machine did. I'd never been upstaged by a fruity before. There's a first time for everything. She was transfixed. I did as she said. One reel came down, a moment's anticipation, then the third. Triple bar, triple bar, triple bar. Jackpot. 'Yee-hah! Doggone critter cleaned up!' The El Dorado spat fifty golden nuggets my way. This was more fun than tracking whores.

I began to scoop the shrapnel into one hand when I felt a heavy paw on my shoulder. I looked round and I was face to chest with a grizzly. I looked up and his moustache was flecked with spittle and other crap I had no desire to identify. I took a step back.

Geezer said, 'I think the lady's rightly entitled to half your winnings, my lad.' He had a proper yokel accent; every vowel an 'oi' diphthong. I didn't know whether to piss or shit myself.

I reached into my jeans and pulled out a wad, two long in twenties, ten and fives. I looked the bear in the eye. I peeled off a pony and handed it to Dirty Harriet without a sideways glance. I pocketed the nuggets. I said, 'I need change for the laundrette, know what I mean?' I was beginning to enjoy myself, serious. Now I turned to Harriet and gave her the estate agent once more. 'There's the same again,' I said. 'If you can help me out.'

She came over all girlish. Her charcoal eyes were like butterfly wings. I said, 'I'm looking for a blonde. Five six. Big habit.'

Harriet played coy. I played along. I pulled sexyrussian's photo out of my breast pocket. 'This is her. Russian.'

The bears were saying nothing. They were circus-tamed.

Harriet said, 'You a pig?'

I gave her a fag. I lit it. I sparked one of my own. I shook my head. 'I'm from London,' I murmured. 'She's from London. I'm an investigator. Enough said.'

I blew smoke-rings; perfect smoke-rings that hung in the air for a full five seconds. I extricated another twenty and another five from my wad. I held them between thumb and forefinger. Harriet stared at that cash like I was some kind of hypnotist. She was small-time in a small town.

She reached for the money. I let her take it. She showed me her teeth. Fifty quid was pissing in the wind of her orthodontic requirements.

She said, 'One of the hotels on the harbour. Dunno which one. The Sea View or the Queens, one of them, I reckon.'

I nodded.

She puffed on her ciggy. 'We had a boy in our class. Right sexy he was,' she said. I didn't know where this was heading. 'What was his name? Mansoor Something-or-other.' Now I knew.

Apparently Mansoor Something-or-other's parents had a swanky pad round Hordle way (wherever that was). Apparently Mansoor got top grades and went to university.

Apparently Mansoor was now an accountant in London. She asked. I indulged her with a moment's consideration before answering. 'No.' I shook my head. 'I don't think I know the guy.'

9

I walked down to the seafront. I was getting bored of the exercise and my feet were starting to hurt. Tommy Akhtar's traipsed days through the wasteland that is Afghanistan, for real; but that was a long time ago. Everyone has a comfort zone but I knew that mine was shrinking. That thought made me uncomfortable, which was a start.

There was a fine mist of rain in the air. It was barely rain at all but I stopped and bought a brolly anyway. I didn't need it but it relieved me of some of my winnings, which were clinking heavy in my pocket.

The Queens and the Sea View were side by side, converted Edwardian houses with pastel-painted woodwork that overlooked the coast road and then the grey Solent slopping against the slimy harbour wall. They both had signs saying, 'Vacancies', that swung gently in the gathering breeze. The Queens also had a sign offering B&B at £39.99, which included a detailed description of their full English: two rashers, two sausages, eggs any style, hash browns, as much tea or coffee as you could drink and as much toast as you could eat. I was surprised to hear my stomach grumbling. I sparked up. Benny told belly to keep it down.

I wasn't sure how to approach this. I decided to wait it out. I settled down on a soggy bench set into the harbour wall beside a bus stop. A bus stopped. I didn't get on. An old codger in a flat cap gave me the suspicious once-over before tottering off home. I read some graffiti markered on to the bench. I wondered if Julie still hearted Gezza. I wondered if David

Miller still loved it up the jaxy. I knew that Pompey were still shite.

Ten minutes turned into half an hour. My backside was getting numb and I was feeling more than a little chilly. I buried my hands deep in my pockets and thought about precisely nothing. It's a skill of mine. It was pushing an hour before sexyrussian appeared from the Queens.

It took me a moment to recognize her. The bird looked nothing like her pictures; not the glamour shots nor the happy snaps neither. But it was her all right.

She was smaller than I'd imagined, thin as a straw and short too. Her hair was scraped back in a limp ponytail and her unmade-up face could have passed for eighteen. She had hoops in her ears that to me made her look like a curtain rail. She was wearing a baggy navy sweatshirt, stonewashed jeans and dirty white trainers with purple flashes. She had a white leatherette bag slung over her shoulder. She sat on the wall of the Queens' front garden. She began to examine a mobile phone like she'd never seen one before. She took out a cigarette and bit it tight between her thin lips. She patted the pockets of her jeans. She put the mobile down on the wall next to her and slipped to her feet. She rummaged through her pockets and then her bag but no joy. Here was my chance. I was across the road before you could say, 'Got a light?'

She said, 'Thanks,' without even looking up. In that one word I heard a familiar accent: a lot of Russian, a little Cockney and a dash of MTV besides.

'You having trouble with your mobile?'

'I just bought this shit one,' she muttered. 'I don't under-stand f__ing thing how it work.'

'Let me have a gander. I'm good with phones.'

Now she looked at me. She blew smoke in my face. I

blinked. She was checking me out. She shrugged and held out the handset. 'I trying to send text message,' she said.

I flipped through the menu to SMS and handed the mobile back. 'Anyone nice?'

'What?'

'You texting anyone nice?'

'My sister.'

'In Moscow?'

She stared at me. I mumbled something about her accent. She licked her lips. Her eyes softened. 'New York,' she said.

She hunched over the phone and began to beep the keys. It started to rain proper. I opened my umbrella. I used it to cover the both of us. I shifted my backside along the wall closer to her. She said, 'Thanks.' She was all wrapped up in her text. She tapped 'Send' and the LCD on her mobile lit up with a flashing message: 'sending . . . sending . . . sending . . . sent.'

I said, 'So. Natalya. My name's Tommy Akhtar. Call me Tommy.'

Sexyrussian's face snapped round to look at me. She jumped to her feet and backed off four or five yards. She had her hand up, her fingers splayed, like she figured she was gonna shoot a bolt of lightning right out of her palm. She looked like she might run for it. I wasn't going to chase her.

'Sorry,' I said. 'Gave you a fright. Should I call you Natasha? Would you prefer it if I called you Natasha?'

The bird was breathing deep but she'd regained her composure. It's not hard to shock a whore but it's definitely tough to keep them that way. 'Natalya . . . Natasha . . .' She shrugged. 'You police?'

'A private investigator,' I said.

She burst out laughing. 'A private eye? Like the movies? In England I don't know you have these things.'

'You're getting wet,' I said. 'You sure you don't want to share my brolly?'

She shrugged again but kept her distance. This whore was good at shrugging. It was second nature. You want me dress up as nurse? You want do line off my backside? You want me wear strap-on? Shrug, shrug, shrug.

She said, 'So who hire you to find me, Mr Private Eye?'

'Call me Tommy.'

'Who hire you, Mr Tommy?'

'Melody.' The bird looked nonplussed. I didn't know what to make of that. 'Your stable-mate,' I said. 'Black girl. Lot of front. You know the one.'

She shrugged.

The rain had plastered her fringe to her forehead and drops hung from her nose and ear-lobes. I was snug under my brolly. 'You gonna catch your death if you're not careful,' I said.

She blinked at me. She suddenly looked terrified. 'Catch my death? What is this?'

'I mean you'll catch a cold,' I said. 'In this rain. You wanna get a coffee?'

We found a greasy spoon one street up from the harbour. Another difference from London after all: not Costa, Starbuck's or Pret but a proper greasy spoon with steamy windows and a fat Fag Ash Lil in an apron and flip-flops.

I asked sexyrussian if she wanted anything to eat. She looked at me like I was a madman, serious.

She took out a Mayfair. Real classy. I offered her a Benny but she wasn't interested. From the back of her fag packet she extricated a small wrap and unfolded it right there and then on the table. We were the only customers. No big deal. She licked the length of her cheap cigarette and rolled it in the cocaine until she had a nice line stuck on the paper. I fired it for her and then sparked a Benny of my own.

I heard somebody humming. It took me a second to realize it was yours truly. 'What A Wonderful World' by Louis Armstrong. Even my subconscious is ironic. What does that say?

Our coffees arrived. They were served black with sachets of sugar and creamer on the side. Sexyrussian sipped hers straight up and said, 'You take me back to London?'

I shook my head. 'Not necessarily. I said I'd find you and I've found you. Job done. I could call Melody right now.'

She stared at me. She pulled so hard on her ciggy I thought her eyes might pop. Her lips were thin and bloodless. Forget different strokes, I couldn't imagine nobody paying for the privilege of her kiss. 'Melody want to find me?' she said. Then she paused all thoughtful. 'Why?'

'Money.'

'Money?'

'You owe her money.'

She shrugged. This whole shrugging thing was beginning to get right up my nose.

'How much do you owe?' I asked. She shrugged. I thought I might be forced to give her a slap.

Then she said, 'Five hundred maybe. Maybe six hundred. No more.'

Suddenly I was shrugging too. Sexyrussian inclined her head like she was saying, 'You see?' And I did see. My head chugged some sums. It didn't take a Fields medal to figure that something didn't add up. You don't hire Tommy Akhtar for three long per diem to reclaim six. No shit, Sherlock.

The whore had found a biro and was scribbling on a napkin. She passed it my way. She'd written a name and a phone number. 'What's this?'

'What Melody want.'

'Who's Gaileov?'

'Just some guy I know.'

'A punter?'

She blew smoke at me. I blew some right back. 'Sure,' she said.

'A Russian geezer?'

She wrinkled her forehead at me. 'Maybe. Maybe not. He says he Russian but . . .' She shrugged. '. . . I meet him in New York first time.'

'Why does Melody need this guy's number?'

'I don't know.' She shook her head. She stuck out her bottom lip. She was looking more like a little girl every second. When she shrugged, that did it. I grabbed her by the wrist and dug my nails into the soft part around her artery. She squealed half-heartedly. She didn't like it but she'd suffered a lot worse. 'I don't know,' she whimpered. 'I tell the truth. I don't know.'

'So tell me what you do know.'

'Gaileov my client. Melody meet him once at the flat. I know she want his number.'

'You don't know much, do you?'

'Let go of me.'

'Why does she want his number?'

'I don't know.'

'Why does she want his number?'

'Please.'

'You always give out your punters' numbers? That in the good tom code of practice, is it?'

'You give Melody this number maybe they don't want to find me no more.'

'They? Who's *they*?'

'Melody and Tony.'

'Who's Tony?'

I thought I had her on the run. I was wrong. She forgot about the pain in her wrist. She smiled at me. She suddenly looked like she was enjoying herself. 'Mr Tommy the private eye,' she said. 'You don't know much, do you?' I squeezed a little tighter but she kept on smiling. 'So you find me. So you do your job. So now I can go.'

I let go of her wrist. I smiled back. 'Not just yet,' I said. 'Tell me about Bailey.'

I'll tell you something free, gratis and for nothing: the whole 'good cop, bad cop' shtick is tough when you're solo but I've got it nailed. I can lurch from enemy to confidant, bully to shoulder, in the breath between questions. I'm not boasting. It's a gift. Way I see it, it's like skippering on a featherbed when they're batting out the last day with no hope of victory. What's your attack? Maybe two quicks, a couple of seamers, a finger spinner and an occasional trundler: you know what you've got up your sleeve and so do the oppo. But you can still spring surprises. It's not just a question of ringing changes. It's a question of timing.

You think sexyrussian had any motivation to talk? No way. But she talked anyhow. Maybe it was my estate-agent smile, maybe it was my winning personality or maybe it was my exotic good looks that made the breakthrough, but I figure (and I've seen it enough times to best guess) that it was my immaculate timing.

Think about it: this whore had seen a bloody corpse, run for her life and then been holed up in some dubious hotel with nothing for company but nosebag; of course she was going to be a sucker for a little Akhtar charm. Think about it: you've batted an hour, seen off the quicks and kept your concentration despite the keeper's endless mouth; of course you're going to be a sucker for some part-time dobber. Think Lords '82: England batted to save the Pakistan test and folded like wet newspaper. Who got the wickets? Imran? Sarfraz? Qadir? No. Mudassar Nazar and his gentle in-duckers with, as far as I recall, six for not many. You can do the sums yourself.

For the most part, sexyrussian only confirmed what I already knew – she'd met Bailey at the Embassy, Melody had taken the table by the door and waited for her signal (the ho-buddy pact was a reality, after all), they'd cabbed it to the Holiday Inn Express at the minister's suggestion, she'd gone out for wine, he'd stayed behind to be murdered, she'd returned to find him battered like cod fillet – but there was one minor difference. According to tom number two, you see, the minister and her had not been alone at their Embassy table the whole time. According to tom number two, they'd spent at least ten minutes in the company of Tunde, the club's resident dealer.

I thought back to my conversations with Melody. I knew I'd asked her specifically about any other characters on the scene and she'd said there were none. Either she was lying, which then begged the question why (which had no obvious answer), or she'd forgotten (which, judging by the detail of her previous descriptions, didn't sound so likely). I ran both these scenarios past Natasha. Guess what? She shrugged.

By now I had Natasha eating out of my hand. I think she liked the way I winced when she described Bailey's corpse. She suddenly smacked powerful about a situation that had left her powerless.

I asked around the subject. I asked her about Tunde, about who else she'd seen in the Embassy that night, about her relationship with her ho-buddy. I was teasing and probing around the off stump. She played and missed, played and missed, played and missed. Then I asked her how Bailey had seemed. Suddenly she came over all thoughtful. It was painful to watch. She said he'd seemed a little tense, especially when they left the club.

I asked her to go through it in detail. I said, 'Humour me.'

She humoured me. She'd gone to the ladies' to do a line. She gave Melody the signal. When she came back, Tunde was gone, Melody was gone and Bailey said it was time to bounce. They left their drinks unfinished. Bailey made a call from the cab. He sounded agitated. I asked sexyrussian if she knew who he was speaking to or could remember what he'd said. Guess what?

I squeezed the whore's hand across the table, real friendly this time. It was small and cool and damp. Fag Ash Lil brought the bill and I paid. I think she thought we were one funny couple, serious.

Sexyrussian said, 'You make me come back to London?'

'How am I gonna do that?'

She nodded. She said, 'You tell Melody where I am?'

'Sure. That's my job. You gonna hang around?'

She shook her head. She said, 'I don't want them to find me.'

'Melody and Tony?'

She smiled at me. Her teeth were yellow. She blinked. Her eyes were yellow too; the colour of turning cream. She said, 'Just give Melody that number. Maybe she leave me alone.'

She said she wanted to go. She said she'd had enough of talking. She said she should get her stuff together because she wanted to leave today. I said, 'Had enough of the delights of the ozone?' She didn't catch my drift. I said, 'Just one more thing. I want Bailey's stuff.'

She tried to brazen it out. She gave it wide-eyed surprise or maybe it was just the coke. Either way, she still hadn't figured out who was in control. Who did she think she was fooling? Some punter who thought he'd just given her the seeing-to of a lifetime?

I rehashed the estate-agent smile: the deal clincher, the signature on the dotted line. I said, 'His Palm Pilot, watch, wallet and phone.' She produced the Palm Pilot and wallet from her bag without a murmur. She said she'd never had the watch or the phone. She said she'd just taken what was in his jacket, that she didn't want to touch the body. I considered. I bought it. I checked the wallet. It was empty. No surprises there. I left the wallet on the table and tucked the personal organizer in my pocket.

We left the greasy spoon. Outside it was still spitting. I gave her the umbrella. Call me big-hearted. We stood and looked at each other. We had a moment. She was desperate but hardier than she looked. I knew how she felt. If I had a waif thing going on I might have been tempted. But I don't so I wasn't. Nonetheless I pulled out my wad and slipped her a ton. Don't call me too big-hearted, I'd charge it to exotic-melody. She'd been lying through her teeth from the outset. I didn't feel guilty.

I left sexyrussian standing in the street. When I looked back she hadn't moved. I felt a moment of melancholy. I almost laughed at myself. Melancholy is emotional luxury.

Before I got on the train I took two deep lungfuls. There's nothing like a breath of country air. I stubbed my Benny and boarded. I bought four baby Jacks and made myself comfortable. I did some gentle thinking. I had three new names to juggle: Tony, Gaileov and Tunde. How did they all fit? None of my business. I took out Bailey's Palm Pilot. Fact is, I was feeling idle and fancied a game of Tetris, but when I switched it on it went straight to the notepad and opened a memo dated the night of his murder. There, in bold caps, was new name number four: AL-DUBAYAN. This was turning into quite some story. It was none of my business but that's never stopped me before. That's always been my problem.

10

I got back to the office to find commotion, serious. It was early evening and the streetlights were humming pink and there was a nip in the air but all the drivers were standing outside Phoenecia in their shirtsleeves. Something must have just kicked off.

I heard Gundappa before I saw him. He was shouting all kinds of unrepeatables. Then I spotted him in the middle of the road ranting like a madman. I was so surprised to see him out from behind his Perspex window that it took me a moment even to clock the object of his anger. My brother had legs after all.

He was bellowing at Swiss Chris who had his arms held out in front of him, partly a gesture of placation, I guess, and partly to repel all the objects that Gundappa was hurling at him: a pair of shoes, four or five bottles of pills, a plastic bag, a Coke can and plenty of abuse besides. 'You stinking monkey! I have to sit in that f——ing office all day, you stinking black shit!' And lots of other stuff that made me proud for real.

Big John was leaning on the roof of his Volvo between Yusuf, a new kid I barely knew, and Irish, a broad Jamaican who was known as 'Irish' on account of being christened 'Patrick'. They were all Cheshire grinning, enjoying the free show. I joined them and just watched for a moment or two before I asked, 'So what's up?'

'I think Gunny sacking Swiss,' Big John said.

'What for?'

'Swiss block the boss's toilet again,' Irish said, and then

creased up laughing. 'Man! I never seen so much shit come out one backside!'

'Is that a sackable offence?'

'You don't smell it, Tommy,' Big John said.

'You ask me, it's practically a hanging offence,' Yusuf added, and the other two agreed.

The row showed no signs of stopping. Swiss was trying to say something but couldn't make himself heard over the insults. Now my brother had picked up a traffic cone and was swinging it like a madman. This was one funny scene.

I looked up and down the street and people were starting to appear in front of the shops and outside their houses to see what all the fuss was about. In front of Khan's, Av was hanging with some other thug-lites, sitting on some upturned crates, smoking and pointing and laughing hard. I knew it was only a matter of time before someone called the Old Bill.

Gundappa took a mighty swing at Swiss. He missed by a good yard but in his follow-through the traffic cone clattered into a parked car. Fortunately it was one of Phoenecia's. I was going to have to step in.

My brother's always had a violent temper. You could – and I know Farzad has – put it down to Mina's death or first-generation identity crisis or whatever. But personally I just think Gundappa's a prize muppet.

Once, when we still had any relationship to speak of, he told me that this was why he'd started smoking weed, to calm himself down. I'm not sure whether I buy that or not but it certainly didn't work and brought problems of its own.

As I approached, I could tell straight away that he was pleased to see me. 'Jesus Christ!' he growled. 'That's all I f__ing need.'

'What are you doing, Gundappa?' I said. 'Put the cone down.'

'Now my f——ing pisshead brother's telling me what to do? Jesus!'

'You know everybody's staring at you, right? You know you look like a total muppet?'

He glanced left and right. Gundappa didn't like to look stupid. 'Who are you calling a muppet?'

'Just put the cone down.' I pointed back to where the Phoenecia drivers were standing. 'Put the cone down and go and sit over there. Count to ten. Relax. I'll sort this out.'

Gundappa threw the cone half-heartedly in my direction. He was staring at me with the pure hatred he sometimes conjures that I always find kind of shocking. If my brother's looks could kill I'd never have made my sixteenth birthday. He did what he was told, though, cursing me under his breath. This wasn't a mark of any kind of fraternal respect but simple recognition of two facts. (1.) He knew that, if push came to smack, big bruv could hand him a pasting. (2.) He had that typical immigrant fear of making a fool of himself.

While we're at it, that's a lesson for life, right? In the absence of trust, fear is a solid basis for a relationship. Ask any world leader from the dark continent to the White House: keep the people scared and you'll keep them in check. And keeping them scared of you is the simplest but keeping them scared of an idea (Communism, Islam or whatever) is the height of progress. There you go: pop political theory; free, gratis and for nothing.

I had a word with Swiss. I told him he'd better unblock the bog sharpish. He said he'd already offered to do that but Gunny wouldn't listen. He grumbled something about the inadequacies of London plumbing. I told him to stop pratting about.

I said, 'I'll tell you something, Swiss. You got to learn to . . . you know . . . do your business at home.'

Swiss looked pained. 'But, Mr T,' he said, 'my wife, she has threatened to leave if I block pipes one more time. I say to her, "It is not my fault that the plumbing is so bad. This is supposed to be Western country." But she doesn't listen.'

I was getting kind of exasperated. I couldn't believe I was standing in the middle of the road with the whole street for an audience discussing this blokey's bowel movements. I said, 'Frankly, Swiss, that's not really my problem.'

'Why are people so offended? It is only natural thing.'

'So stop at McDonald's or something,' I said. 'Early morning. On your way in. Get a coffee. Use the facilities.'

He brightened up a bit at that idea.

I always find it odd that bods justify stuff they do by saying it's 'natural'. In my line of work I've discovered that lots of things – from infidelity to murder – could be described the same way. But I've always figured that just because it's natural that don't make it right, know what I mean?

By now I had a headache, serious. I glanced at Gundappa. He'd regained his composure and was barking at the drivers to get back to work. Swiss Chris headed into the office to try his hand at some plumbing. I strolled over to Khan's for some painkillers and a packet of fags.

Mrs K said, 'What was all that about?'

'You know Gunny, Mrs K,' I mumbled. 'Always had a short fuse.'

'Thank you for talking to Av, Tommy.'

'No problem. Any improvement?'

She gave me a look. I smiled and said, 'He'll grow out of it.' We both knew I was just making the right noises, for real.

When I came out of the shop, Av stood up. He tried me with some convoluted handshake but I wasn't in the mood. He said, 'Yes, Tommy man. How was the whore?' I regretted telling him about that. His boys were sniggering. I shrugged.

He said, 'When you gonna work with me, man? You and me, Tommy. What what what. James Bond and shit.'

'Yeah, Av,' I said. 'Whatever.'

I took out the packet and popped two pills right there and then.

Back in my office the ansaphone was winking. Two messages. Number one was Cal Donnelly again. His voice was urgent and he called me 'Tommy'; not 'my immigrant friend' or 'the Paki PI'. Something was definitely up. He left his mobile number and told me to call him straight back. The second was Ms Melody Chase. She said she wanted a progress report. She sounded strung out too. It was a flip of the coin who to ring first. Heads up was Donnelly. Turned out to be a wise choice.

I dialled on speaker while I checked my desk for sustenance. I was all out of Turk and even any substitute. That made me feel bitchy. I sparked a cig. He answered.

I said, 'Yes, Donnelly. So what's so urgent?'

'Tommy? That you?'

I pulled hard on my tab. The poor Benny was tasting lonely. 'So it's Tommy now, is it? What's with the respect, Cal?'

'You got me on speakerphone? Can you pick up?'

'Why? There's nobody here. Besides . . .' I exhaled. '. . . I'm doing my circuits.'

'Don't be funny, you IC2 prick. Pick up the f__ing phone.'

I picked up. 'IC2 prick?' I said. 'That's better.'

He said, 'That's better.'

'What's up?'

'Bailey.' I felt my heart quicken. I took my guard. I watched the ball closely. Short of a length just outside off stump. I left it alone. Good judgement but it didn't solve anything. 'Bailey.' He said it again. 'Anthony Bailey.'

'Who?'

'The minister who met his maker on my patch. Don't be

105

funny, my immigrant friend. I know you've been poking your big brown nose in. Don't play games with me.'

'It's all games, Cal,' I said. 'You know that.'

Donnelly sighed. 'Look. This is on the level, right? I don't know what you're mixed up with but I reckon you don't know either. This isn't my case and it's not my business so I'm just telling you this as a friend, OK? Steer clear. And if you're not gonna steer clear then you'd better watch your back. This is attracting all sorts of attention –'

'What you saying, Cal? Course it's attracting attention. Blokey was an MP. Goes with the turf.'

'I'm talking other attention, Tommy. The cloak-and-dagger kind. Not what you want. And what I'm saying to you is that your name's already been bandied so much it's practically quarter to three.'

I stubbed my smoke. I didn't know what to say to that. Fact is, I wasn't quite sure what he meant. But I gave it a respectful moment's silence. 'Right,' I said at last. Then, 'Thanks, Cal.'

'Just look after yourself, my immigrant friend, OK?'

'Sure,' I said. 'Nobody else gonna do it.'

'My point exactly.'

I gave him my mobile number. I asked him to call me any time he heard my name being bandied; quarter to three, ten past five, whatever. He gave it the Irish chuckle.

I returned the phone to its cradle. My head was splitting. It was a cartoon headache, the kind when you can picture your head pulsing – swelling and contracting – with every heartbeat. I tried to swallow a couple more painkillers but my mouth was dry and they took an age to go down and left a bitter taste on my tongue.

I went to the fridge more in hope than expectation. Nothing doing but an onion, some cheese and the remnants of a fortnight-old Chinese.

I filled a glass with tap water and took a swig. The water had that vague but unmistakable smell of sewage. I closed my eyes but found I could think of nothing but the number of Londoners who'd already drunk this same glass of water. This city: endless cycles of swallow, piss and chemical purification. I found myself wondering whether this water was still water at all or if it had somehow lost its essence on its journey through a million different guts. Now I felt like I might puke. Strange that when you feel sick you can only think about nauseating things. Strange, too, that sickness seems to sensitize your nose. So doesn't a sickness like mine make me the perfect private eye? Yeah, right. And a comedian with it.

Whatever. I figured I was in the perfect state of health to bell exoticmelody so that's what I did. I didn't consider the conversation in advance – like what I would tell her and what I wanted to learn. I guess that, on the surface of my headache, I mostly thought that my work was done and I'd just give her what she needed and move on to another job (other adulterers to catch, amateur blackmails to unravel, you know the score). But, in all honesty, somewhere behind that headache, I suppose I knew that I wouldn't let this go until the story was all told. That's just me. I had four names and no faces to stick to them, right? And, frankly, Donnelly's warning was, if not a red rag to a bull, certainly a four-pack of Special Brew to a drunk flush from the DSS.

As it turned out chit-chat was limited. The tom asked me if I'd found her ho-buddy. Her voice was strained. When I said I had she told me she'd be straight round and she'd hung up before I could protest.

I turned the lights off. I sat behind my desk. I smoked a Benny. I might have dozed a little. My headache receded.

I heard the door of the waiting room open and shut. There

was a knock. I said, 'Come in,' and there she was silhouetted in the doorway. I couldn't make out her features but she looked somehow different. Then again, each time I'd seen her she'd looked somehow different. Maybe this was just a trick of the trade in tricks. I lit up. Booze makes me smoke, lack thereof makes me chain.

'You're sitting in the dark,' she observed.

'Yeah. Had a headache. The switch is on your right.'

She flicked it. Everything was illuminated. She was wearing a loose, man-sized T-shirt, jeans and trainers. She was off duty. Her left eye was a mess. A purple swelling surrounding a weeping pink slit. No wonder she looked different. In spite of myself I thought she looked better than ever. What does that tell you? Like I said, sick.

I said, 'Have a seat.' She sat. I gathered my thoughts. I figured I'd try my luck with something. 'Tony lose his temper, did he?' Little response. Her good eye blinked. Working on its own, it looked kind of saucy. I ploughed on regardless. 'I mean, I don't know much about pimping. I mean, I know that sometimes you gotta tenderize the meat a little but I wouldn't have thought that beating the merchandise to that kind of state was a hundred per cent clever.'

Why was I saying this? I guess because she'd lied to me about the whole pimp thing and I wanted to confirm my suspicions. I guess too because I was feeling a little bitter. For someone who's surrounded by lies, I've got a strange affection for the truth.

She looked like she was about to say something. Then she thought better of it and the smallest shiver ran through her whole body, like somebody stepped over her grave. Maybe it was an act and maybe it wasn't but I felt momentarily guilty. I'm all heart. I offered her a cigarette and she took it without a word.

She said, 'Where's Tasha?'

'Natalya,' I said. 'Natalya Kuzmin.'

'Natalya. Whatever.'

'Sexyrussian. Sexyrussian.co.uk.'

'Whatever. Where is she?'

I shrugged. I played it late, soft hands dropping the ball down to gully. 'Dunno. She's probably half-way to Moscow by now if she's got any sense. Or New York.'

'You said you found her.'

'I did. But she didn't want to be found. I let her go.'

The hooker stared at me. She pursed her lips, then her tongue flicked out, then she pulled a face half-way between a grin and a grimace and her tongue danced behind her teeth. Headache or no headache (mine), bruising or no bruising (hers), I could've watched those oral gymnastics for ever. I crossed my legs.

I said, 'Let me tell you something. I'm not in the judgement business, you know? If I was in the judgement business I'd have to find myself another business, you get me? But when I take a job it doesn't half make it easier if my client tells me the truth, know what I mean? And you, Miss High-Class-Exotic-Escort, you fed me a load of crap from the start and that's liable to piss a geezer off, even an immigrant geezer like me what's used to being force-fed bullshit.'

Exoticmelody said nothing. She clearly wasn't in the mood for a barney. Her silence only wound me up.

'You lied to me about your pimp, you lied to me about why you wanted to find Natasha, you lied to me about what you saw the night the MP got whacked.'

'So?'

The tom was pouting. When a tom pouts, you know about it; a black tom especially. You could have thrown her at a window and that mouth would've stuck fast.

'So nothing. But now you're getting beatings for your trouble. Looks like your life is getting a little complex.'

'So?' She carefully fingered her swollen eye. For just one moment she looked scared, all little-girl-lost. I wasn't falling for that. It passed in a heartbeat. She blew smoke my way. She said, 'I told you what you needed to know.'

By now she was confrontational. By now I was done for the day. I shrugged. I rolled my neck. It pop-pop-popped like bubblewrap. I took out the napkin sexyrussian had given me. I copied the name and phone number on to a scrap of paper and handed it to Melody. She took it, glanced at it and sucked her teeth.

'Natasha said that's what you were after,' I told her. 'She said when you had this you'd leave her alone.'

The tom slipped the paper into the back pocket of her jeans. From the same pocket, she produced an envelope. She didn't say anything.

I half-heartedly tried, 'So who's Gaileov?'

'You don't need to know.' Then she looked at me and blinked. 'You don't *want* to know,' she said, barely above a whisper.

She leaned forward and handed me the envelope. I could see right down the neck of her XL T-shirt. I could see her silicone chest mummified in a sports bra to keep it under control. Those puppies were strictly creatures of the night.

I took the envelope. 'What's this?'

'Five hundred. Call it a bonus.'

'Right.' I slipped the envelope into my desk drawer. In other circumstances I might have refused it. After all, she'd already overpaid me. (Yeah, right. Who am I trying to impress?) But she'd been lying to me from the start and I wasn't feeling so generous and, besides, I was a ton down to sexyrussian, wasn't I?

She stood up. I stood up. She offered me her hand and I took it. She said, 'Goodbye, Mr Akhtar. Thanks for your help.'

'You never did call me Tommy.'

'You'll survive.'

'Yeah,' I said. 'I always do.'

She turned for the door. I thought I'd press one more button and see what lit up. The big Q. I said, 'Let me ask you something. You know this geezer . . . what's his name? Al-Dubayan? Something like that.'

'Who?'

'Al-Dubayan.'

'Never heard of him.'

I studied her. She studied me right back. Zilch, zip, zero. She might have been faking, of course, but you can only go with your instincts and mine told me she'd never heard that name.

As she finally went to leave, I called her back again. 'Hey! One more thing.' And she stopped. It was strange because even as I said it I didn't know what that one more thing would turn out to be. She looked back at me and raised the good eyebrow above her good eye. I said, 'Just look after yourself, OK?' She snorted at me derisively. She made me feel like I was three inches short of worth it. She walked out.

I stood there a full minute. Then I flicked the light. Then I stood a further five in darkness. I didn't know what to do with myself. When I don't know what to do with myself, I know what to do. I belled Farzad. I got his ansaphone. I told him I was on my way over. I said, 'I come bearing gifts,' as if he were in for the jolliest night of our lives.

I opened the desk drawer and found myself some pocket money. I went down to Phoenecia. The office was quiet, all the commotion forgotten. Gunny had left and the repentant

Swiss was in charge. To be fair to my brother, he'd had a point: the office stank like a turd's wedding.

The only driver was Yusuf. That was fine with me. He was a quiet sort of kid and I had nothing to say. I got him to stop at an offy in Earl's Court. I bought fags and Turk and twelve cans of Genius. Farzad would have preferred Scotch but it was my money. We headed on to Acre Lane.

I banged on the door of the old man's but he wasn't answering. I couldn't see any lights on and I couldn't hear jack but I knew he was there. Where else would he be? I banged harder. I shouted, 'Farzad! It's me! Number-one son!' Eventually he came and answered. It was the first time in ages I'd seen him out of the Bob Marley T-shirt and pinstripe boxers. I'd been hassling him to get rid of them. Nonetheless, I'd imagined he'd wear something else instead. But right now he was naked. He was a state. He had the waterworks going, tears pouring down his cheeks. I'd never realized he was so skinny. I was scared a gust from the street might blow him away.

I ushered him off the doorstep. He was sobbing. He said, 'I've got no booze, Tommy boy.'

I held up my carrier-bag. 'Glad to be of service, Dad.'

I followed him into the living room. The place was a dump. There was a dust sheet on the floor beneath his painting wall and a pot of white matt on the dust sheet. He was almost finished painting over the portrait of my mother as Frida Kahlo. Only her face remained untouched. His shoulders were shaking. 'Simplicity,' he muttered. And he left it at that. My old man can be enigmatic when the mood takes him.

I cracked him a can of the black stuff. 'I've told you not to paint when you're sober,' I said. 'It always messes you up.'

I went up to his bedroom and found a green polo shirt and an old pair of cords hanging in the wardrobe. To look at the size of those trousers, I couldn't believe they'd ever sat snug on his waist but I remembered them from years ago so I knew that they had. When I got back downstairs he was sitting on the sofa and he seemed a little calmer. He'd opened the Turk. I threw him the clothes and he shrugged his way into them.

He pointed a bony finger at the picture. 'My Mina,' he said. 'She can stay there till morning.'

While Farzad started to drink, I hunted through tapes to find us something to watch. By the time I selected Lord's 1990, I knew I'd mostly be watching alone as the old man was half-way to unconscious. He was sweet dreaming before Goochie reached three figures but I stayed and watched and drank for most of the night. After the skipper reached his triple (I figure it must've been tape five), I fast forwarded through the Indian innings to the end and I watched Kapil Dev's cameo again and again. One, two, three, four times he smashed Eddie Hemmings for six to save the follow-on.

Sitting in the old man's couch, at least part bladdered, I considered Kapil's innings. It was brutal, it was heroic but, above all, it was pointless. It was no more than one minute of pointless heroism, the kind of minute when the brilliance is in the action and the end result reduced to an afterthought. I knew then that I couldn't leave exoticmelody's case with something as feeble as 'Just look after yourself, OK?' The triple team of Benny, Turk and the Haryana Hurricane would never allow it.

There was a load of Asian kids, Indians especially, at my school but I didn't hang around with them much. This was partly because of Farzad's impact on the PTA. He only stuck it about six months but in that time he vexed just about everyone. A lot of the other parents on the committee were Indian dads and Farzad couldn't help looking down on them even as he claimed they looked down on him. He used to say, 'The trouble with that lot, Tommy boy, is they're too full of gratitude. They think they're here by good fortune rather than right. This is the most pernicious effect of colonialism: the inferiority complex. Those with the complex themselves need somebody else to look down on to maintain their sanity. And that's where Farzad comes in.'

The old man found the PTA meetings frustrating, serious. According to him, the 'Asian gentlemen' (as he called them) 'played silly buggers' (as he called it), taking turns to pontificate at great length and in ever more flowery English on the subject at hand before acceding to whatever Mr Hopkirk, the headmaster, thought best. Then, at the end of the meeting, they'd all congratulate each other and acclaim the merits of fine debate. Of course I was never present at these occasions but I don't find it hard to imagine how Farzad got a reputation as a troublemaker. Nor, while we're at it, am I particularly bowled over by the fact that the Asian gentlemen didn't consider yours truly an appropriate friend for their precious offspring.

Farzad eventually jacked in the PTA over what he described

as an 'incident of racial bullying'. A teacher had come across it in the boys' changing room where one kid was repeatedly flushing another's head down the bog while shouting, 'Wash your hair, you smelly f___ing Stani!' When Farzad heard about this via the boy's shaken mother (who used to come into Akhtar's occasionally), he raised it at the next meeting and demanded to know what was being done. On being told that the culprit had been punished with nothing more than a fortnight's detention, he made a valedictory speech (at great length, no doubt, and in the most flowery English) and resigned in disgust.

I was relieved twice over. At a general level, with Farzad off the PTA, he had less access to what his number-one son got up to. At a specific level, I was chuffed that Farzad's protest had such little impact since Wayne, the so-called racist bully, was one of my three best mates. In fact, had the teacher who'd caught Wayne opened the door of the adjoining cubicle, he'd have found Lovely, Stuart and me practically exploding with suppressed giggles. The kid with his head round the U-bend? I can't remember his real name but he certainly had issues with personal hygiene and scalp problems, serious. Everybody knew him as Snowstorm.

Wayne Sullivan was the school tough guy. He'd learned how to fight, or at least how to take a punch, from his old man, a sometime builder and full-time tyrant. Wayne lived on the Attlee and we'd all go round there because Wayne's mum was all right and didn't mind us drinking tea, watching telly and smoking. But if his dad came home when we were there, he'd poke his head into the living room, take one look at Lovely and me, and shout at his missus, 'Bernadette! Why's that pair of f___ing Stanis in my house again?' Then we'd have to scarper sharpish to save Wayne and his mum a pasting.

Apart from being hard as nails and using the odd racist

expletive (which, let's face it, was hardly unusual in Blighty in the seventies), I never figured Wayne took after his old man at all. Which just goes to show.

Lovely was my only Indian mate and, now I come to think of it, I can't remember his real name either. Stu christened him Lovely after Windsor Davies's catchphrase, because Lovely's dad – one of the Asian gentlemen – sounded like the char-wallahs in *It Ain't 'Alf Hot, Mum*. There's kid logic in there somewhere.

The nickname stuck, however, because Lovely was lovely. He was the best in class, the best at sport (except football where Wayne was untouchable) and the best-looking. He was tall with a broad chest, narrow hips and his black, glossy, slightly dishevelled hair surrounded Bollywood hunk features. Even the white birds fancied him, though few of them dared admit it.

Stuart Parsons was the middle-class kid with a sharp sense of humour. He always had a little money to spend, the latest stuff (like a waterproof watch and a real Adidas sports bag) and a collection of experimental rock LPs by the likes of Frank Zappa, Captain Beefheart and the West Coast Pop Art Experimental Band. Actually, the albums really belonged to Stuart's dad, who was a producer on *Tomorrow's World* at the BBC. Stuart never called him 'Dad', though. He always called him 'Graham'. In fact, everybody called him 'Graham' or 'Gaffer' when we were at Duke's Meadows where he coached the Sunday-morning football team. At the time this informality was unique. I only started to call Mum and Dad 'Mina' and 'Farzad' after the former died. And I don't know why I did really.

The four of us played regularly for Ravenscourt Park Rovers. Or, at least, Wayne and Stuart did. Wayne was centre forward and Stuart hid at left back because his old man was gaffer. Me? I never got a look in but stood on the touchline, rain or shine, with my hands buried in my pockets, sneaking the odd fag when I could. It was OK. I was rubbish at football and I only went along to be with my mates and get a morning out of the shop.

As for Lovely, he didn't play much either. After Wayne and this black kid called Charlie, who went to another school and played wide right, Lovely was probably the best but he was our supersub; week in, week out. Believe it or not, it took me more than twenty years' distance to figure out the reasons why.

I remember this one cup game in the driving rain. I remember it partly because it was the only time I got on the park and partly because it was, coincidentally, the only time Mina came to watch. No idea what Mum was doing there but I can picture her now, holding Gunny's hand, shivering beneath a brolly and all wrapped up in this massive black overcoat she wore every winter, indoors and out.

Apart from Mina and little bruv, the crowd consisted of Wayne and Lovely's dads and Graham, of course. Me and Lovely tried some half-hearted little jogs and stretches up and down the touchline but mostly hid under a tree behind the goalposts at one end. Twenty minutes to go and we were getting stuffed. It was only one–nil but we'd hardly had a kick. Then Wayne picks up the ball on half-way, drops his shoulder and he's gone. Keeper comes out but Wayne's ice cool in situations like this and he picks his spot and clips it sweet as you like into the top left-hand corner.

I cheered like Wayne's own personal fan club but I remember Lovely said, 'Shit!'

I turned to him and I was, like, 'What?'

Lovely goes, 'I don't care whether we win or nothing but if it stays like this we'll be standing in this f___ing rain for extra time.'

117

Me and Lovely trotted back to the crowd.

Lovely's dad went up to Graham. Graham was shouting instructions to our back four, who were looking increasingly miserable and bedraggled in the sheeting rain. Lovely's dad said, 'Excuse me, Gaffer, but will my son be having a run out this morning?'

Graham ummed and erred and said something about how the conditions didn't really suit Lovely's style, which was, in retrospect, obvious bullshit since the conditions suited nobody but the blackbirds looking for worms.

Lovely's dad would have left it at that but then Wayne's old man got involved. He went up to Graham and poked a finger in his chest and said, 'What the f__ are you talking about? Stick the f__ing Paki on. At least he can play the f__ing game.'

Lovely and Wayne's dads made for an unlikely alliance.

Graham looked terrified but he muttered something about how he was the gaffer and he told Lovely and me to go for a jog to keep warm. Then, ten minutes to go, Graham makes a double substitution (like it was all his own idea and something he'd been planning all along). I replaced Stuart (presumably to demonstrate there was no parental bias) and Lovely went on for Charlie (presumably because Charlie's style didn't suit the conditions either).

You can guess what happened, right? It's not so far-fetched since sport, by its nature, creates heroes and villains in almost every game. Into injury time and Lovely skips one tackle and makes it to the byline. He pulls back the perfect cross and Wayne meets it smack in the middle of his forehead and the ball flies past the keeper's outstretched hand. The referee's whistle goes for full time and we celebrated like we were Kevin Keegan. I don't think I'd even had a touch.

We had chips and beans in the clubhouse after, and Mina

waited with Gunny to catch the bus home with me. Outside it was still tipping it and then, just as we were standing in the doorway about to brave the weather, Wayne's dad pulls up in his Capri and offers us a lift.

I didn't want to but what was I going to say? I thought that if we got in that car, chances were Wayne's old man would drive us down some deserted alley and beat us all to shit – Mina, Gundappa and me; most likely Wayne as well. You think I was having a laugh? Well, I could see Wayne's face through the misty car window and his eyes were wide and I could tell he was thinking the exact same thing, serious.

As it turned out, of course, Wayne's old man just drove us home. Total silence the whole way. Wayne, Gunny and me were squashed up on the back seat, Mina all demure with her hands in her lap in the front. When we reached the shop Mina said, 'Thank you very much, Mr Sullivan.' But Wayne's dad just grunted and sped away. The next day at school, Wayne told me that his dad said they'd have to air the car for a week to get rid of the smell.

In the shop, Mina stood in front of the little electric heater to warm herself up and rubbed a towel vigorously over Gunny's wet hair. 'That was very kind of Mr Sullivan, Tommy,' she said. 'To go out of his way for us like that.'

I couldn't hold back then, I was bursting with the injustice of it, and I told Mina all the things Wayne's old man used to say when we were round his flat on the Attlee. I remember the look on my mum's face. She could look so serene sometimes: beatific, almost like a weary angel. She said, 'He's not so bad. At least we know where we stand with him. Not like that one you call Gaffer.'

I didn't really know what Mina was going on about. I thought I knew exactly where I stood with Graham, didn't I? Right between him and Lovely on the touchline every Sunday.

She said, 'Do you remember Mr Kumalo, habibi?'

I shook my head.

'Of course not,' she said. 'A South African gentleman. A friend of your father's. He used to visit us sometimes at the Kampala mansion when you were still very young.'

Now I remembered him. He was this black guy with the biggest, whitest smile I'd ever seen who used to come round and 'talk politics' with the old man. I remembered that he always brought ice-cream, and whenever he left, Farzad would shake his head and say something about 'life in exile' (wherever that was).

'Mr Kumalo said that in South Africa the blacks like the Boers more than the Brits,' Mina continued. 'He said that the Boers always say what's on their mind and you know what they think of you, but the English say they think one thing and then act out another. I never understood what Mr Kumalo meant until I came to this country and saw for myself. Mr Sullivan? He is like a Boer. And that other one is like an Englishman.'

I still didn't get what Mina was on about. In fact, at the time, I was more confused than ever. I didn't know what a Boer was and as far as I knew Mr Sullivan was mostly Irish. As for Stuart's dad? Of course he was like an Englishman. He was English, wasn't he? But I just nodded at Mina like I understood and took the towel she'd been using to dry Gunny's hair so that I could do my own.

Why am I telling you all this? Various reasons.

First, when you look at history, personal or otherwise, it's always sobering (yeah, yeah . . . I know that's pushing it) to realize that what makes sense in a given moment can seem downright surprising in the future, for good or bad. Like, when I was studying Islam in my late teens, I read about the Constantinople empire of Suleyman the Lawgiver. Did you know that after the Jews were expelled from Spain in the late fifteenth century they found refuge in the Muslim world? That's quite a thought, right? Like, when the gaffer never picked Lovely for the team even though he was the third best player, it never occurred to me that it was because Graham (a dad so liberal we called him by his first name) figured that Pakis were genetically crap at football. It certainly never occurred to Graham.

Second, now I look back on this case, which began with a hooker in my office and me stinking hung-over like a wet towel on a radiator and eventually spiralled almost out of my control (or anyone else's for that matter), it's important for me to remember the lies, bullshit and denial I come from in order to salvage a little pride.

I don't know much about what happened to my mates after we left school. I heard that Wayne married young and then got himself sent down for three to five after he broke his wife's jaw and a rib that punctured her lung. Which just goes to show (although what it shows I'd rather not see). Gunny told me that Stuart went to college, became a smack addict and died in a car crash while I was in Afghanistan. I wonder what the gaffer made of that. I still look out for Graham's name on TV credits. I've never seen it and he must be pushing retirement by now. I don't know anything about Lovely and it's probably just a desire to borrow a positive Paki stereotype that casts him in my mind's eye as a high-flying lawyer or an accountant (like Mansoor Something-or-other from Hordle). Perhaps he's a loser too. Whatever. I guess the point is that my life – a spell as mujahideen, a spell looking up from the gutter and now a spell looking down into it – doesn't seem so bad by comparison.

Third, I told you all this because it led right up to Mr Kumalo's comment about the Englishmen. Now, I don't agree with him wholeheartedly. After all, I'm a Paki-immigrant-Ugandan-Indian Englishman myself. Rather, I take his point more generally to apply to those who find themselves in seemingly preordained positions of power (I know who the Boers are now, of course, and I know that, for all their wealth and influence, they were always on the defensive). Sure, the weak try to deceive the powerful and the powerful the weak. But I've learned that it's much more significant the way the powerful so successfully deceive themselves.

Sometimes now, at night when I lie awake and no fantasy Test innings is going to bring me peace, I look out of my bedroom window and across London. Do you know that Zappa song, 'City of Tiny Lights'? That's what I think about. Not the song itself; just that phrase, which sounds so vulnerable. I think about this city of tiny lights that was on the verge of who-the-hell-knows and how many of those lights might have been and, I guess, might yet be extinguished. Then I think about the lesson of the self-deceiving powerful and how, if I'd figured it out before I started poking my nose – unpaid I might add – into the murder of Anthony Bailey, MP, I'd have saved myself a whole lot of grief and all.

12

After I gave the tom Gaileov's number, I didn't think about the case for a bit. Because there wasn't any case, right? I was done. Nobody was paying me to discover who'd killed Bailey or why and nobody was paying me to find out jack about mysteries called Gaileov and Al-Dubayan. I'd found the Russian hooker, I'd been well remunerated and now, as far as I was concerned, that strung-out piece of stringy flesh could breathe in the Hampshire ozone or the Colombian marching powder to her damaged heart's content. As for Ms Chase? Judging by the bruising, she was clearly neck deep in a London sewer. But it was none of my business. Besides, when I tried to leave the old man's after my night watching the Hurricane make a fool of Eddie Hemmings, I ran straight into Trinidad Pete sitting on the wall outside.

Trinidad said, 'Hello, Tommy man. And how's Farzad this morning?'

'You know Farzad.' I shrugged. 'He's nearly done white-washing Mina. He's got a lump in his throat. He'll swallow soon enough.'

'Seen.' Trinidad nodded at me. He's got these big sleepy eyes, whites so dirty you're surprised he can see out of them. If you got any reason to be guilty, one look from Trinidad will make you feel it. He had me feeling it.

I fired a Benny. I said, 'What?' Trinidad licked his lips. I handed him the cigarette and sparked another for myself. 'What you staring at?' I said.

'Tough times, man.'

'I suppose so,' I said.

I sat next to him on the wall. I've never much understood Trinidad's affection for my dad, who treats him like a piece of crap. We smoked and argued the toss over the merits of Lara versus Kallicharran, who had the quicker feet. I championed Kalli just because Trinidad had given me the guilts and made me, therefore, a little confrontational. When we stubbed our fags I went back inside and left him practising his Lara cover drive: down on one knee, high follow-through, ball rocketing past point before the fielder can move.

I owe my dad a lot and I'm not just talking my peerless genetic make-up. I owe him my business (if that's not too grand a term). I owe him several years' aftercare (albeit of an eccentric variety) on my return from Afghanistan via the London streets. I owe him the judgements he made and the questions he asked and especially the ones he kept to himself. I owe him my uncanny ability to address problems armed with no more than a cricketing metaphor and a quote from Churchill. And, of course, I owe him a full explanation of the precise circumstances of his wife's death. Fortunately the old man seems unaware of these debts so I can pay them back as and when and if I see fit.

I stayed with Farzad another three days. I followed reports of the Bailey murder but it was soon shuffling off the front pages. For all Donnelly's worries about yours truly, the police didn't seem to have no leads (none the press knew about anyway) and there was certainly no mention of a handsome Ugandan-Indian geezer sniffing around the scene.

To be fair to him, Trinidad had it right. It was tough times for Farzad. Fact is, it was always tough times for Farzad when he reached the point to return his painting wall to its pure state. But I'd never seen him as bad as this. On this occasion, for reasons known only to himself, the old man couldn't seem to bring himself to whitewash Mina as Frida Kahlo and it was eventually left to number-one son to paint away his mother's face.

When I'd done it, though (day two), Farzad suddenly seemed as happy as a fat kid in McDonald's in an elasticated shellsuit and he was sketching the next portrait of his dead wife before the white paint was dry. I went out for a bottle of Turk and then ordered takeaway from Dad's favourite dodgy Indian.

By the time I left him to it (day three), Farzad was back to his normal self (normality being, I've come to conclude, an entirely subjective state) and well into his next picture. He'd abandoned Rivera (perhaps it had been this new style that had thrown him) and reverted to one of his more typical techniques with Mina represented as a Shetani after the post-Tingatinga school. As he worked, he told me about his two favourite painters for, like, the five-thousandth time.

Farzad's favourite painters were, jointly, Paul Gauguin and Eduardo Tingatinga. 'It's not enough to be an artistic genius, Tommy boy,' he said. 'You have to be a cultural genius as well.' According to Farzad, these two were years ahead of their respective times. Farzad told me how Gauguin had fled to the South Seas to, he quoted, 'escape everything that's artificial and conventional'. Farzad thought this was the most hilarious thing he'd ever heard. 'One man's exotica is another man's convention, Tommy,' he said. He explained how critics were fascinated by Gauguin's non-naturalistic use of colour. He thought this was hilarious too. 'Does a conception of natural colour really offer anything to the way we perceive the world, let alone represent it?'

Farzad then drew comparisons with Tingatinga. 'What was natural colour for Eduardo?' he ruminated. 'What was convention and what was exotica? Was his muse any greater

125

than the Tanzanian shilling and should it have been so?' I listened with one ear max.

Farzad's argument was if not well thought-out then at least well practised and it had a certain immigrant rationality. Nonetheless I do wonder if Tingatinga reached the pinnacle of the old man's artist chart purely because he once met him in the late sixties in Dar es Salaam. And haven't I heard about it enough times?

Farzad was on some medical jaunt with his mentor Arshad Patel. He went for a walk along the seafront in the posh white suburb of Oyster Bay. He came across Tingatinga flogging his work outside a convenience store. He bought half a dozen pictures that then decorated the Kampala mansion. I remember two of them well: a friendly-looking lion that hung in Farzad's study and an iridescent peacock that overlooked the front hall. The old man claims it was the finest collection in the whole of Uganda. The fact that we couldn't take the paintings when we fled is on Farzad's list of regrets. This is, however, a long list.

Farzad was sketching on his painting wall with a pencil. This time Mina was to be a fertility spirit, a symbol of life's circularity and richness. He talked at me as he worked. He talked at me as I drank. 'Nobody says Eduardo's colours are non-naturalistic!' he exclaimed. 'He used bicycle paint, Tommy boy. Bicycle paint! And didn't the whites think he was marvellous! They thought they were getting an authentic piece of African culture. But Eduardo only gave them what they wanted. He needed to earn a living for his family and that was the most authentic thing about him.' Farzad paused and turned to look at me. 'Eduardo Tingatinga knew there was no such thing as authentic culture, son. Paul Gauguin was the same.'

He began to draw again with ever more flourishing strokes of his pencil. 'Two genii with the united hope that can be found in disillusionment. There is no authentic culture, Tommy boy. It is an international ice rink and that is how you and I manage to skate across it with such ease and grace. Look at this! My Ugandan-Indian wife as a Shetani! How beautiful! We're ice dancers, Tommy. Ice dancers.'

I didn't say anything. But as I watched the manic movements of my father's ghost, loosely defined by his baggy cords and green polo shirt, and stared into my half-emptied Turk, I have to say that I didn't see a whole lot of beauty and, like most Englishmen, the only dance I've ever perfected is the pisshead shuffle.

For all the lack of thinking, I guess the whores, the dead politician and the various mystery men must have been nagging at the back of my mind because when I finally got back to my Chiswick office I found I was somewhat surprised by the lack of ansaphone activity. Three days away and I only had two messages: one was my accountant, who wanted to know the whereabouts of my tax return, the other a solicitor I'd done odd jobs for in the past. Blokey was a tame brief for one of the south London firms and he said he had a mis-per for me to track. It took me less than a minute to decide I wasn't going to do it. What with exoticmelody's generosity, I was currently flush and, besides, the last time I'd found a witness for this geezer, said witness turned up a couple of months later in a shallow grave at the Devil's Punchbowl.

I didn't feel too guilty about it because everybody makes errors of judgement. But there was no need to repeat the mistake. I'll tell you this: a normal guy with a normal job? He rarely faces a moral decision to keep him awake at night so, in my experience, he typically doesn't have much in the way of morality at all. But the dirtier your business, the more important your morals become. So whatever you make of me, you should trust I'm a man of principle.

I spent the afternoon twiddling my thumbs. I guess I knew I was only delaying the inevitable. I guess I knew I was going to stick my nose right into the stink of it and the only question was how. Of course, with the benefit of hindsight, a better question would have been 'Why?' But at the time I didn't know what I was getting myself into and the combination of my affection for the truth and the intoxication of Kapil Dev's heroism seemed like reason enough.

I took out Bailey's Palm Pilot from where I'd stashed it in my desk drawer. I flicked it on. I browsed through his diary and contacts. I learned nothing useful but it gave me a good laugh. The geezer had just spent five grand on a bathroom suite for his King's Road apartment. How the other half had lived. He'd been on a health kick and recently jacked in smoking and taken up Pilates. Ha-ha. He bulk bought Vi from a website in New Zealand. He appeared – I was guessing here from his shorthand – to have seen a call girl every fortnight or so; a different one each time. He had a standing account with a Westminster florist and sent his wife lilies once a month. He had personal contact details for every editor of every national paper. By one name he'd written the word 'C –' in capitals with four exclamation marks after. I pictured Bailey standing at the dispatch box trying to control his chemical erection, the smell of a hooker still on him, all kinds of curses battling it out on the tip of his tongue. It made me proud of our democratic process, serious. Gives hope to all us lowlifes. I played a couple of games of Tetris and beat Bailey's top score. I played a few more until it was Tommy Akhtar, Tommy Akhtar, Tommy Akhtar all down the page.

What next? I could go after Gaileov. I had his mobile number. What was I going to do? Ring the geezer up and ask him out for coffee? I fired up my desktop and it spluttered into life. I clicked connect and lit up while my modem sang its

Hindi chorus. I really should embrace the information age with a little more enthusiasm. My computer reminds me of those old geezers you see at club cricket grounds, perambulating around the boundary, too myopic to make out the action in the middle.

When I'd finally connected, I Googled 'Gaileov'. One match. A list of Russian surnames. I flicked my ash. You don't say. I Googled 'Al-Dubayan'. Forty thousand matches. I skim-read the first ten. Sure, with hindsight, I should have looked a little harder but my myopic eyes were already glazing. Instead I zapped the computer, reacquainted myself with a swift dose of my amber friend and caught a nap. Seventy-two hours of Farzad's familiar stories had knackered me, serious.

I woke up around eightish with a plan. It works like that sometimes.

I took a shower and scraped my cheeks, leaving myself the shadow of a neat goatee. I found an old tub of Black and White that hadn't seen a lot of service. I slicked back my hair. I found a white shirt that fortunately seemed to have survived from the days when I had an iron. I took my one decent suit out of its polythene wrapper and it fitted just fine. Navy, single-breasted, three buttons. Weddings, funerals, court appearances. I dropped a handkerchief into my breast pocket and slid a black belt through the loops at my waist. I had a thought. I replaced the black belt with a brown one. It didn't look so good but the heavy buckle might come in handy. I slipped on a pair of black loafers. I stuffed the rest of Melody's bonus payment into my wallet and the wallet into my inside pocket. I checked myself in the mirror. I looked none too shabby, all things considered. There were a lot of things to consider.

I headed downstairs to Phoenecia. Gundappa made some comment about how I was dressed up like a dog's dinner. I didn't rise to it. I adopted my Indian accent and asked him for a cab please thank you sir. He rose to it and called me a dumb Paki w–er. Decades of the same dynamics and he never learns.

Big John said he'd take me. We walked out to his green Volvo side by side. 'Where we going, Mr T?' he asked.

'Shepherd Market, Big John,' I said.

I was going to Shepherd Market. I was going to the Embassy. I was going to look for Tunde, the coke dealer who'd sat with Bailey and sexyrussian.

I had it figured like this. I figured Tunde was, excepting sexyrussian and the murderer, the last person to see the MP alive. I also figured Tunde had most likely worked this out for himself and chosen to lie low for a couple of weeks. I finally figured that Tunde wasn't so bright (he was a frontline pusher, after all – never, in my experience, the sharpest tacks in the box) and was probably back on his patch now the initial heat had cooled. I figured I'd see for myself.

We got to the Embassy. Big John was impressed. 'You going up in the world, Tommy.'

'Yeah. Sure,' I said.

I told him to pull up directly opposite on a double yellow. I told him to wait until I'd got in and then find parking round the side. I gathered myself and thought for a minute. This was going to be tricky and I'd have to play it just right. There was no queue. I wasn't sure if this was good or bad. I don't reckon it was just my refugee past that had it figured as most likely bad.

I got out of the car, checked left and right and sauntered over to the entrance. There was a velvet rope and two monkeys in monkey suits. They both balanced cue-ball heads on steroid-pumped necks.

Monkey #1 said: 'Can I help you, sir?'

I took my time. I looked him up and down, arrogant for real. The way I was behaving? If I didn't get in, I was due a hiding.

Monkey #2 said: 'This is a members-only establishment, sir. I'm going to have to ask you to step away from the door.'

I smiled like we were best mates. I said, 'DS Akhtar. Special Branch.' I fetched out my wallet and extracted my warrant card. I'd bought it online, www.fake-id.co.uk. Like I've said, good fake documents are harder to come by than you might think. And this one? I've seen Rolexes down the Bush more convincing. I handed it over. There was no point attempting a quick flash because I knew that would only make them come over all pedantic.

Monkey #2 made a show of examining my ID. I prayed he was as dumb as he looked.

'The Bailey case,' I said.

Monkey #1 said, 'Nobody told us you'd be here tonight.'

I gave it the sarcastic ha-ha. 'No shit, Sherlock. We always tell you boys what we're up to, do we?'

Monkey #2 was still examining. He was dumb all right. Monkey #2 said, 'We'll have to get the manager up here. Run it by him.'

I was feeling a little dizzy and a little high with resignation. They were going to clock me as a fraud, they were going to take offence, they were going to take me out back and give me the mother of all kickings. I felt like laughing. 'Be my guest,' I said. I was overdoing the sarky. 'Broadcast it over the sound system while you're at it. Let everyone know I'm here. That'll make my job a whole lot easier and I'll tell the club squad all about your co-operation.'

Monkey #2 said, 'You trying to be funny?'

I was getting desperate. I tried indignation. 'Look here, sunbeam, I could have this joint crawling with uniform in five minutes tops. Just say the word. All I'm gonna do is glance over your clientele for half an hour.' I turned round and looked at Big John in his cab. He was watching me. Good. I shrugged at him and raised an imaginary phone to my ear. He looked bemused but lifted his Phoenecia radio to his mouth as I'd hoped. I turned back to the monkeys. 'You gonna let me in or not?'

It was touch and go. The monkeys were thinking about it. I heard their brains working. The speed of the process, I could have been standing on that knife edge all night. Then I saw three young women approaching the door. They were all blonde and all underdressed in necklines too low and skirts too high. They might have been hookers until I heard the boarding-school accents. Then again, they might still have been hookers. Women like that sum up a place like the Embassy: whores act and dress like ladies and vice versa. It's enough to make a faithful boy's eyes pop. But not mine.

I saw my chance. I spoke again, raised my voice a notch: 'You gonna let me in or not?' Monkey #2 handed me back my Mickey Mouse warrant card and stepped aside.

I headed downstairs before the primates could change their minds. The carpet was deep purple and soft underfoot. The fittings were chrome, the walls mirrored and the lighting sombre enough to tempt a stumble. But if you checked the mirrors by each honey bulb, you could see the residue of years of smoke. This joint might have been class by night but it would be just another shithole come morning.

I pushed open the double doors to the bar. It was busy but hardly rammed. I guessed it was early yet. It was busy enough to be anonymous. Perfect for my purposes. To my left there was a row of booths along the far wall on a platform raised six inches. One was free and I headed for that. A panda-eyed waitress came to take my order. What do you think I had? A piña colada with a cocktail umbrella? A martini with a twist, shaken but not stirred? Wrong and wrong again.

I scoped the geography. I tried to figure how this would have looked to sexyrussian, exoticmelody and pre-mortem Bailey. Coming in the door, the bar was directly opposite you. It was long and chrome, lined with bar stools along a mirrored façade. In front of the bar in the main space, there were maybe twenty tables of different shapes and sizes with two, four or six chairs around them. I guessed that Bailey and sexyrussian had sat at one of these. There was also a table flush to the wall next to the door. I figured this was Melody's spot. To the left of this main space were the booths: six of them in all.

To the right of the entrance, at the far end from where I was now sitting, there was what looked like a small dance-floor. It was hard for me to see from my position but the fact that it was the one bit of empty space gave me a fair clue. I didn't figure the Embassy crowd was much of one for dancing, not at this early hour anyway. Behind the dance-floor there was a DJ booth and two doors that must have been the loos.

Now I clocked the clientele. They were pretty much what I'd expected. There were a lot of young Arabs with long noses to look down over and chunky jewellery that could have come straight from a Christmas cracker. They were surrounded by plenty of poppets, the pert and the less so; pro, semi-pro and even the odd amateur. There were City boys wearing braces that were stretching either side of spreading guts, bright young things in the latest hip gear (a lot of dirty denim, it seemed) and a few middle-aged jokers who thought they could still kick it. Gunny would have loved this place. Yours truly found himself wearing a sneer. What did I expect? I wasn't here to make friends. I necked my drink. I ordered another. I sparked a fag. Defence mechanisms, serious.

It took me about a minute to spot Tunde. It would have

been quicker but it was about a minute before he walked in. He might as well have been wearing a sandwich board. For starters, he was one of only two black dudes and the other I recognized as the star of a daytime soap. For seconds, he had the idiotic cocksure swagger of the coke pusher: nice suit and tie, narrow eyes, rolling shoulders and fixed grin. I watched him closely. He had tight little dreads, good teeth and bad posture. He was brazen for real. He was dealing around the place with little attempt at discretion. I figured the monkeys were definitely getting their cut.

He came to the booth behind mine. I didn't turn round, just pressed my head back and listened. I heard his voice and had his number. How? Just like that. Named for Tommy Cooper, aren't I? He was one of these well-to-do Nigerians who's posher than posh, more English than the English. I wondered what his good African parents would make of his career: first-class education turns out a second-rate bum. You may have figured that I wasn't much taken with Tunde, which, come to think of it, was no bad thing considering what I was going to do next.

I downed my drink. I downed another. I was waiting. I knew I wouldn't have to wait too long because there was no way this geezer didn't enjoy a dab or two of the sherbet himself.

It was twenty minutes before he headed to the bogs. I was three drinks in and had a nice buzz on. I slid the belt out from round my waist and wrapped it round my fist, the buckle on my knuckles. I stubbed my tab and followed him.

The bogs were all bright lights, white tiles and mirrors and they had me blinking for a moment. I checked my reflection and smiled. I looked as good as I felt. I was in luck. Apart from Tunde, who'd already locked himself in a cubicle, there was only one other geezer in there, a smart little dude taking a leak at the urinal. I stood next to him and had a sprinkle myself. He was done sharpish and was gone without washing his hands. Typical Londoner: strong on tidy, weak on clean. I zipped up. I knew I had to work fast. I didn't know how much time I had but it wasn't going to be a lot.

I pressed my ear to the locked door of the cubicle. I couldn't hear nothing. I wasn't half going to feel stupid if I opened Sesame to the dealer having a dump. But I trusted my instinct.

I was really in luck. The lock was easy access, barely a lock at all: a simple hook that flipped over into an eye. I took out my video card from my wallet and carefully slipped it through the slim crack between the door and the frame. I slowly lifted the hook. I listened again. Still nothing. I gently pushed the door. There was Tunde, as expected, bent double over a thick line of charlie racked up on a pocket mirror on the top of the cistern. He was engrossed. I could have stood there five minutes and he wouldn't have noticed. I didn't have five minutes. I wasn't even going to need the belt buckle.

With my left hand, I reached between his legs and grabbed him tight by the nuts. At exactly the same moment, my right hand caught a fistful of locks, lifted his head and brought his nose down square on the edge of the cistern. I heard it break. His nose, that is. Hopefully, the coke numbed the pain a little. I held him there a second. I gave his bollocks an exploratory squeeze. No response. The geezer was out cold. I let him slump to the floor, his head by the toilet bowl. I quickly shut and locked the cubicle door behind me.

Before I continue, I guess you're wondering what this poor sod had done to deserve a lifetime of sinus problems. Let me put it like this: I'm a pragmatist. This is useful for a private investigator and not so handy for a Muslim, which is why I'm good at my present job and bad at my one-time faith. I am, like I said, a man of principles. But principal among these principles is the code of the lesser of two evils. It is what you might call a pragmatic principle. Fact was, I needed to talk to blokey, right? Fact was, he might not have wanted to talk to me. Fact was, I needed to control the situation. You can like that or you can loathe it but it doesn't stop it being true.

By the time Tunde came round, I had him trussed up good. I sat him on the bog and bound his hands with his tie underneath his thighs. Then I slipped my belt behind the pipes on the wall and around his neck and lashed him tight so that his head was jerked back. I don't know if you can picture this but if you can you'll figure he didn't look too comfortable. Finally, I wedged my handkerchief in his mouth. Not too tight. I knew his nose wasn't up to much breathing but I needed to make sure he didn't scream or nothing when he came round.

I lit a fag. I gently placed my thumb into the squidgy mass of bone and cartilage where the bridge of his nose had once been. The pain soon woke him up. I held a finger to my lips. Two geezers had just come in and were chatting at the urinal a few feet away. They were talking, believe it or not, about the huge expense of fitting a stairlift into an elderly granny's house. ('I mean, why the old girl won't consider a bungalow is beyond me.' 'They're stubborn at that age.' 'Quite.') I don't know about the dealer but for me this added a touch of the surreal to our situation, serious.

Actually, I don't think it bothered Tunde much. He just looked terrified. I stared at him and signed blabbing mouths with my hand and rolled my eyes as if to say, 'How long are these chumps gonna be?' I wasn't trying to make him feel comfortable, just convince him I was a headcase. To judge by the way he was beginning to hyperventilate, I was a little too successful.

When the doting grandsons were gone, I started talking. Again, I knew I had to be quick. I mean, I guess I could have taken as long as I wanted but there was just too much to go pear-shaped. I talked fast and low.

'I'm gonna ask you some questions,' I said. 'And you're gonna answer them. But before I take that rag out your mouth, let's get a few things straight. I'm not gonna kill you, OK? So you don't need to be scared. You do, however, need to know that I can cause you enormous amounts of pain. If you don't believe me, ask your poor nose. If you answer my questions quickly and concisely, I promise you that I won't hurt you one bit more than I already have. Cub Scout's honour: I say "dip", you say "dib". If, on the other hand, you don't answer my questions, you scream or you make any noise at all when I put my finger to my lips like this, then, my friend, I will cause you so much pain that you'll start wishing I hadn't promised not to kill you. You get me?'

Tunde tried to nod. The belt restricted his movement. He looked like he was about to faint.

'Don't pass out,' I hissed. 'You remember how much it hurt when I was messing with your nose? That's how I'll keep you conscious. Trust me, it's better for all concerned if you stay awake.'

I was beginning to enjoy myself. I had to rein that in. I know there's a vicious bastard in each and every one of us but that doesn't make me any more proud of mine.

As it transpired, Tunde was the ideal interviewee. He didn't struggle, he shut his trap any time we heard the door to the loos swing open and when he shat himself he was profusely apologetic about the smell. Most of all, though, he talked like it wasn't just his arse that was out of control. And this is what he told me.

He remembered sexyrussian and Bailey all right. He'd had a drink with them while the hooker bought a gram with her john's cash. He'd never seen Bailey before but he'd dealt with

Nadia – that's what he called sexyrussian. How many names did this bird have? – a few times. He remembered exotic-melody too, sitting by the door. Another familiar face. She didn't buy dope but I guess they had that black acknowledge-ment thing going on.

Now it got interesting. Sexyrussian went to the loo for a quick line, leaving the dealer and Bailey alone. This must have been when she signalled to Melody. It tallied with the story she'd told me by the sea. But then, while Natasha/Natalya/Nadia/Whatever was Hoovering her blow, another geezer had appeared with Melody. Why had Tunde noticed? Because they'd been arguing, hadn't they? Caused quite a ruckus.

I asked Tunde what this geezer looked like. Descriptions weren't his strong point. In all seriousness and in his RP accent, Tunde said, 'Sleazy.' This from a second-rate dealer who was currently sitting in his own shit. It was a struggle not to smile. I zipped it. What happened next? Another geezer came in. He took Melody by the arm and led her out with no protest. What did he look like? Smart. I needed more than that. I was told he looked like me. Indian? Maybe. Or Arab. I remembered what Melody had told me the first time we met. How she didn't go for ethnics. How there was one exception and I wasn't it. I was making connections.

I nodded. I thought for a moment. I knew there was something else. I do this for a living. I said I knew there was something else. I said, 'What else?'

Apparently Bailey clocked this Arab-Asian geezer. Appar-ently this Arab-Asian geezer clocked Bailey. Apparently Bailey tried to make a call. According to Tunde, he didn't get through. According to Tunde, he was somewhat agitated. According to Tunde, he took out his Palm Pilot and made a note. We know what it said, right? Al-Dubayan.

I looked at the dealer. I told him he done good. I said,

'Good. I'm sorry about the nose.' He looked at me. He told me he was having trouble breathing. He said, 'Please. Can you untie me?'

I thought about it. It had been a productive night's work, better than I had a right to expect. But I didn't know blokey here from a bar of soap, I didn't know what he'd do when he was free and I had to get out of the Embassy in one piece. I considered the loss of my belt and handkerchief. No big deal. So I stuffed the hankie back in his mouth. I said I was sorry but when I was gone he'd be able to squirm himself free or squeal himself a rescue.

I left him there without a whole lot of guilt and I have subsequently learned that he did indeed escape with the loss of nothing but his dignity and his septum (for which I am surely only partially responsible at most). But what happened next? I still should have seen it coming. I may not be a Hindu or even a real Indian but I know a thing or two about karma.

13

I've seen more than my quota of death and most of the masks it fashions for the dying: from the concentrated horror on the face of a legless new mother to the serene acceptance of a devout young freedom fighter; from the terrified gape of another devout young freedom fighter to the extreme yet seemingly thrilled lottery-winner surprise of a Soviet trooper in whose chest I'd just blown a hole the size of my fist. Guerrilla wars are messy like that.

There is all sorts of talk about what you see at the precise moment of your demise. Over here, the most common suggestions are your life flashing before your eyes, a tunnel with a bright light at its end or some kind of manifestation of God. But it's not just the cynic in yours truly that leads me to suspect these visions may be, to use the current politically correct argot, culturally specific.

I once read this newspaper article about some new-age cult (in the States, obviously) who got into trouble with the law for their death rituals. This cult didn't so much bury its members as just lay them, no coffin or nothing, on the ground and then cover them with compost. Real dignified, serious.

The idea was that the spirit of the earth would eventually open its dark mouth and swallow them whole. Something like that. Well. I couldn't help wondering if, just before they snuffed it, members of this cult found themselves in bright light looking towards a tunnel, know what I mean? Did I say I'm no comedian? Correction. I'm so funny you best be careful not to split your sides.

To put it another way, it would be quite a shock if the Dalai Lama found himself eyeballing St Peter ('Sorry, bruv,' he says. 'But what about you and the crowing cock?') or the Pope came face to face with his ancestors in the animist tradition.

As for this 'life before your eyes' thing? I'm not sure I buy it. In my (mostly vicarious) experience, these moment-of-death visions boil down to just four. One: you don't see anything (freedom fighter #2). Two: you see nothing (new mother – if, incidentally, variations one and two sound kind of the same to you, think again). Three: you see the face of a loved one (Soviet trooper). Four: you indeed see a manifestation of God (freedom fighter #1).

I wonder what Anthony Bailey, MP, saw as he tried to haul himself up on the window-sill of a room in the Holiday Inn Express. I don't know why but I imagine he held a momentary image of his wife as she looked when he first met her at an Oxbridge garden party or suchlike. Perhaps I'm going soft as a toff. Perhaps I'm a closet romantic. Either way, perhaps I'd best keep it to myself.

As for me? In my brief instant as a corpse, I guess I saw a combination of visions three and four. First, I saw someone I love. It was me. I was seventeen years old. I was standing in the doorway of the Akhtar family kitchen, which is now my kitchen, this expression of twisted confusion and pain on my face. It took me a moment (if momentary visions have separate moments) to realize that I was looking up at myself from the position of Mina as she lay on the floor, her eyes wide and staring, her right arm extended behind her, palm upturned. It was like she'd dropped dead waiting for me to hand her a relay baton. Then I saw God. Or at least his messenger. I found myself in the beer garden of this country boozer, the kind of boozer I've never been to, the kind of boozer that only exists in the English collective unconscious. There was this geezer staring at me, a City gent dressed in a three-piece suit with bowler and cane. It was the angel Gabriel. How do I know? Because he spoke to me in the comforting words of the Qur'an.

So there you go. Who knows where I was heading, whether paradise or hell? Because at that moment I came round to a rough moustache and the bitter taste of tobacco on a pair of Polish lips. Funny the things you think. I remember that the first thing to enter my mind was one of Farzad's Churchill quotes: 'There are few virtues that the Poles do not possess.' And I couldn't remember the rest.

What do you make of all this? To be honest, I try not to think about being brown bread too much. But I can tell you how it looked to me through a blinding headache in the cold light of A and E before the anaesthetist came visiting: it looked like a field day for any jobbing shrink. Perhaps I'll go see one some day. Just for a laugh. But having had my head physically reassembled with all the appropriate nuts and bolts by the cream of Anglo-Asian medical science, I've no pressing desire to dismantle it again.

Let me tell you how it happened.

Having left Tunde all tied up in the bogs, you can bet I made my way out of the Embassy sharpish. There was now quite a queue at the entrance so the monkeys took no notice; they were having too much fun patronizing the weak-chinned geezers who could have bought them several times over and chatting up each and every glamour puss. Power is funny like that. It's situation specific.

I took a left and went looking for Big John. I was exhilarated and breathing heavy. I was exhilarated partly because I felt I was getting somewhere but mostly because I was revelling, like the monkeys, in the exercise of specific petty power.

Maybe that explains why my senses were on mute. Because you know what they say about pride, right?

I took another left down a narrow side-street that headed back towards Park Lane. It was only then and way past too late that I realized I was being tailed. I heard the quickening footsteps behind me. I stopped. I turned round. I caught a glimpse of something swinging. I should have known it would be the until-now-anonymous Thug #1 and I should have known he'd bring his old lady. Mrs Hammer was coming at me hard and fast for a kiss. I didn't have time to get out of the way but I managed to turn my head slightly, which took a little, and I mean a *little*, force out of the blow. I still hit the pavement like dropped shopping.

Something Ms Melody Chase had said to me flashed through what was left of my mind. 'You'll survive,' she'd said. 'I always do,' I'd replied. This now sounded somewhat presumptuous.

I was lying face down in what must have been roughly the same position as Bailey before the hammer released his brains; roughly the same position, come to think of it, as the one in which I found my dead mum.

Instinct or raw fear (if there's a difference) took over and I rolled right and thrashed out my right leg as hard as I could. It caught my attacker square on the kneecap and I heard him curse and stumble. I sat up. I immediately felt nauseous and dizzy. I wasn't seeing too good. It looked to me like I was being attacked by several identically dressed geezers, all of them dropped to one knee like the front row of a cricket photo.

Automatically my hand went to my head. My hair was wet and warm and sticky and I found that blood was already seeping down my shoulder and left sleeve. Even if I lived, this was going to take more than a couple of stitches to fix. Even if I lived, my best suit was definitely a write-off. I suddenly felt very cold and the thought that I was dying came calm and clinical.

The cricket team of Thug #1s were getting to their feet. They didn't seem in much of a hurry. I reached for the nearest but picked the wrong one and found myself grasping dizzily at thin air. I could hear blokey laughing.

Strange that although I was seeing in sextuplicate my hearing was clear as a bell. I had one chance. I launched myself head first at the giggling geezer's hammer. I got my fist clenched around its head while my other hand splayed itself across Thug #1's face. My index finger came across something soft – an eye – and I pressed as hard as I could. To judge by the screams, Thug #1 had lost his sense of humour.

I found my mouth was right next to his hand where it gripped the handle of the hammer. This was fortunate. I opened wide and bit down hard on the knuckle of his thumb. He tried to jerk it away but I just bit harder and heard the crunch of cartilage and kept biting until I hit bone. Now he was yelping, fast and high, like a toddler. He let the hammer go and it fell to the pavement and he finally got himself something like free. I was grappling desperately to get another hold. I was doing OK but I knew the damage I'd done to him was cosmetic compared to the state of my poor bonce.

You know those Hollywood punch-ups? It's not for nothing that the guy who puts them together is called the 'fight choreographer'. They're typically elegant affairs where the combatants dance around each other throwing the occasional stiff jab or arcing roundhouse kick. You don't need me to tell you that a proper scrap is no more like that than proper sex is like Hollywood sex. A proper scrap (like, some would say, proper sex) is a madcap wrestle that's all cursing and sweating and biting and scratching and panting. If you ever see a proper scrap it can look somewhat hilarious so long as you're not involved and you can handle the gore. This was a proper scrap and I knew that if Thug #1 escaped my grasp and managed to get to his feet I was screwed. He escaped my grasp. He got to his feet. I was screwed.

I was looking up at him. I would have stood up too but my legs weren't working. I grabbed the hammer from where it had fallen and began to whirl it round my head, shouting all kinds of crap as loud as I could: insults, prayers and even the odd plea for mercy. I was in a sitting position. I must have looked somewhat hilarious.

At least my vision was clearing and, despite the blood that was streaming from his left eye socket and his generally rumpled appearance, I knew I'd seen this guy before. I trawled my addled brain. I came up with two matches. This was the lanky, eighties-style geezer who'd been hanging around outside Khan's the first day Melody came to see me. This was the geezer I'd seen in the hallway of the tom's mansion block in South Ken. This was clearly Tony the pimp. Unfortunately it was a little late for introductions.

My mind was racing. To judge by the fact of this attack and the hammer I was currently brandishing, it was odds on that Tony was the one who'd offed Bailey. That didn't make a whole lot of sense to me when I wondered about motives. It might seem peculiar that I should have thought about this at such a moment but I guess that an investigator is never off duty; not even when he's dying. Call me a workaholic, serious.

Tony came for me then and I swung that hammer as hard as I could. Unfortunately my co-ordination wasn't up to usual standards and I played and missed. Next thing I knew, one of his size-ten brogues was leaving a dent in my guts. There was nothing for it but to try to cover my head and go foetal.

Judging by the military two-four rhythm Tony played on my ribcage, he wasn't a happy chappy. On each upbeat,

I realized that I was about to be marched off the face of the earth. On each upbeat, I couldn't help thinking that this was a somewhat ignominious way to go: kicked to death by a lowlife pimp in a Mayfair back-street. Farzad would be proud, for real.

I began to lose consciousness. I began to stop caring. One kick broke through my hands and caught the side of my jaw. I bit half-way through my tongue. That woke me up for a brief second; very brief.

Then, suddenly, I was vaguely aware of a loud crack in the air. Was it my imagination or had the battering stopped? Maybe I was just too gone to feel it any more. I felt myself slipping away. It was a gentle and not, I'm pleased to report, altogether unpleasant sensation. Next thing I knew, I was staring at my younger self in the kitchen doorway. Next thing I knew, I was listening to Gabriel. Next thing I knew, I was tasting a warm, wet ashtray. I coughed. Big John sat back. I threw up.

It turned out that Big John had talents beyond his gargantuan dick. Back in Poland, he'd trained as a nurse. What with Farzad and Big John, I suspect NHS problems might be solved by untapped immigrant labour. One day I might write someone a letter.

Big John hauled me vertical. I couldn't stand and he had to take my full weight; not bad going when you consider how completely his physique contradicts his nickname. He'd double-parked his cab in the road and he dragged me towards it.

He told me that he'd come looking for me when he heard the gunshot. And it *was* a gunshot as was evidenced by Tony the pimp's corpse lying flat on its back with an oozing red stain spreading across its shirt front.

I was confused, serious, and it wasn't just the concussion.

I tried to ask something but Big John told me not to speak. I tried to tell him to take me home but the words wouldn't come out. As he bundled me on to the back seat of the Volvo, Big John said, 'We must get you to hospital, Mr T.' Fair enough. I wasn't in the mood to argue.

14

Including the surgery, I was unconscious pushing seventy-two hours. When I finally came round, I discovered that I had, among other injuries, a broken middle finger on my right hand (that they'd set in a way that might be described as expressive), a couple of broken ribs (symmetrically distributed) and a skull that appeared to have been put back together with bits and bobs liberated from a Meccano set. It struck me that I wasn't going to be travelling to the USA any time soon, what with the Yanks' noted paranoia and my new head, which would set off a metal detector at forty feet. I also discovered that I had doctors (Asian, mostly) and nurses (Nigerian, mostly) queuing up to tell my battered self how lucky I'd been. It wasn't long before I began to find this tiring so I went back to sleep for a further day.

The second time I came to, I found Farzad standing next to the bed arranging a jolly bunch of yellow daffodils. He'd lashed his cords at the waist with an old cricket club tie and found a V-neck jumper and overcoat. He'd also shaved, albeit patchily, and brushed his hair. He'd made an effort.

I watched him for a couple of minutes before I spoke. There was a kind of calm precision to his movements, a care for detail that smacked of satisfaction (without smugness) and good sense. He looked, I considered, a bit Jewish. This is not as strange an observation as you might imagine. If you take the firebrands out of the equation, I reckon Jews and Muslims have a whole lot of things in common. Most important among these is that they don't think they're in control, at the heart of it all, and this breeds a commensurate level of humility that Western Christians, post-Christians, atheists and agnostics can only dream about. Just a thought.

Eventually I said, 'Thanks, Dad. I wouldn't have figured you the kind of geezer to bring me flowers.'

Farzad turned to look at me. His eyes were sunken and knackered. 'You're awake, Tommy boy? And, goodness me, but your first words are sarcasm.' He stopped what he was doing, pulled up a plastic chair and sat down. 'Your girlfriend brought the flowers, son. Not me. I told her I'd put them in water.'

'My girlfriend?'

'The black girl. She smelled delightful. A little powerful but delightful.'

'Melody? She was here? What did she want?'

'Melody? She never did tell me her name. Melody, eh? That's the trouble with blacks in this country, they just make up names. Back in Uganda, all the names meant something. "Strength Through Struggle". "Eternal Light". That kind of thing. But over here? Blacks just make up names like there's no tomorrow. So Melody, eh? Can I expect little negro grandchildren? Don't interrupt, Tommy boy. Negro, coloured, black, whatever: you know it doesn't make any difference to me. What is it they say? I'm a beggar, son, not a chooser. I'd quite given up on playing grandpa with you so morose and Gundappa so revolting.'

I had a headache and it had nothing to do with my injuries. I said, 'In the first place, Farzad, she's not my girlfriend, she's a client. In the second place, I'm sure it's not her real name. In the third place, Melody does mean something so what the hell are you talking about? And, in the fourth place, what did she want?'

Farzad had stood up again and was now taking a professional

interest in the medical handiwork that had gone into repairing my head. He bent right over me so that I found myself looking up his nostrils and I could smell the whisky on his breath. I'm so gross it gave me a thirst.

'I don't know what she wanted, Tommy boy,' he said thoughtfully. 'Perhaps she just wanted to leave you some flowers, although she seemed a little upset. That's why I thought she was maybe – what do they call it? – your other half.' He paused. 'Have you looked in the mirror?'

'No.'

'That's good.' He ran a light finger along the seam of stitching that ran from my ear to my crown. 'They did a nice job, these chaps. Very impressive.'

I said, 'So how did you know I was here?'

He said, 'Gundappa telephoned me.'

'That's a first.'

'I tell you . . . This is what he says to me . . . "Dad? I thought you'd like to know . . ." Like that. "Dad? I thought you'd like to know that your number-one son's in hospital." He's a bleeding numbskull, that one. You must talk to him.'

'Yeah,' I said. 'Yeah, right.'

Farzad took out his hip flask then and had a swig. He offered it to me but, in spite of myself, I shook my head. 'Better not.' He brought out a packet of fags and began to finger them nervily. He said, 'I want to smoke,' and licked his lips at me.

I said, 'No problem.'

He said, 'I'll see you tomorrow, Tommy boy.'

He kissed my cheek. I watched him go. Sure, I was missing my old mates Benny and Turk, but you know what? Morphine's not a bad supersub; better even than Lovely down Duke's Meadows. I hadn't had the pleasure since those cold nights in camp, side by side with Agent Stanton. But now I had this valve by the side of my bed that I could release to up my dose. I gave myself another squirt and lay back in the mist. That's luxury, serious.

The Old Bill came calling, which was no surprise. Their uselessness, however, was (and that from a geezer who takes a basic level of police incompetence as given).

I got an ageing DS and a young DC from the Marylebone nick. The former seemed so downtrodden he must have been serving time to retirement, the latter so enthusiastic he should have been serving alcopops to last orders. Farzad was hovering in the background. He was trying to play the concerned parent but the way he was tap-dancing foot to foot? Frankly he came across as a cod short of a fish supper.

It turned out that Big John had just left me in A and E and then scarpered. He hadn't told the doctors his name or nothing, just that he'd found me in Mayfair and tried to do the right thing. I figured John hadn't fancied an examination of his own credentials. This was fine with me; in fact, it suited me down to the ground.

The cops asked me to confirm my name. I confirmed it. They asked me what I did for a living. I told them I co-owned Phoenecia, a minicab firm just off Chiswick High Road. Farzad started coughing. DC Barman fetched him a glass of water.

They asked me what had happened. I tried to shrug. It hurt like hell. I told them I'd been jumped, hit from the side, taken a kicking, hadn't seen a thing. They asked me where. I told them somewhere round the back of Shepherd Market; I didn't know the name of the street. They asked me what I was doing there. I gave them a look. I was trying to seem shifty. Battered like I was with my head half-shaved and covered with more needlework than the dayroom at an old folks' home, I'm not sure I could have looked any other way. I glanced at Farzad. I raised the eyebrow I could raise. The doleful DS finally got the idea and asked his mate to 'take Mr Ahktar senior outside. Perhaps he can clear up a few of the personal details. Save us bothering Tommy more than we have to.'

Farzad, though he'd barely been listening anyway, managed a brief but plausible fatherly protest before being escorted from the room. The DS followed him out with his eyes and then said to me, 'Go on.'

I said, 'What do you think I was doing there? You know the neighbourhood, right? I was heading for a walk-up, wasn't I?'

The copper nodded with some relish; like he thought he'd got to the bottom of this issue with the acuity of his questioning. He didn't know that he was a dog fetching a stick.

He asked if I'd seen a girl. He suggested that maybe I'd been followed out. I told him it hadn't happened like that. I told him I hadn't made it in to see any girl.

He said they'd found a lot of cash on me. He asked how come my assailant (only policemen use that word, *assailant*) hadn't taken my dough if it was a common or garden mugging.

I told him I'd had other money in my hip pocket; money I'd separated to pay for my punt. I said, 'The geezer who attacked me probably found that and assumed it was all I had.' DS Carriage-clock bought that, no trouble.

There was a lull in our joyful exchange.

'So that,' he said eventually, 'just leaves this little item requiring explanation.'

He reached into his pocket and produced my iffy warrant card. He looked so pleased with himself that what could I do but look appropriately horrified? I even gave him the 'but . . . but . . . but . . .' and the 'what . . . what . . . what . . .' that he so wanted to hear. He was such an excited pooch that I half expected him to start sniffing my groin.

'I'm sure you don't need me to inform you, sir,' he informed me, 'that impersonating a police officer is a very serious offence.'

I gave it the bluster and panic. I told him everything. I begged forgiveness. His smile was so fixed, he wouldn't have looked out of place at a daytime telly convention. I told him it was just a cheap copy. I told him it wasn't illegal. I told him I'd bought it online at fake-id.co.uk. The geezer couldn't stop grinning. I said, 'Look, Sergeant, it's cheap. Look how cheap it is. You couldn't fool a monkey with that thing.'

He said, 'So what's it for, then?'

I dropped my head. I wrung my hands. I said, 'I use it on the girls. Sometimes, when they think I'm a policeman, I get a free service.'

The DS was staring at me, like he'd just elicited a truth he'd known all the time. He gave me a look like he was inwardly laughing at a private joke. The geezer was a chump. He returned my warrant card and said, 'It's a dangerous neighbourhood, sir. I suggest that in future you steer clear and take your, shall we say, proclivities elsewhere?'

'Yes, Sergeant,' I said, real humble.

He leaned into me. 'I'm not joking. Last night we had a murder in Mayfair. Found a hammer at the scene. It's gone to Forensics and I wouldn't be in the least bit surprised to discover it was the same weapon used on you.' He paused. 'You, sir . . .' He came even closer. I knew what he was going to say and I was scared I might lose my rag and punch him, just like that. '. . . you, sir, were very, very *lucky*.'

He left the room. I wanted to laugh but my broken ribs weren't having it.

Let me tell you something (I should collect all these somethings into a book of some kind, *The Little Book of Tommy* or whatever): if you want to lead the Old Bill up the proverbial garden path, tell them a crock that makes your good self look like an idiot. It's a simple principle: give your interrogator information (albeit bullshit) that (a) they think you wouldn't want them to have and (b) apparently disempowers you and they'll be satisfied. Works every time.

Nonetheless, on this occasion I was genuinely incredulous at the credulity of this copper. Of course I knew I was only buying time. There would be plenty more questions if, as I expected, the lab connected the hammer to Bailey, me to the hammer and consequently Bailey to me. But no rush.

When Carriage-clock and Barman had gone, Farzad hurried back into the room before I could dose myself again. For all his eccentricities and drunkenness, he can do a mean straight-up and sober when he chooses. And now he was choosing. He said, 'What's going on, Tommy boy?'

'What do you mean, what's going on?'

'You know what I mean. Why are you lying to the police?'

'Force of habit.'

I stretched (in so far as I was capable of 'stretching') for my morphine valve but Farzad got there first and moved it out of reach. He snapped at me, 'Stop playing silly buggers!' So I knew he was serious.

For longer than I can remember, the catch-all phrase 'playing silly buggers' has denoted, in Farzad's parlance, only the gravest or, at least, the most unignorable of crimes. When Stuart and me were caught reading porn in the alley behind Akhtar's, when Mina spotted me and Wayne having a fag at the bus stop, when Gunny was first busted with an ounce, when I ventured to the subcontinent and returned a few years later half-way mad with post-traumatics and reeking of vagrancy: all these were 'playing silly buggers'.

I said, 'I told you I was working on a murder, Dad. And that's what I'm doing. And it's not entirely surprising it's turned somewhat gritty. And it's not entirely surprising I don't want plod knowing what I'm up to.'

Farzad said, 'And what are you *up to*?'

This was the big Q. I looked at him, I thought about it, I decided to give him the book jacket if not the whole story. Farzad listened to me, he thought about it, he quite clearly concluded that I was mad (which was surely a case of pots and kettles if ever there was one).

He said, 'So. You're looking into the murder of a junior minister?'

I said, 'Yes.'

'You do not think the British establishment has enough resources to investigate the killing of one of its own?'

'I know more than they do.'

'As far as I can tell, Tommy boy, you don't even know what you know. And what are you doing this for? You found the prostitute for the prostitute. My heartfelt congratulations. But what are you doing this for now?'

'I have what I call a strange affection for the truth.'

'You like to play silly buggers . . .'

'That's another way of putting it.'

' "The truth is a lie nobody contests." Who said that?'

'No idea.'

'I did. Originally, however, it was the Emperor Napoleon who said the same of history. I have merely updated his maxim for our accelerated culture.'

I stared at my old man. For an alcoholic widower who spends most of his time dressed in no more than underpants, he has what I find a surprising tendency towards pomposity. He stared back at me. He went on: 'If the truth did not exist we would have to invent it.'

'Voltaire,' I said. 'But I thought that was God.'

'It *was* God. I have merely updated it for the twenty-first century. We live in Godless times.'

'I never had you down for such a cynic, Farzad.'

'So now you insult me? You insult your own father? I'm only concerned with your well-being.'

'If you're so worried about me, can you let me have my drip?'

'Your what?'

'The drip. You're giving me a headache again, Dad. I need to boost the analgesics, serious.'

'You just don't want to face reality.'

'Look who's talking.'

'What's that supposed to mean?'

'Look . . .' I said. 'Look . . .' In any other situation, I'd have just walked away. Trouble was, walking wasn't one of the talents I currently enjoyed. 'Look,' I said. 'You were always a walker, right?'

'What the hell are you talking about?'

'Batting, I mean. You were always a walker. If you nicked it, and you knew you'd nicked it, you walked.'

'Of course. That's the rules.'

'But it's not the rules, is it?'

'Custom, then.'

'But, Farzad, it's not even custom. By the time you stopped playing, nobody walked except you. But you kept doing it. That's like me when I say I have an affection for the truth, know what I mean?'

The old man stared at me and the beginnings of a smile played at the corners of his mouth. I considered I might have made an impression until he said, 'That, Tommy boy, is the most ridiculous and meaningless metaphor I've ever heard.'

I thought about it. He had a point. 'Yeah,' I said.

Farzad seemed to have chilled, though. He seemed to have unilaterally decided that our conversation needed to move on. So he moved it.

'It seems to me,' he said, 'that the key to your investigation is this Al-Dubayan fellow.'

He'd passed me my drip. My thumb was poised over the valve. 'So?'

'So it's not a common name, Tommy boy. Is it not possible that the gentleman in question is Azmat Al-Dubayan? Now, that's a face a government minister might recognize.'

'Who's Azmat Al-Dubayan?'

'Azmat Al-Dubayan.'

'Azmat Al-Dubayan? Look, Dad, we can repeat his name all day but I still don't know who he is.'

'Don't you read the papers?'

'Not if I can help it.'

Farzad looked at me like I was an idiot. It was OK. He wasn't the first to do that and he wouldn't be the last. In fact, he wasn't even the first or last that day. But he told me what he knew nonetheless and I listened. I left the morphine well alone. I was getting somewhere all right. The only question was where and would I like it when I got there?

15

'According to the British media,' Farzad began. 'Azmat Al-Dubayan is a notorious fundamentalist terrorist.'

He held up a finger like I was trying to interrupt. I wasn't.

'I said *according to the British media*, Tommy boy. In my humble opinion, however, this Al-Dubayan fellow represents a phenomenon that is altogether more modern and, indeed, dangerous.'

I felt I was supposed to say something. I said something: 'So?'

'So he's an opportunist, Tommy boy. An *opportunist*.'

The old man nodded at me like he'd delivered a punchline. I raised my eyebrows. Even that tiny movement stretched the stitches in my scalp.

'Permit me to elucidate,' he said. And I knew I was in for the long haul. I tried to make myself comfy. Who was I kidding?

'You know I am not a religious man. Nonetheless, I don't like this term "religious fundamentalism". It is surely tautologous, is it not? If you're religious, you're a fundamentalist and that is that. If not? Just join the Church of England and take tea with the vicar.'

I kept my eyebrows up there. That was a thought: Tommy Akhtar, pillar of the parish.

'Therefore I dislike the way the establishment and the celebrated fourth estate in this country – *my* country – use the word "fundamentalism" when their meaning is "fanaticism". It is yet another example of every Tom, Dick and Harry playing silly buggers with the English language. Fundamentalism is, after all, inherently rational within the parameters of a closed belief system. *Ipso facto*, if you want to imply a person is irrational or misguided, then they are not a fundamentalist but a fanatic.

'What is more – don't look at me like that, Tommy boy, this is important. What is more, since fundamentalism (albeit as it is currently misapprehended) is always associated with religion, it excuses us Godless British citizens from any reverse accusations. But isn't our democratically elected government (relatively speaking) guilty of democratic fundamentalism? Or rather, to use the correct terminology, are they not democratic fanatics? The gall of this nation, Tommy boy. The gall of it!'

Farzad was getting quite hot under the collar. He'd picked up the corner of one of my blankets and was squeezing it in his fist. I was somewhat concerned that the old geezer might do himself a mischief. That was the last thing I needed: my dad in a bed next to mine. I decided I should express some mild agreement. I said, 'Serious.'

'And terrorism!' he went on. 'That term is no better.'

I blinked. I thought, Here we go again.

'The "war on terror", Tommy boy? The "war on terror"? What is that?'

I didn't have an answer. Fortunately none was expected.

'I tell you, son. The "war on terror" is a contradiction in terms. One . . .' Farzad dropped the corner of my blanket and began to wag a finger. 'One: when someone is labelled a terrorist, they are immediately removed from the rules of humanity that regulate us all. Two: the nature of war as agreed by civilized society is that it is fought within just such a set of rules. *Quod erat demonstrandum*, the phrase "war on terror" is a contradiction in terms!' Farzad was staring at me. I was struggling to follow. He said, 'Are you following?'

I said, 'Sure.'

'The meaning of the word "terrorist" depends entirely upon context. Nelson Mandela? Mahatma Gandhi? These fellows were once called terrorists too. One man's terrorist is another's freedom fighter, Tommy boy. Are you following?'

'Sure.'

'"Sure," you say. Sure. Don't humour me, you numbskull! What about *you*? When you decided to play silly buggers with the Soviet Union, what were you doing? Were you a terrorist? Were you a freedom fighter? Answer me that.'

I thought about it. I rewound a couple of decades. 'I was just a kid,' I said.

Farzad was still staring at me but it was as if something had suddenly given in his expression, some barrier had dropped, and I found I couldn't look at him. I examined the splint on my finger. 'Look . . .' I said. 'Look, is there a point to all this?'

He sighed. I wasn't looking at him but I heard it. 'Have you ever been clamped, Tommy boy?'

'What?' Where was this going? I was thrown. I suddenly thought about Mrs Y's husband and the Bayswater bamboo with their various vices, grips and other forms of restraint.

'Your car. Have you ever been clamped?'

'You know I don't have a car.'

'But you have seen a car clamped?'

'Sure.'

'When a car is clamped they place an enormous sticker on your windscreen. Religious fundamentalist? Terrorist? These labels are just the same: easily applied, hard to remove and designed to obscure your view.'

'So?' And he had the cheek to say *I* had no talent for a metaphor. I looked up at him again. Whatever had fallen from his expression was back in place.

'You're very slow, Tommy boy. The doctors are sure there is no brain damage?'

'Dad . . .'

'So before I tell you what I know of this fellow Azmat Al-Dubayan, it is vital you bear these things in mind.'

'OK. So tell me what you know.'

Farzad told me what he knew. Some of the following is what he told me and some I found out later, potholing online on my steam-powered PC. But even in my hospital bed, with my skull screaming and the morph fading, I began to see that the old man was on to something. Al-Dubayan was not really a fundamentalist or a fanatic, not really a terrorist or a freedom fighter. But he was certainly an opportunist. And, what's more, let's call a spade a spade: the geezer was also a 100-per-cent, no-holds-barred, buy-now-pay-February nutter. And here's how.

Azmat Al-Dubayan was a Saudi by birth and a Brit by adoption. His old man was a top Medina architect turned wealthy property developer. The youngest of six sons, Azmat was the only one who didn't follow in his father's footsteps. Instead he studied for a degree in retail administration at King Abdul-Aziz University in Jiddah.

Some of the British broadsheets have suggested that this demonstrated early rebellious tendencies. But that didn't sound so likely to me. I mean, retail administration? It's hardly running off to join the circus, is it? I preferred the explanation I found on a website run by the Jewish-American Alliance. According to those nameless netheads, the real reason Al-Dubayan didn't become an architect was because he was a lazy daddy's boy who figured the world owed him a living.

He arrived in the UK in the mid-eighties with a sackful of family cash and a place on a master's programme at Brunel. He met and married a local bird and took British citizenship.

A year later he found a job in junior management in the London arm of a Scandinavian firm that sold mid-range kitchens from out-of-town retail parks. The couple dropped a couple of sprogs and bought a couple of cars. I'm guessing the geezer was something of a flash Harry by retail-park standards; but a candidate for terrorism? Frankly, Swiss Chris struck me as more likely, what with the combustible deposits he made down Phoenecia's bog every morning.

It was only at the beginning of the nineties, therefore, that Al-Dubayan became 'politically active' or 'radicalized' or 'plain pissed off' and one can assume it was the result, as these things often are (and I'm speaking as a geezer with the knowledge), of a succession of unhappy circumstances. Of course I don't have the full lowdown but I've done enough swotting to piece together that it went a little something like this . . .

One day, Mrs Al-Dubayan arrived in A and E with a tall tale of falling down the stairs in place of her two front teeth. It was the third time she'd come a cropper on these treacherous stairs inside a couple of months but this time she caught the eye of a sympathetic social worker who called the Old Bill. She got the necessary prodding and within the hour she'd decided to, in no particular order, leave her husband, take the kids and file a complaint. Two. The missus eventually dropped the charges but not before our boy suffered the humiliation of fingerprinting, mugshots and so forth. Then, like he was asking for trouble, he chose to go round and see her where she was staying at her sister's, to 'work things out' (so he later told PC Burly). At one point, his hand (open, at least) just happened to connect flat with her cheek. Plod were called. This time she decided not to pursue it but she did tell her estranged that she was damned if he was going to see his kids any time soon. Three. A-D began to lose the plot in predictable and belligerent daddy's boy style. It didn't help that Mrs Roy, one of the secretaries from HR at the kitchen firm, knew his wife's sister and soon the domestic-violence angle came free with the canteen coffee. The geezer was disturbed to find his colleagues whispering about him behind the low-level partitions of the open-plan office but it only increased his belligerence and he started to arrive late and leave early and treat everyone from the cleaners to senior management with undisguised contempt. Per Pedersen, group sales director for the South East (amazing what you can find on the web), was only too happy to have justifiable reasons to fire him. Four.

Unemployed and unrepentant (but still not short of a bob or two), A-D found solace, as you do, in religion. He became a regular at the Willesden mosque and met numerous mujahideen vets who were streaming into London in the hope of finding a false this or prosthetic that (or, in my particular case, an artificial soul). These guys empathized in their coincidental joblessness: him, made redundant by a Scandinavian kitchen manufacturer; them, retrenched by the Soviet withdrawal from Afghanistan. Some of them stayed at his Neasden house for as much as six months at a time. These included a couple of characters who were fast-tracked on the terrorist career ladder and have since died deaths meaningful or meaningless in parts of the world obscure even to me (and I'm a cosmopolitan geezer, serious). A-D was somewhat star-struck by these dudes.

Like I said, it went a little something like this: a one, a two, a one two three four . . .

Fleet Street has drawn comparisons between Al-Dubayan and Abu Hamza Al-Masri and even with Osama bin Laden himself. The comparison with Abu Hamza seems to be on the basis that both men married British; the comparison with bin Laden because both men are Saudis who went to the same Jiddah university (which is, I admit, quite some jolly coincidence). But Fleet Street (again) is missing the point as only Fleet Street knows how. I mean, just because Michael married Catherine, and Imran Jemima, it doesn't imply that the former can bowl a snorting bouncer any more than the latter thinks lunch is for wimps. And just because Dick Francis was born like my namesake in Caerphilly, does that mean Tommy Cooper could have written a formula thriller called, say, *True Form* just like that?

Besides, if you ask me, Al-Dubayan's long-term Islamic fanatic credentials don't stand up to a whole lot of investigation. After all, while he was trundling out to Brunel's Uxbridge campus on the Metropolitan every day, alongside students with the latest haircuts and various piercings, yours truly was belly-down in Ghardiz dirt taking potshots at pallid Russians looking lost a long way from home. So who's the real fanatic? You may as well book me full board into that nice resort in Guantanamo Bay or a fortnight's self-flagellating in Abu Ghraib because compared to me this geezer's just a Johnny-come-lately. Like Farzad said: an opportunist.

Al-Dubayan was a Supporter of Shariah between '94 and '96. But I suspect his membership was more stance than substance and the forces of law and order took no notice of him before '97 when he went back to Saudi after his dad popped it. It turned out that although his old man was quite the entrepreneur he was no judge of character since he'd planned for his youngest son to take over the family business. Exactly what transpired thereafter is murkier than Mrs K's espresso. However, by the time Al-Dubayan returned to the UK in early '98, there was no family business, his brothers were on the warpath and more than twenty million US had gone walkabout. The Saudis attempted to extradite him but our boy was a British citizen and, if there's one thing you can say for us Brits, we look after our own (unless, of course, it's the Yanks who want to look after them for us).

Al-Dubayan was now *persona non grata* at the Willesden mosque, partly because of his Saudi misadventures but mostly because his views of both the world and his place in it (which he was none too shy about sharing) were increasingly bizarre. Nonetheless, whatever you make of this geezer, he was no muppet. He didn't splash his cash in a way that might attract unwanted attention but kept his Neasden semi and formed what he called 'a study group' that met weekly under the name of the Post-Western Alliance (or PWA). From what I gathered, A-D started to rewrite his CV for real, telling Afghan stories like he'd been there himself to impressionable young men who were certain of just two things: that life was unfair and that they were on the wrong side of it.

It was around this time that he began to blip on the media radar. Of course he did. The papers knew that if sex is a bestseller then fear runs it close and in Al-Dubayan they had a ready-made bogeyman who represented the irresistible alliance of Islam (if only because he said so) and anti-capitalism in all its forms (always easy for a multi-millionaire) and would happily mouth off about anything from the corrupting influence of soap operas to South East Asian sweatshops via the May Day protests. His oratory was hardly worthy of Mike Gatting let alone Winston Churchill but he was a polyglot of resistance-speak (wheeling out vocab from 'imperialism' to 'cultural hegemony' and even 'holy justice' when required) and there was always a lazy editor ready to bring him out front and centre. What's more, where so-called fundamentalist leaders typically adopted religious dress of appropriate gravitas, the anarchists were mannequins of crusty chic, and the anti-capitalists post-rave refugees, A-D appeared in sharp suits somewhat reminiscent of movie Mafiosi, or even combat fatigues, which made for a different kind of photo op or top TV. There were also, of course, those titillating rumours of his activities in Saudi Arabia and his vast personal wealth. The geezer was a media natural and he knew it and his head swelled in direct proportion to both his profile and his following.

Nonetheless, I don't reckon the intelligence boys took him 100 per cent serious. After all, the Muslim community (particularly the so-called extremists with whom he occasionally tried to align himself) found him ridiculous and embarrassing and, the way I read it, MI5, MI6 and the CIA mostly figured he was just a loudmouth prat whose hybrid bull – 'the historical dialectic will crush the infidels of imperialism', all of that – was no more than they required to protect their annual budgets. So it wasn't until a couple of years ago that Al-Dubayan finally graduated from prick in the media bubble to full-blown threat to national security.

In the aftermath of 9/11, of course, anti-Western rhetoric (however incomprehensible) was hardly soup of the day and Al-Dubayan's pronouncements in support of the hijackers went down like a tom on the unwashed (i.e., with an expression of professional disgust). A couple of the red tops even posted his picture on the front page beneath headlines questioning his residential status. I'm guessing he loved that.

However, the proverbial only really hit the rotating when Italian intelligence uncovered a plot to blow up some of Florence's finest history. They turned over a studio flat just north of the Ponte Vecchio and found among the rudimentary bomb-making kit some photocopied PWA agitprop. This included a verbose essay from the man himself which, to give you the potted version, expounded the argument that a new world order was only possible when built on a level playing-field, which could not exist until the heritage of 'Western anti-civilization' (both ancient and contemporary) had been razed to its foundations.

All this would have been kept under wraps but for a low-level Italian cop who just happened to let it slip when hitting on a low-level British hack who just happened to be holidaying in the city. The press had a predictable field day, making connections that leaped like a Shane Warne flipper. Several commentators, for example, proposed links to Al-Qaeda with the unintentionally racist reasoning that the geezer was an Arab after all and the unintentionally comic reasoning that there was no reason to believe links didn't exist since Al-Qaeda is (allegedly) a network of unknown links. Farzad explained it as follows: 'It is the new principle, Tommy boy. If you believe that something is undetectable, then the fact that you can't detect it becomes evidence of its existence.' Don't you just love the journalistic mind? This kind of stuff must have had bin Laden rolling in his cave.

It's fair to assume that UK intelligence was more than a little surprised when their Italian counterparts named our boy as the hub of a terror cell. For starters, they'd assumed Al-Dubayan was all fuse and no bang, and for seconds they typically accorded Italian secret services with respect on a par with that granted to, say, the Saudi fraud squad.

I'm guessing the round-table meetings that took place at MI5 over tea and Jaffa cakes must have been kind of testy for a week or two. I'm guessing being told their job by a bunch of wops introduced a fair few faces to a breakfast portion of egg. I'm guessing there was most likely a spell of self-justification that went something like this: 'Al-Dubayan is small fry. We missed him while looking for the big fish. He must be small fry because otherwise he'd have been harder to catch. And he can't have been hard to catch if the wops caught him since they couldn't catch a cold in Glasgow in January.' I have certain experience of the clandestine world of espionage, remember, and I know that, like journalists and politicians, circular logic is their forte, for real.

Why do I suspect this prevarication? Well. It's the only way I can explain the acknowledged fortnight it took between the authorities receiving the Italian intelligence and their attempt to arrest the geezer. By the time they got to the Neasden semi, you see, they found the house stripped clean and none of the neighbourly curtain twitchers could tell them diddly. Al-Dubayan had gone into hiding. He was climbing the most-wanted chart. He was nowhere to be found and had a few million quid to make sure it stayed that way.

I guess I might have known all of this from the start if I was your common or garden news junkie. But I'm not. Besides, the bluster was short-lived since the media, like your average chippie, always have other fish to fry. Instead, therefore, the bare bones were told to me by the old man as I was propped up in my hospital bed; a captive audience, as it were. It would probably have taken quite some processing even without the bolts in my bonce and my permanent migraine. As it was, my mind seemed to be working on slow-mo.

'This is all, of course, assuming we are talking about Azmat as opposed to Kevin Al-Dubayan . . .' Farzad concluded.

'Hold on. Who's Kevin?'

'My joke. Assuming we are talking about Azmat Al-Dubayan, it strikes me that you may be up to your neck in it.'

I got the feeling he was patronizing me. I didn't like it much and I considered a witty riposte. I couldn't come up with one. My poor sore brain was chugging through a few equations and wasn't up to multi-tasking. I said, 'Yeah.'

I ignored Farzad and thought it through; the Xs and the Ys and the sum thereof.

Anthony Bailey, MP, was at the Embassy with sexyrussian. Melody was watching them, fulfilling her ho-buddy pact. Melody had a gig with Al-Dubayan, her lone ethnic punter. She was running late. Tony the pimp came in. Maybe he'd sorted out the liaison for A-D. Maybe it was an ongoing arrangement and Tony worked as his driver on such occasions. Maybe A-D was waiting in the car.

Tony had a go at Melody for holding up her client but Melody was a loyal tom and refused to leave. Al-Dubayan – London's most wanted – made an appearance. Bailey spotted him, thought for a moment, put a name to the face. A-D clocked the recognition. He took off with exoticmelody. He had a word with Tony and I guess he gave him the nod and promised him decent wedge.

Bailey made a call. Who did he ring? Perhaps his personal security, perhaps his secretary, perhaps even his wife. He didn't get through but he left a message. He said, 'You'll never guess who I just saw . . .' He wrote the name on his Palm Pilot: Al-Dubayan.

He took off with sexyrussian. They went for a 'Businessman's Special' at the Holiday Inn Express on the south side of Battersea Bridge. Tony the pimp followed in the company of Mrs Hammer. The couple checked in, sexyrussian went to the offy, Tony went to the room, Bailey was permanently checked out.

Exoticmelody suspected nothing. She approached Tommy Akhtar. Yours truly got in the mix and tracked down sexyrussian with, though I say it myself, efficiency and aplomb. I got Gaileov's name and number. I passed them on to Melody. One question: who the hell was Gaileov? That would have to wait.

After all, there were other questions of a somewhat rhetorical bent. I approached them. I began to feel a little nauseous. Could Al-Dubayan have figured that yours truly had his nose in the stink of it? Had it been the sometime punter who persuaded his sometime pimp to give yours truly the Bailey treatment? Did the opportunist send another henchman to shoot holes in Tony when the deed was done, to spring-clean, as it were? Was the alumnus (master's programme) of Brunel University aware that yours truly had been resuscitated by a sour-breathed Pole and bolted back together with Meccano? If I answered 'yes' to those four queries then I had to concede that the old man maybe had a point: I was up to my neck in it.

I stared at Farzad. I said, 'So you reckon that Al-Dubayan had the money and the balls to have an MP done in?'

He shrugged.

'Why?' I asked. 'I mean, why would he do that? What was Bailey gonna do? Make a citizen's arrest? I mean, it's not like the powers that be didn't know Al-Dubayan was in London, is it?'

'You're the detective, Tommy boy.'

'I mean, unless he's up to something major. Unless he's really gotta keep it shtum right now. Unless he couldn't afford to be seen at the Embassy or with that particular hooker right now. I mean, what do you think?'

The old man was delighting in being unhelpful. He gave me the famous Akhtar eyebrows: 'Like I said, you're the detective. What do *you* think?'

I thought about what I thought. I thought various things. These were three of them. (1.) I probably preferred the old man when he was naked and tearful on a Brixton doorstep. (2.) I needed to get out of this hospital sharpish. (3.) I had to find Al-Dubayan before he found me and I hadn't a clue where to start. I said, 'I think I have to find our terrorist friend.'

Farzad chuckled at me. 'Were you not listening, Tommy boy? I told you I don't like that word. It is just a noise. Meaningless. Like a bowler's appeal. The young cricketers these days have quite forgotten what they're saying. I would always say, "How is that, sir?" It is, in fact, a most polite enquiry.'

'You don't seem to be taking my problem seriously any more.'

'I'm an old man, Tommy boy. I don't take many things seriously. And those that I do? I cannot afford the time to take them seriously for long.'

Farzad took his hip flask from his pocket and gulped a mouthful. That was OK. In some ways it was easier to deal with him when he was on the sauce. He offered it to me. I thought about it for less than a blink. I took it. Morphine was running low and, besides, it was easier to deal with him when I was on the sauce too. The Scotch was rough on my throat. Scotch isn't really my flavour but even so. I realized I hadn't had a drink for however long I'd been in hospital, which was now pushing a week. That had to be a first in more than a decade.

'Look,' I said. My voice came hoarse. Whisky is rough. My throat felt like it had been ploughed. I took another swig. 'Look. I need to find Al-Dubayan.'

'And what are you going to do when you find him?'

'Dunno yet. Work out what he's up to. But first I need to find him, don't I?'

'That's easy, son.'

Farzad had his cigarette packet in his hand. He was turning it in his fingers. The Scotch had given him the taste for a smoke. I knew the feeling. His fidgeting was irritating me. 'Easy? How you figure that, Dad? From what you say, the law's been looking for this geezer two years.' He raised his eyebrows at me. 'What?' I said. 'What's that look for?'

If Farzad's eyebrows had got any higher they'd have jumped, cartoon-style, right off his forehead. He took his time explaining something I already knew but hadn't clicked.

Law enforcement in this country – whether we're talking cops or intelligence services – has its strengths and its weaknesses. Typically, it is good at what it's done for a long time. Burglars? It gets burglars. Armed robbers? It gets armed robbers. But kids who shoot each other with bastardized replica guns for the sake of a gold chain? These it doesn't get. Similarly, those intelligence boys have got used to dealing with structure and hierarchy. KGB? No problem. IRA? Easy. But lone bandits with gargantuan egos and money to burn? Not so hot. Thus the Russian Mafia and the Real IRA can pose a bit of a problem.

Although MI5 has all sorts of geezers who speak all sorts of languages and all sorts of computers that perform all sorts of analysis, they're lacking in cultural knowledge, so to speak. Although Farzad is an alcoholic sometime artist who's no longer a doctor or a shopkeeper and hasn't darkened the door of a mosque in a decade, he is who he is and where he comes from nonetheless. So it was that the law hadn't found Al-Dubayan in two years of looking. So it was that Farzad knew the Post-Western Alliance still met regularly in a backroom at Kilburn Library. I had a lead.

Farzad left soon after. He poured me a Scotch and said he'd better make tracks. He wanted to get back to his painting. I asked him if he was still working on the Tingatinga. He said, 'Of course, Tommy boy. Your mother as a spirit? She is looking more beautiful than ever.'

With Farzad out of the way, I immediately tried to leave too. I figured one of Al-Dubayan's cronies could turn up any second to finish the job Tony started. Unfortunately, before I even reached the door of my room, I was frustrated by a combination of dizziness and a Nigerian nurse called Gloria who was of a size and temperament that brooked no argument in my current weakened state. I say 'unfortunately' because if I'd left I wouldn't have been there when my next visitor arrived. It wasn't a terrorist brandishing a blunt instrument. It was a stroppy Paki teenager brandishing a bunch of grapes.

'Boy!' Av exclaimed. 'I tell you, Tommy man. You look mash up. Gunny told me you'd been f__ed but you been f__ed *up*! What the f__ did you do to some f__ to get yourself so f__ed?'

I tried my shrug again. It was still too painful. 'That's exactly the question I've been asking myself,' I said. 'In exactly those words.'

'F__ man. I mean, f__!'

'Keep it down. I got a headache and you're not helping.' I pointed to the grapes. 'Those for me?'

'Yeah, man. Sorry, man. Here. My mum sent them. She told me to say get well soon and whatever. She said, you need anything, you just gotta say. You know the score. All of that. You get me?'

'Thanks,' I said. 'Tell her thanks.'

I ate a grape. It was cold and sweet. I peered out of my room into the corridor. There was a blonde teenager hovering nervously. She was wearing too much makeup, a pastel blue velour tracksuit and bright pink trainers. She was the kind of colour scheme that a new dad paints the nursery, hedging his bets.

I said, 'She with you?'

Av looked round. 'That's Michelle, man. You know. I told you about her. That girl from the Attlee who been f__ing with me. We're tight now, boy. I thought about what you said, know what I mean? I thought about what you said and I forgave her.'

'And what about her?' I ate another grape. It was as sweet as the last. 'She forgive you?'

'Of course! I thought about what you said, Tommy man. I gotta be a man, right? She knew it wasn't nothing personal.

She knew I was just handling business, what what what, you get me?'

'Right,' I said. Av's language was rattling around the metal in my head like a pinball chiming special features: you-get-me what what what you-get-me you-get-me f___!

'Michelle!' Av called to his girlfriend, then kissed his teeth long and wet. 'What you doing out there? What the f___ you doing? The least you can f___ing do is come and greet Tommy, know what I mean?' He looked at me and rolled his eyes. 'F___ing birds, man. They extra, you get me?'

'Right.'

Michelle came and stood at my bedside. She was chewing gum vigorously. Up close her makeup did her no favours. The only girls of that age I'd seen in that much slap got paid to look like that. This kid could have earned tidy cash around the back of Queensway.

She said, 'Pleased to meet you, Mr Akhtar,' and I liked her immediately. When you get used to thug-lites like Av and his gang, it's amazing how many barriers a 'please' and a 'Mr' can break down.

I said, 'Av's told me a lot about you.'

And Av immediately protested: 'No, I ain't, Tommy man. That's f___ing bullshit.' And then to Michelle, 'That's bullshit. I ain't told him nothing.'

Michelle ignored him. 'Avid has told me a lot about you too.'

'Yeah?'

'He says you're a private investigator.'

'That's right.'

'Like on telly.'

'Not really.'

She narrowed her eyes. She said, 'Did you have a metal plate put in your skull?'

'Yeah.'

'My brother had that. After he fell off his bike. He's fine now. He even looks pretty normal and everything.'

'That's good to know.'

'So . . .' She took a tissue out of her pocket and carefully spat her chewing-gum into it before discarding it in the bin. There was something totally endearing about the action. I came over all paternal. I looked from her to Av. Av was rolling his tongue around his gums and fiddling with the stud in his ear. Part of me thought she'd be a good influence. Part of me wanted to tell her to run while she had the chance. 'So what happened to you, Mr Akhtar?'

'Call me Tommy.'

'What happened, Tommy?'

Yet again I tried to shrug. I tell you something: you don't notice how often you do something until it hurts to do it. I winced. 'Bad karma.'

'What happened?'

'You should have seen the other guy.'

'What happened to the other guy?'

I replied without thinking. It just fell out of my mouth. 'He got shot,' I said. 'He got shot dead.'

Av jumped in, overexcited: 'You shot him?'

'No.'

'Who shot him?'

'I dunno. I had other things on my mind.'

Av came up behind Michelle and gave her a squeeze. She was looking at me but she seemed to enjoy his attention. 'Other things on your mind?' he scoffed. 'Like what, Tommy man?'

'This and that,' I said. 'Trying not to die mostly.'

That wiped the smile off his face. He murmured, 'F__!' And then, 'F__ing . . . I mean, f__!'

'Yeah,' I said. 'You got a real way with words, Av, know what I mean?'

'You should have let me help you, boy. I told you that. You should have f___ing let me help you. Tommy and Av, what what what. You got grief? Call Tommy and Av. You need to find some f___ ? Tommy and Av. You need to lose some f___ ? Tommy and Av. We could be a team, you get me? We'd rinse it, serious.' He lowered his voice. 'I know people, Tommy man. I know the sort of people who know the sort of people who do this sort of thing, know what I mean? I could sort this. Even now, I could sort this.'

Av was staring at me earnestly. I was staring right back. I had no idea what he was on about. Luckily my face was so swollen that expressions like 'bemused' and 'bewildered' were hidden by the bruising. I don't know which hurt more: my poor broken ribs when I started to laugh or my poor broken ribs when I tried to hold it in. My laughter turned into a cough and the pain had tears pouring from my eyes. Michelle took my hand. Her slim pink baby-girl fingers were warm and slightly damp against mine.

Maybe it was her touch, maybe the pain, maybe the cocktail of drugs and alcohol that was buzzing round my system, maybe my pragmatism or simply a deranged reaction to Av's endless deluded babble but it was at that moment that I had what is probably the worst idea of my sorry existence to date. Now, I've had some crap ideas before – like when Wayne and me covered Stuart's bollocks in Deep Heat, like the time I padded up to a straight one last ball before tea, like when Mina asked me to take her to the doctor and I suggested she rest upstairs because Farzad would have a fit if he found the shop shut when he came back from the cash-and-carry – but, however I think about it, I reckon this was the worst. I mean, even though I feel responsible for Mum's death, she was my mum and she could have made me take her if she'd wanted, right? That's how I've therapized myself for the last decade anyway. But Av? Av was just a kid. In fact, that was kind of the basis of the idea.

I turned to Michelle and asked her if she'd leave us alone for a minute. Av was looking at me curiously, like he knew something was up. With Michelle out of the way I said, 'Maybe you can help me, Av, know what I mean?'

I gave Av a bit of background, not the whole story but enough that he knew the score. I told him a little bit about Al-Dubayan. I told him a little bit about the PWA that met in a back room at Kilburn Library. I suggested he check it out for me.

Av was hyped. He said, 'No problem. I'll check it out. What what what. No f——ing problem.' He said, 'What you wanna know, Tommy man?'

'I dunno. I just want you to have a look, that's all. See who's there and what they're talking about.'

He said, 'What about cash?'

'Cash?'

'Yeah. Cash. We all gotta get paid.'

'I thought you wanted to help.'

'Course I wanna help. What you saying? But there's expenses, you get me?'

I pointed him to my jacket. He looked in the inside pocket and found my wallet. He emptied it. It must have been at least three long but I didn't complain. Av was taking the piss but it's not like I was doing any different. In fact, maybe I was already paying off my conscience.

I had it figured like this. I wasn't going to be up to much espionage for a little while what with injuries sustained and, besides, Av was perfect recruitment material for a bunch of terrorists/opportunists/nutters/whatever. I reckoned he'd fit in at Kilburn Library better than Catherine Cookson. He was young, he was dumb, he was angry and he needed something to follow, right? And aren't those the very qualities that geezers like the PWA know how to exploit? Of course, if I'd thought about it, I'd have realized those were exactly the same qualities I was exploiting too. But I didn't think about it. I guess you could put this down to my pain, painkillers or pragmatism but, after everything that's happened, I can only tell you this: none of these explanations enables me to feel 100 per cent proud of myself.

16

It took a few days to wean me off the morph. I cried like a baby, serious. Gloria was sympathy itself. 'Thomas!' she exclaimed. 'You complaining again? But you're troublesome! You don't know what pain is. You should try childbirth, my friend.'

I suffered a severe sense-of-humour failure. I'm not proud of it. I told her my name was Tommy. I told her I wasn't her friend. I told her where she could stick her troublesome. She came over all pouty and suggested my bed could be put to better use by the more deserving. So at least we agreed on something. I had to get out of there. I had work to do. I needed a drink and a fag. But the doctors made me wait.

In the meantime, Farzad didn't come back. I knew he hated hospitals. They reminded him of Mina: pacing corridors the best part of certain his life had just fallen apart. Fair enough. Then again, everything reminds him of Mina from the bottom of a can of Genius to the wall of his front room, know what I mean?

There was no reappearance by exoticmelody either. I somewhat regretted that I'd been comatose when she'd dropped by. Her flowers sat in the vase until they started to smell rotten. Even then, it took a comment from the registrar before Gloria chucked them. My only visitor, therefore, was Av. No sign of Michelle this time and no fresh fruit from Mrs K. He was on his own.

Av had been to his first meeting with the PWA. Av was overexcited. Av talked faster than usual and, with my brain working slower than usual, it took me a minute or two to decipher whether he was hyped by his first venture into the thrilling world of espionage or what he'd heard at the Kilburn Library. But I figured it out.

'So I went down there, Tommy man. And I was all, like, "I hear this is what what what." And they were, like, "What of it?" But I was cool, you get me? So they let me in and they all calling me "my brother" or whatever and I'm, like, this is extra because I'm not no f—ing sucker, right? But I tell you, Tommy man, there was 'nuff youth down there of all flavours, you know what I mean? I mean, from what you said, Tommy man, I was expecting some c—s talking religious business and what what what. But there was none of that. They was just cool, you know?

'It was like college. Not like college college. But like *college*. It's like what they said, man: "This is schooling they don't teach you in school." That's what they said. They said, "We teach you history and science and mathematics but not like that bullshit you learn in school."'

He paused. He took a deep breath. He was going to tell me something important. 'You know where they had the first library in the whole world?'

I said, 'No.'

'Timbuktu. You know where that is? Africa. *Africa*. And you know where the world's oldest university is?'

I didn't say anything.

'Egypt. They told me that. It's not Cambridge or nothing but this Muslim university in Egypt. They told me that. And did you know that the CIA has been behind ninety per cent of all wars started in the last fifty years? Fact.'

'I didn't know that.'

'That's because you ignorant, Tommy man. It's not your fault. You been brainwashed. You a sheep. It's OK. Most people is sheep. That's why the Post-Western Alliance only looks out for young lions, you get me?'

'Like you?'

'Yeah. Like me.' He paused. He looked momentarily embarrassed. 'Don't take the piss, Tommy man.'

I pushed my thumbs into my eye sockets until I saw paisley. I didn't like what I was hearing. I should have seen this coming. I'd sent Av to the Kilburn Library because he was young, dumb, angry and therefore perfect fodder for the PWA. Turned out he was a bit too perfect. I said, 'I'm not taking the piss.'

He said, 'Yeah, you are. But whatever, man. It's all gravy. They told me about your kind of geezers anyway. They said there's always geezers what say this and that is bollocks and the worst ones are ignorant motherf__ers what look just like you. It has to be like that because the *West*' – he spat that word – 'is based on keeping the players in power and the weak in chains and there's a whole lot more weak than players, you get me? So the players gotta keep the weak ignorant, otherwise they f__ed. It's anti-civilization. But Babylon gonna fall, Tommy man. It's inevitable. That's what they said. They called it a historical diuretic.'

I stared at him. Take out the earring, the swagger and all the 'f__s' and 'c–s' and I could've been looking at myself in the mirror twenty years ago, serious. I had new respect for the PWA too. A couple of hours with a junior hooligan and they'd taught him the A to Z of global capitalism. In fact, I might have joined up myself if (a) they weren't out to kill me and (b) I still had enthusiasm for such certainties.

Av was shifting from foot to foot. His lips were curled half-way to a sneer. I had to be careful what I said next. If I contradicted him, the sneer would harden, for real. Besides, what was there to contradict? To be honest, I even liked the idea of a 'historical diuretic'. I may be a proud Englishman but I know we have a tendency, historically speaking, to take the piss. Too right we do.

I needed, therefore, to focus on Al-Dubayan. Because as far as I was concerned this wasn't about which race, class, nation or continent was doing what to the other but about a geezer who'd murdered (or, at least, had had murdered) two fellow geezers and yours truly was next on the list. As simple as that.

'Dialectic,' I said. 'It's a historical *dialectic*.'

I shut my eyes. My perma-headache was kicking in big-time.

I said, 'Look. I'm not taking the piss. Why would I take the piss? We're a team. Like you said. Av and Tommy. Tommy and Av. What I *am* saying is that you need to choose your side. Because for all their moral this and dialectic that, you need to remember that these are the geezers that tried to off me and they're liable to try again and next time I might not be so lucky. What I'm saying is that we're a team. And if we're a team, we're a team. Because if we're not a team then you'd better tell me so I know where I stand. What I'm saying is, I like to know who my friends are. Look, what I'm saying is this: are we a team?'

Av looked at me sideways. He seemed momentarily confused, then a little crestfallen. I knew I was winning. Then he shook his head. 'Course we a team, Tommy man. Don't even kick it like that.'

'Right.' I had to press home my advantage. 'So did you see our boy?'

'Our boy?'

'Al-Dubayan.'

'Nah, man! Geezer's on the run from the filth, innit? Whole thing was run by his left tenants, Ali and Brian.'

'Ali and Brian?'

'Yeah.'

'Young guys?'

'No way. Old guys. Almost as old as you. But they kitted out like f——ing rappers, in combats and shit, only without the ice.'

'Right.' Almost as old as me? I didn't have time to nurse my bruised ego. I had worse injuries to worry about. I was beginning to get the picture. 'So, no sign of Al-Dubayan?'

Av shook his head. 'They talked about him, though. Loads. You should have heard the stories, blood. I'm listening and I'm, like, this geezer's a *geezer*, you get me? Like this geezer's been everywhere: Somalia, Iran, Iraq, Chechnya – all those places. And Afghanistan. Just like you, Tommy man. The geezer's f——ing nails.'

I saw my chance. I took it. I watched Av shrink as I gave him the potted biography. I told him about Al-Dubayan's upmarket Saudi credentials and his pampered life as the son of a property magnate. I would have told him about the job in Scandinavian kitchens but I didn't know about that yet. So instead I had to make do with how the geezer got his marching orders from the Willesden mosque and how the geezer was a bullshitter. What really pushed buttons, however, was when I told him Al-Dubayan had been busted for knocking his missus around. Av jerked his head like I'd just cussed his mother and I knew I'd won.

He muttered, 'If you think you a man after you smacked a bird, you still a kid, serious.'

I said, 'Serious.'

I was staring at him but he didn't want to meet my eye. I figured we were on the same side again. After all, he was quoting *Little Book of Tommy*, right? I figured it would be OK.

He said, 'So what you want me to do?'

'Just keep doing what you doing. You doing good.'

'Yeah?'

'Better than good. This is a big boys' game, Av, know what I mean?'

'And what if I meet Al-Dubayan, Tommy man? What do I do?'

'Nothing. Just listen, remember and tell me what's going on.'

''Cos I could have him f__ed up for you, Tommy man. Like I told you. I know people. What what what.'

I shook my head. I fixed him with a look until I was sure he got the message. 'No. Just listen, remember and tell me what's going on, OK?'

He shrugged.

'I'm serious, Av. You understand?'

He said, 'Sure, Tommy. We a team.'

'Exactly. Don't let me down.'

'I won't. Don't *you* let me down, boy.'

'Right,' I said. At the time I didn't know how I could.

Av didn't hang around. I meant to ask him how it was going with Michelle, to send my best to Mrs K, all of that. But my mind was full of thoughts that competed like charity muggers for your cash. Besides, Av seemed incapable of anything but parroting PWA rhetoric. His parting shot was, 'If the Vice President and the President of the one superpower are called Dick and Bush, no wonder we're all f__ed, you get me?' That kind of thing.

I said, 'Whatever,' and repeated my mantra: 'Just listen. Remember. Tell me what's going on. OK?'

The thoughts that I was thinking went like this: did I have a problem with Al-Dubayan beyond the regrettable fact that he wanted to kill me? And, if not, wouldn't I have been better off doing a sexyrussian and just heading out for a spot of sea air? After all, from what I'd gathered off Av, it didn't sound like the PWA and I were what you might call ideologically opposed. But I wasn't going to leave town, was I? And I figured there were two reasons for this and I worked out which one weighed more.

In the first place, as I'd said to the old man, I suspected Al-Dubayan was up to no good and what if he was planning misbehaviour of the kind that had almost seen central Florence blown to the great renaissance in the sky? I thought about this and I wondered if, as something of a sympathizer (albeit of the passive variety), this would have been adequate to spur me to intervene. Fortunately there was the second reason and that was reason enough on its own. You see, what really got me about A-D was not what he'd done, not what he was doing and not what he might yet do (whatever that might be). Instead, what got me was the fact that the geezer was a bullshitter. Him and me could have philosophized until we were blue in the face about the moral degradation of the West and his proposed solution, which, to judge by Av's quotations, was a mixture of Islamist, anarchist, Communist, terrorist and Rastafarian at least. However, such discussions would have meant nothing if I was expected to follow a leader who was a wife-beating, family-conning, kitchen-fitting, tom-punting fraud. It made me realize that there's no such thing as corrupt ideas, only corrupt people. It made me realize that my real problem with A-D was not that he was a fundamentalist. The real problem was that he wasn't.

I suspect that a head full of sheet metal means that thinking will now require a fair amount of lubrication. Maybe this is just the drinker talking but that was how I explained the piercing migraine that had me puking within half an hour of Av's departure. I figured his visit must have set back my convalescence a week at the very least. Turned out I was wrong. They discharged me the very next day.

I belled Phoenecia. Gunny said, 'Well well well . . .'

I said, 'Not too bad. Thanks for asking.'

Gunny cackled at that. He said he'd have a car with me in half an hour. He said it would be a tenner, flat rate. I didn't haggle.

He sent Swiss, who parked up and came right to the ward. I could have hobbled but I thought I might as well make the most of my last opportunity for stylish travel. When Swiss saw the state of me his big eyes got bigger. I thought he might burst into tears. But then he met Gloria and his big eyes got bigger still. They hit it off, for real; a sofa of a man and an equally comfortably-shaped woman, each the wrong side of forty, getting all dewy-eyed across the prostrate form of a crippled Paki. It was somewhat filmic in an arthouse kind of way.

I guessed Swiss was having problems with his missus again and the nurse was just what he fancied in the way of extra-curricular. He didn't know what he was getting himself into. This woman wasn't no hobby.

Gloria walked us all the way to pick-up and set-down. While Swiss pushed the wheelchair they talked over the top of my head like I wasn't there. Gloria told stories about my moaning in the third person and Swiss found them funny. Swiss asked her questions and learned more about the nurse in that short journey than I'd found out in however many days bedridden. She had two teenage sons: one was studying chemical engineering at Manchester University, the other was still in Lagos with her ex but she hoped to get him over to finish his schooling. I may have been the detective but there's nothing like a few rattling hormones (even of the middle-aged variety) to catalyse the release of information. By the time we reached the automatic doors, I swear I could smell love in the air. Or maybe it was just disinfectant.

Swiss threw my bag and walking-stick into the back and helped me into the passenger seat of his motor. My head was throbbing and my ribs giving me gyp but Swiss was surprisingly gentle for such a big geezer. He shut the door on me. I buzzed down the window. Gloria was telling him her shift finished at six. He looked as coy as a pretty little schoolgirl asking Dad for a fiver just out of Mum's earshot. I leaned out of the window. My bust ribs protested. My tone was chatty but loud enough. 'Hey,' I said. 'Did Mrs Swiss ever forgive you for the drains?' Gloria's eyes darkened and Swiss was already stuttering as I buzzed the window shut.

You can make your judgements but I didn't have no axe to grind. I just don't like lazy infidelity, that's all. If you can't stand the heat, get out of the kitchen, for real. But, conversely, if you can't stand the cold, don't put your nuts in the fridge, know what I mean? This is one reason why I'm 'Tommy Akhtar, Bachelor' and that's that. Maybe I was sticking my oar in but that's what detectives do, right? Besides, whatever you might think, I had a lot of time for Swiss, a little spare for the nurse too, and I knew I was doing them both a favour.

Swiss didn't talk all the way back to Chiswick. I didn't know whether he was angry with me for grassing or ashamed of his game. I'm not convinced he knew either. Six of one and half a dozen of the other, I guess. When we pulled up outside Khan's, however, he turned to me and took hold of my right wrist and gripped it in one of his great big beanbag paws. His eyes were suddenly raging and I thought he was going to give me a slap. I winced. I could already feel my stitches bursting. But instead he hissed, 'If I ever find the man who did this to you, Mr T? I'll wring his neck like a chicken.'

Although the man who did this to me was long since found, dead and buried, I enjoyed the sentiment nonetheless.

Unfortunately Swiss seemed determined to practise his wringing on my poor wrist. I said, 'Thanks. You're a mate, Swiss.' Then I had to ask him to let me go.

Swiss offered to help me out of the car but I said I'd manage. It took gritted teeth and a couple of minutes but I did. I even grabbed my own bag and stick from the back seat and left him perusing page three. I'm guessing Sophie from Chigwell was a poor substitute for the glorious Gloria.

I peered into Khan's but Av was nowhere to be seen and Mrs K was busy with a customer, weighing up some dusty-looking produce on the scales. I limped across the road. Irish was smoking in Phoenecia's doorway and I could see Yusuf lounging on the one chair inside. Irish smiled at me without teeth and said, 'Yes, Tommy.' Yusuf got up and then sat down again and raised a limp hand. Sure I wasn't tight with either of these guys but I was still surprised by the lack of hoopla. I mean, my story must have been doing the rounds and, besides, I'd seen my boat, right? I knew that my patchwork bonce merited more than a 'yes' and a half-hearted wave.

Then I spotted Gunny's mug, smug and puffy, behind the Perspex screen. I expected a 'Look what the f——ing cat dragged in' or a 'Jesus H, bruv!' at the very least. But he didn't say a word. Momentarily I wondered if my gruesome appearance had even shocked him to silence (which would have been a first) but then I saw something like fear flash behind his eyes. I was somewhat taken aback. Nothing scares Gunny. He doesn't have the imagination.

I just had time to pull bewildered-of-Bangalore and consider the possibility that a certain Saudi (or more likely his associates) was about to reacquaint my brains with the pavement when I heard a voice behind me say, 'Hello, Tommy.'

I turned around real slow. (I wasn't playing it cool. 'Real

slow' was all the turning my body could manage in its current state of repair.) When I saw who was talking to me I was relieved I can tell you.

Little Book of Tommy, #27. There are many things that the movies get wrong most of the time. I've already touched upon Hollywood fist fights and Hollywood sex and, off the top of my head, you could add nightclubs, gun battles, torture, police chiefs, Nazis, American presidents and annoying younger brothers to the list. There are also, however, certain movie archetypes that seem to reflect reality with surprising accuracy. I have never, for example, come across an intelligence agent of any nation who didn't look like he or she had walked straight off the set (even Stanton, whom I'd respected, played hard-bitten field agent to a T). And the 'he and she' who now confronted me outside Phoenecia, backed up by a pair of uniform, did nothing to contradict this assertion. He was six foot plenty with a square jaw, a side parting and a bored look that he practised in front of the mirror. She was five foot nothing with pinched features and hair scraped back off her head like she was determined to punish it. She had bad posture, which might have been down to the burden of expectation or the weight of the chips on her shoulders. She was too short on the one side and too female on the other. I could say she was 'well balanced' and give it the ha-ha. But I'm a better comedian than that. They both wore dark suits and white shirts and arrogance like it was standard-issue underwear. The two plod looked somewhat intimidated and I knew it had nothing to do with me.

'Hello, Tommy.' It was the woman doing the talking. She had an *über*-posh voice that tinkled like a crystal chandelier. 'We wanted to have a word. Shall we go inside?'

Six foot plenty had manoeuvred himself behind me in case I made a run for it. He was having a laugh. I grinned. 'Sure.

Especially if one of you helps me with my bag.' Oversized blokey obliged. 'So,' I said, 'who are you guys?'

'Jones,' said Jones, and she gestured to six foot plenty. 'And this is Aldridge.'

I might have cracked up laughing if I hadn't been in so much pain so I settled for a skew to my smile and the line, 'And I'm Akhtar.' Yeah, right. No funnies there. You're only as good as your last gag.

Movies and life: sometimes I suspect they're a chicken-and-egg type scenario. Let me tell you a story . . .

One time Tommy Akhtar took part in the ambush of a unit on the Salang Highway. It could have been done the easy way, a charge set on the road and anti-personnel mines scattered around the vicinity. But that wasn't how the Mujahideen liked to do things since it diminished chances of personal glory. Instead, therefore, they opened fire with RPGs and machine-guns and the troopers piled out of their mobile coffins like they thought there was somewhere to go.

The road ran through a shallow gully and the mujahideen had the high ground so the Soviets were pinned down in seconds. But this mob weren't your average band of reluctant conscripts and they were tougher than expected and they slowly began to inch their way up the slopes. This was, all things considered, a pointless exercise. After all, the mujahideen had the position and the firepower. Nonetheless, Tommy couldn't help but admire their resolve. It took about twenty minutes to pick them off one by one. And that was that.

Anyway, the point of this is as follows: as the battle was running out of steam, Tommy had this geezer pinned down on his lonesome behind a rock. The soldier was no more than twenty-five metres away. Frankly, he'd worked miracles to get so close but now he wasn't going nowhere. He shuffled left and Tommy spat dust by his foot. He shuffled right and

Tommy splintered stone by his ear. So what did blokey do? He stood straight up and started running towards Tommy's position, rattling off round after round like he thought he was Rambo.

Surprised by his recklessness, Tommy's aim was squonk and his first bullet caught the soldier in the lower abdomen. The geezer stood bolt upright for a second before stumbling backwards and collapsing like a drunk. That should have been the end of it. But then he started twitching like a salted slug before slowly hauling himself to his feet. Tommy watched in admiration as he began to zigzag forward again, trying to raise his gun to his hip. Tommy even let him get a little closer before he popped him twice in the chest.

With the benefit of more than a decade's distance, it strikes me that there are two ways you could interpret this Soviet soldier's death throes. Either he was like a headless chicken and these were the last vestiges of instinct pulsing through him like an electric current. Or – and this is the interpretation I favour – he really did think he was Rambo and, at some subconscious level, he was reliving the bootleg he once saw in a blackmarket cinema in the heart of Moscow. It was a case of life – or in this instance death – imitating art.

Jones and Aldridge were the same. It wasn't like Tinseltown had sent down their finest producers to model Agent X or Agent Y in Movie Z on a couple of MI5's jobbing pros. No. If anything it was the other way round. Jones and Aldridge wore dark suits, white shirts and arrogance because they thought it (literally) made them look the part. Same goes for the whole surname thing. Mulder and Scully, serious.

There was a time when I would have theorized this role play. There was a time when I would have come up with a confident hypothesis about how it reflected the Babylonian nature of Western society when everyone thought they were the film stars of their own, personal, straight-to-video classic. But that time is long gone. Besides, it's not like I figure I'm any different. Mornings when I look in the mirror before Benny and Turk get their hands on me, I see a lonely, lowlife investigator with a dangerous taste for alcohol and an even more dangerous penchant for rumination. I'm the latest in a long line of Marlowe wannabes. Only trouble is, the title 'private dick' has an altogether different connotation in this neck of the woods.

Jones suggested we went into my flat. I couldn't get over her accent. It was like being ordered around by the Queen; a post-colonial fantasy waiting to happen. I said no problem.

I was playing it nice and easy but you know my mind was strategizing. I got away with it on account of my injuries. I knew they'd done their sums on the Mayfair murder but I didn't know what they knew and what they suspected. In situations like this, experience told me that the safest option was to say as little as possible.

I shuffled towards my door. Jones, Aldridge and the two plod followed. I was moving so slowly that they were almost tripping over each other trying not to step on my heels. I put the key in the latch but I couldn't resist playing some games. I said, 'Hold on,' and turned and shuffled over to Phoenecia where Irish and Yusuf were watching every move and acting like they weren't. As I approached, they looked away and pretended they were deep in conversation. I don't know how many of Gunny's drivers are legal but I do know that none of them likes the Old Bill nosing around their motors and documentation. I asked Irish for a smoke. He wanted to be somewhere else but he handed me a battered packet of Lambert and Butler. I took one and he sparked it. I winked at him. He raised his eyebrows at me, a look that said, 'Who the hell do you think you are, Mr T?' He had a point but I was having fun.

I hobbled back to my door, really hamming the agonized limp. Jones was so impatient she might as well have been tapping her foot. I knew I'd got to Aldridge too because he didn't look so bored any more. 'A fag,' I said, by way of explanation. 'Sorry.'

I opened the door and led the way up the stairs to my flat. It's a narrow flight – strictly no overtaking – and, with me at the front playing the cripple, it took us the best part of ten minutes to reach the top. I could hear Jones and Aldridge seething behind me and I slowed down and muttered a few Farzad-style curses – 'I'm an old bugger', 'Goodness me, my ribs' – that kind of thing. Like I said, I was having fun. It didn't last.

When we finally got inside I said, 'So what can I do for you?'

I didn't get a reply. The two plod disappeared into my flat while Aldridge dropped my bag (no doubt Farzad would say 'unceremoniously') and made straight for the office. There were soon occasional bangs and crashes; the sounds of breakable stuff meeting unbreakable stuff at careless velocity. Jones and me were left in the waiting room, sizing each other up. She was short; I was knackered and hunched and leaning on a stick. It didn't take long.

I tried a smile. I'm charming, serious, but she didn't seem to notice.

I tried politely inquisitive: 'What's this all about? I answered questions in the hospital. DS Something-or-other from Marylebone. I told him everything. You should talk to him.' Nothing. I tried mild indignation: 'I said, what's this all about? I'm the one who was mugged, you know. And now I have to put up with this nonsense?' Nothing. I tried defensive blather: 'What are they doing in there? This is my home. You haven't even shown me any ID. If you don't tell me what's going on I'll . . .'

I petered out. Jones was staring at me impassively. We both knew that sentence had nowhere else to go. At least it drew a response. She said, 'Why don't you relax, Tommy?' She pointed at my waiting-room bench that I'd salvaged from Holy Trinity. She said, 'Why don't you pull up a pew?' Real funny. We could have dovetailed on the stand-up circuit, serious.

I shook my head. I was beginning to feel more than a little uncomfortable. I was indecisive, which is not like me and a sure sign that there was nothing to be done.

I peered through the door of my living room. The two plods' style of searching was not what you could call systematic. It seemed to involve taking all my possessions from wherever they sat and distributing them evenly, although with little care for their well-being, around the floor. Even my TV was face down on the grubby carpet. It looked like it was praying for forgiveness. I figured it was a good job I'm not house-proud. I could see one copper's legs poking out from beneath my bed. Even in my state of growing agitation, I could see the funny side. I hadn't been under there for at least five years. I didn't know what he was looking for but whatever he found *chez* Tommy he was welcome to, for real.

Jones had gone into the office. I followed. It looked exactly like I'd left it. Clearly Aldridge was better raised than the uniform. I saw the case folder titled 'Sexy Russian' face up on my desk. No big deal. I knew that, besides the photo of the hooker holding someone or other's baby and the bank statement, there was just a few notes that had been scribbled in various states of inebriation. Nothing instructive.

Her Majesty's most secret were both studying my computer. I went to join them. Aldridge had fired my Internet connection, checked my web cache and brought up exotic-melody.co.uk. I ha-hahed. 'It's been a while. What can I say?'

Clearly I needed to work on my timing. I said, 'Look, I'm not being funny . . .' Like *that* was something that needed clearing up. '. . . but if you told me what you were looking for, I'm sure I could help out.'

Jones smiled at me. It was the first time I'd seen her cheeks move. It was an expression that gave me the fear, serious. 'Later, Tommy,' she said. 'There'll be plenty of time for talking later on.'

I began to feel sick. My ribs were hurting and my tongue was hurting. My head was hurting and itching all at once. Intensive care was starting to catch up with me. I had some anti-nausea pills and some painkillers in my bag. But my bag was next door and next door seemed a long way away. This was a big boys' game and I was losing out to a pint-sized bird. There was nothing to be done. I pulled up a pew.

Aldridge opened my desk drawer. There were only two things that I didn't want this geezer to find and he was just about to find both of them. But my head was pounding so hard that I was struggling to concentrate and struggling to care. I was beginning to feel more than a little detached.

First things first, though. Aldridge produced a bottle of Turk that was two-thirds clapped. My stomach lurched at the sight of it. I must have been sick. Aldridge looked at me and gave me the bored eyebrows. He said, 'So the man likes a drink?' I realized this was the first time I'd heard the geezer speak. You could have knocked me down with a feather and not just because I was already half-way unconscious. For all his side parting, fringe and old-school-tie demeanour, blokey was a Mick; somewhere round Belfast with not much give in the accent. Books. Covers. Judgements. All of that.

I didn't have the time or inclination to dwell on it. Aldridge had now located incriminating item number one: the napkin from a Lymington greasy spoon with a name and number in a Russian tom's handwriting. Aldridge handed it to Jones, who held it up for me to see. She looked so pleased with herself you could have been misled into thinking she'd done something clever. I said, 'What's that?' and pulled a puzzled face. I heaved myself to my feet and lurched towards them as if I had to check it out up close. I'm no superhero but this took some kind of Superman effort. I found the floor of my office was now rolling like a cross-Channel ferry. I supported myself on the edge of my desk, looked at the napkin and tried a 'no idea' shrug.

Aldridge was already on to item number two and cradling Bailey's Palm Pilot in his hand. He said, 'And what do we have here?' I was just about to be caught with a murdered MP's personal organizer. This wasn't a good thing. I didn't have a clever answer. I said, 'That's mine.'

The six-foot-plenty Mick flicked it on. I was struggling to stay vertical. He snorted like something was funny. He showed me the screen. He said, 'You like Tetris?' The Palm Pilot had opened straight to Top Scores and it said Tommy Akhtar, Tommy Akhtar, Tommy Akhtar, all down the page. I was in luck and I was about to double up and I'm not even a big believer in the phenomenon.

I'll try not to get all ruminative on you again but it strikes me that the whole idea of luck and the subjectivity therein is peculiarly revelatory of the British psyche. For example, you ever see one of those wildlife films where a buffalo is brought down by a pride of lions? The animal struggles until it's vain to do so and then lies back and accepts its fate as the cubs chew on its innards. For the buffalo this is just the ongoing cycle of hunters and hunted. But if it was a Brit getting eaten you can bet they'd thrash around long after it was pointless purely on the basis that they couldn't believe their misfortune. For example, when I came round in hospital after my pasting at the hands of Tony the pimp, there was a bunch of do-gooders just queuing up to tell me how lucky I'd been. How do you work that out? I get battered within an inch of my life and I'm *lucky*? For example, coming through Heathrow is always a riot if you're of ethnic persuasion. You can almost see the Immigration officers rubbing their hands in anticipation. You can almost smell their disappointment when they clock your British passport. You can almost hear them thinking, Lucky bastard. You can almost be bothered to tell them that there's no luck about it and they should read their colonial history. Almost. For example, Aldridge would typically have given the Palm Pilot more than the cursory once-over and I'd have been even further up the you-know-what without a paddling implement. In fact, typically, Aldridge and Jones would have gone through all my stuff with a fine-tooth comb or even taken it all away for further examination. But now, as I stared at Tommy Akhtar, Tommy Akhtar, Tommy Akhtar and relief fizzed up in me like indigestion after a kebab, I saw my name divide and multiply and begin to butterfly around the room until I figured I must be tripping. The good ship TA Services was now pitching and tossing in a storm and my sea legs weren't up to it, let alone my sea belly. My knees buckled and I slumped against the desk and threw up my hospital breakfast into my intray before sliding on to the floor.

I heard Aldridge say, 'Oh, for f___ 's sake.' And then, accusingly, 'I told you he wasn't up to it.'

I heard Jones tut and say, 'He'll be OK. Just get him cleaned up and we'll take him in.'

So they dosed me with coffee and painkillers and gave me ten minutes to recuperate. So I was helped into a clean set of clothes by two plod, who looked just about as happy about it as I was. So Jones and Aldridge left for Paddington Green nick with nothing in the way of evidence but yours truly. So I was arguably saved from even more problematic investigation by the grave extent of my injuries. Aren't I one lucky geezer? Yeah, right.

17

The short drive to Paddington Green was small-talk free. Even in my poorly and somewhat frazzled state, I noted this and considered a wry smile until I realized there was nobody to smile wryly at. I'd never been picked up by MI5 before but I'm a pro when it comes to being taken in for questioning by the Old Bill and it's always struck me how the car journey to this or that factory is, without fail, conducted in absolute silence.

Typically, there's all this aggro before you get in the car, right? 'We'd like you to come down the station.' 'What if I don't wanna come down the station?' All of that. But then, as soon as you get in, it's like someone hits mute. The logic is fairly obvious: there's only one reason they want to speak to you, the same reason you don't want to speak to them and this reason can only be explored on tape and in the correct setting. The car journey is, therefore, something like half-time without the team talk. Nonetheless, it's a funny kind of situation if you think about it. Both peculiar and ha-ha.

This time, however, I was grateful for the space to think. Aldridge was driving, Jones riding shotgun, and me in the back alongside one of the plod. I don't know what happened to Plod #2. I'd lost track as I was bundled out of the flat still feeling all nauseous. But I knew I'd only seen one car so Plod #2 was either still in my place, feet up in front of the three fifteen at Epsom or, more likely, wee-wee-weeing all the way home. I leaned forward, shut my eyes and covered my face with my hands. Aldridge said, 'Jesus Christ! Our man better not puke in my car.' These were the only words spoken the whole way. In fact, I was feeling a little better and simply pondering the ponderables.

I decided that I'd got myself all hot and bothered over nothing while Aldridge and his tame uniforms were giving my place the once-over. I blamed my injuries. I wasn't match fit. After all, I'd done nothing wrong and didn't have much to hide. Even if they'd found Bailey's Palm Pilot (or, rather, found that it *was* Bailey's Palm Pilot), surely they weren't so dumb as to try to tie me to the gory scene in the Holiday Inn Express . . . Hold on. I did the intellectual equivalent of a double-take. Who was I kidding? Overestimating competence is an easy mistake to make; although rare, you would think, for my father's son (what with Farzad's Steve Waugh fascination). Underestimating prejudice is similarly straightforward; although rare, you would think, for an immigrant.

But whatever the situation, I knew that the important thing now was to figure out how I was going to play it from here on in. I figured. It didn't take long. I decided I'd play it straight as Geoff Boycott on a muggy day at Headingley. I needed to know where my off stump was.

I thought, I've got nothing to hide. I'm looking for Bailey's killer. They're looking for Bailey's killer. I thought, Our motivations might be different (mine? Self-preservation. Theirs? A monthly pay slip/national security/whatever) but our aims are the same. I thought, I'll tell them the truth, the whole truth and nothing but the truth, so help me God. I thought, If it's Al-Dubayan that needs catching then no skin off my nose if it's MI5 who do it. I thought, We're all on the same side, right?

Wrong. We weren't far into the interview before I concluded, We're not on the same side and, frankly, this bunch of stuck-up unrepeatables can kiss my furry backside if they think I'm going to help them out.

Of course, looking back at what happened beneath the unsympathetic strip-lighting of hindsight, I've wondered whether events might have unfolded differently if I'd told them everything I knew right then and there in that box room with minimal furniture. Typically it's a late-night thought when this insomniac looks out at London's tiny lights and they wink back at me through the window like they're in on a secret. Because when I open that window it's not long before the sting of a brisk night grants me, shall we say, a more sober appraisal?

The truth is that even if I'd sung like the barmy army it wouldn't have made the blindest bit of difference in the long run. But guilt? I can't get enough of it. I should have been born a Catholic, for real.

Jones vanished into the heart of the nick while Aldridge checked me in and showed me to my quarters: concrete walls and floor, four plastic chairs around a solid-looking table, DV kit, two-way mirror and a single bulb of inadequate wattage that swung a little every time the door was opened. Even the room had thespian pretensions. It wasn't the kind of bachelor pad I'm used to but fortunately I'm adaptable. Blokey fetched me a coffee. I took it sweet and black and made myself comfortable. While I sipped, he lurked in the shadows in one corner. He wasn't much in the way of company.

I said, 'This gonna take long?'

He shrugged. I nodded.

I said, 'You got a fag, mate? I'm gasping.'

He shook his head. I nodded.

I said, 'Do you come here often?'

He didn't react. I nodded and then chuckled for my own benefit. I'm so hilarious I'll have my own show on a seaside pier come November.

Time flies when you're having fun. The converse is also

true. I guessed they were trying to intimidate me, let me know who was boss. But I had no issues on that score so I was just bored. I sat in that interview room with nothing for company but the silent Mick for what must have been pushing an hour but it felt longer, serious. Let me put it like this: when Jones finally appeared, I ran my hand over my chin figuring I must need another shave.

Aldridge left the room. He was replaced by another matinée idol. This one had a nuclear tan and radioactive teeth. Jones sat opposite me with her fingers knotted on the desk between us while he kicked back and crossed his legs like he was only there for the hell of it. They both had official-looking briefcases that they laid on the floor next to their respective chairs.

Jones said, 'So, Tommy,' and smiled. She could have learned a thing or two from her new partner about top-of-the-range dentistry. I remembered Dirty Harriet in the White Horse. What is it about Brits and their teeth?

I smiled back and said, 'So, Jones.'

'We'll keep this very informal, OK?' Her accent was so posh that when she said 'OK' it sounded confusingly like 'hair care'.

I said, 'Sure. First-name terms.' She didn't get it.

'We're not going to record what is said so you should feel free to speak openly. It's more of *a chat*, if you will.'

'I will.' I leaned forward and raised my eyebrows at her. It was an expression that put strain on the surgeon's needlework. 'I want my brief.'

'I'm sorry?'

'I said I want my brief.'

Her face was a blank page, inscrutable. 'I assure you, Tommy, there's no need . . .'

I gave it the ha-ha. I said, 'Only kidding. I always wanted to say that. "I want my brief." Like in the movies, know what I mean?'

She gave it the Queen Victoria: not amused and then some. She licked her lips. She said, 'You're here of your own volition. You're not under arrest and you're free to leave at any time.'

I smiled again. I pushed my chair back and started to stand up. It was a struggle. Was it my imagination or did her mouth shrivel a bit? She said, 'Another joke?' I sat down and looked suitably abashed.

You may wonder what I was playing at. I'll tell you. Although I'd decided to bat out this session showing the maker's name with my left elbow high, I figured it wouldn't do me any harm if she thought I was an idiot. And, what with me being a Paki immigrant and her being impatient establishment (albeit of the kind that's paid to be suspicious), I figured it wouldn't be too hard to convince her.

She said, 'I'm afraid this is no joking matter, Tommy. But you're no fool. You know that.' So much for my figuring. 'As you know, we're investigating the death of Anthony Bailey, MP, at the Holiday Inn Hotel in Battersea. I know you know that because you yourself have looked into it and stayed at this same hotel two nights after the murder under the name "Younis Khan". Don't look surprised, Tommy. Of course we know that. You know we know that. You're not surprised.'

She was wrong. I was surprised. In fact, my gob was smacked. There was I trying to convince this posh bird I was an idiot and all along she'd thought me smarter than I am. In other circumstances I might have considered this amusingly ironic.

She reached down and opened her briefcase. She produced a polythene evidence bag that she placed carefully on the table between us. I peered at it. No surprises there. It contained Mrs Hammer, the pimp's partner in crime. Jones said, 'As of now, of course, we're also investigating the related murder of Tony Simone on Avlon Street, Mayfair. He was shot, Tommy, and we found this near the corpse. We've been able to remove various physical samples and we know beyond dispute that this is the instrument of Bailey's death. However, we also found secondary and as yet unidentified DNA evidence. Naturally we could engage further testing but, as I'm sure you'll agree, one look at you suggests such efforts are . . . what shall we say? *Unnecessary*, if you will.'

'I will,' I said. I was desperate for a fag. I said, 'Any chance of a fag?'

'I'm afraid not, Tommy.'

She picked up the hammer and examined it like she'd never seen it before. 'So you can see our interest in you. A government minister is murdered and two days later you're poking around the crime scene. Then Tony Simone, a nasty piece of work but strictly small-time, is found shot dead and the implement that killed the aforementioned MP is by his body with half your head attached. You can imagine we have some questions.'

'Serious,' I said. 'And I bet you already got some answers too. What you need me for? You guys should be talking to yourselves. Left hand, this is right hand. Pleased to meet you.'

It came out stroppier than I intended. What can I say? I'm a nicotine addict and my spell in hospital hadn't helped the pangs. I was feeling somewhat stroppy.

Jones looked at me and then at the matinée idol on her right. He didn't acknowledge her but this was clearly his cue to get involved. He leaned into the table and his expression suddenly animated, like someone had flicked his switch.

'So,' he said, *'you*'re Tommy Akhtar.' And he even made it sound like he gave a toss.

He was an American. First, Aldridge was a Mick and now this geezer was a Yank and I hadn't spotted either. Clearly I was off my game. I looked at him a little more closely. Besides the tan and teeth, there was the stain of a recent moustache on his upper lip, his neck was fat in his collar and his suit had a slightly shiny quality and the vague suggestion of a tasteless blue check: now I could see it. So the Yanks were involved? OK. I did some recalculations. That wasn't so surprising.

He caught me staring. He said, 'Something interesting you?'

I blinked. I touched a thumb to my brow. I said, 'Headache. You know.'

He nodded. Now it was his turn to reach for a briefcase. He extracted a thin cardboard folder and laid it on the table. My name was written on the front in thick black marker. I ran a few equations. I was surprised by the rudimentary nature of MI5 filing. I was surprised they had a file on me. I was disappointed it was so flimsy. I figured it might be just for show. Off my game or not, my processor's second to none.

The geezer offered me a hand across the table. I took it. His fingers were Cumberland sausages and his palm was a side of beef.

He said, 'Chip Paradowski, CIA.'

Chip? He wasn't trying to make friends so, clearly, this was about to get meaningful. I said, 'Tommy Akhtar, TA Services.'

'So you're Tommy Akhtar.'

The brief surge of animation in his face had played out and his expression was now frozen in this weird fixed smile. He looked like a photo of a geezer at his own leaving-do from a job he'd never liked.

'Tommy Akhtar,' he said again. It was like he was trying the name out, seeing how it fitted his gob. 'Tommy. That's a funny kind of name, right?'

'Funny. Right,' I said. 'Whereas Chip is gravitas in a box.' I met his eye. He didn't blink. He figured this was a *mano a mano* kind of scenario. Typical Yank: full of macho bollocks.

'Easy, son. What I meant was that it's an unusual name for someone of your *extraction*.'

I was already taking a dislike to this geezer, serious. 'Son'? This wasn't the English version of the word as in 'my son' as in 'mate' as in 'like-minded individual', this was the patronizing American version as in 'Just you remember who you're talking to, son.' 'Son'? I doubted the geezer was even as old as me and I knew he hadn't seen anything like the realities of yours truly. My back was now officially up and my nose was on its way to out of joint. But I wasn't going to show it. I'm a pro. Yeah, right.

'Not so unusual,' I said. 'My old man's a fan of Tommy Cooper.'

'Tommy Cooper?'

'The comedian.'

'A comedian. Right. I confess I've never related to the British sense of humour.'

'You don't say.'

Paradowski sighed. He adjusted his position and crossed his legs. 'Look, son, can I be straight with you?'

'Sure, Dad.'

'Your attitude is about to start ticking me off. Do you understand what I'm saying? What is it the Brits say? "Winding me up"? That's it. You're *winding me up*. Now, I'm a straight-talking kinda guy so I'm gonna tell this to you straight: my colleague Jones here? She thinks you're just some hopeless bum who's stumbled over a situation. She thinks you're a nobody, a nothing, not worth our time. I have a lot of respect for my friends in British Intelligence and I think she may well have a point. But, hell, you know what? I'm tempted to f__k up your life anyway and I'll tell you why. Because I can, Tommy. Because I can. I've been dealing with pieces of crap like you my whole professional life – not just ragheads but all varieties of the terminally pissed – and the one thing I know for sure is that nobody in the civilized world is gonna give two hoots if I make your life a misery.'

I nodded like he was talking sense.

'There's a lot to be scared of these days, Tommy. Ordinary folk in a city like London don't know it or they choose not to admit it but there's danger on every corner; danger from people just like you. It may be from you or it may be from people *like* you but, frankly, I don't give a rat's ass. Because if I f__ you up? If I make an example of a piece of shit like you? The way I see it, I'm doing the honest citizens of the free world a favour.

'One, they see you and your pals as the morally bankrupt SOBs you really are. And, two, they come to realize that there's another enemy just waiting to perform some heinous act and they will react with appropriate fear. You see? What is it they call it over here? "Defence of the realm". That's my business. "Defence of the realm". Are we on the same page here, Tommy? Do we understand each other?'

I stared at him. I turned my attention to Jones but she was doing inscrutable again. As a fellow Brit, I felt like I should ask the bird, 'Is Senator Joe McCarthy for real?' I wondered if I should laugh. I wondered if I was on one of those practical-joke shows they have on prime-time telly. I'll tell you for nothing that I was shocked by what he said to a proud citizen like yours truly. I shouldn't have been but it's easy to forget that the Yanks are the founding fathers of extremism. And now he was asking me if we understood each other.

I kept my face straight and said, 'I understand you, Mr Paradowski. I really think I do.'

He liked my use of the 'Mr'. I've talked to ansaphones more intuitive. So much for my resolve to play it straight. If I'd had a sturdy bit of willow in my hands, I'd have opened my shoulders and swung his head high over cow corner.

I said, 'So what do you want to know?'

Paradowski smiled. He looked at Jones and then back to me. He looked pleased with himself, serious. Guess what? Although Chip was a chip off the old block and Jones had a chip on each shoulder, at this point in our exchange I still would have told them everything that had happened and everything I suspected, if only because I was keen to get out and spark a smoke. Guess what else? Turned out Paradowski wasn't done with loving the sound of his own voice and, what with Jones's occasional interjections, I couldn't get a word in edgeways.

In my early teens I used to go round Wayne's on my way to school so we could idle in together. There was always fighting at his gaff, usually between his mum and his old man but sometimes involving Wayne as well. Add on the fact that Wayne's dad had no affection for my heritage and you can understand I typically chose to wait on the doorstep. I remember this one time, though, when Wayne answered the bell and he wasn't ready and he told me to come in and wait for him. I didn't want to but he insisted. I could hear his old man shouting from the kitchen so I just stood with the backs of my legs against the radiator in the small hall, staring at the framed postcard of a laughing leprechaun that said, 'Irish eyes are smiling', ready to bolt in case of emergency.

Wayne was looking for his maths book or something and he was shuttling between his bedroom and the living room while his dad broadcast a one-sided argument with his mum that made my ears burn: 'Bernadette! Can you not keep that c– of a son of yours under control? You know the little f__er's been at my fags again? Jesus Christ, Bernadette! Are you listening to me? You better get yourself in here, woman, or you'll be f__ing sorry. You hear me?' Pause. 'Wayne? You still here, you little c–? You better not be here when I'm done with my breakfast or I'll make you eat every last butt in that f—ing ashtray and then break the f—ing thing over your head. Wayne? *Wayne?*'

Wayne had found his maths book. We headed out; him a couple of steps in front of me. We went down the four flights in silence. As we walked across the patch of green where the pensioners were standing around while their dogs did their morning business, I said, 'You all right?'

There must have been something in my voice because Wayne turned and looked at me and said, 'Yeah.' And then, 'What's up with you?'

I said, 'Your dad. What he was saying.'

Wayne looked surprised. He said, 'Dad? That c–? Why? What was he saying?'

I figure Wayne learned to block out the worst of his old man's anger until it intruded no more than the lift music in a cheap hotel. I'm not saying it had no effect (I don't think Wayne's later conviction for marital GBH, for example, was the result of some hard-wired character flaw) but, over time, the precise wording of the abuse was less important than the overall atmosphere of hatred. I reckon the same happened to me while Paradowski and Jones were talking (only a whole lot quicker). I mean, I can remember what they said, I just can't remember what they *said* – the words, I mean. It's a pity because it was the precise words that showed them up as evolutionary throwbacks: king and queen of the Neander Valley when Tommy Sapiens Sapiens came visiting from the south. It's a pity because when I tell you what they said in all it's naked absurdity (i.e., without the threatening glances, linguistic tics and so on), you'll think I must be telling porkies, for real.

So the CIA man Chip Paradowski opened my file. It might have been thin but it contained an astonishingly accurate picture of my past, my war record in particular. He told me everything I'd been up to and he had most of the facts down pat. It was the interpretation that left more than a little to be desired.

He told me the exact date I'd flown to Pakistan. He told me the exact date I'd crossed the border and the exact date I'd hooked up with Hekmatyar's party. He reeled off names of guys I'd fought alongside and listed them by nationality: Afghans, Iranians, Uzbeks, Pakistanis, Turks and Algerians. A lot of them were new to me but I didn't blink. He told me the locations of the camps I'd trained in, the operations I'd fought in, the route of my eventual escape.

He showed me a copy of the application I'd made in Islamabad for a new British passport. He showed me a copy of the arrest document after I was picked up for vagrancy in Charing Cross. I'd only been back in London a few weeks. I'd forgotten all about that. He showed me copies of my driving licence, phone bill, bank statement. Finally, he showed me a blurry fifteen-year-old photograph of my Yank friend, Stanton, and me standing side by side in front of a burnt out T-55 somewhere near Ghazni. The sky was bright blue, the Yank was smiling and he had his arm round my shoulders like it was a holiday snap. I looked skinny to the point of malnutrition, deadly serious and very young.

I'd never seen this picture but I remembered it being taken. I was driving the agent to some pow-wow and we came across this tank and he told me to stop. Stanton gave his camera to a local kid and insisted we pose. I remember he said to me, 'For God's sake, smile, Tommy. This is one for the album.' Within a couple of months, yours truly was back in Blighty and the Yank's body was scattered in the Afghan dirt. Clearly he hadn't had his camera with him when he'd stepped on that mine.

I glanced up from the photograph. Paradowski and Jones were watching me. If they'd looked any more pleased with themselves, they'd have had to run for political office. I licked my lips. Injuries or not, I was ready for this, in top form. Bring it on.

They began to ask me questions of the rhetorical variety. Only these were rhetorical questions to which they had all the wrong answers. They questioned my past moral, religious and political motivations. They questioned my current philosophies, faith and affiliations. They asked me what I thought freedom meant. They asked me whether I believed in democracy. They asked me what I thought of terrorism. They asked me whether I believed in fundamentalism. They asked me what I thought of foreign policy. They asked me whether I voted in the last election. They questioned my family's decision to come to this country. They questioned my decision to leave. They questioned my decision to come back. They questioned my nationality. They asked me what I thought of patriotism. They asked me whether I felt British.

Finally they created a series of bizarre, barely hypothetical scenarios: if So-and-so says, 'Do such and such,' and Wotsisname says, 'No. Do thingummyjig,' do you do such and such or thingummyjig? Or, say X declares war on Y, and Y on Z, do you think you should support X, Y or Z? That kind of thing. I didn't think much beyond the fact that their grasp of algebra was basic, for real.

This whole sorry process dragged, serious. So when Paradowski finally said, 'So you can see our problem, Tommy,' it took me a second to realize that I was actually expected to respond. I looked at the Yank. I looked at the posh bird. I thought for a moment. Where to start?

Did I point out that their doubts about me came from my past as mujahideen, a past they only knew about because

211

of my associations with the CIA in their support of the mujahideen? Did I really need to point out the paradox or should I just have reminded them of their history? The ill-fated Abraham Lincoln Brigade, for example, Jarama Valley, 1937? Or would it have been better to draw attention to their overt equation of religion with ethnicity or their apparent incomprehension of a secular state? Or maybe I should have just introduced them to Farzad and he'd have given them the benefit of his considerable about the way ideas like 'freedom' and 'democracy' only exist relatively.

Maybe I could have explained Farzad's 'decision' to come to the UK with an idiot's guide to Idi Amin. Maybe I could have explained it with reference to half a millennium of European colonialism in Africa and the by-products thereof. Maybe I could have just told them to leave my family out of it. Perhaps I could have hypothesized about the limitations of their take on nationality. Perhaps I could have hypothesized that a conception of British patriotism depends on a conception of what it means to be British. Perhaps I could have just told them that it wasn't so much rich as downright unpalatable to have my patriotism questioned by a foreigner (albeit one, ironically, of immigrant extraction himself – as if there's another kind of Yank). Perhaps I should have said something like 'You guys can stand shoulder to shoulder until your feet are numb but, if you ask me, you need to check out who's standing behind you, know what I mean?'

I might have said all of that. Of course I said none of it. Instead I figured it was time to wheel out the wry smile I'd been saving since my ride in to the nick: 'To be honest, Chip, I can't see your problem. To be honest, I've no idea where this whole terrorist crap came from unless you've just got a thing for my – as you put it – *extraction*. But you tell me what you wanna know and I'll do the best I can. Can't say fairer than that, can I?'

There was a moment's silence. American Intelligence and British Intelligence shared the moment and they decided not to include Ugandan-Indian lowlife.

Then Jones said I should tell them exactly what I knew in my own words. Like I had anyone else's. As for the terrorism? She said that obviously they had to consider all angles in an investigation into the murder of an MP.

I said righty-ho and told them exactly what they wanted to hear.

I told them that I'd been hired by exoticmelody to find sexyrussian. I told them that's what I do: look in sewers for shit. They enjoyed my turn of phrase. I told them that the hunt for sexyrussian had led to Bailey but I was guessing they knew that already. I told them I'd tracked Natasha/Natalya/Nadia/Whatever to the Hampshire coast. I told them she'd given me Gaileov's name and number and I'd passed them on to her ho-buddy. I told them that should've been it, case closed, but I'm an inquisitive geezer and I wanted to figure how Bailey got into the mix. I told them I'd poked around at the Embassy and it was on the way out that I'd been jumped by the pimp and Mrs Hammer. I told them I reckoned, therefore, that the whole terrorism thing was the wrong trunk to woof at because Bailey had been done in by a pimp and the pimp ... well ... he who lives by the whore, dies by the whore (metaphorically speaking). Enough said.

What I didn't tell them was jack about Al-Dubayan. They may or may not have known what I knew but they didn't know what *I* knew (if you see what I mean) and I had no desire to enlighten them. In the first place they'd pissed me off and in the second place I needed to look after myself and

I had no reason to suppose those two had the will or the skill to help.

Thereafter my innings was just about as easy as batting gets. To push the boundaries of the metaphor, it was a sunny afternoon, the ball was old, the field back and the strike bowlers had lost their zip.

The Yank and the posh bird asked me what I knew about Gaileov. I said, nothing. I guessed he was one of sexyrussian's regulars, a fellow countryman. I was well set but my judgement outside off stump was as careful as ever. They asked me if I'd called the number on the napkin. I said I hadn't. It was none of my business. They asked me if I knew what Gaileov looked like. I gave it the knowing smirk and questioned how the hell I'd know what he looked like. They asked me if I knew where they could find sexyrussian. I told them to shake up coke dealers from Lymington to Penzance and see what frothed. They asked me if I knew where they could find exoticmelody. I ummed and erred at that. I had no debt to the whore but figured she had enough problems of her own making. I told them to look online. They could guess the URL.

We agreed a draw, honours even. They'd decided I was small-time. They were on to something. I'd decided they were idiots. I was on to something too. We were all smiles.

The CIA geezer even said he was sorry he'd come on strong but I understood, right? I don't know why he said that because he wasn't sorry and I didn't understand. The MI5 bird told me to keep my nose out of it from now on and then gave me her card. I don't know why she did that because we weren't going to hook up for dinner and a movie any time soon. I touched my chin with my splinted finger. I figured it sent appropriate subliminal messages.

Paradowski said, 'That wasn't so painful.'

I said, 'I've got broken ribs and a piece of metal in my head. Everything's painful.'

He laughed. I've always thought I'm a comedian but that Yank was my first and last independent confirmation. So much for him not getting the British sense of humour.

Jones walked me to the exit. I hobbled out into the early evening. They didn't offer me a lift and I didn't have my mobile to call Phoenecia. I've had better journeys home. On the bus, some thug-lites decided to take the piss and impress their groupies with a chorus of 'Frankenstein's a w–er'. I was too knackered to correct the literary reference. Because I wasn't the deranged genius trying to control life itself, was I? I was the monster dreaming of humanity rebuilt from its constituent parts.

18

I stopped in at Khan's. Mrs K was stacking shelves with Benzi. Av's little sister has storybook pigtails, these permanent wide eyes and an expression that's too innocent to be innocent. Mrs K dotes on her like she's a prize puppy. No wonder she drives Av round the bend.

I drummed my fingers on the counter, pretended to examine the various brands of chewing-gum and waited to be noticed. Eventually Mrs K looked up from the tray of blackcurrant jam and said, 'Tommy!' all overexcited, like I was her baby brother just back from the front line.

She rushed over and for a second I was worried she might try to give me a hug or something. But she headed behind the counter and satisfied herself with taking my right hand in her two and squeezing and patting it. Then, suddenly, even this action felt too intimate and she let go and I don't know about her but I felt embarrassed. I mean, I saw her every day and had more information about her and her family than seemed totally kosher and I was sure the same was true vice versa; but it wasn't like I actually knew her at all, right? When all's said and done, she was just my local shopkeeper and I was her best customer and that was that. The lights in this city are tiny but distinct. So no wonder we quickly resorted to tried and tested patterns of interaction, even if our words and gestures were laced with a bit more engagement than usual.

She said, 'And how are you, Tommy?'

'Mustn't grumble, Mrs K. You?'

'Just the same. Mustn't grumble.'

We looked at each other. I smiled and unconsciously traced my fingers along the canyon in my scalp. The hair was growing back and beginning to thicken and soften. Mrs K couldn't help but watch and, now that she was watching, she had to say something. She furrowed her brow to preface the only two things she could say in whichever order she chose to say them.

'So are you feeling better?'

'Yeah. I feel fine. Really.'

'But what happened?'

I shrugged. I said, 'You know.' Obviously this was a ridiculous response since she didn't know and I wasn't even sure I knew myself. But it let her off the hook.

She said, 'Terrible.'

I said, 'You know.'

She nodded and I nodded and we nodded together. After an appropriate heartbeat in respect of just how terrible it was, she allowed her face to brighten. 'Av tells me you have given him some work in your company, Tommy. He has been really quite excited, I must say.'

I looked at her. She seemed sincere. So why was I embarrassed all over again? I guess I hadn't figured Av would tell his mum about our arrangement. I guess I knew our arrangement wasn't an altogether good idea.

'He's a good boy. But you know that, Tommy.' Mrs K was now well into her stride. 'This is what I say to his teachers all the time. He's a good boy but he needs discipline. He has nobody to look up to apart from those rap stars so, I am asking you, is it a surprise he goes off the rails? That is why it's most kind of you to take an interest in him, Tommy. Most kind. If you take him in hand then it gives me renewed confidence.'

I was examining my fingernails. I made the right noises. 'Sure,' I said. And 'He's a nice kid.' We tried some more nodding but it didn't feel as comfortable as before. We were done.

'So,' Mrs K said, 'is there anything I can do for you, Tommy? Of course you only have to ask.'

I glanced up. 'I just came in to say hello. And pick up a few supplies.'

'Of course. And what supplies do you need?'

'Twenty Bensons,' I said, 'and the usual if you've got it.'

She smiled. 'I was at the cash-and-carry last week. I thought, I wonder if Tommy Akhtar will be home soon and wanting his favourite bourbon. I bought two bottles just in case.'

'You're an angel, Mrs K.'

She called to Benzi. From where she was standing, she couldn't see her daughter. But I could. She was hidden down one of the aisles, sitting on an upturned milk crate and blowing sullen bubbles with her bubble-gum. She grouchily hauled herself to her feet but, as soon as her head rose above the biscuit and coffee shelves, her expression was replaced by a shy smile and willing eyes. Mrs K sent her down to the cellar to play 'hunt the Turk' with the words, 'No. My daughter is the angel. Did you ever see such a face, Tommy? And so helpful too.'

Mrs K reached for my fags. I told her to make it forty. She rang up the till. I'd been to the cashpoint on my way back from the nick and I paid in three crisp notes. Benzi returned with the Turk. I know it was only my imagination but I swear I could smell it, serious. Almost hear it too. Mrs K began to put one bottle in a bag. I told her she might as well make it two. She looked at me curiously for a second. I couldn't read what she was thinking. She said, 'Are you sure you should be drinking, Tommy?'

'I'm fine,' I said. 'It helps me sleep anyway.'

Mrs K nodded. Whatever that look was about, it had gone

now. She smiled. She murmured, 'You like a drink and a smoke. Many people do. It's a healthy thing for a man to have hobbies.'

I don't know who she was saying *that* for but it wasn't me and, excepting Benzi, there were only the two of us there.

I said, 'Thanks, Mrs K. I'll see you soon. You take care. You too, Benzi.'

I limped out, my stick in one hand, supplies in the other. As the shop bell rang, Mrs K called, 'See you soon, Tommy.' I looked round but she was already heading back to her shelf-stacking. Benzi watched me leave while she helped herself to whatever she wanted from the selection of confectionery by the till.

I crossed the road. This time the Phoenecia drivers gave me the welcome I'd been expecting when I originally got back from hospital, crowding round and asking questions and pulling faces; first horrified, then amused, then horrified again. Or at least they would have done if my lovely brother had let them but he immediately started barking through the Tannoy: 'Two-five! What the f— are you doing? You got a pick-up at the health club on the Great West Road. No, I've no idea where it is so you better get a f—ing ripple on.' And 'Two-zero! Mrs Thomas at the Brook Green Tesco's. Some time in the next f—ing year would be nice. We're a community service, aren't we? So don't keep the old cow waiting.' And 'Jesus H, bruv! Do you have to stand round here like a f—ing freak show? You'll scare the punters away.'

The knot of interest dispersed and left me alone with Big John who was shifting from foot to foot. Last time I'd seen him we'd been mouth to mouth on a Mayfair pavement. I felt on the excuse-me side of awkward and so, it seemed, did he.

I said, 'Yes, Big John.'

'How are you, Tommy?'

'Good. Yeah. I'm good.'

He shook his head. 'When I saw you –'

I cut him off. 'Look. I just wanted to say . . .'

Big John looked away. He held up his hand and said, 'Don't worry about it, Tommy, OK?'

We were having one of those emotionally retarded English male moments, which was, when you think about it, somewhat strange since Big John's a Pole and yours truly a notorious cosmopolitan.

I said, 'Sure.' And then, 'So how's it hanging, Big John?'

He grinned at me. 'To my knees.'

My flat was as left by the Old Bill's makeover team. It was depressing, for real. I've never been big on attributing sentimental value to inanimate objects and, not for the first time, I felt this was fortunate since a lot of my possessions – from the set of tumblers I'd got free from a garage to the magnetic travel chess that Mina gave me for my twelfth birthday (in, I now see, a last-ditch attempt to make me amount to something) – were broken. Nonetheless, I did discover a couple of things that made me come over a little quivery-lipped.

First, in my bedroom, I came across this statuette of a footballer in moulded gold plastic that was now detached from its elegant marble plinth that bore the following inscription: 'Tommy Akhtar. Ravenscourt Park Rovers U-12s. "Supersub".'

It wasn't that it was broken that bothered me. In fact, truth be told, this was the first time I'd seen the damn thing in more than a decade and I'd forgotten I had it. Furthermore, despite the award, I knew I hadn't been a 'supersub' at all since Lovely was the supersub whereas I hadn't got on the park once that whole season and the trophy represented nothing but guilty charity on the part of Graham the manager.

What bothered me, therefore, was the pointless destruction on the part of the coppers. I mean, there was no room to hide anything in a moulded-plastic statuette, was there? And the plod were not to know that I am not nostalgically inclined. So breaking the trophy was no more than an attempted (albeit failed) act of cruelty. This only reinforced my feeling that most people who want positions of authority should be automatically banned from applying.

Second, my telly was still praying face down on the carpet. Again, it wasn't the fact of this that depressed me as such. Rather, I felt more than a single shot gloomy when I discovered there was no way in hell I was going to be able to help said telly to its feet in my current state of repair. This then led me to thinking just how vulnerable I was and then to the realization that, as far as I knew, a certain opportunist still had my card marked for death.

As you know, I typically left my doors – both the external and into the waiting room – unlocked when I was inside but I figured that now was not the time for such an open-house policy. First things first, though. I needed a drink, serious. I cracked Turk and sparked a Benny. I took a mouthful and a drag. They felt like home, which was more than could be said for home.

Avoiding the chaos of the flat, I made for the comparative order of the office. I rested Benny in an ashtray and Turk on the desk while I went to see about the doors. Despite my best efforts, it took me a good five minutes to get down and up the stairs and, by the time I got back, Benny was cremated. Turk, however, was a good and faithful friend and there were, of course, plenty more Bennies where Benny had come from.

I settled back in my chair and enjoyed the company. It was approaching dusk and I watched the outside world turn grey. Then, after ten minutes or so, the streetlights began to illuminate one by one; first pink, then orange, then a burning yellow. They led up the street and down the street, left and right, mapping out every route, no matter how complex, across London town. I must have been feeling a touch emotional because that idea struck me as little short of miraculous.

I poured myself another and sparked myself another. I fired up my PC and potholed for information about Al-Dubayan. I was less efficient than usual because typing's tricky when you've got one finger locked in the up-yours position. I found out all sorts that backed up everything the old man had said. The geezer was an opportunist all right.

The Turk was going about its business. I was tired but I didn't feel like sleeping so I played out Nasser's last test innings in my mind's eye. Again and again, I rocked on to the front foot and sent the last delivery skimming past cover with his trademark inside-out off drive that had won the Test match and had the Lord's crowd rising to a man.

I had a thought: Nasser Hussain's whole career was a thing of prosaic beauty, an internal and eventually successful struggle against his own lack of genius that was worthy of great literature. And yet, in that last instance, that last innings, that very last shot, he embraced poetry and the Kapil Dev theory of momentary greatness. This suddenly struck me as somehow disappointing. Wouldn't it have been more appropriate if his swansong had been scratching his way to twenty over four hours to save a Test match, cussedly refusing to blink beneath the glare of greater talents? Instead he chose to accept others' definitions of glory and I don't begrudge the geezer the decision. But I resolved then and there to remember him for his career-long battles with all-too-evident failings.

Like Farzad says, you can learn everything you need to know about life from the game of cricket.

I must have fallen asleep in spite of myself. Not surprising when you consider that I was out of practice with booze and still pumped full of painkillers besides. In fact, I suspect my

doorbell must have been buzzing some time before I eventually jolted awake like a dead dude in resusc.

I'd been slouched with my head lolled to one side and I'd
given myself a crick in the neck. I gave it a rueful rub and
swallowed some of the glutinous matter that seemed to have
coagulated on my tongue and gums. I checked the time. It
was only just past midnight.

Obviously, when you're scared for your very life, sleep
is like a blink between spells on high alert. Obviously I have
less affection for my very life than I'd imagined since, despite
a vague awareness that this could be my killer come visiting,
I still felt like I was under water. Then again, I guess it would be
an amateurish kind of assassin who felt the need to announce
his arrival by ringing the bell.

One reason I usually left my doors on the latch was that I'd
never got round to installing one of those intercom/buzzer
things. If the street door was locked, therefore, I had to trot
down the stairs to let someone in. This was a hassle at the
best of times. This was not the best of times.

I hauled myself out of my chair to the window and heaved
it open. I leaned out and shouted down, 'Hello?' Whoever it
was, they were hidden in my doorway. The doorbell stopped
ringing. I shouted again. Nothing. I could see the top of a head
and the burning cherry of a cigarette just outside the Phoenecia
office. I strained my eyes. It was Yusuf. I called his name. He
looked up. I said, 'Yusuf! Who's at my door?' He had a peer.
He said something indecipherable to whoever it was, then
pointed up at me. My visitor emerged from the doorway.
Guess who?

I said, 'Give me a minute and I'll come down.'

19

So exoticmelody and me sat either side of my desk exactly as we had just a few weeks previously. Only a lot had changed in the meantime. Then, I'd only been a hangover shy of suave (yeah, right) whereas now I was Frankenstein's monster. Then she'd been a brassy whore with bought-the-T-shirt cynicism whereas now she stank of terror and, as much as you can fake the appearance of fear, you can't simulate that smell.

She was wrapped up in jeans and a baggy hoodie and her face was mostly hidden by a baseball cap. She could have passed for a teenage boy but for the flat pumps. I guessed that was the point. She was in disguise.

I poured two Turks and lit two Bennies. As she took her first drag, her hand was shaking. I said, 'So what you want?'

She exhaled. She sighed. She fidgeted in her seat like she couldn't get comfortable. She didn't say nothing.

I rinsed my teeth with bourbon. I said, 'Sorry about my appearance. In fact, sorry about the mess. I wasn't expecting company. It's been one of those days. In fact, every day's been one of those days since I got mixed up with you, know what I mean?'

She didn't say nothing, just twitched her head like I'd slapped her. Eventually she looked up at me from beneath the peak of her cap. She looked rough. She had panda and frog eyes all at once. She looked like she hadn't slept since the late seventies. She was trying to compose herself. When she spoke, her voice was a single sidestep from panic. 'Mr Akhtar . . .' she began.

I said, 'Call me Tommy.' It was just a reflex.

'Mr Akhtar. I've come to ask for your help.'

She was struggling to keep control. Her tone was strung out like a tightrope across Niagara Falls. I kept shtum.

'I don't know . . .' she tried. 'I don't think . . . I don't know . . . I think . . .'

A deep breath. I got a first glimpse of her man-made chest rising and falling beneath the sweatshirt. She appeared to have run out of words. She fidgeted a bit more. She dug her hand in her hip pocket and produced a dirty-looking wad of cash, which she now waved at me like a question.

I said, 'Just tell me what you want. Take your time. I've got all night. I'm not sleeping so well, know what I mean? What with my head full of metal and a tendency to pick up *The Archers*.'

I laughed at my own joke. Someone's got to. If I sounded less than sympathetic it's because I was less than sympathetic. I tend to get like that when some geezer's out to kill me.

It took some time but the tom caught me up with her life story, which was not the stuff of fairytales, and her news, which would have made more of a postcard than 'wish you were here'. I'll give you the reordered version minus the false starts, tangents and lies. I'll give you the clarified version with pseudonyms replaced, assumptions verified and the like. I'll give you the précised version minus the sniffs, occasional sob, packet of fags and drained bottle. You can fill in my pertinent questions and subtle prompting depending on your opinion of me. This is what she told me . . .

Exoticmelody had been on the game three years. She was twenty-two years old. I'd had her down as twenty-eight and thought that might be generous. It must have been a tough three years.

She was from Essex originally but had moved around a lot

as a kid, both with her mother and in various short-term fosters when she or, more likely, Mum or, more likely still, Mum's new man decided they couldn't hack it. She relocated to London as soon as she turned eighteen, partly to escape home and partly because she got a job in a mobile-phone shop in the West End.

It wasn't long before she met a geezer and caught a bad case of teenage love. Said geezer told her to jack in her job and promised to take care of her. Nobody had ever promised her anything before, let alone that. Unfortunately, said geezer turned out to be Tony the pimp although she still referred to him as 'my boyfriend, Tony'. At first I couldn't tell whether she was taking the Michael.

The way she told it, turning pro was something of an accident (like she'd slipped on a banana skin and ended up flat on her back, legs spread). The way she told it, when she moved into Tony the boyfriend's Vauxhall pad, he'd had a good job in the City and ample folding to look after the pair of them. Then, surprise surprise, Tony lost his job and things had quickly got desperate. They had no cash to pay the mortgage, the phone bill, the instalments on the motor. The way she told it, it was her idea to go on the game. The way she told it, Tony hadn't liked it at first and he did his best to dissuade her. Then again, he didn't want her to try to get her old job back either. He said that she was worth more than that. He said that flogging mobiles was never going to pay enough dosh to keep them afloat anyway.

Tony the boyfriend said he'd find her first punter. In fact, he insisted on it. For his 'peace of mind', he said. Turned out that one of Tony's City mates had fancied the trainee tom all along and was only too happy to part with a bit of wedge in exchange for you know what.

She said it wasn't that bad. She said she knew her motivation so she just lay back and thought of the flexible-rate mortgage. What happened to lying back and thinking of England? Such is the state of the nation.

Turned out that Tony the pimpfriend had a few other mates who felt exactly like Punter #1 and they had mates who felt likewise. Exoticmelody was soon turning tricks like a magician.

Then Tony the pimpfriend went, I quote, 'funny'. He'd always left the flat when she was working, of course, but now he stayed out all hours of the night too. When she asked what was up, he said it was nothing. When she pushed, he said he couldn't even look at her, let alone sleep with her, knowing all these geezers had banged his woman round his yard. She said, what am I supposed to do?

They talked it through, as couples do, and they agreed that maybe it would be better if she worked out of somewhere else, if he could find it. He found it within twenty-four hours: a poky two-bed in Kennington where she'd share rent and maid's fees with an older Brazilian called Gabriella or, on occasion, Madame G.

After her first day working there, she returned to the Vauxhall flat and the couple had the mother of all rows. She didn't remember what it was about but she remembered that he hit her all right. She ran out crying without thinking where she was going. When she thought about where she was going she realized she had nowhere else to go. She caught a bus to Kennington.

She didn't see Tony the pimpfriend for about a week. She didn't call and he didn't drop by. Finally she cracked and headed over to the flat. Her keys didn't work any more. When she got back to Kennington, she found him waiting for her. He was distraught at having hit her and begged forgiveness. He said he was weak. He said he was sorry but he couldn't cope with it all. He'd brought her stuff over in two bin-liners.

He said they needed a break from each other if it was ever going to work out OK in the end. He hugged her and held her tight and then they had sex on the bed she shared with at least a dozen men every day. I figured it was unnecessary to point out that such niceties seemed to have stopped bothering him.

Afterwards, she asked him why he'd changed the locks on their flat. He made some excuse that didn't make a whole lot of sense. She pushed and he flipped out and gave it that tired 'You calling me a liar?' spiel. Then he hit her again. This time, when he'd dazed her with the flat of his hand, he tore off her T-shirt, wrapped it round a coat-hanger, and whipped her bare back. He didn't worry about scarring since he was only adding to her mother's artistry anyhow. Such a professional beating (and she'd taken enough to know) was hardly a crime of passion, was it? She suspected Tony the pimp had done this a time or two before.

I don't know how you're reading this, but I should point out at this juncture that exoticmelody neither admitted nor denied any gullibility on her part, nor did she ever refer to Tony as anything other than 'Tony' or 'my boyfriend'. The way I figured it, this wasn't because she didn't think she'd been gullible and it wasn't because she still thought of Tony as anything other than 'Tony the pimp'. Rather, I figured it was because there was no gain in such admissions and, in fact, they might even force her to confront certain issues (like a lost three years supporting the weight of countless men) that, if examined too closely, might break her.

I tell you this because I don't want you to think that exoticmelody was stupid because she wasn't. And, before you get any ideas, I don't want you to think she was stupid only because I have, as I've said often enough, an affection for the truth. Besides, it's too easy to say, 'She's a sucker,' without knowing what you're talking about, right? Like, it's never a good idea to comment on the quality of the bowling before you've gone out to bat. Like, that's the kind of thing that provokes the exchange, 'Was that A Fall I saw coming in before?' 'No, no, old bean. I think you'll find that was Pride.'

Exoticmelody worked out of the Kennington two-bed for the best part of eighteen months. Typically she saw Tony once a week when he pitched up to collect his cash and, every now and then, stake his claim using a coat-hanger or his dick as the mood took him.

She learned several important lessons during that time, one of which was that a crack whore is not your ideal flatmate. Gabriella accepted visitors of all degrees of dubiousness at all hours. One night, when Melody returned from an outcall way past two to find a strung-out zombie making himself comfortable on her bed in a warm deposit of his own shit, she decided enough was enough.

Melody called Tony. She told him she needed to move. He said, so? She suggested that maybe she could move back into his place in Vauxhall. He laughed at that. She told him, whatever but she couldn't stay with a f__ing Brazilian crack whore a moment longer, could she? He spoke quietly. He said he thought she knew better than to talk to him like that. He said he'd let it slide just this once. He said he'd see what he could do.

Tony found her a bedsit in Charlton and she moved within a fortnight. This was a definite improvement. She was staying on her ownsome in a tree-lined suburban street and she had young families and OAPs for neighbours who had no clue how she earned a crust. There were, however, a couple of drawbacks. In the first place, the new joint was on the junior side of bijou and, by the time she'd moved in all her accessories, uniforms and the like, it was impossible for her visitors or, indeed, the tom herself to escape the bare facts of what she did (which was what she wanted most). More to the point, though, when it came to punters' paradise, Charlton was way off the beaten track. So, in spite of her recent tit job, exoticmelody had to drop her rates, I quote, 'commensurately'. I was impressed by her vocab.

It was also, incidentally, in this Charlton spell of whoring that Melody was visited by an earnest young tech-head called Graham (and if he was lying about his name he either had no imagination or a whimsical sense of humour). He told her a lot of hookers had websites. He said he'd do the same for her if she'd let him buy one get one free. She did and he did.

Anyway. What with the lack of cupboard space and declining returns, Melody was not averse when Tony suggested she start working out of a South Ken mansion block alongside a new Russian bird he was running fresh from New York ('he was running' apparently did not conflict with 'my boyfriend' in the tom's phraseology). He said she could keep the Charlton bedsit and commute. He seemed to find his use of the word 'commute' hilarious. That was about nine months ago.

It turned out that the establishment of exoticmelody.co.uk (closely followed by sexyrussian.co.uk in exchange for an hour's threesome) revolutionized working practices for the pair of whores. Where before they'd relied on Tony for all sales and marketing, they could now attract punters without his help and, as a consequence, there was a distinct power shift in the relationship between prostitutes and pimp. This is, I'm guessing, an unsung by-product of the Internet revolution.

Although Tony still tried to dominate their lives, taxed their incomes and handed out the occasional thrashing, he could no longer keep easy track of their bookings. The relationship between toms and pimp, therefore, became more of a partnership (albeit one that would hardly have seemed familiar to anyone who knew squat about company law) in which they provided the services and he provided the muscle. For exotic-melody this meant a much healthier bank balance and a better class of clientele. For sexyrussian this meant a much unhealthier coke habit.

So much for the back story, on to the main plot.

Although Melody now attracted the majority of her punters via the web, it was Tony who introduced her to an Arab geezer – calling himself, bizarrely, Teddy – who had a notorious penchant for all things ebonic.

At first, the tom was none too keen, what with her indiscriminate policy of racial discrimination (i.e., apparently she couldn't tell an Arab and an Asian apart). However, when she measured the length of his preferred booking (three hours including sometimes drinks or even dinner) against the length of his average performance (three minutes including foreplay), and compared the size of his wallet (large) with the size of his dick (small), she soon changed her mind. I tell you, I learned so much about what pushed Teddy Al-Dubayan's buttons that if he'd turned up to kill me right there and then I might have died laughing and saved him the trouble.

Seemingly seduced by exoticmelody's ability to yell, 'Come to Mummy! Come to Mummy! Split Mummy in two!' in a thick Jamaican patois, he was soon a weekly regular. Wednesday nights. Three hours incall. One quick tumble. Six long. Close the door behind you.

Typically, exoticmelody and sexyrussian didn't take incall bookings at the same time. Although this hit their earning capacity, the average punter's desire for anonymity would have turned such an undertaking into something like *Carry on Hooking*. And these two were supposed to be high-class whores, weren't they?

One Wednesday, however, Melody returned to the South

Ken flat with only ten minutes to spare before her weekly rendezvous with Al-Dubayan and found Natasha and one of her regulars, a Russian geezer she'd known from her time in New York, at the tail end of a binge. The place was a municipal tip: bottles, drugs paraphernalia, and half-eaten snacks from the Greek deli down the road littered the coffee-table. Natasha was prostrate, naked apart from a suspender belt. Her eyes were wide, like she was contemplating the final line that sat untouched on a glossy magazine on the floor under her nose. The Russian, however, was fully *compos mentis*, taking it easy with a beer and watching porn on wide screen. He stood up when Melody came in and introduced himself like he owned the joint. He said his name was Dimitri Gaileov.

Melody was somewhat vexed but she shook the geezer's hand and then tried to sort things out before her own punter arrived. It didn't take her long to tidy up but, when she'd finished, she looked at the living room and thought there was still something not quite right. What could it be? Oh, yeah. There was some dude making himself at home in an armchair, apparently playing with himself through the pocket of his cords (touchingly coy in front of a couple of pros, serious), and a coked-up whore comatose on the sofa.

She suggested to Gaileov that he might have outstayed his welcome. He kept smiling and told her he'd booked Natasha for the rest of the night and he wasn't going nowhere without a refund, which would be tricky since most of his cash was now deep inside the tom's left nostril. She suggested to sexyrussian that she might shift her scrawny backside and take a shower but her ho-buddy wasn't up for much in the way of conversation. Eventually she managed to cajole sexyrussian into a sitting position and manhandled her to the bathroom. Then the doorbell rang.

Melody tried to direct Al-Dubayan straight into her bedroom but he'd brought flowers and was having none of it. He was all, like, don't I even deserve a cup of tea? He barged past her and headed for the lounge at which point there was a crash from the bathroom where sexyrussian had just collapsed while standing under the full force of a cold shower. Oh-so-exoticmelody then had to leave him to his own devices while she made sure that oh-so-sexyrussian hadn't impaled herself on a bog brush. *Carry On Hooking* doesn't even cover it.

When she'd checked on her fellow tom (and relished giving her a slap around the face while she heaved her into a sitting position on the toilet), she went, somewhat nervously, to track down her punter only to discover that he seemed to have hit it off with Gaileov and the pair of them were now deep in conversation.

The Russian left soon after when he realized that no amount of alcohol, cocaine or semi-consensual sex was going to revive Natasha that day. Al-Dubayan then opened a bottle of wine and patted the sofa next to him. Exoticmelody did as she was told and they made awkward small-talk for half an hour like they were an old married couple. Later, post-coital ('Come to Mummy! Come to Mummy!' – that cracks me up every time, for real), A-D mused aloud that maybe he should be doing unspecified business with the Russian geezer.

Over his next few punts with exoticmelody, that 'maybe' became a 'definite'. Unfortunately, Melody told sexyrussian; unfortunately, sexyrussian told Tony the pimp; unfortunately, he wasn't one to pass up the opportunity for a skanky blag. Tony therefore made sure he was at the flat for Al-Dubayan's next visit. Melody recalled that he looked somewhat nervous. He probably knew more about the Arab than she did. That wasn't saying much.

When Al-Dubayan arrived, it was like Tony had prepared a speech cobbled together from soundbites he'd picked up along the way (from his 'good job in the City' perhaps. Like such a job ever existed). He said he'd heard that the client was interested in establishing ongoing business relations with another client for mutually beneficial ends. He said that this kind of gentlemen's networking was precisely the kind of service he provided as a fellow businessman and, that is to say, an entrepreneur. He said that he was an experienced facilitator and was only too happy to arrange a meeting at a venue of the client's choosing, subject to an appropriate facilitator's commission.

Exoticmelody was sitting next to Al-Dubayan while Tony made his pitch, holding his hand and occasionally nibbling his ear. The opportunist barely moved a muscle throughout and his hand was cold like dead meat. It was, she said, the first time she figured this geezer wasn't 'your average Paki wide-boy'. I was charmed.

Al-Dubayan asked Tony what kind of commission he had in mind.

Tony licked his lips (in my Hollywood imagination anyway) and tried his luck. He said that would obviously depend on the size of the deal but, seeing as they were serious business-men, they would surely only deal in serious business in which case he'd expect a serious commission for his services. Serious. He said that he imagined they'd be talking about a minimum ten grand up front with the same to follow when the deal was done and dusted.

There was a moment's silence. Exoticmelody half expected her punter to laugh in her pimp's face. But he didn't. He just said something to the effect of 'So. For ten grand you introduce me to someone I've already met? What sort of an arrangement is that?'

Tony blustered. He said that he'd misunderstood and what in fact was on offer was a comprehensive facilitation package that would smooth the progress of the deal from start to finish, beginning to end; from A to Z, so to speak. What's more, he, himself, Tony Simone, guaranteed he'd be available 24/7 for his client's every requirement.

Al-Dubayan stared at him and smiled. Exoticmelody described it as 'the kind of smile that makes babies cry, know what I mean?'

Al-Dubayan said, 'Twenty-four/seven? That's quite a commitment.'

They shook hands. They agreed the first meeting should be organized sharpish but Al-Dubayan said he needed to sort out a few things first, stuff to do with financing and whatever. Tony spread his arms magnanimously: 'Anything I can do, just say the word.'

Al-Dubayan left. He had business to attend to. He didn't even hang around for his session with the tom. He said they should reschedule. He told Tony he'd call him in the morning. Tony said he'd look forward to it.

When the opportunist had gone, the would-be opportunist was even more pleased with himself than usual and, having dismissed his new client as a 'f___ing sucker', insisted they go out for dinner. He took exoticmelody to a nearby bistro and ordered champagne that he clapped single-handed. After the meal, he took her back to the mansion block for celebratory sex. He was drunk and she almost locked her jaw getting him hard and almost locked her hips getting him to finish. He fell asleep on top of her but when she tried to move him he muttered, 'Lie still, you cheap c–.' It was a romantic celebration that made me come over all cuddly.

At this point in exoticmelody's story, the details get a little furry so I'll just give you the basics. This is partly because it was, by now, something like four a.m. and partly because we were now down one pack of Bennies and one bottle of Turk. You'll understand that these factors had equal impact on the tom's capacity to tell it like it was and my own to listen and recall.

Melody knew that her punter rang Tony the pimp the very next day and she knew that he paid him a sizeable sum up front and had him do a couple of errands. She didn't know what these were. She figured just driving, mostly. For all that Tony had said about the geezer being a 'f__ing sucker', she reckoned he was somewhat star-struck. She couldn't put her finger on why unless it was simply the dude's cash. I figured that as the Afghan vets had been to Al-Dubayan, so he was to Tony: it was all a question of aspiration and authenticity for bullshitters.

Having abstained from his previous session, Al-Dubayan booked exoticmelody through Tony for the Monday following. She said fine but she knew she had to accompany sexy-russian who was meeting a newbie at the Embassy first. She told Tony that he could pick her up from there at such and such a time. But then Bailey was twenty minutes late, wasn't he? So Tony came down and lost his rag and then A-D too (who, mind you, she still referred to as 'Teddy'). She left with them and that was the last time she saw sexyrussian. She got into A-D's motor while punter and pimp had a private chinwag on the kerb. Then, leaving Tony outside the bar, A-D drove her back to the South Ken mansion block for a dose of 'come to Mummy'. She commented that it had been a particularly frenzied liaison that night (although the words she actually used weren't half so pretty).

Don't get me wrong, exoticmelody's naïvety and seeming inability to run the equations stretched my credulity, serious. Then again, I knew that she didn't have the academic record of yours truly: five O levels and two A levels, thank you very much. She may have been a student at the University of Life but all the signs were she'd been bunking seminars.

So Bailey got bludgeoned, sexyrussian scarpered and Tony had got himself into more of a pickle than you find in your average pub ploughman's. Look at it like this: one day he was a small-time pimp, the next he was a part-time facilitator and part-time rent-a-thug in hock to a wife-beating, opportunistic millionaire would-be terrorist with a god-complex named Azmat, a.k.a. 'Teddy', Al-Dubayan (although Tony's familiarity or otherwise with any of these labels is anyone's guess). What's more, in murdering Bailey he'd misplaced his one trump card, i.e., the cokey Russian tom who knew how to get in touch with a certain Dimitri Gaileov.

So what did Tony do? He put the squeeze on hooker #2. And that was where yours truly came in. I'll put it like this: if you have a problem, if no one else can help, and if you can find him (*Yellow Pages*: look under 'Private Investigators'), maybe you can hire Tommy Akhtar. Yeah, right.

Are you following? I'll keep it simple.

So Mr T (to my friends) found sexyrussian, who gave up Gaileov's number, which was then passed on via exoticmelody to Tony the pimp and thus the meeting between Al-Dubayan and Gaileov could finally go ahead.

It took place at the South Ken mansion block. Exoticmelody played hostess. She didn't hear the ins and outs but afterwards all parties seemed happy and toasted with champagne.

The Russian geezer was the first to leave. Tony the pimp then demanded settlement from his new boss. Al-Dubayan told him there was a loose end that needed seeing to. I guess we can call me a loose end. I guess we can call my confrontation with Mrs Hammer a seeing-to. All departed, leaving exoticmelody to wash the plastic flutes.

A couple of days later, Al-Dubayan pitched up with Melody for a seeing-to of his own. Melody claimed he was behaving really weird. I suggested that the whole 'come to Mummy'

237

thing was hardly two kids and a Volvo but she said that was nothing on the freakydeak barometer and she didn't mean weird like that anyway. I asked her what kind of weird she meant then. She said that he seemed melancholy and everything he said sounded portentous. Even in my drunken state, I remember thinking that maybe the tom had just bought a thesaurus, know what I mean? I said, like what? She told me that when he left he'd said he wouldn't see her again but he was extremely grateful for her services. He'd gone all formal. I agreed that was weird.

Of course it all seemed a lot less weird when exoticmelody headed back to Charlton only to find two geezers equipped with cricket bats and balaclavas waiting inside her bedsit. She may have been a whore with a wider knowledge than most of the freakydeak barometer but she didn't figure they'd dropped round for a spot of role play. As far as she was concerned, they must have been sent by the opportunist. I took a little more convincing (possibly on the grounds that, if they played the gentlemen's game, they were OK with me) but when she told me they'd greeted her with a straight drive and a hook shot (both, fortunately, played and missed) I had to concede she was on to something.

Every good tom has survival instincts to balance their self-destructive streak and exoticmelody was no different. She flailed and kicked out as their swinging bats forced her across the bedsit and into the kitchenette. She picked up her frying-pan and caught one of them flat round the head. She managed to make it to the door and threw it open screaming before the second batsman managed to grab her by the arm.

Luckily the ruckus woke Kiri, the toddler downstairs, and Kiri's dad, Dennis, emerged from his flat wearing an expression that was none too chirpy. When he saw Melody grappling with the hooded batsman, he looked like he was about to wade in but then a gunshot cracked and he disappeared back inside. In the bedsit, the tom saw the batsman she'd just lamped struggling to his knees, gun in hand, adjusting his aim. She saw the doorframe splintered where the last bullet had just bit. She saw that the geezer holding her was just as shocked as she was and had loosened his grip. She saw her chance and legged it down the stairs and straight out the front door.

An aside: at some point in our conversation, me and the tom debated why the gun-toting geezer hadn't just shot her as soon as she walked in. She said she figured guns are noisy and liable to attract attention. As far as I was concerned, two swinging cricket bats hardly sing a song of subtlety but I had no better explanation.

The tom bolted into the street. She said she felt calm. She considered running but didn't think she'd get far if they decided to chase. Instead, she just sprinted across the road and into the front garden opposite where she ducked behind the hedge.

Ten seconds later the two geezers emerged from her house, arguing and shouting at each other and looking up and down the street. The upstairs window behind her lit up and she could see an old dear peering down at the action and then directly at her, cowering behind the hedge. She held her breath. The two geezers looked like they didn't know what to do. Then they took a decision and ran off down the road. A moment later, she heard an engine roar and tyres squeal as a car sped away.

Now Melody felt sick but her mind was still clear. She said it was strange how quiet the road was and you might not have noticed anything had happened but for her front door swinging wide and the lights that were now flicking on in bedrooms up and down the street.

Dennis met her at the door holding Kiri in the crook of his arm. He was ranting at her: that he'd called the cops, that he wanted to know what the f__ was going on. She walked straight past him and up to her bedsit where she packed a handbag and was gone in less than a minute. She didn't wait for the Old Bill.

The tom had nowhere to go so she spent the night on a bench outside the bowling pavilion in Hornfair Park. She said she got so cold that she could barely feel her extremities. I said I thought that was par for the course when you'd had a boob job. She didn't find me funny so I quickly asked her if she could tell me anything about the geezers who'd attacked her beyond the balaclavas and the bats. She thought about it and told me they'd had London accents and, when they were arguing on the pavement, she thought she'd heard one of them call the other Brian.

I ran this information through the sophisticated processing equipment that is Tommy Akhtar's bonce (metal plate and all). I remembered Av telling me that one of the geezers at the PWA was called Brian. There are a lot of Brians in London, for real, but this was evidence enough for me. I decided the Post-Western Alliance were ready to tear down the citadels of capital, starting with a Charlton bedsit. I assumed they planned to work their way up.

The next morning exoticmelody belled Tony on his mobile but it was answered by a voice she didn't recognize. She asked if he was there. The voice said, who's asking? She said, it's me, who are you? The voice said he was DI Such-and-such and was she a friend of Tony Simone's and did she know anything about the previous night's events? She cut the call.

She didn't know what to do. She had some cash so she checked into a cheap hotel locally. There was a *Standard* on the coffee-table in the lobby. She flicked through it. She came across a report about a fatal shooting in Mayfair. The victim was named as the pimp formally known as 'my boyfriend'.

When she got to her room, she locked the door, curled up under the duvet and had a think. She concluded as follows: Al-Dubayan or his cronies offed Tony on the grounds that it kept him quiet and was a whole lot cheaper.

She came looking for yours truly. Yours truly was not at home and his door was locked. She said that some geezer in the cab office downstairs told her I'd taken a battering and gave her the details with something like relish. He claimed I'd be out of action for a while, perhaps even permanently. He told her that, if she wanted his opinion, I'd had it coming. I asked her which geezer she'd spoken to. She shrugged. She said she didn't know but he was a pervy little p__k with an attitude problem. Gundappa has rarely been so concisely described.

She came to visit me in hospital. I asked her why she'd bothered. She said she knew it was a risk but she felt somewhat responsible and wanted to check I was OK. I told her it wasn't her fault and I was fine. We had a moment. If this had been a movie, she'd have fallen in love with me right then and there. It wasn't a movie and I reckon I had a lucky escape.

I asked her what she'd been doing since. She hadn't been doing anything. She'd been staying in her crappy hotel room and catching up on daytime telly. I asked her why she didn't go to the Old Bill. She looked at me like I was an idiot. Fair enough.

I checked the time. it was past five a.m. I checked the Turk. It was clapped. I looked out of the window and the sun was struggling out of bed and the birds were starting to sing. Did you know that the birds in this city sing louder than anywhere else in the country? They have to if they're going to be heard above the hubbub. There's a metaphor in there somewhere.

I looked at her across the desk. She looked like I felt. It was past five a.m., I was drunk and I was as yet unrecovered from the worst symptoms of attempted murder. I felt like shit. I thought about what I should ask her next. I realized I was back to square one. 'So what you want?'

'Help,' she said.

I pondered. I figured Al-Dubayan had had Tony killed and tried the same with the whore and me. At least, therefore, we had something in common. I also figured that he was 100 per cent certain to try again, which meant that my cosy flat with the praying TV and crap everywhere could hardly be described as a safe haven. I said, 'OK', and played the nodding game a while. I wondered where I could drop Melody while I worked out my next move. I wondered who I knew who'd definitely be awake at this hour. There was only one answer. I said, 'OK.' I picked up the phone and dialled the old man.

20

Farzad sounded surprisingly sparky, all things considered ('all things' being, in fact, only two: the time of day and his habitual state of mind). I didn't know whether this was a good sign or not. Generally speaking, Farzad's only sparky when he's standing on the edge of a precipice, looking down and preparing to jump, but I usually figure it's best to appreciate these brief spells because what else are you going to do?

He picked up the phone with the words, 'Goodness me! So they let you out of hospital, Tommy boy? How are you feeling?'

Presumably, just like I knew he'd be awake, he knew there wasn't no one else who'd be calling him round five a.m.

'All right, Dad. You?'

'I am . . .' he gave a theatrical sigh '. . . in the pink, as the saying goes. But have you found Mr Al-Dubayan? Are you still up to your neck?' He stopped himself. 'No. You tell me, son. What can *I* do for *you*?'

I thought about what exactly I should tell him. I decided on the bare minimum. I told him I had a client who needed a place to crash for a few days. I told him she wouldn't be any trouble. I told him the company wouldn't do him any harm.

He said, 'Who is she, this client?'

'You met her at the hospital. Her name's Melody.'

'Ah,' he said, a touch wistfully, I thought. 'The delightful-smelling negress.'

'Farzad . . .'

'Yes, Tommy boy?'

I had nothing to say.

He said, 'Might I enquire if your use of the word "client" may be somewhat euphemistic?'

'What the hell are you talking about?' I knew he knew she was a hooker. But I was surprised to find he would reference it so overtly. Turned out he wouldn't.

'You cannot blame an old man for asking, son,' he said. 'Your mother and I always wondered how we would feel when you brought a woman home for the first time. I must say, it has been quite a wait.'

I tutted into the mouthpiece but the tut turned into a splutter and then a full-blown coughing fit.

'You sound sick, Tommy boy.'

'I am sick. And drunk.'

'And in the morning you'll be sober. But will your client still be beautiful?' He paused. 'Who said that?'

'You did. And it's already morning. Look, we'll see you when we see you, OK? You gonna be there?'

'Are you making fun of me, Tommy boy? Where do I ever go?'

'Right,' I said. 'Thanks. We'll see you.'

I rang off. I considered whether he'd still be sparky when we got there. I realized I should have told him to make sure he put some clothes on. And Farzad wondered why I never brought a woman home.

While I talked to him, I was looking out of the window. The road was already busy with early risers heading to work and the night shift heading home. Amazing all the worlds you never see in this city because of your own particular London lifestyle.

Now I turned back to exoticmelody only to discover she was fast asleep with the brim of her cap pulled low and her chin in her cleavage. It looked like a comfy resting-place. Her every outbreath was interrupted by these little snorkelling sounds that I thought were kind of cute. I blinked. I checked myself.

I wondered if we should get going. Then I figured that Al-Dubayan and his cronies weren't likely to come tom and Tommy hunting so bright and early and a couple of hours' kip wouldn't do either of us any harm. How did I figure that? Like time of day makes a difference to a bunch of nutters. I was cream-crackered, wasn't I? And my logic wasn't up to its usual rigorous standards.

I hobbled over to exoticmelody and gave her shoulder a gentle shake. I whispered, 'Don't sleep there. You'll be stiff as a board.'

She looked up at me all bleary-eyed. She whispered, 'F__, man! Where's your toothbrush? Your breath f__ing mings.'

I let exoticmelody take the bed. It was the first time I'd had a woman in there since God knows when. I sat in my chair in the office. I thought I'd snooze but I didn't.

I wasn't on intruder alert. I didn't think. I didn't play a momentous innings. I just sat and marvelled at the fact that time passed without any help from yours truly. Life, like cricket, will always make you humble if you think about it too much. Maybe I should be a Catholic but I was born a Muslim.

I stirred around ten. I dug around in my closet in the bedroom for clean underwear, shirt and jeans. The tom was out cold. I reckon I could have redecorated without waking her. I went to the bathroom and shaved my face left-handed. I'd had a few goes in hospital but I still wasn't much good at it and it left my cheeks patchy and uneven like I was an inept old man; my old man, in fact.

I brushed my teeth. I had a shower. However gentle I was, the combination of new hair growth with soap and hot water made the scar on my head itch like hell. When I got out, I stood naked on the bathmat for a full five minutes, biting on a knuckle. The idea was that the pain would stop me thinking about the itching. It was semi-successful. I dried myself carefully and got dressed. Although my ribs were healing well, it still took five minutes of wincing and uncomfortable contortion to get both arms into a shirt. I resolved then and there not to get beaten half dead again any time soon. It was inconvenient, serious.

I woke exoticmelody. It took a minute or two's prodding but then she snapped alive with a big gasp of breath like she'd just heard a gunshot. She looked confused by her surroundings. I knew the feeling. I told her it was time to go. I gave her a towel. She took half an hour in the bathroom without the excuse of life-threatening injuries. I swear that if Al-Dubayan or his rent-a-thugs had turned up, the poppet would have shouted, 'What? Just give me a minute, OK?' All irritable.

Nonetheless, when I finally heard the bathroom door open and the bedroom door close, I revelled in the smell of clean woman that permeated the whole flat and reached my nose in the office. It made me feel nostalgic for a live-in lover, marriage perhaps. Strange you can feel nostalgic for a life you've never known.

It was another twenty minutes before the tom appeared. I began to get irritable. I wasn't being paid to hang around for some hooker. In fact, I wasn't being paid.

When she finally emerged, she looked altogether different. For starters, she'd taken off the baseball cap (which, I now realized, she'd even been wearing in my bed) and I saw that she'd chopped out her fake ringlets and replaced them with neat little cornrows, tight to her scalp. She still had on the same jeans but she'd raided my wardrobe for a shirt (sky blue with pink check – not one of my favourites) that she'd knotted at the waist. Her face looked different too. She wasn't wearing any makeup but it wasn't that. It was more like her expression had lost some of its attitude; like some of the muscles in her cheeks that she'd been working out every day in three years' whoring had finally relaxed. Look at it like this: for the first time since I'd met her she actually looked twenty-two years old. She looked scrubbed and clean and presentable. Which was only right and proper because she was about to meet the in-laws, wasn't she? Yeah, right.

She tutted at me. She said, 'What are you staring at?'

I said, 'Let's get out of here.'

We went down to Phoenecia. Gunny was reading a porn mag like it was the *FT* and he didn't look up. 'Yeah?'

'I need a cab, Gundappa.'

Now he looked up so he could give me the full value of his sneer. He said, 'My f__ing brother!'

Exoticmelody nudged me. She was looking somewhat shocked. I was somewhat shocked myself. It wasn't like Gunny to acknowledge the connection. I said to her, 'I know. You can see why I keep it quiet.'

Momentarily that brought Gunny up short. He said, 'F__ you, Tommy.' And then, under his breath, like it added anything to the preceding, 'F__ing Tommy Akhtar.'

I was still looking at the tom. 'As you can see, charm runs in the family.'

Gunny leaned forward a bit, all conspiratorial. He said, 'A word in your f__ing shell-like, bruv.'

'Sure,' I said. I didn't move. Gunny glanced at the hooker and then back to me. I said, 'Spit it out.'

Gunny raised his eyebrows at me. He was trying to look cool but his voice came urgent, serious. 'I dunno what the f__ you up to, bruv, but you better f__ing sort it out because I don't like filth sniffing round my shit, you know what I mean?'

He nodded at me. I nodded back. He added, 'We clear?'

'Crystal,' I said. Then, 'I need a cab, Gundappa. I'll be away a few days so you won't have to worry about anyone sniffing round your shit or otherwise. Well away from here, OK?'

'Where you going?'

'Why you care? None of your business. I'll pay the driver.'

'Who you want?'

'Big John around?'

He turned to his radio mike. 'Two six, two six. Pick up from base. How long to base?' Big John's unintelligible reply crackled through the speaker. Gunny said to me, 'Five minutes, OK?'

'Sure,' I said. 'We'll be outside.'

I reckon this was both the longest and the most civilized exchange my brother and me had shared this side of the millennium. We left him to his porn.

On the other side of the road, I spotted Michelle hanging outside Khan's with some of Av's fellow thug-lites. There was, however, no sign of the stroppy Paki teen himself.

I told exoticmelody to wait there and crossed the road. Michelle saw me coming and stubbed her fag. She was wearing the same blue velour tracksuit, the same pink trainers and the same surplus of makeup she'd had on in the hospital but she had a new hairstyle too. Clearly there was something in the air. Two blonde bunches poked out of the side of her head like handlebars. It made for a disturbing effect: makeup from a King's Cross walk-up and hair from primary school. Give me a couple of years and I'll be trying out phrases like 'kids these days'.

She said, 'How are you feeling, Mr Akhtar . . . I mean, Tommy?'

'Fine,' I said. 'Good. Better.' I realized I must be feeling better because if one more person asked me about it I was going to start to get irritable. I said, 'You seen Av?'

She frowned at me. The expression made her makeup cake on her forehead. 'Not for a couple of days. He's working for you, right?'

'Right,' I said. 'Right.'

Mrs K was peering out of the shop window. She waved at me and smiled. I waved back. Big John pulled up outside Phoenecia in his Volvo. I said to Michelle, 'Gotta go. You see Av, get him to call me, yeah?'

'Sure,' she said. 'Whatever.'

'Right.'

I turned and crossed the road to Big John's cab. As I went, I heard one of the thug-lites ask Michelle who I was. She said, 'That's Tommy Akhtar.' He said, 'Seen.' All respectful. I knew I was something of a hero for West London's proper little gangsters. It was all I'd ever wanted.

Exoticmelody sat in the back and I rode shotgun. Big John said, 'So where we going, Mr T?'

'The old man's.' He'd driven me there before. I had a thought. I said, 'You know what, Big John. You keep this to yourself, OK?'

'What?'

'I mean, if anybody asks where you took us, keep it to yourself. Or tell them you took us to a station. Victoria or whatever, OK?'

'OK.'

'I mean, don't even tell Gundappa.'

Big John glanced at me. He looked more than a little offended. He said, 'Tell Gunny? Why I tell Gunny? I'm sorry, Tommy, but your brother is w–er.'

'For real.'

'You know I won't tell nothing. You know you can trust Big John, Mr T.'

'Sure,' I said. 'Sure. I know I can. That's why I asked for

249

you. Gundappa said, who do you want? And I said, Big John. Sorry, man. It's just important, know what I mean?'

'OK. You can trust me.'

'I know,' I said. 'I know.'

We didn't talk the rest of the way. Every now and then I looked back at exoticmelody but every time I did she was staring out of the window. After a while my neck started to hurt so I stopped bothering.

When we pulled up outside Farzad's, I paid with a purple queen. I tried to persuade Big John to keep the change but he wouldn't.

The old man opened the door promptly, wearing a smile and, I'm pleased to report, his green polo shirt, cords and even a pair of plimsolls that, to judge from the way they gleamed, he'd just painted white. He was holding a brush in one hand and a large plate in the other that was chock-a-block with biscuits and Battenburg cake and Madeira cake and individual jam tarts in individual foil trays. He said, 'Come in. Come in both of you, please. I've just made some tea.' I wondered what the act was for. I'd got out of Big John's cab and straight into a parallel universe.

Farzad had even tidied the living room. He'd Hoovered the carpet, straightened the rugs and plumped the cushions. He'd cleared away his cricket tapes too and I could see a couple of them poking out from where he'd chucked them behind the curtain. There was a pot of tea steaming on the occasional table and the only ashtray in sight was empty and clean. He was making an effort, although for what was anyone's guess. When Dad makes an effort I never know whether to be grateful or worried. I mean, the geezer's at best odd and at worst a full-blown nutter, right? And it'll come out some time so what's the point of playing nice?

For the moment, however, the only sign of the old man's

eccentricity was the freshly whitewashed living-room wall, which was shimmering and tacky. Farzad caught me looking at it. I said, 'What happened to the Tingatinga?'

He regarded me disapprovingly and then spoke to Melody like I was an idiot to be benevolently patronized. 'He always asks stupid questions, my dear. He knows, of course, that the wall desires nothing more than to return to its pure state.' He offered her the plate. 'Biscuit, cake or tart?'

She looked up at me, confused. I tried to adopt an appropriate facial expression. There wasn't one. She chose a slab of Battenburg.

I'd been thinking about what I was going to do. I mean, if the opportunist/terrorist was after exoticmelody, then he was also after yours truly and if she needed a place to lie low, then so did I. I guess I'd assumed that I'd just stay with Farzad too but the next half-hour of torturous conversation changed my mind. The old man seemed to have adopted a peculiar persona that occasionally made him sound like a rural English vicar as borrowed from various seventies sitcoms.

For example, he asked exoticmelody where she came from. She said, Ilford. He said, no, originally. She looked nonplussed so he said, your parents, where did your parents come from? She told him that her mum was Jamaican. This was, according to Farzad, a pity.

He said he didn't understand the Caribbean mentality. He said, 'The average Caribbean person is intrinsically idle, isn't that so? Why is that? I have always thought it is most likely a by-product of slavery. What do you think?' Exoticmelody sipped her tea. Farzad said that you could take his neighbour, Peter from Trinidad, as an illustration. 'Very nice chap,' he said. 'We watch the cricket together and so forth. But that black bastard's never done a day's work in his life.'

I told him to shut up.

He said, what? Couldn't he even talk about his own friend? He said, we're having a conversation here, three people of the world, a triumvirate of immigrants, so why should we be afraid to speak our minds? He told exoticmelody that I found him embarrassing. He adopted a confidential tone of voice like I wasn't there and couldn't hear him.

He said he wasn't being rude, he'd just hoped she was African. He said Africans were his people, more even than Indians who always wanted to look down on everybody. He said, Africans are as honest as the day is long and, if they're not, you can tell straight away because they have such honest faces that they're unable to hide it. As for the English, how could you relate to a race who didn't know who they were? He said, 'Isn't that so, Tommy boy?' I didn't respond.

He said to her, so your name is Melody? What's your real name? For some reason, I decided to join in. I watched her curiously and asked, 'What *is* your real name?' She answered the old man. She said Melody was her real name.

Farzad said he'd never remember that. He announced that from now on he'd call her Melanie if it was all the same to her. His eyes lit up with the idea. He said, 'You see? Melanie comes from the Greek meaning "dark skin". It's perfect.' Exoticmelody said it wasn't all the same to her, her name was Melody. The old man looked disappointed. He suggested that maybe they could compromise and he could call her Mel. The tom said, no, her name was Melody. She said it was easy to remember because you only had to think of a tune. She said, 'I know, Mr Akhtar. You think of a tune, whistle it and I'll come running.' I looked at her in surprise and saw a giggle twitch her cheeks. She was one funny hooker.

I had to get out of there. I had an idea. I left them to it and went to the kitchen to make a call. I hoped I had the number in my mobile. I did.

Cal Donnelly must have had my number in his mobile too because he answered with the words, 'My immigrant friend.' Either that or he moves in very cosmopolitan circles.

I said, 'All right, Detective.'

'I heard what happened. How you doing? You still in one piece?'

'Don't ask.'

He said, 'And what the hell were you doing, you IC2 prick? This must have been about Bailey, right? I told you not to stick your big brown nose in the f__ing mix.'

'Yeah,' I said. 'I've never been much good at taking advice.'

I wondered where he was. I knew he couldn't be at the factory because he was talking so freely. Besides, I could hear him sucking on a tab and I knew CID was no-smoking. The sound made me want one. That's addiction, serious. I took out a Benny and sparked up. I said, 'Where are you?'

He said, 'At home. Day off. Julie's got me putting up a coat-rack.'

'How's that going?'

'The coat-rack?'

'No. With the missus, I mean.'

He laughed. 'Fine. So long as I can keep proving I have my uses, and isn't that the truth?'

'Sure.'

There was a beat's silence but that was all it took to make me feel uncomfortable. We'd only been talking a minute but that was all it took to remind me that I barely knew the geezer and we weren't friends. And now I was about to ask if I could crash round his gaff.

He said, 'So what can I do for you, Tommy?'

'I need a favour.'

Another beat's silence. More discomfort. Then he said, 'So?'

'I could use a place to crash. Not long. A couple of nights max.'

'And you're asking me?'

'Yeah.'

'OK.'

'Yeah?'

'Yeah. Fine.'

He gave me directions to his house in Streatham Hill. He said he was no good with Rawlplugs so he'd be in all day. He asked if I was any good with Rawlplugs. I said, no. He said, whatever, I could come any time. I asked him if he wanted to check with Julie. He said she'd be fine with it. I said, 'You sure?'

He said, 'Course I'm sure, you IC2 prick. I'll just remind her who pays the mortgage.' He sounded unconvincing and unconvinced.

'Thanks, Cal.'

Farzad came into the kitchen. He went to the fridge and extracted a four-pack of Genius. He said, 'I've never had much of a taste for tea. Melody and I thought we might have a small tipple.'

He offered me a can. I shook my head. I said, 'Actually, Dad, I'm gonna shoot.'

He examined me closely, like he'd spotted a bit of spinach between my teeth. He said, 'What's going on, Tommy boy?'

'Nothing.'

He sighed. 'I am old and sad and increasingly, I find, highly strung. I am not, however, stupid.'

I said, 'You know what's going on. I'm looking for a geezer called Al-Dubayan and said geezer is looking for me. It's nice and simple.'

He nodded. 'What else?'

I told him about MI5; about Aldridge, Jones and Paradowski. I told him what I'd told them and what I hadn't. He frowned at me. I said, 'What?' He shook his head. I said, 'What do you expect? An MP gets bumped off, they gonna call the intelligence boys, aren't they? Look. Those guys are after Al-Dubayan, just like me. Whether they find him or I find him, it's the same difference, right?'

He sniffed at me. The action took me straight back to numerous careless dismissals at numerous junior cricket matches around London. 'I knew Gundappa was a numbskull,' he said, 'but I expected better from you, Tommy boy.'

'What?'

'I'll just say this, son. You and the "intelligence boys", as you call them, you're not on the same side. You had better remember that.'

I looked at him. You'll remember that this was a thought I'd already thought. I knew why I thought it, but not him. I said, 'What are you saying?'

'Just that, Tommy boy. No playing silly buggers. I had to go to Mina's funeral and I don't want to have to go to yours. Because who will be left to attend mine? Gundappa?'

'Point taken,' I said.

I followed Farzad back into the living room. Exoticmelody had been browsing the bookcase and was now flicking through something I recognized immediately. It was a heavy hardback tome about Paul Gauguin, full of pictures of his pictures. The old man had owned it since I was a kid.

Farzad opened a can of Genius. He began to pour it expertly into a glass and said, 'I'll be mother.' Exoticmelody looked up. He said, 'You like Gauguin?'

'Yeah,' she murmured. Her voice was almost reverent. 'I did a project. When I was at school.'

I couldn't take my eyes off the tom's face. She was getting younger by the second.

Farzad handed her the glass. He said, 'Which do you like best?'

She held the book open for him to see.

'Excellent!' He sounded like she was his star pupil. '*D'où venons-nous? Que sommes-nous? Où allons-nous?* Where do we come from? Who are we? Where are we going? Did you know that Gauguin himself said of this picture, "I shall never do anything better"? And he was right. For me, however, the interest is in the intention. The whole premise is the collision of innocence and knowledge; a state of nature, if you will, colliding with the terror that accompanies experience. There is a fascinating connection to be made with the artist's own imagery that reflects the naïve and jaded sensibilities of colonialism, isn't that so?'

Melody looked from the old man to me, like she was trying to check whether he was joking. She said, 'I just like the colours.'

'The colours? Precisely! What do you like about the colours?'

'I dunno. It's just you can't tell what time of day it is. If you think it's morning, that works. But it could be afternoon or evening or even night too.'

'Such erudite analysis!' Farzad grabbed the book from her and began to flick through its pages. 'Do you know *The Seed of Areoi*?'

Exoticmelody came over all thoughtful. She said, 'Yeah, right. The same thing.'

Farzad was in his element. He went over to the bookcase and started thumbing spines. He asked her if she knew a Mozambican-Tanzanian artist by the name of Eduardo Tinga-tinga. She said she didn't. He said there was a book here somewhere that he had to show her. He asked her who else she liked, apart from Gauguin. She said, Edward Hopper. That seemed to please him. 'Ah, Hopper!' he said. 'Solitude and introspection!'

I told them I was leaving. They barely acknowledged me. I lit a fag, nicked a can and made my way out.

21

I can't remember who – Aggers, Boycs, Richie, one of those dudes – but there's one commentator who has a theory about cricket that gets me thinking every time. I'm not quoting verbatim but it's something like this. Basically, if you want to know your position in the state of the game, you imagine two wickets falling quickly. So, for example, if you're sitting in the pavilion, padded up at fifty without loss, you can feel like everything's peachy, but when you realize that the score could be fifty for two, you're prepared to get your head down as required. Alternatively, if you're out in the field, patrolling the boundary while their middle order picks off the third change, you imagine 150 for three becomes 150 for five and you buck your ideas up sharpish.

I guess the point Aggers or Boycs or Richie is making is that the game can change just like that, to coin a phrase. Don't think you're out of it when you're only a good over short of being back on top. Don't think you're bossing things when you're only a couple of loose shots away from being up the axiomatic without the proverbial.

Cricket. Life. Farzad. Do the sums.

I bussed it to Donnelly's. He'd given me directions but it still took me half an hour to find his Streatham yard in one of those dead-end streets of purpose-built, identikit townhouses that don't qualify for the A–Z. You can picture the kind of thing: rows of homes like boxes that stand behind boxes of lawn and next to box garages housing a variety of mid-range hatchbacks. This is suburban London as Toy Town, only without the cartoon characters.

Donnelly opened the red door with the stained-glass panel holding a beaker of something strong and amber. My tastebuds fidgeted like kids in a movie queue, serious. He was wearing tracksuit bottoms, a vest and a resigned expression. I figured the last of these was either the result of the coat-rack that sat on the floor behind him in its own patch of drill dust, defiantly unaffixed to the wall, or the row between the geezer and his missus that had undoubtedly resulted from said coat-rack's intransigence in the face of DIY. Donnelly smiled at the sight of me, like I'd cheered him up. He said, 'You look like shit.'

I followed him inside. I stepped over the doormat that said 'Home Sweet Home' on to the cheap beige carpet. From the narrow hall, the staircase ran straight up the left-hand wall lined with photographs in frames. They were family snaps; hers, I was guessing. The one above the bottom step was a group picture taken in someone's garden on a bright sunny day. Most of the faces were saying cheese. Donnelly was in the back row, far left, caught looking out of shot with a glass half-way to his mouth.

The kitchen was first on the right – pristine baby blue Formica beneath *faux*-granite work surfaces – then the loo opposite the cupboard under the stairs. This cupboard door swung open and a Hoover was trying to escape. I had a peer inside as we passed. Behind the ironing-board, step-ladder and open toolkit, I spotted a couple of crates of vinyl gathering dust. His, I reckoned.

The living room was at the end of the hall. It was spacious and airy and carefully decorated. The marigold of the three-piece suite was subtly picked up in the hint of colour in the off-white walls. There were more photographs and a large kitsch mirror – the frame carved with flowers and foliage and butterflies – that hung above a cheap fireplace that held a cheap gas fire full of imitation logs. Every surface – mantelpiece, bookcases and window-ledges – held small porcelain horse figurines of varying degrees of ugliness although uniformly naff. But all these lovingly realized details were almost rendered invisible by the imposing form of the home cinema TV system (with VHS, DVD and Surround Sound) that was plonked in the middle of the room like it was a meteorite that had just crashed through the ceiling. It was currently showing high-powered motorcycles zooming around a track at maximum speed and maximum volume.

I'd been in the house less than a minute but I'd clocked the situation and could have dispensed some marriage guidance if asked. Cal and Julie were one of those couples who, ten years in, find they've nothing in common but an address. Full-time investigator? One-time confessor? Sometime comedian? Part-time counsellor? Yours truly is an all-rounder, serious.

Donnelly offered me a drink. I accepted. It would've been rude not to. It was Jack not Turk but better than Jim.

I said, 'Where's Julie?'

He said, 'What?' His eyes were glued to the telly.

'Your missus.'

'Gone to her sister's.'

'My fault?'

'You never met her,' he said. The motorcycles screamed. The commentator was overexcited. 'You like bikes?'

'I'm more a cricket man.'

'Cricket?' he scoffed. 'Stupid game.' I'd forgotten we weren't friends. I suspected we had even less in common than him and his old lady and that was saying something.

We sat on the sofa. We watched the remains of the race. Occasionally Donnelly got excited and said things like 'Look at that! Would you look at that,' before shaking his head. I tried to get into it but no joy. The geezer who was leading when we sat down won, the geezer who was second came second, and the geezer who was third, third. There aren't no metaphors in motorsport; at least, not for an immigrant raised on dreams of social mobility.

At the end, Donnelly clicked mute and clapped me matily on the thigh. I realized that he wasn't just drinking, he was drunk. Unusually I may have been cream-crackered but I was stone cold sober. He said, 'So what's going on, my immigrant friend?'

I told him. At first his eyes were continually flitting back to the edited highlights on the screen. But the ins and outs of what I'd been up to soon had his full attention and he pulled that intensely serious face that the half-cut do best.

When I'd finished, he said, 'F— me!' And tried out a laugh. It didn't work. He said, 'F— me, Tommy. You best go back to that woman.'

'What woman?'

'MI5.'

'Jones?'

'Yeah. Jones, You best go back to MI5 and tell them what you know.'

'What do I know?' I said. 'They know what I know.'

He said, 'And you know that for sure?'

I said, 'Look, Cal, they didn't seem entirely sympathetic to my position, know what I mean?'

He shook his head. I didn't know what that meant. He said, 'So what was the Russian selling Al-Dubayan?'

'I dunno, but I doubt it was hooky fags straight out of Calais.'

'Guns? Explosives? Worse?'

'Worse how?'

He shrugged. 'No idea, my immigrant friend. But Russian Mafia? Nuclear this, biological that. Who the f__ can tell?'

'You got quite an imagination. Al-Dubayan? The geezer's just an opportunist.' I'd finished my drink. I made myself another. 'Whatever. It's a job for the intelligence boys.'

'And you sent a kid into this?'

'What kid?'

'I thought you said you sent some kid under cover?'

'Av? I didn't say I'd sent him under cover. I never said that. He's just checking out a few things on my behalf, what with me being somewhat incapacitated; the lie of the land, as it were. He'll be all right. He can look after himself. He'll be fine.'

Donnelly blinked at me. He said, 'Are you f__ing crazy?'

The conversation changed tack. Despite impending nuclear or biological terror, Donnelly was drunk so he needed to talk about something more interesting. Himself. I kept shtum on the grounds that I was a house guest and it was only polite.

The geezer asked me if I knew the answers to various questions and then told me that I didn't. He was on to something, serious. He asked me if I knew what it was like to get into bed every night with a woman who wouldn't even talk to you. He asked me if I knew what it was like to hear her chatting to her sister or her mum – he said, 'Her mother, for f__ 's sake!' – about all the ways you didn't measure up. He asked me if I knew how long it was since he got laid. No, no and, let me emphasize, there are few things in the world I care less about.

I could have given the geezer some daytime-telly advice. I could have told him that him and Julie needed a shared hobby – the garden, local amdram, swingers' parties or similar. But I had something else on my mind and I wasn't really listening. Suddenly, all I could think about was whether I was actually, as the drunk detective suggested, 'f___ing crazy'. Suddenly, all I could think about was the well-being and whereabouts of a stroppy Paki teen by the name of Avid Khan.

Donnelly got drunker and less coherent. If I'd had a sister, I'd have gone to stay with her too. But I don't.

By half ten he'd given up on consonants and was only using vowels. I told him he looked knackered.

He drained his glass and got unsteadily to his feet. He said, 'That, my immigrant friend, is a sign of wedded bliss.'

At least, I think that's what he said.

He told me I could have the sofa. He said they had another bedroom but he was decorating. If the coat-rack was anything to go by, it would take a while. He told me that the other bedroom was supposed to be a nursery but that was a f___ing joke. He said that if Julie wanted a kid she'd better read up on the f___ing facts of life. He said, 'It takes two to tango if you get my meaning.' I got his meaning. He started to laugh and then looked like he might burst into tears. I took the opportunity to shove him in the direction of the stairs. I followed him up to grab a duvet and a pillow.

He said, 'My immigrant friend . . .'

I said, 'Thanks for letting me stay, Cal. I owe you one.'

I left him swaying on the landing.

I closed the living-room door behind me. The air was heavy with smoke. I know I can be as gross as a Highbury toilet on match day but even so it's always been a principle to avoid sleeping in an ashtray (literal or metaphoric). I considered opening the windows and clearing away the ashtrays (literal) but I couldn't be bothered. I thought, not for the first time, that there's no point having principles you haven't got the discipline to stick to. The scar on my head was irritable. I gingerly ran my fingers across its ridges. It was weeping for me but I didn't want its pity. I lit a Benny.

I belled Av. It went straight to voicemail. His message involved thirty seconds of grimy dance music with a bass to make you feel seasick before his voice kicked in with: 'I'm busy!' Then the beep. I was disconcerted. I used to be a teenage boy. I remember being a teenage boy. I can't figure teenage boys. I left the following message: 'Av, it's Tommy Akhtar. You better call me soon as you get this.'

I sat back on the sofa. I let my brain tick. I realized that the situation, while as yet undisastrous, was no more in my control now than it had been that first day I found exoticmelody sitting in my waiting room. I realized that the whole scenario needed an injection of impetus, courtesy of yours truly. I got my wallet out of my pocket. I got the MI5 bird's card out of my wallet. I looked at it. It simply said, 'A. Jones', and there were two phone numbers: landline and mobile. I must confess I thought that was somewhat stylish. Whatever I thought and Farzad said about who was on what side, I figured I'd have to give her a call.

I switched off the lights, stubbed my Benny and tried to catch some zees. They were as elusive as ever. It didn't help that the Donnellys had a motion sensor in their back yard that triggered an outside light. Every couple of minutes or so, a bird or a fox or a tooled-up thug with designs on yours truly trod in the wrong place and the whole room was washed yellow. It didn't help that in the semi-darkness the subject of every photograph transformed into one or other of two middle-aged ladies of Indian extraction. To the left of the fireplace, for example, it seemed that Mina was rocking one of Julie Donnelly's nieces to sleep while her eyes were fixed on me, full up with disappointment. Meanwhile, above the telly, Mrs K wagged her finger at me disapprovingly as only an Asian mother knows how.

I turned over, face to the back of the sofa, and tried a

favourite innings: a Caribbean dustbowl, mid-eighties, you know the score. It worked for a while as I pulled and hooked with all the flair of Gavaskar in his pomp. But then, as I began to doze, so my subconscious began to play tricks on me and soon I was fending off bumpers from Roberts or Croft or Holding or Garner; only now each and every one of them had the face of Mrs A or Mrs K. You can imagine that a night spent ducking bouncers bowled by Joel Garner wearing my mum's boat was not the most restful.

22

I was awake at half eight. It was Donnelly's fault. He was late for the factory and he came in to hunt for his mobile, making pantomime efforts to keep quiet in the best tradition of the worst hangovers. When he saw my eyes open, he put a set of keys on the coffee-table and muttered, 'Make yourself at home.' His face looked like yesterday's washing-up.

I dozed a couple more hours. Then my phone rang. It knew the number. It was a west London thug-lite. 'Av,' I croaked.

He laughed. He said, 'What's up with your voice, Tommy man? You sound f___ed up, know what I mean? You gotta lay off that tramp juice, man. That shit rots your brain.'

I gathered myself. 'So what you been doing?'

'What the f___ you think I been doing? I been doing this and I been doing that. I been doing what you told me. What what what.'

I said, 'You all right?'

'All right? Course I'm all right. I'm having a f___ing laugh, Tommy man. This is f___ing easy, man. I tell you what this is: this is f___ing gravy, know what I mean? I can't believe people pay you for this shit. You extra, man. I tell you: we a team. It's Av and Tommy, Tommy and Av, all the way, what what what, we'll f___ing smack it.'

'What's going on?'

'What's going on? I don't know what's going on. But I know it's about to kick off, know what I'm saying? But I was thinking. You know your company, right? You know how it's called "TA Services". I was thinking . . . well . . . you know what I was thinking? I was thinking that's f___ing perfect. "Tommy and Avid Services". That's what I was thinking. A lot of companies do that: leave out the "and" in their name, whatever. Tommy and Avid Services. What you think?'

I thought several things. I thought that trying to clean my teeth with my tongue was like trying to clean crap from the toilet bowl with a stream of hot piss. I thought that this was a gross thought and unworthy of a man of my sensitivity. I thought that a restless night on the sofa had done nothing for my broken ribs. Most of all, I thought that Donnelly was right and I must have been crazy to think this junior gangster could look after himself.

'Av,' I said. 'Just back up, reverse, rewind, restart, reboot. Just keep your wet dreams to yourself and tell me what's going on. Have you seen our boy?'

'Nah. Not yet. But I'm gonna, Tommy man. I tell you, shit about to go down. And when I say go down, I mean go *down*. Serious, boy. These geezers is extra, know what I mean? They is f___ing *extra*.'

I noted the admiration. I'd come back to it. I said, 'What shit?'

'I dunno. That's what I'm saying. I'll find out when I meet the man himself. And I'm gonna meet him. I tell you, man, I'm like their star pupil, *numero uno*, top of the f___ing class. Ali says I'm a natural.'

'A natural what?'

'Don't take the piss. Serious, I'm on it. Ali says they been doing deals, what what what. He says they got their hands on state-of-the-art shit. All kinds of fun and games.'

'Right,' I said. I paused. 'What's he like?' I was back to it.

'Who?'

'This Ali geezer.'

'Ali? He f___ing cracks me up. When he's off on one he talks like he's a f—ing professor or something. He's all, like, "It is ironic that the extension of global capitalism into the former Eastern bloc should play its part in its downfall." And then he takes his glasses off, right? And he's all, like, "Babylon gonna fall, my brother." And I'm, like, "Yes, my brother." But at the same time I'm thinking, I've no idea what you're on about, you mad c–, but as long as I got an ounce of skunk and I can chirps some bird, it's all good, know what I mean?'

I checked myself. I was reassured. Av was like me at his age but he had a dash of my brother too and right now that seemed like a good thing. I said, 'So what they got their hands on?'

'You listening to me? I think you lost some brain cells, serious. When they f—ed you up they f—ed you up *good*, know what I mean? I told you, Tommy man. I dunno what they got their hands on. That's why I gotta meet the man himself. Al-Dubayan.'

I considered the options. I realized there weren't any. I took a deep breath. I said, 'All right, Av. We gonna call it quits.'

'What?'

'I said we gonna call it quits. I know everything I need to know. Game over.'

Av got irritable. I should have seen it coming. He said, 'Know everything you need to know? You don't know nothing. I haven't even met the boss yet. What the f— you talking about, Tommy man?'

I had to figure my tactics. I'm usually good at tactics. This time I got it wrong. I adopted didactic-of-Delhi: I said, 'Game over. TA Services stands for Tommy Akhtar Services. Are we a team, Av? Sure we're a team. But you gotta do what the captain says and I'm the captain and I say game over, OK?'

There was a pause. Then, 'Whatever.'

'Don't say "whatever". What you doing?'

'What you mean what am I doing?'

'I mean what you doing? We need to hook up. We need to debrief.' I was trying to get him back onside with the technical talk. And bribery. 'And I need to bung you some wedge.'

'Whatever.'

I checked my wrist. I still wasn't wearing my watch. 'I'll come meet you. Where are you?'

'Around.'

'Don't give me the Chiswick roundabout, Av. I'm gonna come meet you. Give me an hour.'

'I'm busy.'

'Busy doing what?'

'Got business.'

'What business?'

'My f___ing business. What's your problem? Look, Tommy man. I'll give you a bell, yeah?'

'Today. We need to hook up today.'

'Today. Sure. Later.'

I sighed. Excepting the false start, my morning was less than ten minutes old and already it was not going to plan. I said, 'OK. Call me later. But listen to what I'm saying, Av. Don't go near the PWA. If shit gonna go down, if Babylon gonna fall, it can do it without Tommy and Av, know what I mean?'

'Whatever, Tommy. I'll bell you later.'

Av clicked the phone. I sparked my thermometer. The first drag made my brain fizz. I had, in the language of mini-series and B movies, a bad feeling about this.

The cigarette started my belly chewing. I needed to give it something to work on. I went scavenging in the Donnellys' kitchen. I made a pot of coffee. They didn't have any bread so I had to make do with cereal. They only had some high-fibre, no-added-sugar organic muesli (hers, I reckoned). It looked like gravel. I added some milk. It tasted like gravel too.

I heard the front door open. Julie Donnelly breezed past the kitchen without stopping. Thirty seconds later she was back and standing in the doorway. She was holding an address book that she waved at me by way of explanation. She looked totally unsurprised to see me, resigned even. I was beginning to suspect that this is a natural reaction to yours truly.

She was neat and petite. Her hairstyle was recent. She was wearing a white blouse, tucked into fitted jeans over cowboy boots. She looked older than Cal but that could have been all the hours she'd spent in the gym or likewise on a sunbed. Her skin was stretched over her bones like orange Cellophane.

She said, 'You're Cal's friend. He said you'd been beaten up.' These were both statements and carried no curiosity. She said, 'He put you on the sofa. There's an inflatable mattress under the stairs. You'd be more comfortable on that.' I nodded. I raised my spoon. She left. I hadn't even managed a 'hello' what with my jaws working gravel.

I gave up after half a dozen mouthfuls and emptied the remainder into the bin. I poured myself a coffee and sparked a post-prandial. Sometimes I suspect I only eat to make the fags taste better.

I took out Jones's card again. I wanted to procrastinate but I couldn't think of anything else to do. I called the landline. She picked up after one ring. She said, 'Jones.' I licked my lips. She said it again: 'Jones.'

I said, 'This is Tommy Akhtar.'

'What do you want, Tommy?' She, too, sounded resigned. I was starting to get a complex.

'I've got some information.'

I told her everything. I told her about Al-Dubayan's connection to Tony the pimp, my theory about Bailey's death, A-D's meeting with Gaileov. I told her everything I knew about the PWA, which wasn't much. I told her I'd had a kid on the inside. I told her about Av and dropped the names he'd dropped. I told her where they met and I told her I thought they were planning something big. She didn't say anything but I felt like she wanted me to go on so I said, 'Like a bomb. Or worse. I dunno. You know the Russians. Nuclear, biological, all of that.' The words sounded somehow stupid coming out of my mouth.

There was more silence on the line. I vaguely wondered if I was being taped. I vaguely wondered who was listening in. I guess I expected her to ask some questions. But she just said, 'Right.' And rang off.

I sat on the sofa. Life was brilliant. I had nothing to do but wait for the stroppy Paki teen (who was now extra vexed) to call me back. But I had to do something. I decided to make some notes. I decided to write down the facts of the situation as it currently stood. I found a paper and pen. I didn't get far. I knew the facts of the situation as it currently stood and writing it down wasn't going to help anyone but my biographer (*Tommy Akhtar, Private I*, something like that). I thought it through. I realized the key to it all was the opportunist. I catalogued what I knew about him and I decided I knew enough. Then I thought it strange to be simultaneously chasing and on the run from a geezer whom I'd never actually seen in the flesh, up close and personal. Then I realized that I didn't actually know what he looked like. I mean, I'd pulled a few press photos off the net but they were all at least a couple of years old and taken before he'd gone to ground. Maybe the geezer had changed his appearance. I decided I wanted to know what blokey looked like. I decided I'd ask the only person who could tell me. I'd already had a couple of weird phone conversations that morning so if this one went pear-shaped I'd know I was on a roll.

I rang her mobile. It went straight to voicemail. I didn't

leave a message. I rang Farzad's home number. Exoticmelody answered, saying, 'Farzad's phone.'

I said, 'You're making yourself comfy.'

'Your father's cooking.'

'Cooking?'

I was thrown straight back into that parallel universe where the old man is normal. She might as well have told me that he was bobsleighing down Brixton Hill. I've never known Farzad boil an egg.

'Yeah,' she said. 'He's making me lunch.'

'Right.' I didn't know what to say to that. I was momentarily discombobulated. I said, 'You two getting on OK?'

'Yeah. He's a nice man.'

'A nice man? Right.'

There was a brief silence. Exoticmelody chose to fill it.

'We been talking about art. And about your mother. She sounds like an amazing woman.'

'I dunno.'

She gave it the incredulous ha-ha. 'What you mean you dunno?'

'I dunno.'

There was more silence. I could hear someone singing in the background. It had to be Farzad. He was singing the theme tune to Morecambe and Wise, 'Bring Me Sunshine'. I felt . . . I didn't know what I felt. There isn't no word for it. Eventually the tom said, 'Do you want to speak to your father, Mr Akhtar?'

I said, 'Call me Tommy.' Then, 'No. I wanted to speak to you.'

I asked her for a description of Al-Dubayan. She gave me one. It was detailed but unhelpful: six foot, twelve stone, bushy moustache, mole on his left cheek, scary eyes, good suits, small dick. Apart from the moustache (new) and the dick (unknown), he sounded exactly like the dude I'd seen in his web shots. It made me wonder just how he'd stayed unarrested for so long. I guessed he did archetypal Arab as well as I did archetypal Paki.

The hooker must have sensed my disappointment because she said, 'What else you wanna know?'

'Not sure,' I said. 'Anything.'

'What kind of phone you got?'

'What?'

'I took a picture of him. The night he met Gaileov.'

'You serious? He let you take his picture?'

More ha-ha. 'No way. He didn't see or nothing. It was on my mobile, wasn't it? If you do picture messaging, I could SMS it.'

I didn't know if my phone did picture messaging. She asked me the make and model. I told her. Turned out our phones, like their owners, were of different generations. I suspected built-in obsolescence. She asked me for my e-mail address. I said what for? She said she'd send it direct to my inbox by MMS. I didn't really know what that meant but I said OK.

She said, 'Your father wants to talk to you.'

'OK.'

'Goodbye, Mr Akhtar.'

'Right.'

She put the receiver down. I could hear snatches of their conversation. She said something unintelligible. He told her she didn't need to worry but she could stir it occasionally if she wanted. She said something unintelligible. He said, 'That? It's a Monet. Adolescent bullshit.' He said something unintelligible. She burst out laughing. He picked up the phone. 'Tommy?'

'You're getting on well.'

'Indeed. Melanie is delightful.'

I heard a whistle in the background. The phone muffled. He'd covered the mouthpiece with his hand. He whistled back. I heard him say, 'Just my joke, my dear.' He was back with me. He said, 'Tommy boy?'

I said, 'Farzad.'

He said, 'Are you fine?'

'Sure. Why do you ask?'

'Why do you say why do I ask? Of course I must ask. You may be a daft bugger but you are still my son.'

'I'm fine.'

'That is good. What is happening?'

I felt reckless. I told him. He went quiet on me. I said, 'What?'

He said, 'I told you about "the intelligence boys" as you call them. They are not on your side.'

I lost my cool. What can I say? I was feeling indescribable. I said, 'You think I don't know that? You think I don't know what I'm doing? It's not about sides, Farzad. It's about trying to stay in one piece without the need for surgical assistance. F__!'

He sighed. 'You have a foul mouth, Tommy boy. You know how I hate it when you use strong curse words. You sound just like every other hooligan in the street. You effing this. You effing that. We both know my failings as a father –' I tried to interrupt. 'No . . . listen to me . . . but we also both know that I did not bring you up like that.'

I shook my head to myself. 'Sorry, Dad, but it's not about sides. Or it is but it's more like a round robin.' I was blustering, serious. 'It's like the NatWest Series. It's like a triangular tournament where England play West Indies and New Zealand and the top two go through to the final. Sometimes you end up cheering for the black caps against the Windies. They're not on your side as such but if they win it helps you out. It's all about staying in the tournament, know what I mean?'

'No, I don't know what you mean. What on earth are you talking about? I must say, your use of metaphor is becoming increasingly eccentric.'

I took a deep breath. When the old man describes *me* as eccentric, I know something must have gone wrong. 'Sorry. I'm just trying to say that I know what I'm doing.'

'I'm sure you do, son. But no –'

'No playing silly buggers. I know.' More silence. I was getting used to uneasy silences. I said, 'Thanks.'

'For what?'

'For taking Melody in.'

'It is a genuine pleasure.'

'Dad,' I said. 'You know she's a hooker, right?'

He sighed harder than before. He said, 'I am going to eat my lunch, Tommy boy. Before you make me ashamed of you.' He hung up.

Ever since I was a kid, the old man's had a thing about what he calls 'strong curse words'. Compared to other Paki-immigrant-Ugandan-Indian parents in our neighbourhood, Farzad and Mina were relaxed, for real. But you didn't want to let the old man hear you swear. That was a sin comparable to playing silly buggers cubed. To be honest, I was pretty good at keeping my tongue in check, but Gundappa? He had been dragged to the sink for a soapy-water mouthwash so many times I'm surprised he's not still blowing bubbles. Come to think of it, no wonder he ended up on the North Bank at Upton Park.

I remember this one time. It can't have been long after Mina died so Gundappa must have been about fifteen and Dad must have just started hitting the bottle. Gunny had been brought home by the Old Bill for, like, the second time in a week and Farzad was giving him hell. Then Gundappa made the fatal mistake of telling him to f__ off. Gunny was already a lot bigger than Dad but the way Farzad manhandled him into the bathroom you'd have thought he was a rag doll. There was no soap, shampoo or washing-up liquid to hand (we were always running out of things after Mum died) and I swear Farzad would have rinsed his number-two son's mouth with bleach if I hadn't stepped in.

At calmer moments, Farzad used to tell us, 'Language like that? It is lazy. Some people can afford to be lazy. You boys cannot.'

I remember on my first morning at secondary school I came down into the shop and Mina knelt in front of me and straightened my tie. She said, 'Habibi! Look at my son! He looks like a proper little English boy.'

Farzad was behind the counter, checking a delivery of cigarettes. He looked up from his clipboard. He said, 'Listen to your mother. You are an English boy because that is the opportunity we have given you with the assistance of my fine friend Dr Arshad Patel. But if you want to stay that way you must be better than all the other boys in your class. Even then it might not be good enough.' Mina shot him a look but he just laughed. 'What? I will always tell my son the truth.'

I thought about these things as I sat on the Donnellys' sofa waiting for Av to call; first, because I hadn't heard the old man use the phrase 'strong curse words' in years and then because of something I saw in a magazine.

I had time to kill, didn't I? So I ended up flicking through the aspirational women's glossies (hers, I hoped) that sat at the end of the sofa in a wooden rack carved in the shape of a horse. I learned several useful tips: how to keep my man faithful, to grow at least one cup size the natural way, twenty tricks to accessorize a little black dress. But mostly I just looked at the pictures.

One of Julie Donnelly's favourite titles (she had every issue from the last six months) was a weird publication that seemed to be some kind of handbook for the upper classes. It devoted a whole section to pictures of people I'd never heard of sipping champagne at twenty-first birthday parties, gallery openings, book launches and so forth; louche geezers with carefully dishevelled haircuts and smug eyebrows and empty-faced blonde birds holding cigarettes in hands attached to the limpest wrists. The captions said stuff like 'Lord Bath and Anoushka Featherstone-Haugh at the Shipshape Club, Piccadilly'. I was class rubber-necking, for real.

Then I came across an image that made me double-take. If I was a cartoon, you'd have seen my eyebrows jump off my head. It was a group shot taken at the engagement of the Hon. What-What and Lady Such-and-Such at a boutique hotel in Fitzrovia. Five people posed for the camera, raising their glasses in a toast. Two were the stereotypically louche and two were the standard empty-faced, but in the middle was this Asian dude beaming into the lens. I checked the caption. Even though I couldn't remember his name, I figured it would come back to me if I saw it. I saw the name but it rang no bells. I looked again. Maybe I'd got it wrong. I stared at his boat and tried to rewind the best part of thirty years.

As I stared, I began to see all kinds of different stuff behind his expression. His eyes began to look a little bemused and his broad grin a little forced. Maybe I was imagining things but I was almost certain I wasn't imagining the dude's identity. He might have been a little heavier and his hair might have turned an elegant shade of grey but I was pretty sure that this was none other than Lovely himself, the loveliest boy at my school.

I smiled like someone was watching. I wondered what the

hell he was doing there. Knowing Lovely as I once did, I wouldn't be surprised if he's now some high-flying venture-capitalist or whatever. Knowing Lovely as I once did, I wouldn't be surprised if he's now the exotic appendage of some double-barrelled aristocrat. I guess what I mean is that I wondered if he was there by right because, after all, he had been, as Farzad wanted for his own sons, better than all the other boys in our class. I wondered if, mixing in high society, Lovely felt more or less English than yours truly. But as soon as I asked myself the question I answered it just like that.

The way I saw it, the toffs on the pages of this magazine did not live in any England I knew. They were Hollywood English just like Jones and Paradowski were Hollywood secret agents. They existed only in a mythologized world of stately homes, tea at the Ritz and boxes at Ascot when in reality, of course, stately homes are the domain of the voracious Japanese, the Ritz is booked out with fat Americans and Ascot boxes are reserved for Arab oil. The England I knew was a cheek-by-jowl kind of place where seemingly polar opposites were wedded by nation, frustration and location, location, location: stroppy Pakis to small-town racists, the morally fundamental to the morally bereft, office juniors to senior management, thug-lites to petrified pensioners, suburban swingers to pregnant pubescents, coke-addled hookers to coke-addled media whores, aspirant Africans to resigned Rastas, loaded gym freaks to obese benefit junkies, entrepreneurs to economic migrants, organized crime to chaotic bureaucracy, politicians to terrorists, hopeless to hopeful. And like all marriages these were for better or worse, richer or poorer, till death them would part as discovered by one Anthony Bailey, MP.

I would have thought about it more. But Av called at half past two.

23

On my way to Knightsbridge I considered how I'd ended up with a fifteen-year-old calling the shots. I didn't come up with any answers. I made the station by twenty-six minutes to four. I remember the precise time, first, because Av told me when I met him by the photo booth, tapping his watch like a school teacher, and second, because the precise chronology of events turned out to be important.

He kissed his teeth at me. He said, 'Wassup, Tommy man? You f—ing late.'

I gave him the amused eyebrows. I said, 'Sorry, boss. I'm carrying an injury or two, aren't I?'

He didn't find me funny. He was tetchy, twitching impatiently from foot to foot. Dressed like he was – bandanna, white T, gold chain, rucksack, baggy jeans pin-tucked into spanking new trainers – he almost looked like he was up on something, like he was dancing a rave soliloquy. His agitated expression suggested otherwise (unless his happy pill had been cut with something dodgy).

He said, 'Let's go.'

'What you mean "let's go"?'

'Let's go, man. Let's go. We could be being watched.'

I gave it the ha-ha and told Av he wasn't in a movie. In fact, his overactive imagination had a point. I had suspicions of my own, what with my dealings with MI5. I looked around. There were businessmen, tourists, shoppers, kids; all rushing past like they were the only people who'd ever been in a hurry. There were a few characters loitering – businessmen, tourists, shoppers, kids. Some of them were staring. Then again, I was Frankenstein's prototype, wasn't I? Half a head of hair, an itchy scar and a limp like a gimp. There was no point making assumptions. If we were being watched we were being watched, and I was in no mood and no shape to try shaking a tail.

I turned back to Av. He was anxious, for real. I couldn't tell if he was about to crack up or wet himself. I tried a concilia-tory shrug. I realized I was physically capable of shrugging again. It had finally stopped hurting. 'OK,' I said. 'I could use a caffeine shot anyway.'

Av kissed his teeth at me. That made twice. The power relations were upside-down, for real. I'd have to have a word or two and one of them would be 'respect'.

He said, 'No, Tommy man. We gotta get a tube.'

'What?'

'We gotta get a tube.'

'What you mean we gotta get a tube? Where you going?'

'Where *we* going, Tommy.' He flashed a grin at me. He looked disconcertingly cocky. 'I got a surprise for you, what what what. Trust me.'

He was through the barriers before I could tell him I didn't trust him and my last great surprise had been the encounter with Tony the pimp and Mrs Hammer. I followed, didn't I?

My disabilities had me struggling with the automated gate before a friendly station guard popped the mothers and babies' exit. He was a black dude, all dreads and teeth. As I passed, he gave me the disbelieving whistle. He said, 'What happened to you, guy?'

'I fell.'

'Yeah?' He peeled his pearlies at me. 'Off a cliff?'

'Right.' Everyone's a comedian.

I caught up with Av on the westbound platform. It was

mid-afternoon quiet but still busy enough. My sense-of-humour gauge was flashing. I said, 'What's going on, Av?'

He didn't look at me. He was checking the electronic board for the next train. 'What you mean what's going on?'

'We need to talk.'

'About what?'

'About you know who.'

The stroppy Paki teen looked at me like I was a stroppy Paki teen. 'Why you sound so vex, Tommy man? We *are* talking. What you wanna know?'

'Where we going?'

He chuckled. Yours truly was struggling to keep his temper and considering how it would look to give the kid a hiding with his walking-stick.

Av said, 'It's a surprise.'

I grabbed him by the wrist. I dug my nails into the soft part just so he knew I wasn't playing. My expression was come-off-it-of-Kampala. I said, 'I don't like surprises.'

His front cracked. He said, 'F__, Tommy man! Chill the f__ out. We gonna meet him, aren't we?'

'Who?'

He widened his eyes and dropped his voice to a stage whisper. 'Al-Dubayan.'

I felt cold and sick. My brain scrambled. I might have fallen over without the benefit of my stick. I said, 'What you talking about?'

Av clocked my reaction and his front rebuilt sharpish. He was back to thug-lite brazen: all bollocks and no brains. 'I told you, Tommy man. I'm the f__ing star pupil, what what what. Brian says they told the boss all about me and now he wants a meet. I'm, like, cool cool, just give me where and when and I'm going down like f__ing Mary J. They, like, four p.m., Hammersmith station, today. *Today!* They fell for it big-style, boy! Like I told you, man, this shit is gravy. So I figure Tommy Akhtar can come along and check the geezer out first hand, know what I mean? McDonald's, four p.m., Hammersmith, and they said he coming on his own for a private meet. They *actually* said that.' He took a breath. 'What you wanna do, Tommy man? You wanna play it nice and easy and sit back and watch? Or you wanna jump the motherf__er?'

I said, 'F__!' but it was drowned by the noise of the approaching train. It must have been the first time I'd used strong curse words twice in a day for pushing fifteen years. Farzad was right. I was just another hooligan in the street.

We got on the train. It was half full. I needed to sit down. We were in the front carriage. We took two seats right up against the driver's cabin.

Knightsbridge to South Ken.

I tried to unscramble my brain. I'd have had better luck trying to persuade the hen to lay me a fresh one. Av was chatting like he was autistic. He told me that, like he said, shit was about to variously go down/blow up/kick off/kick in. He was excitable to the point of incoherence. I told him to calm down and lay it out for me like a corpse on the slab.

South Ken to Gloucester Road.

He told me that Ali said they were just finalizing their targets and they needed to know which of their young brothers were ready to take part in the PWA's greatest assault on Western anti-civilization so far. Ali patted Av on the shoulder and said if they had more like him the new front would be won sharpish. Av thought this was hilarious. He told me that Ali asked the young brothers if any of them could tell him their greatest weapon. Said young brothers played dumb convincing, for real. Ali said their greatest weapon was the cowardice of the enemy and the ease with which they could be terrified and divided. He said the biggest mistake of many

so-called terrorist organizations was their insistence on attacking major targets like embassies or the fortresses of global
capitalism; high-risk strategies that required excessive planning. He said that these so-called terrorist organizations failed
to understand that the structures of Western anti-civilization
were all pervasive and therefore endlessly vulnerable. He said,
for example, it might be tricky to take down Parliament (just
ask Guy Fawkes) but it was easy and just as effective to blow
up a suburban fast-food joint. He gave it the ha-ha and said
the PWA would even be improving the national diet. What
Ali was saying, Ali said, was that the PWA's targets would be
small, numerous and diffuse. Ali said that the assault was ready
to begin any day now. Ali asked the assembled young brothers
who was ready to join them. Avid Khan, undercover employee
of TA Services, was the first to stick up his hand.

Gloucester Road to Earl's Court.

Av said he'd taken a call that morning, eyes bright and tail
bushy, arranging the meet with the PWA boss/terrorist/
opportunist/nutter. It had been right before he'd rung me. Av
said he knew I'd told him it was game over but I wasn't gonna
miss an opportunity to meet the subject of my objections, was
I? My brain was ticking. I felt like I was watching an alarm
clock for the five minutes before it went off.

I asked Av why the hell our boy would want to go face to
face. Av looked at me like I was slow. My expression was
reflective. He said he was the star pupil, wasn't he, what what
what? Besides, he was making a drop. Tick tock. Tick tock.
The second hand was loud in my head. I said, 'What drop?'

He said he'd met one of the PWA left tenants at Knightsbridge at three fifteen; a white dude who listened to maximum
gangsta rap and called himself Akhbar. He laughed and said,
'What's that about? Geezer's f___ing –'

I interrupted. I said, 'What drop?'

Well, he said. He'd made a pick-up, hadn't he?

I said, 'Pick-up? I thought you said it was a drop?'

He kissed his teeth at me for a third time. My clock was ticking too fast to spare a second to give the stroppy Paki teen the slap he deserved. He told me to chill the f__ out. He said, 'It *was* a pick-up, *now* it's a drop. Pick-up. Drop. You get me?' Sarky, for real.

I said, 'What drop?' I was on loop.

He took the rucksack off his shoulder. He raised his eyebrows at me. My alarm clock went off and I jerked awake and straight into a nightmare. Wakey-wakey. Rise and shine. Earl's Court.

Earl's Court to oblivion.

'Give me the bag.'

'What?'

'Av. Just give me the bag.'

He was laughing. He said, 'Wassup, Tommy man? You look like you just shat yourself, boy.'

I tried to keep my tone even as I explained the following: Av is told he's meeting the opportunist. Av is not meeting the opportunist. The PWA are planning attacks on suburban fast-food joints. The meeting that is not happening is not happening at Hammersmith McDonald's. Said information is multiplied by the fact that Av has just picked up and will drop. Logical conclusion? Strong curse words.

Av slowly handed me the rucksack. His hand was shaking. He looked like he was about to puke. I knew the feeling. I opened the bag. If I was right it was going to take a whole lot more than a length of twine and a Meccano set to put yours truly back together again. I admit I'm often wrong. Unfortunately, this time I was bang on the money.

Av said, 'What is it?'

'Dunno. But it's not clean underwear and a toothbrush.'

Av peered into the bag with me. He tried out a selection of his favourite vocab.

There was a shoebox. There were wires. There was a mobile phone attached to said wires and taped to the lid of said shoebox. Call me daft but I opened the shoebox. I'm daft but nothing blew up in my face. Inside there were more wires, putty and two blocks of what could have passed for New Forest nougat fresh from Lymington high street. Even if I'd eaten the whole lot I couldn't have felt more nauseous.

Av was hyperventilating. He said, 'Do something.'

I said, 'What you want me to do?'

He raised his voice. He said, 'Come on, Tommy man! You're the ex-terrorist!'

There was nobody in our immediate vicinity but he'd spoken loud enough for the whole carriage to hear. I glanced down the aisle. Not an ear was pricked, not a word said, not an eyelid batted. Welcome to London: city of the deaf, dumb and blind.

Av sobbed, 'Something!' And then again, 'Something!' He was getting more than a little hysterical.

I said, 'Shall I cut the red or the blue?' I didn't have any scissors and all the wires were brown. I was getting more than a little gallows.

The train slowed as it emerged overground approaching Barons Court. Then it stopped. Our carriage was in daylight, the rest was still in the tunnel. The driver came over the Tannoy. He said something about an unscheduled delay and could we all remain in our seats and he was sure we'd be moving again shortly. I don't know about Av but I wasn't really listening. I was watching the mobile phone, which was starting to flicker into life. I watched the reception bar click up from zero to five strong. I watched the mobile's clock display click over from 15:57 to 15:58. I looked at Av. For once we were on the same wavelength. He said, 'F—!' I couldn't have put it better myself.

Av took the bag off me and zipped it. I said, 'What you doing?' He stood up. He didn't answer. He was crying.

Now people were staring: businessmen, shoppers, tourists, kids. One 'businessman' was going for his pocket. One 'tourist' got to his feet. Two badges were flashed. I couldn't take it all in. The doors of our carriage slid open. Two black uniforms vaulted in the nearest door SAS-style. They were wearing body armour, helmets, earpieces and radio mics and their fists were wrapped around standard-issue semi-automatics. Av was already past them and into the middle of the carriage but two more cops had also jumped in at the far end. Av was doing the terrified pirouette; brown boy in the ring, tra-la-la-la-la.

I hauled myself vertical. Someone shouted, 'Armed police!'

I said, 'You don't say.' Danger was making me facetious. One of the helmets turned to me. The geezer looked so scared that he scared me right back. He stuck his gun in my face and thrust his fist up sharply into my chin. He didn't hit me hard but I still dropped like a drunk's kebab. What can I say? I was ring rusty. I sat on the floor and dizzily fingered my new bruise.

The 'businessman' with the badge was talking to Av, the 'we're all friends here' routine: 'Just put the bag down, son, and step back. We can all walk away from this. Just put the bag down.'

But Av clung to that bag like it was his only hope. He was muttering to himself, snotty nose and tears streaming down his cheeks. I have since read 'eyewitness reports' claiming that he was reciting verses but I only remember hearing a lot of 'shits' and 'f—s'.

I said, 'Av!' And he looked at me like I might have something useful to say. I didn't have anything useful to say. All I could think was that there was a bomb in that rucksack and it was attached to a mobile phone and we were all going to die when the opportunist or one of his henchmen took the opportunity to make a call.

Fortunately, Av seemed to find some courage in my uselessness like he realized that if anything was going to be done he'd have to be the geezer to do it. He sniffed and he shivered like a kid that's all cried out. He turned to the 'businessman' with the badge so that he had his back to me and when he spoke his voice came like the snow in the carol; deep and crisp and even. 'Bomb,' he said. 'I've got a bomb.' He unzipped the rucksack wide enough for all the coppers to see. One of the coppers swore. One of the passengers began to scream. Av slowly started to make his way towards the other end of the carriage.

The 'tourist' with a badge backed off. The 'businessman' with a badge backed off. The coppers with the shooters backed off. When he passed them, they sort of shuffled after him with their guns raised and aimed like this was all part of the plan and they were actually backing him into a corner (as opposed to down the train). Av was saying things like, 'I've got a bomb! I am holding a f__ing bomb! That's right! You'd better back the f__ up, boy! I'm holding a f__ing bomb.' He sounded half cocky, half insane and half like he was trying to convince himself. If that's too many halves it's because Av was suddenly larger than life.

I tried to get to my feet but I was feeling woozy and my feet weren't co-operating. I started to crawl up behind the coppers for a better view. It wasn't dignified but no one was watching me, were they?

Av reached the connecting door to the next carriage. The way the train was positioned, he was already within the jaws of the tunnel. He kept checking the bomb in the bag. He kept saying, 'It's a f__ing bomb! It's a f__ing bomb!' Occasionally he'd sniff. Occasionally he'd giggle.

He opened the connecting door with one hand. The passengers in the next carriage had already all shifted up the far end. A lot of them were screaming and shouting and now they set off the businessmen, tourists, shoppers and kids in my carriage who had previously, for the most part, been remarkably calm. There was a lot of panic, anger, terror and prayer. Tommy Akhtar's always known that the base human expressions are highly contagious, for real. He saw it in Afghanistan. He could tell you stories.

Av was now a couple of metres into the next carriage. The plods shuffled after him. The 'businessman' with a badge was trying to dialogue again. He was saying, 'Don't be silly, son.'

Av was saying, 'It's a f__ing bomb!'

I crawled forward. I was watching the action through a forest of plod legs. I wondered about the time.

Av clearly wondered the same thing. He peeked into the rucksack again. He was checking for something. He was a kid who knew a thing or two about mobile phones and network coverage. He lifted the rucksack close to his face for a better look. That action switched the screaming up another notch. It was so real we could have been in a movie. The 'businessman' with a badge was getting jittery. He said, 'I'm not gonna tell you again.'

Av lowered the bag. Av licked his lips. Av blinked. Av slowly put the bag down on the floor. Av was about to speak. I heard one, two, three, four armed plods yelp into their radio mics: clear, clear, clear, clear. One plod fired one round. I couldn't see anything. There was a moment of silence long enough to hear a fifteen-year-old body hit the deck. Then there was more screaming. I might even have screamed myself. The plods rushed forward. I was up on my knees. I was speaking in tongues. I found myself face to waist with the 'tourist' with a badge. He introduced my ribs (that were still more than a little fragile) to his size tens. They didn't get along. He only kicked me the once and I spat blood. I'm told he was pulled off by a couple of French students who knew a mismatch when they saw one and had heard a great deal about the British sense of fair play.

24

I was held in a maximum security cell at the Paddington Green factory. I exchanged my clothes for a greaseproof jumpsuit. A uniform plod said I looked like a takeaway. I didn't get it but his mate laughed. I gave them the pacifist Paki grin regardless.

I was locked up pushing thirty-six hours. In that time, I was passed fit by a medical examiner and interviewed twice. The first interview was less than a minute long. Some junior paper shuffler asked me to confirm my name, address, nationality and date of birth. I confirmed. That was that. I half-heartedly tried kicking up a fuss, demanding to know what was going on, my rights, all of that. I was told to shut up. I shut up.

The second interview must have been a full day later. I guessed it was early morning but I didn't have a watch or the benefit of natural light. By now I was feeling more than a little various. This one was with the posh bird called Jones and Aldridge, her mick sidekick. It lasted all of ten minutes. She thanked me for my assistance. She apologized for my latest beating. She said such mistakes were regrettable but often unavoidable in such confusing situations. She told me they wouldn't hold me long. She said they were just processing the paperwork. I came over obstreperous and suggested several creative destinations for said paperwork.

Aldridge got to his feet and told me to calm down. I wouldn't calm down. I asked Jones what had happened to Av. She looked nonplussed, which did nothing for my pulse. I said, 'The boy I was with. Avid Khan.' She looked nonplussed again. I said, 'Is he alive?'

She glanced at Aldridge. She glanced at her watch. Apparently I was boring her. She said yes he was alive. She said he'd been in surgery and he was still unconscious but they were confident he'd make a full recovery. She sounded like a recorded message. If she'd told me to press the hash key to return to the main menu I wouldn't have been entirely surprised. She said that he was receiving the best possible care and when he was sufficiently strong he would be transferred to a secure location pending further investigation.

I said, 'What?'

Jones repeated herself. Her tone was irritating me. I questioned her sanity, intellect and parentage. She questioned my attitude. She told me she understood I was angry but we were on the same side here. Warning bells rang, serious. I needed to stay in control.

I reminded her that I'd told her about Av and how he was working for me. I reminded her that I'd been none too shabby with the info. I reminded her that cricket was a team game and I'd batted for the team so what about her. I reminded her that Av was a born and bred Brit and fifteen years old.

She told me that since he was still unconscious they hadn't yet established his identity. I snorted at that. I couldn't help it. She ignored me. She said the facts were these: an as yet unidentified suspect was restrained using necessary force at 3.59 p.m. on the day in question on a Piccadilly Line underground train while threatening the use of a bomb. Upon his arrest it was discovered that he was indeed in possession of a simply constructed device built from an as yet unidentified plastic explosive (presumed Russian) primed for remote detonation. She smiled at me. I could surely agree, therefore, that it was natural for the subject to remain in custody but this did not mean that he would not receive first-rate medical attention.

Self-control was proving tricky, for real. I was tenderizing my gums with my molars. I said, 'What about Av's mum? Does she even know what's going on?'

Jones looked at Aldridge. They seemed to come to a decision. Jones told me that since I had been so co-operative she could confirm that a Mrs Khan had been brought in for questioning.

'But has she seen him?'

She couldn't confirm that.

I shook my head. My skull hurt, my ribs hurt, my jaw hurt. Now my gums hurt too. I was suddenly knackered. I felt like the Don after a ton against Larwood and Voce. The opposition – and they were the opposition – might have been playing by the rules but they'd abandoned the spirit of the game.

I said, 'This is bullshit. You know that Av is Av, you know he's a kid and you know this is bullshit.'

'Tommy,' she said, 'I don't think you understand the . . . the *gravity* of the situation, if you will. And why should you when we've kept you here since your arrest? You are therefore unaware that the attack on the tube was far from an isolated occurrence. Rather, it was part of a co-ordinated series of bombings across the South East: one of five, in fact, all within minutes of each other. The PWA also hit fast-food franchises in East Grinstead and Cheam, a video shop in Luton and a minimart on the Seven Sisters Road.'

I took this in. It didn't take long. It made sense and was hardly a surprise. Five gullible kids. Five bogus meetings with the opportunist. Four successful phone calls. Four successful detonations. I said, 'How many dead?'

'Twelve. Including the suicide bombers. And three others who are still touch and go. It would've been many more but these were, shall we say, rudimentary devices.'

'Suicide bombers? I doubt they were suicide bombers.'

Jones raised the painted lines where her eyebrows were

supposed to be. 'They blew themselves up. What nomenclature would you consider more appropriate?'

I shrugged. What with my latest kicking, shrugging hurt all over again. I let it pass. I couldn't see any point trying to explain. Besides, Jones wasn't finished.

'That's why Avid Khan (if that is indeed his name) is important to us. He's the only frontline operative we caught alive, thanks, I might add, to your information. If he was working for you and answers our questions satisfactorily, I'm sure he'll be back with his . . . his mother, you say? . . . back with his mother very soon.'

Av as a frontline operative? Ha-ha. Only internal. I said, 'So you're expecting more trouble?'

'I don't think so. We've picked up the PWA hierarchy.'

'Al-Dubayan?'

'Not yet. But we will. We've got his aides and they'll talk. Take a fundamentalist out of his cadre and they tend to enjoy conversation.'

'Fundamentalist? Fundamentalist what?'

'What do you mean?'

'I mean, fundamentalist what?' Sure I was knackered, but Jones was so full of the brown and foul that she was giving me a second wind. I was changing roles like a one-man show. 'Islamic fundamentalists?'

'Quite.'

'But they're not, are they?' I wasn't confrontational. I was sincere and questioning. I was now acting the suck-up schoolkid, hungry for knowledge.

'I take your point. Although I'm sure many of them are, in this context I take the term to mean that they are fundamental in their opposition to our way of life.'

I tried to smile. It didn't work. What with my sore jaw it was just as painful as shrugging. Probably no bad thing since it left my options open for the next role. I had to decide how to play this. I could, of course, have asked her what the hell she was talking about. I could have asked her if she'd listened to herself lately. But I decided to play it elbow high and back where it came from. There is, you will be unsurprised to learn, a decent cricket principle here: survive one delivery and you're still there for the next, know what I mean? 'Right,' I said. 'So it's been a successful operation?'

'Yes, I think it has.'

I shook my head. I pulled a tired face. It was just about the only expression I hadn't tried. It was just about the only expression that didn't hurt. 'Twelve dead, though. I mean . . .' What did I mean? I didn't mean anything. I left it hanging.

Jones sighed. Jones smiled. Jones picked her words slowly like this was fridge poetry. 'You have been very helpful, Tommy, and I believe we understand each other and there's no reason to suppose you might not be helpful again.' As questions go, hers was barely interrogative. I blinked at her. As answers go, mine was barely affirmative. She continued, 'Of course, the deaths of innocent civilians on British soil is a tragedy. Of course, I wonder whether, had we been able to act sooner, these awful murders might have been avoided. But I'll be candid with you, Tommy: I sincerely believe we have escaped lightly and if the events of two days ago, horrific though they were, increase understanding of the undeniable realities of our present situation, then the victims will at least have died . . . or, rather, if you will, will not have died . . .'

I prompted stage left: 'In vain.'

'Quite. We are in a war situation. We are fortunate that much of this war is currently being fought abroad. But we are not so fortunate that this has led to increasing apathy and even, shall we say, negative enthusiasm among sections of the media, government and, indeed, population at large. Nonetheless the dangers here at home are, as you and I know, just as real and it is of paramount importance that we acknowledge this and allocate adequate resources to address the developing situation.'

I was staring at her. I couldn't help myself. I blinked again. I kept my tone even, noncommittal, unquestioning. 'Everyone should be scared.'

'Scared? No. We want people to go about their daily business as normal. All we hope for is heightened awareness of the threat from the PWA and similar fundamentalist groups. All we hope for is to protect our way of life.'

I fixed on a point somewhere over her shoulder while I nodded. I thought about her definition of the word 'scared' and her professed desire for 'people to go about their daily business'. I remembered Afghanistan. People (including a certain Tommy Akhtar) went about their daily business in a state of permanent terror. It sounded to me like she wanted people to be scared. I thought about her use of language: euphemistic, for real. I wondered if she believed what she was saying. I wondered if she even understood what she was saying. I thought about 'our way of life', hers and mine. I wondered if we shared one. I thought about my way of life as, variously, a Ugandan-Indian, a Paki, an immigrant, a Londoner, an Englishman. I wondered if it was worth protect-ing. I would have shrugged but it hurt.

I remembered Paradowski, the CIA man who talked more crap than Gundappa after six pints and an eighth. It seemed that Jones had read the same primer. I started to make some loose connections but I couldn't snap them together. I guess years of alcohol abuse combined with recent beatings to stop a lifetime of low-level cynicism working its irrefutable logic.

I licked my lips. Aldridge produced a packet of fags. 'You want a smoke?' Apart from telling me to calm down, it was the first time he'd spoken. So now I was allowed to smoke. So now we were all buddy-buddy.

I took one and he sparked it. It was a Silky. I've sucked straws more satisfying but in the absence of trusted friends it would have to do. I exhaled. I said, 'So what happened to Chip?'

Jones said, 'Who?'

'Parawotsit. Paradiddle. Paranoid. Whatever. The American geezer.'

'Mr Paradowski? He was only briefly seconded to our operation as part of an inter-agency skills initiative.'

'Right.' I nodded. More alarm bells were ding-a-linging. They were tolling so consistently I wondered if I had tinnitus. 'An inter-agency what what? Right. If you ask me, Chip could use an interpersonal skills initiative. But you're not gonna ask me, are you?'

She smiled. She shrugged. She stood up; the Mick too. I'd had my ten minutes. We all shook hands. We exchanged pleasantries so fake it was a struggle not to laugh. She told me I had her number. She was right in more ways than one. She told me they'd need to interview me again at some future point. I said they knew where to find me. I considered raising the Av issue again – fifteen years old, bullet wounds, unwitting political prisoner, all of that. I decided there was no point. If he lived to tell them, he'd have tales for thug-lites from Chiswick to Chislehurst.

I was taken back to my cell. I paced another half-hour. The junior paper shuffler came by and swapped me an oversized sweatshirt, undersized jeans and brand new Marks and Sparks underwear for my greaseproof jumpsuit. No sign of my own clothes. I figured I'd been had. Then he signed me out.

I walked out into the car park. I took a few deep breaths and the air tasted good. I cracked my neck and my knuckles (excepting the broken one), index to pinky. I looked around. I saw what looked like Gunny's old Merc parked on the far side. Maybe he'd come to find me in a fit of fraternal love. That didn't seem so likely. I hit the streets on foot. It was morning rush-hour only nobody was rushing. I would have caught a bus but there were body searches before you could get on and the queues were crazy. London was on high alert. London was scared.

I switched on my phone. I had a message from Donnelly asking where I'd got to. He was cagey. His tone suggested he'd already figured the answer. Donnelly could wait. I belled Phoenecia. I said, 'Gundappa?'

A voice said, 'This is not Gundappa.'

'Who's that?'

'Christopher.'

'Swiss? Swiss, it's Tommy. Where's Gunny?'

There was a pause. Then, 'He's not here.'

'Right. Any danger of a car? I'm in –'

He interrupted. 'I'm sorry, Tommy. We have nothing right now.'

'Really? OK. How long?'

There was another pause. There was a sigh. 'I'm sorry, Mr T. I think it is two hours at least.'

'Right.'

He smacked uneasy, for real. I didn't dwell on it.

I figured I'd have to catch a black cab. There were plenty flying past, lights winking, but it was twenty minutes before one stopped. I'm sure this had nothing to do with recent events, nor the colour of my skin, let alone my monstrous appearance. Yeah, right.

The geezer who eventually picked me up looked unreconstructed, serious. From the back seat, his number-two cut and the folds of skin that rolled on up his neck smacked British bulldog. He had yesterday's *Standard* on the dashboard. The headline read, 'Terror Threat Strangles Capital'. I knew he'd have something to say. I sat back and thought of England.

He gave me his world-view. So much for my assumptions. He blamed the media. He blamed the government. He was my kind of guy.

He asked where I was from. I said Chiswick. He said he meant my parents. I said Uganda. He told me he had an eight-year-old. He told me his son's best friend was from Bangladesh. He said, 'Nice kid, nice family, all of that.' He told me that yesterday he'd caught the two boys having a right old barney. Turned out that best friend was throwing a wobbly because he was fed up of playing the terrorist and being repeatedly blown up, shot or arrested. He said, 'I mean, what's that all about? Where do they get that from? It's not from me, is it? In my day we were happy with cowboys and Indians. No offence.' None taken.

When he let me out we shook hands. He waved his paper at me. He said, 'I tell my boy you can't judge a book by its cover but look what I'm up against, know what I mean?' I felt guilty and tipped 20 per cent. We bonded patriotic.

25

Swiss and Yusuf were hanging outside Phoenecia. I said, 'You all right, Swiss? Yusuf?' They looked embarrassed. Yusuf turned away. Swiss raised a hand uncertainly. Something was up. Whatever.

I clocked Khan's opposite. It was lights off and grille padlocked. It looked totally unfamiliar. I realized I'd rarely seen it without a bunch of proper little gangsters killing time out front and never shut up before dark. I felt sick to my stomach and more exhausted than ever.

I let myself in to TA Services. The stairs looked testing so I left the door on the latch in case of visitors. I figured it was no longer likely that Al-Dubayan would be coming Tommy-hunting, what with all forces, constabulary and clandestine, out to get him.

My flat and office were still suffering the after-effects of the plod makeover. This was no surprise but it hardly lifted spirits. I considered tidying up. I considered settling back with old friends. Whatever the time of day, guess which option got the nod?

Benny gave me clarity, Turk gave me the guilts. I remembered how Mrs K said she'd picked it up for me special.

I checked my messages. I had three. They were reverse chronological.

First up was Donnelly. It was the same as on my mobile. Second was some dude who left his name and number. I heard confidence, middle-age and wealth. I figured he wanted help with his divorce. I noted the digits absentmindedly like I actually intended to call him back. I was going through the motions. The third churned my guts. It was Mrs K. It was from a couple of days back. She didn't know where Av was. It was getting late. She'd been watching the newsflashes of three or was it four bombs exploding. She was fretting. She was sorry to interrupt my undoubtedly busy schedule but she just wanted to enquire if her son was with me because if he was then at least she could stop worrying. I raised my glass and toasted the Khan family. I could tell you my heart was broken because it was. But it had already been broken a long time.

There was a knock at my office door. I hadn't heard anyone come in the waiting room and my churning guts suddenly lurched. What if it was Al-Dubayan after all? I didn't have any way to defend myself so I thought of exoticmelody and 'come to Mummy'. If it was my time, I'd go with a smile. I said, 'Who's there?'

It wasn't the opportunist. It was a teenage poppet modelling a familiar pastel blue tracksuit. It was clearly a favourite. If it hadn't been for the outfit I might not have recognized her. Maybe it was her hair. She had yet another new look: plaits scraped off her face, black-girl style. More likely it was her face; the absence of slap and the circles rubbed raw pink around her eyes. She looked fourteen years old. I considered it an improvement. She was fourteen years old.

She said, 'I'm sorry.' She gulped a sob. Then, 'I'm sorry. I saw you come in.'

I said, 'Michelle.' It felt somehow undignified to be drinking and smoking in the face of such evident grief so I downed Turk and stubbed Benny. I stood up. I said, 'Michelle. Sit down.' She flopped into a chair. I sat down again. She looked at me. She started crying. I realized that I wasn't going to hack this without a drink and a smoke so I poured another and sparked another. Buy me a car sticker: 'Pragmatists do it as and when.'

She said, 'I'm sorry.'

I tried variations of 'no problem', 'there there' and 'take your time'. I couldn't get any of them to sound right but she pulled herself together on her own.

Michelle said she didn't know what was going on. She asked if I knew where Av was. I told her I didn't. She said he could be dead or anything. I told her he wasn't dead. She asked how I knew. I told her I just did. She asked me what happened. I took a mouthful and had a drag. Fortunately she had more to say.

Michelle said that after the bombings, when Av didn't come home, Mrs K called the police and everything. She said she'd waited up the whole night with Mrs K. She said that Mrs K was like a mother to her. She said they'd come the next morning and taken Av's mum away in a flash car. She said Mrs K had been screaming that she just wanted to know where her son was and she thought he was with Tommy Akhtar and who was going to look after Benzi? I drank and smoked. I was Tommy Akhtar, Private Dick.

Michelle said that she called Mrs K's sister, whose number was on a sticker by the till. She hadn't known what else to do. Mrs K's brother-in-law came for Benzi. She said that she ran to Phoenecia. She hadn't known what else to do. She said that my brother was kind and he told her he knew a lawyer. I poured another and lit another. She said that nobody had been at the shop since yesterday. She said that Gunny hadn't been at Phoenecia since yesterday. She said she didn't know what was going on. She said it again: 'I dunno what's going on, Tommy.'

I got up. I walked round the desk and stood in front of her and opened my arms. I said, 'Come here.' She fell against me and I stroked her hair in so far as it was possible with her tight new plaits. I said, 'It's my fault. But it'll be all right. Serious. I promise it'll be all right. Av'll be all right.' Rash promises and desperate situations walk hand in hand to God knows where.

She wept into my chest. She squeezed me so tight that my bust ribs protested and my eyes began to water. She looked up at me. She thought I was crying for Av. I wish I had been. She trusted me more than ever. She said, 'I know it will.'

'What?'

She said, 'I know it'll be all right.'

We parted uneasily. I was embarrassed. I poured myself a Turk. I poured her a Turk. I gave it to her. She said, 'It's a bit early for me.' She was fourteen going on forty. I said, 'It'll do you good. Calm you down.' Who was I kidding?

She asked for a cigarette. I gave her one. She smoked and sipped in silence. Occasionally I said, 'It'll be all right.' Who was I trying to convince?

She gave me her phone number. I scribbled it on my pad. She told me to call her as soon as I knew anything. I said I would. I had no idea what I'd know or when.

She dabbed her eyes with a sleeve. She sniffed. She asked me if I had a tissue. I didn't. I said, 'Come through to the flat.'

She spent five minutes in the bathroom. I spent five minutes trying to resurrect my telly from its prone position on the carpet. I was fighting a losing battle. When she came out, Michelle said, 'Let me help.' We had the TV back in its rightful position just like that. I said, 'Thanks.'

She stifled a giggle. She said, 'You look terrible.'

'Thanks.'

She was suddenly calm, verging cheerful. It seemed the situation looked rosy now that Tommy Akhtar was back on it. Yeah, right. She made for the door. She said, 'Thanks, Tommy.' I shrugged. It hurt. Karma. I said, 'Soon as I know anything.'

I smoked. My guts were chewing. I went into my bedroom, sat on the edge of my bed and looked out the window. As I sat down, exoticmelody's scent wafted up from the sheets; thick and sweet and fresh. I was tempted to bury my face in those bedclothes. I wasn't no freakydeak. I just wanted to lose myself in a smell other than my own. I resisted the temptation and peered out at London.

Was it my imagination or was it different somehow? I figured that it looked peculiarly uncertain, nervous, temporary. Even if it was my imagination did that make the perception less real? *Little Book of Tommy*, #33: don't communities, cities, countries and whatever primarily exist in the imaginations of their residents? I shook my head. This was no time to come the pseud.

Nonetheless, I did figure that something had changed, for real. London was now a city where gullible kids carrying bombs blew up in your local neighbourhood. That was a shift. Check the understatement. It struck me that the PWA had got their way. It struck me that Jones and Paradowski had got their way too. They were all on the same side. London was scared.

It made me think of Sir Garfield Sobers. I grew up with his 365 against Pakistan in '58 as the benchmark for Test batsmanship. It was a record and one that stood for so long that it seemed like it would never be broken; in fact, it began to seem like it *could* never be broken, like 365 was the pinnacle of human batting, a run for every day of the year. Then Brian Lara broke it in '94 and thirty-six years of received wisdom, consensus and myth was suddenly shattered. Lara's new record stood for a decade before it was broken by Matthew Hayden. Hayden's record stood for less than six months before it was broken by Lara again.

Certain commentators have written that the game has

changed: Test batsmen score quicker these days and there are some weaker teams so the opportunities for massive innings have increased. Certain commentators are missing the point. The point is that when Lara creamed England's finest to all points Antiguan in '94, he crossed an invisible line of the imagination, and when it had been crossed once, it was a whole lot easier to cross it again. So London was never a city where opportunists exploded kids on your doorstep; not because it couldn't happen but because it didn't. And then it did. So London was different.

I didn't know what to do with myself. I looked at the Turk and considered drinking it all away. Typically self-hatred helps me to drink; this time it stopped me. I couldn't condone blotto when Av was lying half dead who knows where and it was all my fault. I sighed. I paced. I took a shower. The itching was preferable to the pain.

It was mid-morning. I switched on the telly. I zoned in to one of those magazine shows that had been given a post-traumatic spin. An ex-MI5 officer, now author of several bestselling novels, was offering practical advice on how to respond to terrorist attack. He waxed obvious and plugged his books while the his and hers TV goons nodded along in awe. They thanked him and plugged his books some more. They said they'd be right back after the news with the latest hit from the latest band formed on the latest reality show, plus tips for concealing your cellulite, plus a phone-in: 'Islam – friend or foe?' It seemed Jones had got her way again: people were going about their business more or less as normal.

I watched the news insert. It's an unusual experience when there are only two items and they both concern you and yours. Check my powers of understatement one more time.

First was what was billed as a 'terror-bombing update'. Police had made further arrests bringing the total number to forty. They flashed up a picture of a black guy they'd brought in who was named as Ali Haqid. He was described as thirty years old, of Afro-Caribbean origin. He was described as a 'ring-leader'. I assumed this was the geezer Av had described as a 'mad c–'. I took in his photo, fascinated. Behind seventies-style specs, his eyes were wide and crazy. Then again, no one looks their best in a mugshot. The report cut to obligatory interviews with his Harlesden neighbours, who spouted obligatory soundbites. They were shocked. He'd kept himself to himself. He'd always seemed very polite.

Cut to police press conference right outside the factory I'd left little more than an hour before. A senior copper in fancy uniform said they were almost certain every attack had been carried out by the PWA. Senior copper said they were almost certain they'd picked up the majority of the group and they were now merely involved in a mopping-up exercise. Senior copper shuffled his papers. Senior copper said they were almost certain that the PWA were not in any way religiously motivated or attached to wider terrorist networks.

I blinked. I asked the TV to say that again. The TV was uncooperative. Had the geezer actually said something worth hearing? He had. No religious motives. No connections to other terrorists. The camera panned the faces of assembled hacks. It was too little too late. Nobody was listening anyway. Today's editorials were already circulating. Tomorrow's head-lines were already written.

Cut back to the suit in the studio and we were already on to 'And in other news . . .' Cut to footage of an all-too-familiar Brixton terrace, a small crowd milling outside, plod posted on the door. Cut to Tommy Akhtar's living room and yours truly frozen to the spot, jaw-dropped and numb.

'And in other news, a man has been shot dead in a house in south London. According to a police spokesman, the victim was found early this morning by a neighbour. Police have yet to establish an exact time of death but suspect it was late last night. The spokesman said it bore all the hallmarks of a contract killing and they haven't ruled out the involvement of organized crime. The victim's identity will not be released until the family have been informed.'

I called Cal Donnelly. He went off on one before I could get a word in. I believe he swore at me. I believe he called me an IC2 prick. I don't remember. I told him Farzad had been murdered. That's how you shut someone up. I heard my heartbeat. He said, 'That was your dad?' He told me it wasn't his patch. He told me he hadn't heard anything about it. He told me he'd meet me there.

I went downstairs. Yusuf and Swiss had been joined outside Phoenecia by Irish and Big John. They were all looking at me funny: one measure sheepish to two measures vexed.

I said, 'Where's Gundappa?'

There was a moment's silence, like I was speaking French or something. Then Big John said, 'We haven't seen him, Mr T. He went yesterday with Mrs Khan.'

'I need a car.' *J'ai besoin d'un taxi.* No response.

Big John approached me. He was wearing an expression like a kid who's just caught his old man in bed with the nanny. 'Tommy,' he said, 'what happened to Avid? We know he work for you but he just a kid. Gunny said you got him f__ed up. You know I think your brother is w–er but I see what happened to you Tommy, remember? And Avid just a kid.'

He wanted me to tell him that Gundappa had it wrong. He wanted me to tell him that it wasn't true. I couldn't do that. I said, 'I need a car. They killed Farzad.'

26

Big John took me himself. I sat in the back to discourage conversation. Big John did ask a couple of questions but I played monosyllabic and he soon got the picture.

Farzad's house was better than TV. It must have been because people had even come outside to stand around, shake their heads and gossip, and watch the succession of forensics guys coming and going like tail-enders on a green top. I asked Big John if he'd mind waiting. He said, 'Sure, Mr T.'

I got out of the car. I stood around for a bit, hovering on the pavement on the other side of the road among the knots of local audience. I wondered where Donnelly was. I wondered if I should go and introduce myself to the plods standing guard, say, 'I'm the family. Inform me.' But I was feeling fragile and I'd had more than enough of the Old Bill just lately. I fired a Benny.

A large woman with a thick Jamaican accent and a head-scarf looked me up and down. She said, 'Terrible thing when you're not safe in your own street.' I agreed with her. I said, 'Serious.' I felt some big bubble swell inside me. I guess it was grief and it was pressing on my lungs and left me short of breath. My eyes were prickling. I turned away. I sucked hard on my cigarette, vengeful like it was to blame and I planned to smoke it to death. The weak-willed only fight battles they can win.

Farzad's front door opened and Donnelly appeared chatting to a fellow plain-clothes. I crossed the road towards him. I said, 'Cal.'

Donnelly saw me. He touched his colleague on the arm. He hurried over. He said, 'It's not your dad.'

'What?'

'It's not your dad. Farzad. The man wasn't Farzad.'

'What do you mean?' I started crying. I couldn't help myself. I'm soft as a toff. I tried to make like I wasn't. I looked away and sniffed. I flicked my butt. I lit another straight away.

Donnelly had his notebook out. He said, 'The victim's name was Peter Ellington, fifty-eight years old, of twenty-three Concannon Road. Just round the corner.'

'Who's Peter Ellington?'

Donnelly shook his head.

'Where's Farzad?'

Donnelly shook his head and raised his eyebrows. 'That's what we'd like to know.'

I tried to gather myself. I asked him details.

It was a professional job. They'd come in the back, jimmying the gate and then cutting a neat hole in one of the glass panels of the kitchen door. It would've taken a minute tops. Peter Ellington had been watching TV. He must have heard the entrance and known it was dodgy because he appeared to have gone at them swinging a tin of paint. They shot him once in the head.

They hadn't left straight away. They seemed to have been looking for something or, more likely, someone. They hadn't ransacked the house and it didn't look like they'd taken anything but every cupboard door was open and the beds upturned. It smacked calm and methodical. They exited by the front door. They were clearly confident because they left it swinging. A neighbour got nosy bright and early. She saw the front door wide and went exploring. She screamed down the phone to the operator on 999.

I said, 'They?'

Donnelly said, 'What?'

'You said *they*. You know there was more than one of them?'

He played sheepish. 'That's just what we say. It could've been a he, it could have been a she, it could have been a they. That's just what we say.'

Everyone thinks they're in a movie. That's just what I say.

I nodded. I had a thought. Don't call it instinct, call it experience: this is what I do for a living. I said, 'Peter Ellington. What was he watching?'

Donnelly looked at me quizzical. This was what he did for a living too. 'Why?'

'Just tell me. What was he watching?'

'There was a video in the machine. Some old game of cricket. England/West Indies.'

I said, 'Peter Ellington. Trinidad Pete.'

'What?'

'The geezer's name: Trinidad Pete. A friend of the old man's.'

'You think they fell out?'

I glanced at him. 'What? And Farzad popped him Mafia style?' Was he taking the piss? 'It must have been Al-Dubayan or his boys.'

He looked at me, eyes dubious. He asked if he could ponce a cigarette. I sprang him one and sparked it. He said, 'I'm trying to give up,' and then dragged hungrily. He said, 'So you reckon Al-Dubayan was going after Farzad and Trinidad Pete just got in the way? Why the f—— would Al-Dubayan wanna kill Farzad?' I'd expected this. His tone washed 'Who's the paranoid Paki?'

I said, 'Not Farzad. Exoticmelody.' Funny. I'd only remembered she existed in saying her name. I'm sure she'd have been flattered.

'Who?'

'Melody Chase. The tom. She's been staying with Farzad. She's the opportunist's ebony fantasy.'

'Who's the opportunist?'

'Al-Dubayan.'

'The terrorist?'

'Right. Whatever.'

Donnelly looked unconvinced. He'd already sucked his Benny to the butt. He could teach me a thing or two about vindictive smoking.

'Same question, my immigrant friend,' he said. 'Why the hell would Al-Dubayan want to kill the hooker?'

I thought about it. I didn't know the answer. I tried, 'Because she knows what he looks like.' But Donnelly laughed at that. He pointed out that everybody who owned a TV or bought a newspaper knew what the opportunist looked like. He suggested that the fundamentalist probably had other shit on his mind right now. He pointed out that the murder was strictly pro and everything the terrorist had done so far sang not so much amateur as total karaoke. He suggested that yours truly was a small-time IC2 prick who'd got mixed up with the big boys but needed to get back to chasing strays and errant husbands. He got no argument from me.

I said, 'So who's your suspect, then?'

'It's not my case and it's not my dad's friend lying dead.' He shrugged at me. 'You're the detective. Go detect.' I let it pass.

When we'd both presumed Farzad was dead, I'd been dazed and Donnelly sensitized, so we'd been shimmying that awkward tiptoe dance typical of the English (strange considering our respective backgrounds). But now that Farzad was presumed alive (if missing), we quickly slipped back into our usual dazzling repartee and it felt a whole lot more comfortable.

I asked him if he'd help me find the old man and the tom. He said he'd love to but he had to get back to the factory.

I said, 'What if they've been kidnapped?'

He said he didn't think that was so likely. He pointed to the police car outside Farzad's house and told me to talk to the boys in blue. I protested. I told him he was my tame copper. He protested. He told me I was an IC2 prick.

He said he had to get back to the factory because all leave had been cancelled, what with certain fundamentalist terrorist opportunists blowing up chip shops, chicken shacks and burger joints. He paused. He noted my new bruising round the jaw. He asked me when I was going to tell him the whole story. I told him he could read my autobiography, *Tommy Akhtar, Private I*. I'd even give him a signed copy.

He asked me what happened to the kid. I said, what kid? He said the kid I'd sent undercover into the PWA. I didn't feel so witty. I said I'd tell him another time.

He said he should go. He pointed out the detective he'd been chatting to earlier and said that was the guy I needed to talk to. He told me I could drop his name and blokey might find it charming.

I said, 'Thanks, Cal. You sure you don't wanna hang around?'

He said it sounded like a dream come true but he needed to get back to his desk. He had a load of paperwork to clear and he'd sworn to the missus he'd finish his shift on the dot. He came over confidential. He told me Julie had come back from her sister's but he was on final, final warning. She'd made him agree to counselling and their first session was that evening. He said he figured it was all bullshit but he was keeping that opinion to himself.

I fed him another fag. I said, 'You know what I think, Cal? You don't need counselling. You just need to get rid of the widescreen, quit the sauce and drop a sprog sharpish.'

For a moment I thought he was going to punch me. His eyes blazed an Irish temper. But he satisfied himself with an Irish chuckle. He said, 'That what you think, my immigrant friend?' More chuckles. A quick puff. 'The day I take advice from Tommy Akhtar is the day I admit defeat.'

Whatever. I gave it the ha-ha in solidarity with the self-deluded everywhere. He made for his motor.

I did my times tables. I got stuck on six thirteens. I thought about Farzad. I remembered his hundred in Hounslow, the way he swept the leg spinner to sleep, the most boring innings in the history of West London club cricket: Farzad the pragmatist. Like father, like son. I had a half-thought.

I made for Concannon Road. I walked past Big John parked up and reading the paper. The terror headlines promised nightmares for sensitive kiddywinks. Big John saw me coming and started to get out of the car. I waved at him not to bother and showed him five fingers for five minutes. He nodded and gave me the questioning thumbs-up. I figured I should let him in on what was going on so I stopped and he buzzed down the window.

I said, 'It wasn't Farzad.'

'What?'

'It wasn't Dad who was murdered. I made a mistake. It was Trinidad Pete.'

'The black man?' He pointed to Farzad's garden wall. 'The black man who sits just here?'

'Yeah.'

'That is good.' Big John shook his head. 'But poor Trinidad Pete.'

But poor Trinidad Pete. I felt more ashamed of myself. I hadn't thought that was possible. I said, 'Yeah.'

I said, 'I'm just gonna check something. Five minutes, OK?'

Big John gave me the thumbs-up and a supportive smile. He still wanted to like me. I still wanted to like myself too but I was both used to and anticipating disappointment.

I turned into Concannon Road. I was working a hunch. I got to number twenty-three and kept right on walking. It seemed my hunch was no good.

Trinidad's gaff was crawling with coppers. Of course it was.

I went fifty yards past and then stopped for a ponder. My half-thought had come to half nothing and I didn't have no others. I didn't have nothing to ponder so I pondered that.

Then I heard a familiar voice say, 'Tommy boy,' right behind me. I spun round and I wasn't sure whether to laugh or cry so I tried a bit of both.

Farzad was lurking behind a white van. He was wearing a baseball cap and this enormous overcoat that must have belonged, I was guessing, to Trinidad Pete. He looked ridiculous. As disguises went it was the equivalent of whistling to play innocent, Stan Laurel-style. In fact, change Farzad's baseball cap for a bowler and what did I get?

He said, 'I'm in disguise.'

I said, 'You don't say.'

He said, 'Come here. Let me look at you.'

I went to him and he kissed my cheek. Then he prodded at my chin. 'You been beaten up again?' He tutted. Then he slapped me around the face. It tickled. I would've laughed only it wasn't funny. He said, 'What are you doing, Tommy boy? What are you *doing*?' Now *he* started crying. He made no sound and his breathing was even but there were tears streaming down his cheeks.

I said, 'Farzad . . .'

He shook his head. 'No, Tommy boy. I know you think "Who's this stupid old git?" but they killed Trinidad and it's your fault. That black bastard was my best friend and they killed him and it's all your fault. You're a numbskull. I knew Gundappa was an idiot but at least he only harms himself. But you? Why do you always want to play silly buggers? You're a bleeding numbskull and dangerous to boot.'

I didn't know what he was on about. I suspected he had a point since right then I was ready to take the blame for everything from Palestine to global warming but I still didn't know what he was on about. I said, 'What are you on about?'

'They killed him, son.'

'Who killed him?'

'What do you mean who killed him? *They* killed him. Who do you think?'

He'd raised his voice. I checked the cop-fest down the road but no one was looking. But I told him to calm down nonetheless. He said he was calm. I asked him to tell me what had happened. He said he didn't know what had happened. I asked him to tell me anyway. I said, 'Just start at the beginning.'

He looked at me, disdainful to the top. He said, 'Don't patronize me, Tommy boy. I'm a sad old man, not an idiot.'

Farzad told me that Gundappa had rung him yesterday bright and early. Little brother only ever rang the old man when big brother had screwed up. He said that Avid had gone missing and Mrs K had been arrested. He gave Farzad the benefit of his considered: he told the old man that big bruv must be to blame so it was lucky that little bruv knew a good lawyer. He said he was about to head down the nick himself. He said it was the least he could do considering the disgraceful behaviour of yours truly. Yours truly could just picture how Gundappa must have loved it: the opportunity to slag me while playing local don added up to double fun.

Farzad said he'd been feeling doubtful ever since I told him I'd spoken to MI5 again. The phone call from Gundappa swung it. I pressed him but he didn't elaborate. He said, 'Just doubtful.'

He said he'd decided it was time for a holiday so him and exoticmelanie went knocking round Trinidad Pete's and asked if they could stay a couple of nights.

I said, 'Melody.'

He said, 'Yes, yes.'

He said Trinidad was only too happy of the company.

Last night they were drinking. Trinidad had climbed inside a bottle and decided he wanted to watch cricket. Trouble was, Trinidad didn't have a TV let alone a video, let alone a collection that spanned most of the best matches of the last twenty years. Trinidad suggested they went round the old man's. The old man suggested that wasn't the best idea. Melanie pleaded exhaustion and said she was going to bed anyway.

Trinidad was half cut and half feisty. He said he wanted to watch cricket and that's what he was going to do. Farzad gave him the keys and said it was up to him.

Farzad was woken by the screams. He went out at the sirens. He caught the Brixton wildfire. His mental arithmetic was flawless. He woke exoticmelanie and they were out of Trinidad's in ten minutes flat.

I asked him where they went. He said it was none of my business. I asked him if Melody was safe. He looked at me squonk. He said, yeah, she was safe.

He was silent, like telling the story had knackered him right out.

I said, 'And?'

Farzad said, 'And? And nothing.'

I stared at him. I was missing something and Farzad wasn't offering no clues. I said, 'So what?'

'What?'

'So who did it?'

He sighed. He said, 'You're the detective, Tommy boy.'

This is a hazard of my profession. Doctors get 'I've got a terrible back', stand-ups get 'Tell us a joke', investigators get 'You're the detective'.

Farzad muttered to himself. He said, 'That's what happens when you raise an Englishman. They think like an Englishman.'

I was exasperated. 'What's that supposed to mean, Farzad? Stop with the gnomic.'

He smiled. He patted me on the shoulder. 'You may not think straight but your vocabulary is flawless.'

'Dad . . .'

'I believe it was your metaphor, Tommy boy. And as far as I remember it was most eccentric. I think you said it was a triangular tournament, something like that: yourself, Azmat Al-Dubayan and the . . . I recall the phrase you used was "intelligence boys".'

'Dad . . .'

'Listen, son. It wasn't Mr Al-Dubayan who killed Trinidad Pete and I trust it wasn't you, so who does that leave?'

I pondered. I said, 'You think MI5 killed Trinidad Pete? Why?' I answered my own question. 'They were after Melody? But why? Farzad, that doesn't make no sense . . .'

'*Any* sense. "This is the sort of language up with which I will not put." Your vocabulary may be impeccable but your use of the double negative is distressing.'

'It doesn't make any sense. What does exoticmelody know that I don't? Nothing. And they just had me banged up. If I knew something, why would they let me go?'

Farzad shrugged. 'You're the detective.'

He started to walk away.

I said, 'Where are you going?'

'I'm too old for this nonsense. My best friend has been murdered and my son is to blame. I need a drink.'

'Farzad . . .'

'You're too comfortable, Tommy boy. This is what happens. I thought you had an affection for the truth. Stop thinking like an Englishman.'

'But I'm English.'

He nodded. 'Of course you are. But does that mean you can't think for yourself?'

I watched his progress until he turned left at the end of the road into Acre Lane. He looked bizarre in his cap and the coat that dragged on the pavement behind him. He looked like a kid gone wild in the dressing-up box. He was gone.

Big John drove me home. He felt free to ask questions. I felt free to ignore them.

There was a reception committee outside Phoenecia. It was unfortunate timing.

Gundappa was just helping Mrs K out of his Merc in the presence of all the drivers. When I got out, there was a nervy silence that number-two son couldn't resist breaking. He said, 'What's going on, bruv? Where's Avid? They won't tell us shit.' He was playing it bemused and distressed. I knew Gundappa's style inside out. I ignored him and made for my door.

Mrs Khan said, 'Tommy?'

I turned back to her. I couldn't look her in the eye. I said, 'Later, Mrs K.' And then, 'I – I just wanted to say . . .' What did I want to say? The sentiment sounded insulting.

I opened the door. I shut it behind me and let the latch click. I took the stairs slowly. I was home but there wasn't nothing sweet about it. I looked out of the window and saw the Phoenecia drivers staring up at me. They looked like they might storm Castle Akhtar. An Englishman's home may be his whatever, but I was unfortified. How much did I care? How much is less than squat?

I was feeling sorry for yours truly. I knew I had something to discover but I didn't know what. I knew it was all my fault but I didn't know why. I found trusty Turk. I unscrewed the cap. For the first time since God knows when Turk wasn't looking like no solution.

I fired my computer. I decided all I could do was trawl the web for inspiration: Google Al-Dubayan and read everything there was to read.

My PC chugged. I connected my modem. It sang the Hindi chorus. I fired Netscape. I fired Google. The machine told me I had new mail. I checked it.

I was offered the chance for new confidence, length and girth that any woman would appreciate. I was offered the chance to buy cheap generic Apcalis direct from a Bangalore laboratory. I was offered the chance to see Earthworm ('Think Pearl Jam? Think again!') at Club Mozaic in Santa Monica tonight. I had only two messages that weren't Spam.

The first was from Mrs Y's husband, the suburban banker with a taste for Bayswater bamboo and CBT. He'd got my e-mail telling him about the photos I had. He'd taken his time to respond. He mixed threats and pleading half and half. It didn't create a good impression but I figured his missus would get her farmhouse Provençale. I didn't care. I simply felt nostalgic for a more innocent time just a few weeks previous, a time of fire escapes and long lenses when pain was only something paid for by rich perverts to teeny Thais. Oh, yeah. My lovely life.

The second was from exoticmelody. It was the message she'd sent from her mobile. It was the picture of Al-Dubayan.

I clocked it. It was thumbnail size, badly lit and pixellated – reflective of its surreptitious origins. But there was no doubting it was two geezers sitting on a sofa, mid-handshake and laughing. And there was no doubting it was Al-Dubayan and Gaileov sealing their deal; mayhem for money.

One of these geezers was the top story, the front-page news, the country's favourite opportunist fundamentalist terrorist. I looked again. My heart was playing an ostentatious drum roll. There was no doubt about it. The other geezer? Guess who? It was the man I'd met in the Paddington Green factory as Chip Paradowski.

I may be a Paki-immigrant-Ugandan-Indian Englishman but I still figure I went pale.

I made connections. I remembered what exoticmelody had told me. I remembered that sexyrussian had known Gaileov from New York. I recalled that Natasha/Natalya/Nadia/Whatever had sounded dubious about his origins. I figured the CIA man had got lucky; found himself caught up in a prime-time sting. I remembered Paradowski saying, 'There's a lot to be scared of these days.' I remembered Jones's spiel about real dangers at home and the need for the allocation of adequate resources. So it turned out my metaphor about the triangular tournament wasn't so off beam after all. Trouble was, while there were two teams playing for the same result, I was on neither of them. Al-Dubayan wanted terror. Paradowski and Jones wanted terror. And Tommy Akhtar? I wanted a double Turk double quick but I figured I'd best stay sober.

More connections. So now I knew why they wanted exoticmelody dead. She'd been the only one who could name Paradowski as Gaileov. Until now. Because now yours truly could name Paradowski as Gaileov and Gaileov as Paradowski too. This was smacking insomnia, for real. So British/American Intelligence were implicated in the murder of an MP. So British/American Intelligence were implicated in terrorist attacks on London. So British/American Intelligence had killed

Trinidad while playing hunt the hooker. I wondered how high up the food chain this went. I stopped myself right there. I had the shakes and they weren't nothing to do with bourbon withdrawal.

The big Q: what the hell did I do now? I figured. Turk was trying to distract me. Benny joined in. I ignored the pair of them. I kept figuring. My brain was accelerating and it wasn't even oiled. I remembered Bailey's Palm Pilot. There it was in my desk drawer. I had an idea. What with my tastes and all the headlines I'd seen so far, I didn't much like it but I now knew this wasn't my game and I hadn't made the rules.

I flicked the device on. It immediately flashed up my top scores in Tetris: Tommy Akhtar, Tommy Akhtar, Tommy Akhtar, all down the screen. I toggled to the main menu and checked Bailey's contacts. I found the list of personal details for every editor of every national newspaper. I picked up the phone. I wondered where to begin. By one name Bailey had written the word 'C–' in capital letters with four exclamation marks after. I figured he might be my kind of geezer. I dialled.

Epilogue

I developed my tastes sleeping in London shop doorways in the late eighties: cigarettes to dull hunger, booze to dull everything else. When religion stopped providing answers, the double team stopped me asking questions.

Amazing the number of my fellow vagrants who were Falklands vets. They'd fought for Queen and country and returned to parades and waving flags but found they couldn't fit back in. And me? What had I been fighting for in Afghanistan? God? An idea? A people? I guess I'd been fighting for my own guilt; not to alleviate it, just to drown it. I guess history makes all wars look inevitable and therefore renders individual motivations superfluous next to the heaving tides of greater interests. But, at the time, individual motivations are all you've got to go on so you'd best nail them down.

Jones – British Intelligence/posh bird/traitor/whatever – said, 'We are in a war situation.' Farzad – alcoholic/artist/shopkeeper/doctor – said, '"We have nothing to fear but fear itself."' Yours truly – Ugandan-Indian/Paki/immigrant/Englishman – said, 'Franklin D. Roosevelt.'

The war on terror? Serious. The old man described it as a 'contradiction in terms' but it's a conundrum too. *Little Book of Tommy*, #50. We're fighting fear but we're the ones who are scared so we're fighting with ourselves. *Little Book of Tommy*, #51. No wonder it's tough to pick a side and I can't help but ruminate on what history's judgement and, more to the point, the heaving tides will turn out to be.

When I played the prodigal in '89, Gunny and Farzad were

already the Brixton odd couple. Adding yours truly to the mix didn't diminish the eccentricity. Gundappa was only there as an ex-gangster, I was only there as ex-mujahideen and Farzad was only there *ex silentio*. For the best part of a year, we didn't communicate jack; just moved around that house like shades; ghosts of a dead family haunting one another.

We were still staying round Farzad's when Norman Tebbit made his infamous remarks about the 'cricket test'. I remember it well because the old man was at the tail end of his minor artistic fame and one of the broadsheets ran a selection of reactions from various immigrants in the public eye. They sent a junior hack to conduct an interview. I remember it too because when she turned up Farzad was wearing his Bob Marley T-shirt and Union Jack boxers, I was drunk and mildly abusive and Gunny tried to hit on her. The poppet didn't know where to look and she rejected offers of a cup of tea or a can of Genius in favour of a few quick questions and a sharp exit.

The old man was at his most vociferous. He said that while, in general, he disagreed with whatever emanated from the black hole that was Mr Tebbit's mouth, in this case he felt he had a point. He said that he was a proud Englishman who had brought his sons up to be proud Englishmen and, as such, we always supported the cricket team even though, let's face it, it was often a thankless task. 'We consider it our duty,' he said. 'Otherwise the Chingford skinhead and similar numbskulls will think England are their team and they are not. They are ours.'

The journalist asked if the England team couldn't represent both the Akhtar family and Norman Tebbit.

Farzad shook his head. 'My dear,' he said, 'cricket is a gentleman's game.'

I have occasionally wondered whether the old man meant what he said then and whether he'd agree with it now. I have occasionally wondered whether he was being ironic, provocative or simply subtle. Frankly I've no idea. Farzad's a contrary geezer, for real. It is true, however, that I mostly support England. Gunny supports West Ham.

When the story of British/American Intelligence selling Russian plastic explosives to an opportunist would-be terrorist broke, I don't know what I was expecting but I guess I was expecting something. In retrospect, however, I confess I'm unsurprised it turned out to be a damp squib. Sure, it was all over the front pages for a few weeks and there were allegations made, questions asked in Parliament and on Capitol Hill, and demands for resignations. But then it wasn't on the front pages and the allegations were denied, questions went unanswered and the only resignations were by junior civil servants I'd never heard of. There was talk of a murder prosecution but they couldn't find anybody to bring charges against. Paradowski, Jones and whoever else were hiding in the bureaucracy. Trinidad Pete didn't have any family and there were only four of us at the funeral: Farzad, exoticmelody, yours truly and Big John. The Government established an independent investigative commission and I believe I'm due to give evidence. But there's been all kinds of wrangling about who's sitting on it and I've heard nothing more. The self-deceiving powerful: they know where I am.

Al-Dubayan still hasn't been caught. Farzad reckons he'll go free until the next foreign-policy disaster requires alleviation. Exoticmelody reckons catching him would require no more than an ebonic hooker shakedown. 'Come to Mummy! Come to Mummy!' That still cracks me up every time.

As for yours truly? I figure it's appropriate the opportunist's still on the loose like a good bogeyman should be. Sometimes, despite the evidence, I kind of wonder whether he ever actually existed at all. Then I figure that if he didn't exist someone would have had to invent him. No restful nights come from thinking like that although the old man would be proud to hear me bastardizing Voltaire, for real.

It turned out that the newspaper editor whose number I lifted from Bailey's Palm Pilot wasn't my kind of geezer after all. In fact, Bailey's one-word description had it spot on. I'd agreed to give him the whole story on the following conditions. (1.) That the most important thing was to get Avid better and released. (2.) That the names of exoticmelody, Av and myself would never be revealed.

The first part of the deal went smoothly enough and on the quiet. But a month into the story, when it was beginning to run out of legs, he blackmailed me into giving an exclusive interview with the threat of printing a who's who. I figured I didn't have a lot of choice.

The interview ran next to a small graphic showing that before the PWA's intervention, 30 per cent of the population regarded Islamic terrorism as the greatest threat to their way of life. Now the figure was 65 per cent. That, even though (and this is my editorial) the police spokesman said at the time there were, and subsequent investigation revealed, zero links between the PWA and any known Islamic groups.

The interview ran beneath the headline 'Fundamentalist Turned Patriot'.

Farzad read it in silence. Then he muttered, ' "*Sed quis custodiet ipsos custodes?*" Who said that?'

I tried a name. 'Cicero?'

He shook his head. 'Not a bad guess, Tommy boy. But no, this is from Juvenal's *Satires*. Endlessly quotable. For example: "*Difficile est saturam non scribere.*" '

'What does that mean?'

Farzad gave it the ha-ha. ' "It's hard not to write satire." '

I decided to spend Christmas round the old man's for the

first time in years. Gundappa was off with his latest bird and her two toddlers (which didn't bear thinking about) so it would just be Farzad, exoticmelody and yours truly.

By now Melody had been staying with the old man for pushing three months. One time when we were watching a cricket video (England/New Zealand, Trent Bridge '83, Randall's cameo against Hadlee), I asked him if I should start calling her Mum. He didn't like my sense of humour. He reacted all feisty. 'How dare you, Tommy boy? You may not remember your mother but you know I think about my beloved Mina for every second of every day. How dare you?' His eyes were filling up. He said, 'Get me another drink before you make me ashamed of you.'

Recently I've been thinking about letting the old man in on my twenty-year-old secret. I've been thinking about telling him how Mina asked me to take her to the doctor and I told her to rest upstairs because Farzad would lose it if the shop was shut when he came back from the cash-and-carry. I haven't found the moment yet. I figure that when something's gone unspoken for so long, maybe there aren't words for it any more.

On Christmas Day, I left it till early afternoon before heading over to Brixton. I reckoned it was worth having a lie-in before hitting the parallel universe.

I needed some provisions. I stopped by Khan's. It was open as ever.

Av and Michelle were working the shop on their own, which was a relief for me, serious. They were smoking fags and sharing an alcopop. 'Tis the season to be jolly. Oh, yeah. I said, 'You OK, Av? Michelle?'

They said, 'Easy, Tommy man.' And, 'Hey, Mr Akhtar.' Michelle had reverted to formal.

I said, 'Where's Mrs K? Everything all right?'

Av sniffed at me. 'She's with Benzi, man. Benzi decided she wanted a Christmas stocking and you know she's Mum's pride and joy, what what what.'

I said, 'Sure.' Then, 'She forgiven me yet?'

Av ducked his chin. He was embarrassed. 'I told her but . . . you know.' He shook his head. 'She got some Turk in, though. She still thinking of you. What you want?'

I took two bottles of Turk, a carton of Bennies, eight cans of Genius and a family pack of luxury turkey and sage stuffing crisps. Just to enter into the spirit.

While Michelle packed me a box, Av and me small-talked.

During his convalescence, we'd got quite tight behind Mrs K's back. He didn't want to hang with the other thug-lites so much any more; just me or Michelle. He told me that while he was laid up he'd done a lot of thinking.

He said, 'I'm the man of the house, Tommy man. You get me? I gotta take responsibility. Anything happens? What what what? I gotta be "Come to Av. Sorted." I changed my attitude, man. I can't be flogging weed or whatever. I already talked to the careers geezer at school. He says I need a "realistic aspiration", know what I mean? So that's what I got.'

I said, 'That's good, Av. Serious.'

He nodded. He leaned forward. He told me his plan. 'The music industry, Tommy man. I'm gonna make beats. I tell you, man, I'm gonna smack that shit.'

Av told me he'd applied for a sound-design course after he'd done his GCSEs. Michelle couldn't take her eyes off him while she wedged in the Turk with a box of Quality Street she'd thrown in for free. She was the pop star's groupie number one.

As I walked out with my supplies Av said, 'Don't forget, Tommy man. TA Services. Tommy and Avid Services. We'll f___ing rinse it.'

I gave it the ha-ha and a slight bow. 'Happy Christmas.'

Av gave it the ha-ha back. 'Whatever.'

Yusuf was outside Phoenecia, looking miserable. He had a beanie pulled low on his head, his shoulders hunched and his hands buried deep in his parka.

I said, 'Yes, Yusuf. What you doing outside? It's freezing.'

He said, 'Swiss Chris is running control.'

'So?'

'So he used the bog, didn't he? It f__ing stinks in there.'

Fair enough.

Yusuf took me to the old man's gaff and I tipped him appropriate to the festive season and he cheered up somewhat.

Exoticmelody opened the front door. She was wearing Farzad's Bob Marley T-shirt, a headscarf and holding a paint-brush. Welcome to the parallel universe. She said, 'Hey, Tommy.'

I said, 'Call me Mr Akhtar.'

She didn't respond.

I said, 'You all right, Mum?'

She thought I was hilarious.

In the living room, the old man was sitting bolt upright on a stool against his painting wall, which was currently in the pure state he liked best. He was staring out of the window. He was wearing his baggy cords but naked to the waist. There was an easel and canvas set up in front of him. 'Hello, Tommy boy.'

'What's going on?'

'No lunch today, son. I hope you brought the booze. Melanie is painting me after Edward Hopper. How is she doing? She won't let me look at it.'

I went behind the canvas. The ex-tom made a half-hearted show of trying to stop me. I clocked the picture. It was primary school, serious. The figure was a peculiar pale blue and his features were indistinct. The window was much too big so it looked like the figure might be sucked through it. Melody looked at me, a touch embarrassed.

Farzad said, 'Tell me. How's it coming? Has she captured the alienation? The loneliness? The urban *ennui*?'

The ex-hooker touched my arm. She was biting her lower lip. We shared a moment. I checked the picture again. I guess it had something. 'Sure,' I said.

I went into the kitchen to fix drinks. It looked different. It was spotless. A woman's touch. I was half-way jealous. I sparked a Benny. I emptied the crisps into a bowl. I poured three Turks, cracked three cans and stowed the rest in the fridge. I filled a tray. I carried it back into the living room. I was bearing gifts. One wise man.

The ex-whore had covered her canvas and the pair of them were now sitting in front of the telly. I put the tray on the table and Farzad took a glass and a mouthful and said, 'Ssh, Tommy boy! The Queen's speech.'

Exoticmelody gave me a look. I shrugged and sat down.

Her Majesty played it scripted and unsurprising. She started with the PWA's attacks on fast-food joints and a video shop. She condemned the subsequent and continuing spate of violence against mosques and Muslim businesses. She championed tolerance and mutual respect. She talked about the greatest threat to homeland security since the heights of IRA terrorism. She told us to be grateful for our way of life. She made only oblique allusion to the scandal uncovered by yours truly, calling for vigilance from all citizens to preserve our proud democracy.

I couldn't help myself. I was tutting like an outboard motor.

Farzad looked at me daggers. He said, '"Democracy is the worst form of government except all those other forms that have been tried."'

I said, 'Churchill.'

'Of course.'

The Queen wished her citizens a merry this and a peaceful that and the shot cut to the Union Jack fluttering above Windsor Castle. The national anthem kicked in.

Farzad got to his feet, thrust out his bare excuse for a chest and raised his Turk in the loyal toast. Exoticmelody pulled a face at me. I pulled one back. We shared another moment. I didn't know whether the old man was being ironic, provocative or simply subtle. A contrary geezer, like I said.